Dear Reader,

This is an especially wonderful month for *Scarlet*. We are *so* proud to announce the publication of our first *Scarlet* hardback – *Dark Desire* by renowned author Maxine Barry. It features determined, angry, clever, sexy and power-packed Haldane Fox – a man with a mission. Fox plays with fire, but always wins. Electra is very beautiful but, due to a traumatic past, has dedicated herself to her career as an orchid grower. When these two ambitious people meet something's gotta give and Electra is determined it won't be her!

Also this month, Sally Steward's *Secrets Rising* gives us a heroine who suddenly discovers she was adopted. She enlists the help of a private detective to look for her biological parents but he is reluctant, knowing her quest may not end happily. And soon it becomes clear that someone else doesn't want Rebecca to find out the truth . . . In *A Temporary Arrangement* by Margaret Callaghan, businessman Alex Gifford seems to be a fairly unusual parent. He denies his young son James nothing – except affection. And he makes it clear that this is part of Stella's nannying job. Not that he is incapable of strong feelings. What he wants, he takes. And he wants Stella . . .

I really hope that you enjoy these exciting titles, and if you are interested in reserving a copy of our second hardback, *Finding Gold* by Tammy Hilz, available in September, send us your details now.

Till next month,

Sally Cooper

SALLY COOPER,
Editor-in-Chief – *Scarlet*

About the Author

Brought up in the market town of Ormskirk, Lancashire, **Margaret Callaghan** trained to teach in the West Midlands. She met her husband Rob at her first teaching appointment and, like all good romance stories, it was a case of love at first sight!

Margaret took a career break to have her daughter Laura, now a teenager. Then she did several years of short-term contract teaching before accepting a full-time position back at her first school in West Bromwich, where she currently teaches 11-to-16 year olds.

In her spare time Margaret enjoys good food, good wine, foreign holidays and spoiling her cats. Margaret had her first romance novel published in 1991. Her most recent novel for *Scarlet*, *Wilde Affair*, won her plaudits worldwide.

Other *Scarlet* titles available this month:

SECRETS RISING – Sally Steward
DARK DESIRE – Maxine Barry

MARGARET CALLAGHAN

A TEMPORARY ARRANGEMENT

Enquiries to:
Robinson Publishing Ltd
7 Kensington Church Court
London W8 4SP

First published in the UK by Scarlet, 1998

Copyright © Margaret Callaghan 1998
Cover photography by Colin Thomas

The right of Margaret Callaghan to be identified as author
of this work has been asserted by her in accordance
with the Copyright, Designs and Patents Act 1988.

All rights reserved. No part of this publication
may be reproduced in any form or by any means
without the prior written permission of the publisher.

This book is sold subject to the condition that it shall
not, by way of trade or otherwise, be lent, re-sold,
hired out or otherwise circulated in any form of binding
or cover other than that in which it is published and
without a similar condition including this condition being
imposed on the subsequent purchaser.

A copy of the British Library Cataloguing in
Publication data is available from the British Library

ISBN 1-85487-570-1

Printed and bound in the EC

10 9 8 7 6 5 4 3 2 1

CHAPTER 1

Hand raised, braced to deliver a short, sharp rap to the solid oak door, Stella Marshall caught the sound of angry voices and paused. More than paused, stepped back, her mind going into overdrive as she moved out of sight of the frosted pane that made up the top third of the door, and, inadvertently, took half a dozen steps closer to the open window.

Women. Two, she decided. Definitely not Carly. Equally definitely not happy. And, faint but distinct from deep within the house, the thin wail of a baby. Ten-month-old James Gifford, poor, motherless mite. The sweetest little baby in the world, according to Carly. And with the baby's cries continuing unabated, Stella felt a prickle of alarm. Just where was Carly?

A sudden lull. The lull before the storm, perhaps. The urge to put her mind at rest, knock and ask for Carly, was outweighed by an overwhelming need to stay out of sight. Eavesdrop. Sly. Underhand. Almost second nature in a job like Stella's. Only this wasn't work, and listening in on a private conversation was distasteful, to say the least. Hardly a conversation,

Stella amended as round two began in earnest, and, since the man on the moon could hear each and every word, hardly private either.

Two voices. The first a high-pitched whine that grated on Stella's ear, the other more modulated, reminiscent of a bright but bored young thing goaded to respond.

'And I'm warning you, Miss Clayton, I've had enough. Thirty years I've been employed by this family, and never so much as a hint of complaint –'

'Then more fool Alex for putting up with you. Naturally when I'm in charge –'

'Only you're not. You're a guest. A house guest. And you've no more right to order me about than the butcher, the baker or the candlestick-maker. I know my place –'

'In the gutter, Mrs Edwards, and sooner rather than later. Because the moment Alex walks in through that door, you'll be walking out of it. Better go and pack,' the younger woman entreated saccharine-sweetly. 'And save us all a lot of bother. And while you're up there, shut the door on that snivelling little brat.'

'James –'

'Needs feeding, or changing, or despatching forthwith to the nearest children's home. Though on second thoughts,' she tossed out harshly, 'an orphanage on Mars might serve a better purpose. Good God, woman, you work here. Can't you do *something*?'

'I'm paid to manage the house. James –'

'Has a nanny. A nanny conspicuous by her absence. A nanny *you* didn't approve of,' she emphasized gleefully. 'And, since the girl has clearly had enough of your sharp tongue, that leaves you holding the baby – literally, Mrs Edwards. Understand?'

'Perfectly. It's twelve forty-five. Mr Gifford's due home within the hour, and I've got work do to. Lunch. Not that I'd expect *you* to do more than push a tomato around the plate.'

'If your culinary expertise stretched to something more imaginative than platefuls of stodge, and grey stodge at that, then maybe I could rustle up an appetite. Like I said, the moment I'm in charge –'

'Over my dead body.' This was Agnes Edwards, sounding every inch the trusty retainer, not so much fixtures and fittings as the centre of the Gifford universe – in this part of the world at least. And why not? Thirty years of loyal and faithful service in a house that wouldn't look out of place on a film set. In the back of beyond maybe, according to Carly, but with a car thrown in with the job that was hardly a problem.

But there *had* been a problem, Stella recalled with a shiver of apprehension. Carly's letters had changed over the weeks from the cheerfully chatty to the downright morose. And, though Stella had probed, Carly hadn't seen fit to confide. Carly. With Tamara Clayton's words echoing in her mind, Stella's unease deepened: *A nanny conspicuous by her absence*.

'Now what are you doing?'

'Like I said, Miss Clayton, one of us has work to do. Work. An honest day's work. Something one of your sort would be hard pressed to recognize.'

'How dare you –?'

'Speak the truth for once? Age, my dear,' Agnes Edwards witheringly informed her. 'Experience. And a knowledge of my worth.'

'You're fired!'

'Not part of your brief. You don't employ me –'

'*Yet,*' Tamara Clayton interrupted tersely. 'But I will. And the moment I do –'

'You won't need to bother. Work for you? I'd rather rot in hell. Only it isn't going to happen. Mr Gifford's no fool. Once bitten, twice shy, and on *that*, Miss Clayton, you have my word.'

'Oh, yes? Privy to his deepest thoughts are we now? Well, for your information, the engagement's set for the end of the summer – and the wedding, I can assure you, won't be far behind. Time to pack your bags and leave, I believe?'

'Wrong. Time to check on Mandy in the kitchen. Young girls these days can't be trusted to boil so much as a kettle. Spineless, the lot of them. Not to mention workshy. Just like that impertinent little baggage who called herself a nanny.'

'Sour grapes, Mrs Edwards? Beginning to feel your age? Time to retire. *Retire,*' Tamara Clayton emphasized slyly. 'Go before you're pushed.'

'I'm going all right. Downstairs. Now. I've had enough –'

'Not half as much as I have. Now, will you please do as you're told and see to that screaming infant before he does himself an injury?'

'You're his stepmother elect – apparently. *You* see to James.'

'I –'

'Oh, for heaven's sake –' A third voice, young, vaguely amused yet authoritative. And the sudden silence was so deafening that for a moment Stella didn't react. And then she darted forwards, rapped her knuckles on the woodwork at the precise moment the battle recommenced.

With a mental shrug of the shoulders, Stella stepped back again. Fine. She'd wait. The row would blow itself out eventually, and until she'd located Carly, Stella was going nowhere – would camp out on the doorstep if that was what it took. But in the meantime she'd listen, she'd learn – and she'd try to stay calm, she entreated wryly, jumping edgily at the sudden slam of car door unexpectedly close.

Wheeling round, she was amazed that a car as sleek as a Jaguar XJ8 could sweep up the drive unnoticed. Not so the devastating man who'd swung himself out from behind the wheel and stretched, as if easing tired muscles. All man. Six feet four inches of rippling muscle, Stella couldn't help but notice. But she didn't want to notice such openly sensuous detail as the shadow of hair at his throat, the powerful thighs encased in moulded jeans. And, since the glance he shot at Stella was instantly dismissive, the fact that she had was all the more galling.

The battle in the house stepped up a gear. The man's chin snapped up. 'What the hell –?'

Hell, indeed, Stella could allow, but hadn't time to allow, since Alex Gifford strode past and, reaching for the handle, threw open the door that opened directly on to an enormous, sparsely furnished room. With barely a pause to weigh up the scene, he stepped silently over the threshold, leaving an unnerved Stella to bring up the rear.

'Can't one of you see to James?' the girl in the wheelchair pleaded, enormous eyes filling with tears, and, though she didn't acknowledge the man's arrival, facing the door fairly and squarely, she couldn't fail but to notice. 'Tamara –'

'Don't even think it,' the dark-haired woman scorned, every inch the up-and-coming model, from the tip of her exquisitely sculpted head to the crimson-painted toenails peeping though fashionably strappy stilettos. 'I wouldn't know one end of a baby from another,' she bit out, 'and I've no intentions of learning. Ruin my figure in childbirth –'

'Mrs Edwards? *Please*. I'd see to him myself only –'

'Of course you can't, my dear. But those who could don't choose to,' the housekeeper sniped with a withering glance at the woman on her left. 'And I –'

'Clearly don't know your place at all,' Tamara Clayton interrupted savagely. 'You're the hired hand. It's high time you learned to –'

'Enough!' A single word, an icy inflection. The result was electric as the women spun round, the flicker of fear on the older woman's face sharp contrast to the ugly flash of triumph shadowing Tamara's. But as for the girl in the wheelchair, though it was not easy for Stella to judge, poised in the open doorway with the width of the room between them, yet with a journalist's eye for detail the word that sprang to mind was 'sly'.

And then the girl's tears spilled over, along with the noise, the rush to get in first with a string of complaints. A raging torrent cut short by the imperative wave of an arm.

Folding arms across a powerful chest, Alex Gifford surveyed the scene, his gaze going from face to face, and, though Stella was standing behind him, three newly wary faces spoke volumes. He was angry, toweringly angry.

Silence, complete and utter. And then the plaintive wail of a child – a sob of exhaustion, Stella decided, amazed any woman worth her salt could choose to ignore a baby in distress.

Alex Gifford nodded at his housekeeper. 'Carly?'

A sniff of disapproval. 'Didn't come home. Friday's her night off. Said she was driving up to London and to expect her when we saw her. Only we won't now. Packed and gone. Every last stitch of clothing, and as for the car –'

'A box on wheels. It's replaceable or recoverable – or writeoff-able. And arrangements for – the child?'

'Are in hand. Darling –'

Another imperative wave cut Tamara Clayton dead in her tracks. 'Mrs Edwards is the hired hand – apparently – Mrs Edwards can explain. Mrs Edwards?'

'I phoned the agency first thing, Mr Gifford. They're sending someone round at once.'

'And in the meantime?

'In the meantime?' Wary. With a trusty retainer's knowledge of her employer, a sudden awful comprehension that the job she'd enjoyed for the past thirty years could well be coming to an end. An abrupt end. She gave an uneasy glance at Alex Gifford, an anguished glance at the girl in the wheelchair – the need for an ally, any ally, pitifully obvious to an impartial observer.

'In the meantime, Mrs Edwards,' Alex Gifford prompted silkily, 'I assume someone – yourself, perhaps – has had the compassion to deal with the child? Feeding. Winding. Changing. Bathing. Do I make myself plain?'

'I –'

'No need to bother,' Stella cut in pleasantly, stepping forwards, amazing the whole room – amazing herself more, since she didn't know what she was saying until the words tumbled out without conscious thought. 'If Mrs Edwards could show me to the nursery, I'll make a start at once.'

'And you are?'

Rustling up a smile, she offered her hand. 'Stella Marshall, Mr Gifford. I believe I am expected?'

'You're late,' Tamara Clayton, back in control of her emotions, though not of that waspish tongue, moved across to a low, generously proportioned chair and flung herself down, allowing a daringly short skirt to ride up over her thighs. 'Four hours late.'

'Better late than never,' Stella countered mildly, wondering how on earth she'd explain away her presence once the real agency nanny arrived. She dropped her hand awkwardly when Alex Gifford made no attempt to take it. Not that she'd need to explain. Given the way he was regarding her, she'd be surprised if the job was hers for so much as a fraudulent half-minute.

Piercing blue eyes. Cold blue eyes. No emotion, not a hint of warmth as they travelled Stella's slender body, assessing, appraising. Not a tangible caress, not even a man's flicker of interest in the woman beneath the layer of clothes. Just a flicker of annoyance quickly masked when the baby's cries began afresh.

Alex Gifford nodded. 'Fine. As you say, better late than never. It won't happen again, Miss Marshall. Understand?'

'Perfectly.' An equally grim nod from Stella. She angled her head, met his gaze unflinchingly.

The nerve of the man. For two pins she'd tell him precisely what he could do with his job. *Carly's* job, she amended silently, tersely. Which settled it. Stella was staying put. Five minutes, ten, half an hour if she was lucky, but she'd take what Fate had offered – a tantalizing glimpse of Carly's world that might just make a difference, yield a few clues to her sister's current whereabouts. Too soon to overreact and call the police, she hastily reassured herself, but the vague unease at the back of her mind was beginning to crystallize.

Tamara Clayton yawned, loudly, pointedly, just as pointedly checked the time on her wristwatch, then stood, stretched, sidled across. 'Alex, darling, let me fix you a drink.'

'Thank you, Tamara. Later. I've been travelling

half the night and I'm grimy. I'll take a shower. Half an hour,' he insisted, dipping his head to kiss her in a casual display of intimacy that Stella didn't want to watch, had no choice but to watch and silently rail against.

Thirty seconds. An interminable thirty seconds. And then Tamara wheeled away, flouncing down into the chair with another display of thigh.

With a lightning switch of focus, Alex Gifford homed in on the woman who'd melted into the background, whose fingers were plucking at the corners of her apron in a giveaway show of nerves. 'Lunch in forty-five minutes, Mrs Edwards?' he murmured crisply. And then it was Stella's turn as cool blue eyes slid across, appraising, assessing, stirring the blood in her veins.

Unnerved, but damned if she'd let it show, Stella raised her head, held his gaze, angled her chin in defiance.

'Oh, yes. And lay an extra place,' he insisted silkily. 'Miss Marshall can join us. Call it a painless way of getting to know one another. I assume that gives you plenty of time?'

'If not,' Stella retorted coolly, 'I'll be sure to let you know. If that's all?'

'For now. Till later, Miss Marshall.'

I can't wait, Stella derided. Only silently. She nodded at Mrs Edwards, nudging the older woman into movement.

It seemed to take for ever to cross the room, and the thought of those cool blue eyes following each and every step was thoroughly unnerving. Only they weren't. The stab of disappointment when Stella glanced back was quickly replaced by another disturbing emotion. For if Stella was forgotten, the girl – young woman – in the wheelchair wasn't.

Another kiss. Hannah's arms creeping up to lock around his neck as Alex leaned over the back of the chair. A long kiss. Overlong, surely, for a man and his sister-in-law? Stella mused sourly. And, sure enough, as she switched her gaze she caught the flash of raw emotion on Tamara Clayton's face and began to make sense of Carly's unease. Undercurrents. And, since she'd been in the house less than ten minutes, all the more worrying.

But no time to ponder now. Stella had problems enough staying one step ahead of the game she was playing. Not to mention finding her way through a minefield of hostility.

'I take it the agency filled you in?' Agnes Edwards, her voice as stiff and starched as the apron she wore.

'Filled me in?' Stella stalled, running the tip of her tongue across her dry lips.

The housekeeper nodded. 'Miss Wesley. She's touchy about the wheelchair. Doesn't like being made a fuss of.'

No. So Stella had gathered from Carly. But quite what else she'd be expected to know was anybody's guess. Still, nothing ventured, nothing gained. With a mental cross of her fingers, Stella took the plunge. 'Her fall from a horse?' she half-queried, half-stated, arching an eyebrow. 'It – was mentioned in the briefing,' she conceded carefully. 'But of course I wasn't given any details.' Just a tiny white lie – the first of many, she was beginning to see. She was used to living on her wits, but uneasy all the same.

Thin lips tightened. 'Precious little to tell,' the housekeeper bit out. 'One minute she's sailing over the jumps like a true champion, the next she's lying in a ditch all twisted and still. Damaged her spine. Not that she's ever let it beat her,' she added with a fierce touch of pride. 'Works her fingers to the bone at the stables, and can't abide being treated as an invalid.'

'And quite right, too,' Stella demurred crisply. 'It's a disability, not a handicap. But you don't need to worry; I'm used to being discreet.' And if by some fluke she did last more than half an hour, that hint about a briefing would help explain any apparent prior knowledge.

Prior knowledge. Like the timing of the accident – just two short weeks before Alex Gifford's wedding to Hannah's sister. Way before Carly's time, of course, but, ever the romantic, Carly had been struck by Hannah's insistence that the wedding go ahead as planned.

Entering the nursery, Stella wrinkled her nose. Little James Gifford was clearly in need of changing, ditto his need for a bath. But far more pressing, for this hungry baby at least, food. So, first stop the kitchen. Less a kitchen than a designated area linked by an arch to a well-furnished living room, Stella noted automatically, but all in all very impressive. A self-contained nursery wing tucked away at the back of the house, carefully located as far away from the family rooms as possible.

Or maybe Stella was being cynical.

There was an awkward pause. The housekeeper darted forwards to flick an imaginary speck of dust with the corner of her apron. 'I'll fill the kettle.'

'Thank you,' Stella said pleasantly. 'But I'm sure I can manage. And with lunch in forty-five minutes . . .'

Another sniff, a definite air of burnt martyr. 'I – did feed James,' the older woman explained defensively. 'First thing. I couldn't let the poor mite starve. Not like some.'

'No.' Stella's lips twitched. 'Quite. But you didn't think to change him?'

A look of pure horror crossed her face. 'Change him? Good heavens. I wouldn't know where to start,' she stunned Stella by conceding. 'And I didn't think I'd need to with that flighty little baggage sure to come home with the milk. After all, it wouldn't have been the first time.'

'Really?' Another shiver of alarm. Stella paused, standing, watching, waiting.

Only the housekeeper had already said more than she'd intended, and her sharp face was closing up again. 'Right. Well, if you're sure you can manage?'

Stella nodded. 'I'm sure. And if there's anything I need to know, I'll ask. Internal phone?'

'Eight for the kitchen, nine for the lounge, ten for the –' Bang on cue, it began to ring. 'That's an outside line. Long rings for out, short rings for in,' she explained, crossing to take it. 'You'll soon get the hang of it.

'Freshfields. Good afternoon. Housekeeper speaking.' A pause, then the tinny sound of a voice in the handset, and the woman's eyes swivelled to Stella, who hadn't moved but, sensing her cover was about to be blown, was instinctively poised for flight. 'One moment.' She was holding out the handset, not a flicker of interest on her face. 'It's for you. The agency. Some garbled message about a flu epidemic.'

'Oh! Yes, of course. Thank you. And thanks for your help. I'm sure I can manage now.'

She paused, pointedly checking the time on the wall clock, praying the woman would take the hint and leave – which she did, doubtless spurred on by the thought of being asked to change the baby, whose cries had abated – through sheer exhaustion, at a guess – but whose needs were becoming more obvious by the second.

The click of a door and Stella was alone – or as alone as she was likely to be. And, since a ten-month-old child couldn't betray her, she took a deep breath. 'Stella Marshall. How may I help you?'

'Marshall?' A moment's confusion, yet then, clearly too polite to ask outright, the woman at the end of the line waded in. Apologies. Profound apologies. For the nanny in residence letting them down, for the non-arrival of the replacement. 'It's this dreadful flu bug,' she explained frantically. 'The staff have gone down like nine-pins and I'm sorry to stay there's not a girl to be had this side of London. Not until Monday at least –'

'Not good enough, I'm afraid,' Stella cut in smoothly. 'Mr Gifford's a busy man. He's also a man with influence. We've made our own arrangements. Just a *temporary* arrangement,' she reassured lightly. 'I'm sure we'll be in touch in time.'

Cutting the connection, she smiled wryly, re-entered the bedroom, placed a mental peg on her nostrils and, praying a three-week stint with her godson would prove an adequate grounding, gingerly approached the cot.

'Poor little mite,' she soothed automatically. He was heavier than expected, and damp and oozing. Stella grabbed the first thing that came to hand – a towel carelessly tossed on the back of a chair. Draping it around him, she tucked James firmly into the crook of an arm.

'Now, then, let's see . . .' She paused, stifled the panic. Think. Baby. Food. She gave a smile of reassurance for James that did nothing for the quiver in that tiny bottom lip, and then, desperate to head off the protest he was bracing himself to make, Stella pounced on the fridge. Thank heavens. Bless Carly for planning ahead. For herself? Stella wondered, placing the ready-made bottle in a jug of boiled water. Or had Carly known that feeding James would be the last thing on Tamara Clayton's mind? And though Tamara hadn't, the housekeeper had – a task clearly beyond her brief, given the simmering resentment.

As James opened his mouth, Stella moved fast. But nothing like as fast as James himself.

'Easy, now,' she entreated lightly, adjusting the angle of the bottle. 'Take a tip from an expert. Guzzle it down like that and you'll end up with wind, and then we'll both be sorry.' Expert? That three-week stint with her godson all those months ago? No doubt her cousin, Beth, would raise a sceptical eyebrow at that precise definition, but since Beth wouldn't know . . . Stella grinned.

Next problem. Nappy. Bath. Not a good idea on a full stomach – so, barely enough water to cover the base, but more than enough to soak Stella who, despite that spot of practice with Connor, was sadly lacking in expertise.

'All done. All dry,' she burbled chirpily. 'Let's leave the nappy off for now, hey? A breath of fresh air and a kick of those heels and little James Gifford will be none the worse for his neglect.'

'I'm relieved to hear it. Less relieved to have my worst fears confirmed.'

Stella froze, the hairs on the back of her neck rising like the hackles of a cat. Because Alex Gifford was standing in the open doorway, seeming ten feet tall to Stella, still kneeling on the floor beside the changing mat – safer on the floor for a novice, she'd quickly decided, and had given the purpose-built cabinet a very wide berth.

No expense spared for this baby – no, sir! Just the odd spot of love, according to Carly. And, since the great man himself had never deigned to show his nose inside the nursery in the three months of Carly's employ, why unnerve Stella on her first afternoon? Easy to unnerve Stella, she was beginning to think, given that earlier overreaction. Absurd. Absurd to allow that reaction to a man – any man. But to this man in particular . . . the implications didn't bear thinking about.

'I was merely thinking aloud,' she murmured pleasantly. 'No blame intended.'

'No blame taken – unless you count the little minx who went off without so much as second thought.'

'Carly –'

'The one and only. Flighty, according to the sober Mrs Edwards, and clearly unreliable.'

'I don't agree. Oh, yes, she's gone,' Stella confirmed, having checked the bedroom herself. 'But she didn't leave James alone and she didn't leave him unprepared. Everything's laid out ready. There's a day's supply of milk made up in the fridge and comprehensive instructions clipped to the pin-board. Oh, yes –' Sitting back on her heels, she smiled grimly, waved a hand to the open door of the bedroom. 'And she left a note.'

He was back before Stella had time to miss him, his expression grim. 'A note? You call this a note?'

'Surely it speaks for itself? "Tell James I love him. Tell James I'm sorry. I really am sorry."' Stella quoted tightly. 'What did you expect?' she couldn't resist needling. 'A map of Treasure Island? Detailed instructions on where to find your precious car? Well, worry not, Mr Gifford, as you said, the car's traceable or replaceable, and if I know –' She pulled herself up short, horrified at what she'd almost blurted out. *If I know Carly*. A moot point, she supposed, given her sister's disappearing act. Half-sister, if she was in the mood for splitting hairs, only she wasn't. In the meantime, Alex Gifford's eyes had narrowed.

'If you know . . . ?'

Stella licked her lips, a nervous gesture this devastating man wouldn't miss.

He didn't, moving away from the door where he'd propped himself and closing the gap between them. 'If you know *what*, precisely?' he enquired evenly, razor-sharp eyes boring into hers, refusing to allow her to look away.

Half-paralyzed with fear, Stella's numb mind seized on the truth. 'If I know Carly. A passing acquaintance, maybe,' she acknowledged pleasantly, 'but in our line of work naturally our paths have crossed. Carly's no thief; I'd stake my life on it. You'll get your car back. And in the meanwhile, as I'm sure you must have noticed, I'm not without the means to get around.'

'No.' Another narrowing of eyes that missed little to start with. 'A Rover 2000. An impressive set of wheels,' he mused. 'Very impressive. And on a nanny's wages . . .' A shrug, an eloquent lift of powerful shoulders. 'Still, you are, shall we say, slightly more mature than the usual run-of-the-mill nanny. Doubtless you've earned each and every penny.'

'Precisely,' Stella clipped, inwardly seething. 'I work for a living, Mr Gifford. I earn the money, I decide how to spend it. And since I tend to move around –'

'You don't stay long, then? In any one establishment, I mean? Strange, I thought nannies grew up with their charges.'

'Doubtless some do,' Stella informed him crisply. 'It just so happens I prefer to move around. No ties, no emotional tug when the job comes to an end.'

'Another day, another baby, another wage cheque,' he scorned. 'And precious little commitment,' he tagged on grimly.

'If you like,' Stella conceded coolly. 'My life, my job, my decision. But if it's worrying you, I don't have to stay. Doubtless the agency will rustle up someone more suitable – someone slightly less mature, perhaps?' she needled lightly. 'Though a difficult balance, wouldn't you say. Stability and maturity set against youthful exuberance? Now, how did you describe the previous incumbent? Flighty? Unreliable? A little minx?'

She smiled sweetly, sat back on her heels, wished she felt as confident as she sounded, wished, too that she didn't have to strain her neck to meet his gaze. Six feet four inches of dynamism, towering over Stella and making not the slightest effort to acknowledge his son, now kicking his chubby little legs and gurgling happily on the changing mat, a towel spread out beneath him to catch any spills.

To her amazement, Alex Gifford's stern expression lightened. 'A little minx indeed,' he acknowledged. 'And I'm beginning to think it goes with the job. But you'll do. Assuming you don't pack up and leave at the drop of a hat. Ten minutes,' he reminded her, turning, and strolling lazily to the door without so much as a sideways glance at the baby. 'Two-fifteen precisely.'

Yes, sir! Stella clipped, only silently. Ten minutes. Barely long enough to dress a wriggling, giggling, newly refreshed James, let alone sort herself out. And, since she was decidedly damp and crumpled, should she waste precious minutes retrieving the suitcase stashed in the back of the car or make do?

Making do won. A peremptory brush of the hair, which she pulled back off her face and secured in an uncompromising knot at the back of her neck, the merest hint of lipstick and bang on time, the clock in the hall chimed the first quarter as Stella approached the top of the stairs.

Pause, deep breath, reassuring smile at the baby, safe and secure in his carrying chair, and Stella was ready – or as ready as she'd ever be. She was safe. She'd cleared the first hurdle, she was here, she silently tallied, and she'd been accepted.

Even so, Stella took the stairs in silence, for all the world as if she were descending the stairway to hell.

CHAPTER 2

It was Hannah who saw them first, her eyes widening like saucers as they switched from Stella's face to the baby she held and back again, her mouth forming a perfect O.

Catching Hannah's reaction, two sets of eyes swivelled round, the shock almost tangible. Silence. Screaming silence. And then the grating sound of metal on wood as Alex Gifford came so hurriedly to his feet the chair was propelled backwards.

'Miss Marshall. Punctual to the second, I see. But I thought you understood,' he murmured tightly, coming forward to meet her, rugged features carved out of granite. 'The child remains upstairs. There's a super-efficient listening device plugged into every room, and I can assure you he's perfectly safe for an hour or so.'

'Maybe so,' Stella agreed pleasantly. 'But James has already spent the night and half the day alone. He needs company.'

'The Mary Poppins school of philosophy?' he sneered. 'And this from the woman ready to tend them and leave them at the drop of a hat.'

'Hardly,' Stella bit out, flushing, though heaven knew she had nothing to feel embarrassed about. 'But if James isn't welcome . . .' She let the sentence hang, searched those cold blue eyes for a hint of a thaw and didn't find one. Without a word, she spun on her heels and retraced her steps, acutely conscious of three sets of eyes boring holes in her back.

She'd reached the foot of the stairs before Alex Gifford's voice sliced across to halt her.

'Five minutes, Miss Marshall. And not a moment longer. Understand?'

Stella nodded grimly. 'Perfectly.'

Five minutes to climb the stairs, walk the length of the house, settle the baby into his cot and make the reverse journey.

Five minutes minus one and Stella had re-entered the playroom. Five minutes minus two and a seething Stella was down on her knees in front of the carry-chair, angling James into an upright position. Five minutes minus three and James was gurgling in delight as Stella played hide and seek from behind a chair. Five minutes minus four and the game had switched to tickling James's feet with an assortment of cuddly toys. At five minutes precisely the door swung open behind her.

'What are you doing?' Alex Gifford. With a voice that would slice through steel.

'Doing? Why, the job that you pay me for,' Stella conceded warily. 'Nothing more, nothing less, I assure you.'

'And I assure you, Miss Marshall, you're expected at the table. Now. I trust I make myself clear?'

'As crystal. Or a bell. Or a dozen and one comparatives. In fact, it's as plain as the nose on my face. James stays up here.'

Alex Gifford smiled. Leastwise, his mouth did. The light simply didn't reach those ice-blue eyes. 'Got it in one. Now if you don't mind, Mrs Edwards is ready to serve.'

'Don't let me keep you.'

'I don't intend to. Believe me, no one but no one keeps Alex Gifford waiting.'

Stella's mouth formed the ghost of a smile. No. She could well imagine. The Alex Giffords of the world snapped their eloquently manicured fingers and everyone jumped to attention. Everyone but Stella. Because Alex Gifford didn't own her and Alex Gifford had unwittingly hit the nail on the head in the first place. Tend them and leave them. Love them and leave them. No involvement, no commitment. One assignment over and time to move on with rarely a backward glance. She felt a twinge of annoyance that she couldn't stick around for Carly's sake, but she'd allow a couple of days for her sister to surface and then if the worst came to the worst, Stella would go to the police. A missing person? Hardly. Clearly absent, judging from the empty wardrobes, but since she *had* taken the car . . . No need for Stella to overreact – yet.

At a definite disadvantage on her knees, Stella came slowly to her feet and, drawing herself up to her full five feet five inches, looked Alex Gifford straight in the eye. And waited. And Alex Gifford waited.

James broke the impasse, giving a shriek of delight

as his outstretched hand connected with the figures swinging on the play bar in front of him.

Stella smiled indulgently, caught Alex Gifford's flash of hatred – or pain – and had to fight the urge to back away.

'You're being obtuse,' he murmured coldly. 'You're an intelligent woman. You don't need me to spell things out to you.'

'Do as I'm told – or else?' Stella challenged calmly – a lot more calmly than she felt. She shrugged. 'You're an intelligent man,' she conceded in turn. 'You hired me – apparently. You're well within your rights to fire me. A quick call to the agency and the regulation nanny is yours for the moulding. Not being a slip of a girl, a flighty bit of baggage,' she conceded flippantly, 'I'm a little bit set in my ways, you see. And since I clearly don't suit . . .'

'Fine.' He nodded grimly, crossed to the phone lifted the handset and held it out for Stella to take. 'Call them. You explain. And make it snappy, hey? Who knows? Mrs Edwards might even treat you to lunch in the kitchen before you leave.'

Stella swallowed hard, licked her dry lips, didn't move, couldn't move. Panic. Call the agency. Greenhavens – the name she recalled; the number she wouldn't remember in a thousand years. Time to come clean, then, not that coming clean would matter now. For, whichever way she played it, she was out on her ear. Unless an irate Alex Gifford called the police? Stella bristled. Even better. He might not know it, but he'd be doing Stella a favour.

Without a word, she took the receiver from his outstretched hand, brushed against his fingers, the skin to skin contact searing, unnerving, the sudden rush of colour to her cheeks an irritation she could well have done without. And, turning her back in an effort to escape his intense silent scrutiny, began dialling automatically. 0181 . . . Her own number, she realized as the dialling tone changed to the robotic chant of the answer-machine. 'Stella Marshall. If you can't reach me here, leave your name and number after –'

A hand reached past her shoulder, cutting the connection. A bewildered Stella spun round, meeting his gaze and reading nothing in the frigid pools that returned hers unblinkingly.

'Mr Gifford?' she queried absurdly.

'I've changed my mind,' he explained without emotion. 'Don't look so surprised, my dear. It's not the exclusive prerogative of the female of the species.'

'You – want me to stay?' she asked, hardly daring to believe it.

'For now,' he conceded with a rare flash of humour. 'Let's just say, I'm intrigued. And better the nanny you know than the flighty bit of baggage you don't,' he added, almost lightly. 'Besides, lunch is getting cold, and I for one am ravenous. Shall we go?'

'I . . .' Stella shrugged, reached for James, discovered Alex had forestalled her and watched in amazement as he led the way across the room.

Pausing at the door, he turned, stepped aside, waved an airy hand. 'After you,' he urged politely.

Only if you insist, Stella derided silently, inwardly

seething, and with a curt nod of assent she swept past, leaving father and son to follow at their own pace.

Unfamiliar with the layout of the house, she followed her nose, the tap of heels on parquet flooring betraying her approach. And sure enough, when Stella pulled up in the archway, Tamara and Hannah were waiting, a look of spiteful enjoyment on one face, thinly veiled amusement on the other.

Stella stiffened. Yet she who laughs last, laughs longest, she consoled herself grimly, and with a regal sweep of her arm turned to herald the grand entrance.

No mood-setting drum roll on this happy occasion, though. Alex and his son stepped into the frame, and into a seething, simmering silence.

'Well, well, well,' Tamara Clayton drawled, recovering fast and masking the shock in an instant. 'Who'd have believed it?'

Lunch. Plain and somewhat unimaginative, but not the platefuls of stodge Tamara had claimed. And no formal introductions, just an assumption that Stella would know the set-up – which she did, thanks to Carly's letters.

Chatty letters, full of life in the big house and life in the village, acidic observations on one lady balanced by the pity directed at another. Only the letters had grown shorter, the cheerful tone disintegrating so slowly that Stella hadn't noticed at first. And, since she'd been working abroad, nothing else for it but to try not to worry and resolve to drop by as soon as she was home. And twenty-four hours earlier, she acknowledged wryly, she'd have managed it.

'Wine, Miss Marshall?'

'Thank you, Mr Gifford, but no. Not while I'm –'

'On duty? How very commendable,' he observed with a thinly veiled sneer. 'But a single glass isn't going to hurt. Unless it turns out you're a closet alcoholic?'

'Stocking the nursery shelves with innocuous little bottles? Pour the gripe-water out and the vodka in and no one's any the wiser? Colourless, odourless, tasteless . . .' Stella shrugged. 'You never know,' she needled lightly.

Alex ignored the challenge, just a tightening of the jaw-line betraying his annoyance. 'Tell me,' he entreated coolly, 'gripe-water aside, what are the attractions of this particular job?'

'Sleepless nights?' she couldn't help but tease, using the banter to cover her nerves.

Inquisition time. Doubtless the first of many, but, since a journalist lived on her wits, no real problem for Stella. Unless someone was suspicious in the first place. No reason to be suspicious, surely. Yet.

'Soiled nappies and mewling, puking infants,' Tamara Clayton observed, her pert nose wrinkling. 'Sounds divine. Thank heavens someone's prepared to take it on. When my turn comes –'

'Only it won't,' Alex reminded her slyly. 'Ruin your figure in childbirth? Heaven forbid.'

Tamara had the grace to blush. 'Maybe. Maybe not,' she conceded tetchily. 'But since fatherhood ill becomes you, darling, it's hardly your place to judge.'

'I was simply making an observation, my dear. But you're right, of course. Fatherhood doesn't appeal.'

'Present tense, or future?' Stella challenged lightly, switching her gaze from Alex Gifford's thunderous face to the baby, carefully positioned in sight of the table and beginning to flag, his presence clearly forgotten by the less than doting papa.

'Mine to know and yours not to enquire,' he rebuked, reaching for his glass and draining it.

'Miss Marshall – Stella. I can call you Stella?' Hannah queried pleasantly, drawing the sting from Alex's terse words.

Stella nodded, swapping Alex's chill gaze for Hannah's openly warm one. Only Hannah's smile faltered, a shadow of doubt crossing her face, and with that guilty conscience prickling, Stella could only sit and squirm.

'You know,' Hannah mused, blue eyes clouding, 'I can't shake the feeling that we've met before.' Half-statement, half-query, setting Stella's nerves on edge as the silence drew out – a screaming, deafening silence. And then Hannah shook her head, the halo of curls glinting gold in the shafts of sunlight streaming through the blinds. 'Of course we haven't,' she conceded doubtfully. 'I'd have remembered. We'd both have remembered. And in your line of work it's all the more unlikely our paths would have crossed. So . . .' Leaning forward, she smiled, banished the awkward moment. 'Is bringing up other people's children really your life ambition?'

'It's – a very rewarding job,' Stella conceded carefully. 'But a job for life in this day and age?' She shrugged, smiled. 'Who knows.'

'Who cares?' Tamara put in rudely.

'Stella, presumably,' Alex chided lightly, the formal 'Miss Marshall' for the present consigned to the nappy bin. 'So, tell me, Stella, how long have you worked for Greenhavens?'

'I don't. I'm freelance.' The truth – and if not the whole truth and nothing but, then as much as Stella could allow.

'You mean the agency doesn't employ you?'

'Not directly,' she conceded warily.

'Which means – what, precisely?'

'Where the job leads, I follow. And, whilst I'm generally independent, I'm happy to pick up the occasional commission.'

'Commission? Looking after babies?' Tamara – voicing her derision. Alex's flash of warning passed her by. 'How grand. How pretentious. How downright ridiculous.'

'Tam –'

'It's quite all right,' Stella cut in pleasantly. 'Miss Clayton is perfectly correct. It's a job, nothing more, nothing less, but it keeps me independent and gives me the means to pay the bills.' She risked a calculated glance at the woman to her left. 'It beats sponging from a man any day.'

'I don't think –'

'No,' Stella cut in coolly. 'You don't. But I do. I put my brain into gear before I open my mouth and that way, Miss Clayton,' she explained, saccharine-sweetly, 'I normally manage to keep the peace. Normally. Naturally there are times when only the truth will do.'

'And, surprise, surprise, this is one of them?'

'It doesn't have to be,' Stella conceded pleasantly. 'Like the job, I prefer to follow the lead that I'm given.'

Tamara flushed to the roots of that stark, stunning hairstyle, jet-black and fashionably short, a boyish, skullcap wedge and the perfect backdrop for the exquisite porcelain face with its discreet application of make-up. Not so much exquisite now as fleetingly ugly, Stella amended as Tamara reached for her glass, draining it in one before pushing it across for Alex to fill.

Alex did, that lazy smile spreading as he held out the bottle in general enquiry. 'Stella? Hannah? No? No,' he agreed, reaching for the carafe of water. 'Much better to keep one's wits. Bad for the company's image, of course, the boss endorsing another product, but even so I think I'll join you. So –' a lightning switch of focus, a lightning return to the subject '– if the agency doesn't employ you, Stella, what's the connection?'

'The c-connection?' she stalled, meeting those razor-sharp eyes with difficulty.

'You know, the link. The method of communication. Don't ring us, we'll ring you – and how convenient you just happened to be free.'

Stella shrugged, vaguely aware of the silence, a loaded silence, and three sets of curious eyes. Four, since the housekeeper had appeared in the open doorway and, sensing an atmosphere, was hovering with tangible expectancy.

Steeling herself to hold his gaze, Stella mentally crossed her fingers. 'All hands on deck in a crisis,' she explained. 'The flu epidemic. But you don't have to take my word for it. Mrs Edwards spoke to the agency just after I arrived.'

'Indeed I did,' she obligingly confirmed, sweeping through in a swish of starched apron and retrieving the plates with an ease born of practice. 'They couldn't apologize enough, sir, and, reading between the lines, we were lucky there was anyone left to send. Going down like nine-pins they are, yet that little madam, Carly, simply ups and leaves at the drop of a hat. Young women these day . . .' Pause, sniff, a pointed glance at a bristling Tamara. 'Bone-idle, unreliable –'

'Thank you, Mrs Edwards. I think we have the picture. And we've just about finished here. If you could serve coffee in the lounge? And thank you. The meal was first-rate.'

'First-rate stod –'

'Precisely.' He cut Tamara short, smiling, a flash of white teeth that would have served a basking shark proud. 'First-rate. Mouth. Brain. Gear,' Alex murmured pleasantly under his breath. 'Advice well worth heeding. Coffee, ladies? If Hannah would lead the way?'

Seeing the baby's head begin to loll on his shoulders, Stella held back, caught between the devil and the deep blue sea. Should she risk disturbing James by taking him upstairs and placing him in his cot? Or leave him to sleep in the carry-chair?

'Decisions, decisions,' Alex scorned, sensing her dilemma. 'Now if you'd left him in the nursery the first place . . .'

31

'Out of sight, out of mind?' Stella needled, reaching for the handle. 'But maybe you're right. And better late than never. If you'll excuse us –'

'And if I don't?'

'Don't what?'

'Excuse you. Allow you to escape. Escape, Stella? The battling nanny's developed cold feet. Disappointing. Most disappointing.'

'Life generally is, Mr Gifford. Things rarely turn out the way we plan.'

'Depends who's doing the planning – or the buying. And you can take it from me, money's a powerful persuader.'

'Bribery and corruption? Depends who's doing the buying – or the selling. After all, one's no good without the other.'

'Meaning?'

'Money. All the money in the world can't buy what isn't for sale.'

'And Stella Marshall isn't for sale?'

'Got it in one.'

'But you do . . . hire out your services?'

'I certainly do. I believe it's called work. Toil, labour, employment, the sweat of one's brow. Occupation, trade, craft, vocation, profession, livelihood. I trust you're getting the message?'

'Loud and clear. So tell me, which of those applies to you?'

'Any – or all,' Stella informed him. 'Why not simply take your pick.'

'Why not indeed?' he mocked, though not unkindly.

'And while we're on the subject, which of those would apply to Tamara?'

'I wouldn't know,' Stella retorted, wary now, sensing a trap – or a reprimand.

Reprimand it was. Alex Gifford's smile spread, but the light didn't reach his eyes. 'Precisely. You don't know. So what gives you the right to sit in judgement?'

'I didn't –'

'Oh, but you did,' he contradicted stonily. 'And furthermore you were rude. Rude to my house guest. You do understand what I'm saying?'

'It's – coming over kind of loud and clear,' she conceded flippantly. 'Whoops! Time to go cap in hand and beg for forgiveness?'

'Hardly, since the damage is done now. Just bear it in mind the next time your brain goes into overdrive. Understand?'

Her response was automatic. 'Yes, sir!' she clipped, snapping fingers to her temple in jaunty salute. Catching Alex's flash of fury, Stella backed away.

'You, madam, are too sharp –'

'Alex?'

Ice-blue eyes released her, switching to Tamara, who was hovering in the doorway, her expression curiously bland.

'Tamara?'

'The coffee's getting cold,' she explained flatly.

'Fine. I'll be with you in a moment.' He nodded grimly at Stella. 'I'll catch up with *you* later.'

He did. Much later. Way past James's bed time. And, since Carly's letters had made it painfully clear that Alex Gifford didn't afford his son so much as the time of day, appearing in the nursery twice in the space of one day had to be nothing short of miraculous. Or part of the Alex Gifford 'put the staff in their place' ploy.

'Sit down, make yourself at home,' Stella invited calmly – a lot more calmly than she felt.

'I think not,' Alex demurred – a weary-looking Alex, she couldn't help but notice. Hardly surprising if he'd been travelling half the night – and half the day as well presumably. 'This isn't a social call.'

Surprise, surprise, Stella derided silently. Stifling the panic, she shrugged, led the way through in any case. She stood like an awkward schoolgirl hauled before the Head, then decided Alex could please himself but she was sitting down.

Another mistake, she quickly discovered, with Alex towering over her, six feet four inches of simmering man. All man. Powerful muscles rippling beneath the fine lawn fabric of his shirt. His open-necked shirt. The shadow of hair at his throat drew her gaze, sending currents of heat rippling through her wayward body. Dark and luxuriant, in erotic contrast to the short blond crop that would serve to please the most fastidious of sergeant majors. Military. Yes, come to think of it, his entire mien was military. Authoritative. Used to issuing orders and having them obeyed. Alex Gifford pronounces, and the whole world jumps to attention. Unnerving for Stella. Devastatingly unnerving for a girl like Carly, she was beginning to see. Yet the man was nothing but tender to Hannah, and as for Tamara –

Ah, yes, Tamara. The stepmother elect – apparently. And reason enough for Alex's grim expression. House rule number one, Stella recalled. Don't insult the house guests, and most definitely don't insult the master's intended.

'If you have quite finished?'

'Ah!' Stella's cheeks flamed. She'd been staring, had probably been glaring, but definitely appraising somewhere along the way. All man, she recalled, shivering despite the sudden surge of heat. Dangerous. Just like the expression in a pair of blue eyes.

'Yes, ah. Coming from anyone else, I'd probably be flattered. But you –'

He broke off, a smile playing about the corners of his mouth, and without so much as a by your leave flung himself down on the chair opposite.

His house, his prerogative, Stella decided sourly, wondering if in the interests of hospitality she ought to offer a drink. She did.

'Only coffee, mind. Or maybe I could interest sir in a neat slug of gripe-water?'

'Coffee will be fine,' he insisted. 'If it isn't too much trouble?'

'Since it's merely instant,' Stella warned, 'the trouble is negligible. Consider it done.'

'Why?'

'Why, what?' Stella stalled, pausing in the archway that divided the room into two – seating area and cooking area.

'Why merely instant? Doesn't the super-efficient and pernickety Miss Marshall prefer perked?'

'She certainly does,' Stella agreed solemnly.

'So?'

'The super-efficient and pernickety Miss Marshall hasn't had time to put a shopping list together. And even if she had,' she informed him sweetly, 'she doesn't suppose for a moment the list of nursery essentials stretches to a coffee machine.'

'You mean there isn't one here already?'

'Kettle, yes. Percolator, no. Fridge, yes. Freezer, no.' She began counting things off on her fingers. 'Microwave: one. Cooking ring: double. Plates: two of each in assorted sizes and patterns. Cups and mugs: ditto. Oh, yes, I almost forget, a drawerful of ancient cutlery. EPNS. Probably worth a small fortune these days.'

'And that's it?' he asked incredulously.

'You mean you don't know?' Stella enquired. 'Well, here's a turn-up for the books. I thought the rich and even richer hung on to their money by fair means or foul and knew to the last penny exactly what was theirs.'

'The exception that proves the rule?' he drawled, the set of his mouth a belated warning for Stella to hold her tongue. 'Well, maybe the super-efficient Miss Marshall is wrong for once. Yet, come to think of it, I poured a small fortune into this suite.'

'Worry not, Mr Gifford. I doubt you've been short-changed. James wants for nothing.'

'Ditto his nursemaid. Tomorrow, Stella, you make a list of what you need – a comprehensive list at that – and we'll have it sorted by the end of the day.'

'Hardly. Tomorrow's Sunday.'

'Never heard of seven-day shopping? Or, since we're barely an hour's drive from London, twenty-four-hour opening. You'll be sorted if I have to do it myself.'

'I guess there's a first time for everything,' Stella teased.

'Meaning?' His pupils were contracting, at odds with the casual enquiry. It was just a journalist's eye for detail picking up the signs. Annoyance. Anger. A simmering resentment. Because Alex Gifford wasn't used to open challenge. Or criticism. Or implicit condemnation. Or banter.

Poor little rich boy, Stella silently jeered. All the money in the world, yet whilst he knew how to make it – and spend it – Alex Gifford clearly didn't know how to loosen up and have fun. A bit of give and take. An innocent occupation, Stella mused, logging the set of his mouth, the needles of ice that passed for eyes, and wondering if that grim expression would lighten in love-play. Love. Man and woman. Alex and Tamara. An exquisite stab of pain.

Banishing the image, Stella forced a smile. 'Nothing. Just a throwaway remark. Ignore me.'

'Difficult, wouldn't you say? Since you're sitting large as life in front of me, disapproval stamped across your forehead, those well-aimed darts subtle enough to parry but impossible to miss. You don't approve?'

'Of you, Mr Gifford? How could I possibly judge on less than a day's acquaintance?'

'Prior knowledge, perhaps?'

'Hardly,' Stella demurred. 'Since I'm new in town.'

'Woman's intuition?' he sneered. 'Or, having crossed paths with the previous incumbent, a snatch of gossip? Gossip, Stella?' he repeated, dangerously coldly.

'Mine to know and yours not to enquire,' she reminded him coolly. 'If I have indulged in a spot of gossip – if,' she repeated evenly, 'it's a harmless occupation. Unless you've something to hide?'

'When it's plastered across the tabloids?' he bit out, coffee slurping over the rim as his untouched cup was thrust roughly down on the table. 'The hell it is. For gossip, Miss Marshall, read slander and defamation.'

'Contestable in law. If someone's spreading lies,' she pointed out coolly, 'the solution's glaringly obvious.'

'But of course,' Alex sneered. 'Just like the retraction. An apology not worth the cost of the ink it takes to print, and tucked inside where the chattering masses wouldn't notice. You saw it, of course?'

'Hardly,' Stella demurred, ignoring the well-aimed insult, 'since I haven't the least idea what you're driving at.'

'Don't lie, Miss Marshall. It really doesn't become you.'

'Slander – or defamation?' she challenged, her chin snapping up in annoyance.

'Clever,' he scorned. 'Very clever. And almost convincing.'

'So let me guess. Alex Gifford isn't impressed?'

'With your naïveté? Got it in one. Unless you've

been living on the moon for the last five months, you can't possibly plead ignorance.'

'I can, as it happens. Not that you want to believe me. Not that I care one way or the other. But if your conscience is squeaky clean,' she couldn't resist needling, 'why the heated reaction?'

'What's this?' he jeered. 'The Stella Marshall school of philosophy? Turn the other cheek while the gutter press wreaks havoc? Well, for your information, madam, I've had a bellyful. Gossip, slander, defamation and lies – lies and damned lies –'

'Precisely. Lies. You know the truth, and my opinion, like the rest of the chattering masses, surely counts for nought?'

'You –'

'Prefer to live in blissful ignorance. Fact, Mr Gifford, believe it or not.'

'You mean you really don't know?'

'How can I possibly know what I'm supposed to know or otherwise,' she pointed out dryly, 'unless you spell it out to me? But you're right, I suppose,' she added softly. 'Since I clearly haven't been living on the moon, I do know that you lost your wife.'

A swimming accident, Stella recalled, but the details were hazy, and, since Carly's employment hadn't started until three months later, Carly's letters had centred on the baby. Leastways, Stella recalled with a twinge of unease, they had at first.

'I lost my wife. Diplomacy at its best,' Alex sneered. 'Lost: one wife. Age twenty-four. Five feet six, slim build, green eyes, long blonde hair. Last seen stretched out on a lounger at the poolside. Reward for information leading to – what, I wonder? The truth, the whole truth and nothing but the truth? Or, since drowned women tell no tales, the sort of sleazy headlines that turn front-page news into a goldmine?'

'I'm sorry,' Stella murmured, sensing the pain behind the harshly spoken words. 'I didn't realize.'

'You mean you don't read the scandal sheets?'

'Not as a rule,' Stella stalled, with another twinge of conscience. The scandal sheets. Gossip and sleaze and Alex Gifford's open condemnation. And, given Stella's line of work, a second major deception. Heaven help her when Alex discovered the truth. Guilty as charged – on both counts. Impersonation of a nanny and a sleazy occupation – the lowest of the low in his eyes. Even to her own mind the plea sounded feeble. Because if Stella had been really so concerned for Carly's safety, she'd have gone to the police in the first place. Yet what does she do instead? Gains access to Alex Gifford's house and family by deception. Deception. If not a journalist's stock-in-trade, then a common perception of it and oh, what a tangled web she was managing to weave. Too late to come clean now, she consoled herself. She'd face the wrath of Alex Gifford if and when it happened.

'No.' He smothered a weary sigh, reached for the cup of coffee, cold and unappealing, changed his mind and shot Stella a rueful grin.

'I'll make some fresh –'

'*I'll* make some fresh,' he insisted, coming leisurely to his feet. 'Unless . . . ?'

'Unless?' Stella probed, forced to angle her head to meet his gaze, the breath leaving her body as her eyes locked with his.

He shrugged, pointedly checked his watch. 'It's late. You must be tired.'

'No more than you,' she countered politely, recalling his overnight flight – from one of the far-flung Gifford vineyards, presumably. 'And since this wasn't a social call . . .'

He smiled then, the light even managing to reach his eyes, she noted, glowing inside. 'So it wasn't,' he conceded lightly. 'But I guess it is now – unless you'd like me to leave?'

The coward's way out, Stella mused. Her reactions to this man she barely knew were thoroughly alarming. But since he was in receptive mood . . . No! Sly. Underhand. A journalist's stock-in-trade. Better to let him go, she decided. And yet even as the thought occurred, she stifled it. Smiling, she shook her head. 'Coffee?' she reminded him brightly. 'Instant, I believe, if sir could manage to boil the kettle?'

'You, madam, would be surprised at what sir could do in a reasonably equipped kitchen. And if you stick around long enough I might even prove it.'

'I doubt it,' Stella countered, flirting, but not the least bit repentant. 'The prim and proper Mrs Edwards wouldn't allow it.'

'Ah, yes, but if I ask nicely, the anything but prim and proper Miss Marshall might prove more receptive.'

'I wouldn't bank on that either. And furthermore, in

this particular kitchen you'd be hard-pressed to boil so much as an egg.'

'Ah, yes, but not for much longer,' he reminded her. 'And that goes for decent coffee. Still, I guess instant will do for now?'

'Sounds perfect.' Smiling? Flirting? At her age. And with this devastating man of all people.

Definitely devastating, Stella acknowledged, sipping the scalding coffee and glancing across through the veil of her lashes. Uncompromisingly grim at times, but surprisingly easy to talk to once the barriers came down.

Barriers. A steel wall around his heart. A heart of stone, according to Carly, who had never managed to come to terms with Alex's neglect of his son. Not physical neglect, since James clearly wanted for nothing, but emotional. Yet perhaps not so much neglect as total indifference. As far as Alex was concerned, the child didn't exist. So – the fifty-thousand-dollar question – why? Unless James was too poignant a reminder of the wife he'd lost? Stella mused, floundering in the dark and beginning to think blissful ignorance was a state she couldn't afford – for her own sake as much as Carly's. Which meant she would have to probe and Alex Gifford wouldn't like it. Ah, yes, but if she was careful, she consoled herself, he might never know.

'You know, you're the most unusual nanny I've ever come across,' said Alex, breaking into her thoughts, triggering a surge of guilty colour in Stella's cheeks.

'I don't see why.'

'Strong-willed, forthright, downright rude when the occasion demands it.'

'I simply give as good as I get,' she informed him crisply. 'If and when necessary.'

'Precisely. Pert. Impertinent. Impudent. If not bordering on the insolent.'

'An unfortunate legacy of my advancing years,' she reminded him, completely unrepentant. 'Not being a flighty bit of baggage, I'm somewhat prone to speaking my mind.'

'Mary Poppins Mark II?'

'No, Mr Gifford. Stella Marshall Mark I.'

'Yes. I do believe you're right. Like I said, unusual. So how long –?'

'Have I been gainfully employed?' Stella cut in, the thought of looking him in the eye and spouting a downright lie more than she could take. 'I guess I always knew what I wanted and let nothing stand in my way.'

'And now?'

'Now?' Stella stalled, feeling her way in the dark.

'You're what – twenty-seven, twenty-eight?' he mused, eyes narrowing thoughtfully. 'And still single. And, since you clearly like kids, have you no plans of your own? No Mr Right hovering in the background?'

'None of your business,' she said politely, pointedly coming to her feet, conversation over and done with. 'And coming from a man who values his privacy . . .'

'You're right. I was prying. My apologies.'

'Accepted.'

'This time.'

'This time?' Stella repeated absurdly.

'The note of warning in your tone. I've given it myself often enough. Don't overstep the mark – or else.'

'Hardly,' she countered crisply, leading the way across the room. 'But –'

'Ah, yes, the but. Point made. Point taken. Goodnight, Miss Marshall. Sweet dreams, Miss Marshall. See you bright and early for breakfast.'

'Why?'

'Why, what?'

'Why breakfast? I'm an employee, not a house guest, and all the nannies that I know eat with their charges in the nursery or join the staff below stairs.'

'My house, my decision,' he reminded her. 'Breakfast. Eight o'clock sharp.'

'Yes, sir!' Stella bit out, too late recalling Alex's fury at the same snappy comment earlier in the day.

Sure enough his face changed, not so much to anger as fury mixed with pain, and suddenly afraid, but not sure why, Stella stumbled backwards, felt the wall at her back bring her up short, and shrank against the plaster as rigid fingers reached out to close about her shoulders.

CHAPTER 3

Breakfast at eight. With or without her charge? Stella wondered, wondering too if Alex would remember issuing the invitation in the first place. Less an invitation than an order, she amended, the heated scene replaying in her mind . . .

Anger, Alex's muffled oath, those rigid fingers digging deep, bruising, punishing, though heaven alone knew why, and yet a moment later she was in his arms, Alex's sharp hiss of breath triggering another surge of emotion. Fear. That Alex was going to kiss her. That Alex wasn't about to kiss her. Yet, body against body, with his open palms sliding the length of her spine, Stella's instinct to bolt was completely swamped by another emotion – want, need. A woman's needs long denied. Madness, she told herself, freezing, refusing to struggle yet determined to deny him. How to deny him, with magic hands gliding over the swell of her buttocks, his lips nuzzling the corner of her mouth, Alex's low words an incomprehensible murmur and yet music to her ears?

And Stella was losing the battle, her tightly clamped

lips no match for Alex's persuasive mouth, insidious, insisting, now the merest hint of connection, now a lightning change of tack, lips nibbling, nuzzling, the follow-on sweep of tongue unnervingly erotic. Stella gasped, allowing his tongue to dart into the secret moist depths, Alex's growl of satisfaction filling her with heat, filling her with dread. Want. Need. A body's needs, Stella's needs long suppressed.

She didn't need a man. Not now. Not ever. She had her life and she was happy, and men, she told herself grimly, were surplus to requirements. Men. Selfish, self-centred and ruthlessly efficient at taking what they wanted, and heaven help the women they trampled along the way. Women. Plural. If Stella's father was anything to go by. Not to mention Toby – no!

She didn't want to remember, refused to remember, hadn't time to remember with Alex's hands sweeping the curves of her body, Alex's mouth invading her own, and, *yes*, she wanted him to kiss her! Shameful, shameless. Had she no pride, wanting the touch, the taste, returning the kiss? Mouth against mouth, lips exploring lips, tongues entwining, exploring, exciting. Mouth, hands, fingers – and Stella's knees had buckled and she was swaying against him, another surge of heat rippling through her because, body to body, Alex's needs were every bit as urgent as her own.

'No! No, no, no,' she murmured in anguish, attempting to pull away.

'Yes!' Alex contradicted thickly, tugging her even

closer, and the shock of connection drove the breath from her body all over again.

'No, Alex,' she repeated, but she was wasting her time, because Alex's mouth was covering hers, lips devouring, the touch exquisite. Stella's need was too real to be playing her false; touch, taste, kiss, touch again – magic hands sweeping into the curve of her waist and on, and upwards, the merest hint of connection at breasts that ached for a touch, a man's touch, barely a touch, a fleeting, bitter-sweet denial.

Control. She had to stay in control – deny him, deny herself just as badly. Woman or wimp? she silently goaded herself, damping down the panic. Because heaven help her she wanted this man, this man whom she barely knew yet had heard so much about from Carly. Carly. The reason Stella was here, now, in this house. Only Carly wasn't here, of course. Carly had bolted. Why had Carly bolted? she silently probed, shockingly aware she was losing the battle to deny him. Want, need, desire. Kiss, touch, taste. Man and woman. Stella and Alex. Alex and Carly. No!

'No!' With a massive surge of will, Stella brought her arms up, pushed hard against him, knocking herself off balance in the process. Stumbling back against the wall, she caught Alex's stunned expression and smothered a hysterical laugh. No time to laugh with Alex's fingers closing round her shoulders.

'You little –'

'Bitch?' Stella supplied, her head snapping up at the hatred in his eyes, the venom in his tone.

He smiled, little more than a contemptuous curl of

lips. 'If you say so,' he conceded, but at least he released her, almost thrust her away and back against the wall.

She leaned back against the wall, struggling for control as the aftershock of ripples continued unabated. How could she? How could she come so close to losing control with a man she barely knew? she silently berated herself, squeezing back the tears. Pride. Little enough to hang on to. Pride. With this man's hatred, his open contempt washing over her? Oh, yes? Oh, no! Stella stiffened.

'Playtime, Mr Gifford?' she enquired icily. 'Amuse thyself with the hired hand? What's the matter? Doesn't the sultry Miss Clayton live up to all that promise –?'

'Don't you dare drag Tamara through the mires of your mind.'

'It was – just a thought,' she sneeringly conceded. 'After all, I can't imagine why else you'd be wasting time with me – unless,' she queried coldly, 'you think it's a social service you're providing?'

'I beg your pardon?'

'Servicing the nanny. Or should that be plural?' she enquired, eyes fastened on his, searching his, logging each and every nuance of emotion. Please, God, let it be no, she silently prayed. But she had to ask, she had to know.

Anger. Disbelief. Amazement. Sheer incredulity.

Alex laughed, blue eyes loaded with scorn. 'Good God, woman, give me some credit,' he entreated harshly. 'The girl was barely out of the nursery. It would have been tantamount to eating my own young.'

'The girl,' Stella reminded him icily, 'was nineteen. And something caused her to bolt.'

'Not guilty, my dear. Not having been around for a week or two, not having chanced my luck when I was. I like my women to be women – not prissy misses with one eye on their virtue and another on a wedding ring. I didn't, I wouldn't, I couldn't.'

'If you say so,' she murmured, in a calculated echo of an earlier remark.

Alex's chin snapped up, the flash of anger in chill blue eyes all the truth Stella needed. Alex hadn't, Alex wouldn't. Not with Carly at least. But Carly *had* taken off without a backward glance, and Carly's letters to Stella had grown more and more disquieting.

'It's this house,' she'd explained, less than a week ago. 'I feel it's closing in on me. There's evil lurking in corners. The place gives me the creeps, Stell, and not just because it's old. The house is creepy, the inhabitants are creepy and especially –' She'd broken off there, had clearly finished the letter later in a hurry. She was heading in to town for a hot date, she'd confided; her whole tone chirpier, but Stella hadn't been convinced, and, arriving unannounced today, she'd hoped to discover why. Only Carly wasn't here. Carly had bolted. Or leastways, Stella amended as an icy finger touched her heart, she hoped she had.

'You know,' Alex murmured coldly. 'You and I must have a little talk. Soon. Only not now. It's late, and, since I was travelling half the night, my body clock insists it's even later. But if you stay – if,' he underlined softly, 'then you need to learn a few ground rules – and fast.'

'Like treat the master with respect? Be seen and not heard? Speak only when spoken to? Lay my humble cloak over any incommoding puddle?' she mocked, folding her arms. A defensive gesture maybe, but it helped her to feel in control. 'Well, fine,' she acknowledged silkily. 'As long as it works both ways. Employees have rights, too, Mr Gifford.'

'I didn't doubt it for an instant. But, since you clearly do, why not check it out with Mrs Edwards? Or Mandy. Or any one of a dozen others who work around the place. Conduct a survey, why don't you?' he scornfully invited. 'Ask away. And if you hear so much as a grumble of discontent, feel free to think the worst. Only you won't.'

'No, since the one person likely to complain is conspicuous by her absence.'

'That flighty piece of baggage who called herself a nanny? Your opinion – or hers?' he queried coldly.

'Mine to know, and yours to find out,' she mocked.

'Maybe. If I thought it mattered. Only it doesn't, of course.'

'And how do you make that out?' she enquired coolly. 'Carly isn't here. She's walked out on a job she loves and *that, Mr Gifford*, takes a lot of doing.'

'And you'd know, of course? Privy to her deepest thoughts? For a mere passing acquaintance, Miss Marshall, you make a lot of presumptions.'

Yes. Stella flushed, aware that over-concern for Carly could give her away, bring her own deception out into the open. No bad thing at the end of the day. One day, she reminded herself. Twenty-four hours. Too early to overreact, so why not simply stay calm and take advantage of the situation that had offered itself? Sly? Underhand? All in a day's work? She could allow that, but it was not something she relished.

'It's the nature of the job,' she retorted coolly, her words unwittingly ironic. 'Nannies are trained to stay cool, calm and collected even in a crisis. They're reliable, stable, overworked, underpaid and, in far too many cases, ruthlessly exploited. And still they do the job.'

'Or disappear without so much as a by-your-leave.'

'Precisely. Out of character, I'd say.'

'I wouldn't know, since I barely knew the girl.'

'And now that she's gone, it's a case of out of sight, out of mind, I suppose?'

'Meaning?'

Stella shrugged. 'Nothing. Why should you care? A passing acquaintance. A hired hand. You paid her wages. End of responsibility.'

'Got it one. Her life, her job, her decision. And if you were to walk out of here tomorrow, Miss Marshall, I'd doubtless think the same.'

'How reassuring to know that you care.'

'I do, as it happens – up to a point. Believe it or not, I've too many demands on my time to worry about things beyond my control. Carly walked out. End of contract.'

'And the reasons why?'

'Her business, I'd say. Not mine – or yours.'

'I don't agree. If I'm taking Carly's place, then I've a right to know.'

He shrugged, an offhand lift of powerful shoulders. 'Stick around long enough, and who knows . . . ?' Another shrug, a faintly mocking smile, and then he swung away, reached the door to the hallway and called without turning, 'Goodnight, Miss Marshall. Sleep well. Sweet dreams.'

Dreams. Nightmares, more like, with Carly and Alex Gifford at the centre.

Late to bed, early to rise, thanks to little James Gifford and his lusty set of lungs, his pressing need for food. A healthy ten months old and with an array of baby foods stacked neatly in the cupboards. Tins, jars, packets – like the bottles Carly had left ready in the fridge, fine for an emergency, but just the sort of processed pap to give Beth a fit of the vapours. Beth. Time to give her cousin a call. Only not yet, Stella decided, and definitely not from the house phone. But with a crash course in childcare as pressing a need for Stella as James's need for food, there was no time to waste.

Nursery breakfast. Rusks softened with formula milk carefully made as per instructions, and as much of the top-up bottle as James would take. Stella sat back on her heels, ruefully regarded the mess she – and James – had managed to make.

'Hardly worth dressing you in the first place,' she conceded, using a damp flannel to wipe his hands, clear away the debris from fingers, face and wisps of hair. And out of the creases of his ears. Heaven only knows how it had ended up there! And then, of course, with one end reasonably clean, the reflex action after food meant there was the other end to attend to. More mess, and a fastidious Stella held her nose, wondering if there was time to give James another bath before heading downstairs.

From deep within the house a clock chimed the hour. Eight o'clock. Risk the wrath of the master and arrive late, plus baby clean and shining? Risk the wrath of the master and arrive on time plus baby slightly grubby? Risk the wrath of the master and fail to arrive at all? But, since Alex had come to find her for lunch less than eighteen hours ago, she might as well get it over and done with. Thank heavens for baby wipes – extra thick or otherwise – she noted, swallowing a smile. Extra thick babies? The mind boggled. But, tired or no, at least she was smiling as she and James pulled up on the threshold of the breakfast room.

'You're late.' Tamara Clayton, alone, bored, hostile. Her plate of half-eaten food cold and congealing and pushed carelessly away.

Stella nodded, noted the three unused place-settings and rearranged her face into what she hoped would pass for deference. 'I'm afraid so. Occupational hazard, you know.'

'No. As a matter of fact, I don't. And if you must dine with the family, can't you at least make it alone?'

'Difficult, I'd say, since James has more right to be here than I have,' Stella murmured pleasantly, taking the chair opposite and angling the baby's carry-chair towards her. 'But if you've finished, don't let me keep you. I'm perfectly happy.'

'I bet.'

'Meaning?'

'You. Here. Wining and dining in style. Didn't anyone ever tell you the nanny's place is below stairs?'

'Upstairs, actually,' Stella corrected mildly, shaking out her napkin. 'In the nursery. Unless I'm told otherwise.'

'By Alex?'

Stella nodded. 'By Alex,' she echoed, daring the younger woman to contradict.

She didn't, simply baring her teeth in a mocking semblance of a smile. 'But Alex – Mr Gifford – isn't here. He's been called away on business. A couple of hours, a couple of days, a couple of weeks . . .' She paused, shrugged, spread her hands.

'And let me guess,' Stella put in dryly, 'you're about to countermand his orders?'

'Hardly orders, Miss Marshall. More a temporary aberration. No offence intended –'

'No offence taken,' Stella interrupted. 'You're perfectly right; I don't belong here. But worry not, you won't be forced to rub shoulders with the hired hand for a moment longer than necessary. Breakfast, I believe? Since I was invited. If you don't mind?'

'And if I do?'

Stella gave a rueful smile, reached for the cafetière of coffee a clearly disapproving Mrs Edwards had set down at her elbow, poured her cup to the brim and spooned in sugar with slow deliberation. 'At the risk of sounding rude, Miss Clayton, the word that comes to mind is "tough".'

'You think you're clever, don't you?'

'Because I speak my mind?' Stella shook her head. 'Let's just say that if life's a battle, then I'm a survivor. I do an honest hour's work for an honest hour's pay and I refuse to allow the world, or anyone in it, to trample over me. It's called "take me as you find me – or leave me alone".'

'No contest. I wouldn't dream of wasting time by even swapping insults.'

'Good.' Stella nodded. 'I'm glad we understand one another.'

'Just so long as we do. And just in case there's a shadow of doubt, that includes Alex.'

'I beg your pardon?' Stella felt a frisson of alarm as she paused, fork half-way to her mouth, the heated scene with Alex weighing heavy all of a sudden.

'Alex. My fiancée. Your employer. *Employer*, Miss Marshall. Nothing more, nothing less. Understand?'

'Hands off, he's yours? But if you're really so sure,' Stella couldn't resist goading, 'why the thinly veiled warning? Unless Alex makes a habit of seducing the staff?'

'Don't be so ridiculous –'

'Exactly. The idea's absurd. Now all you have to do is start to believe it.'

'You little –'

'Tamara! Good heavens, what on earth are you doing up at this time?' Hannah, appearing in the archway, her approach out of nowhere strangely unnerving.

Sheer imagination, Stella mused, as Hannah glided forward, or did a set of green eyes flash their derision?

'Good morning, Hannah,' Tamara retorted sweetly. 'And you're right. That makes two of us up bright and early. But you could have saved yourself the effort. Alex isn't here.'

'Oh?' Hannah wrinkled her nose, allowed fleetingly cloudy eyes to rest on Tamara. 'You mean –?'

'Duty calls,' Tamara told her crisply. 'Problems in France. The workers at one of the bottling plants are threatening a walk-out and Alex has been called to intervene. But then, doesn't that speak volumes? Staff these days,' she declared with a withering glance at Stella, 'just don't know their place.' Smothering a yawn, she crumpled her napkin into a ball and came lazily to her feet. 'Now, if you'll excuse me, I think I'll catch up on my beauty sleep.'

'Something I said?' Hannah enquired with a conspiratorial wink as Tamara ambled out.

Stella swallowed a smile. 'Staff these days,' she echoed wickedly, 'just don't know their place, I'm afraid.'

'Ah. The lady of the house has pretensions of grandeur. Only she isn't, of course.'

'No.' Lady-elect maybe, in Tamara's eyes at least, but if Stella was reading things right, that particular role fell to Hannah. Undercurrents. She'd been right. The place was almost awash. Understandable in a way, given a houseful of women and a man as dynamic as rugged Alex Gifford, but surely not enough to unnerve Carly? Unless Alex really had made a pass? Impossible thought. Stella's stab of pain instinctively suppressed it. 'Correct me if I'm wrong,' she mused, 'but there is a happy announcement in the offing?'

'A happy –? Oh, *that*,' Hannah scorned, her heart-shaped face fleetingly ugly. 'Well, Tamara isn't the first, and, knowing Giff, she won't be the last. A bit like the string of nannies, I suppose. Here today, gone tomorrow,' she carelessly reminded her, blue eyes oozing challenge.

Stella felt a prickle of alarm. Giff. A pet name. And another thinly veiled warning unless she was mistaken. Hands off, he's mine, perhaps. Definite shades of Tamara. 'Like Carly, you mean?' she enquired carefully, pulling a freshly baked croissant apart with her fingers. 'Strange, according to the agency, Carly'd been here some time.'

'Three months,' Hannah allowed. 'Which is two months, three weeks longer than the rest. This poor little mite's had more nannies than I've had hot dinners, haven't you, poppet?'

The 'poor little mite' chose that moment to sneeze, and, fishing a tissue from a pocket, Stella crouched down, gently wiping his nose and tickling beneath his chin as James squealed out a protest at the one, squealed in delight at the other. She resumed her place at the table as Agnes Edwards sidled in with a freshly cooked plateful of sausage, bacon and eggs.

'About lunch,' she murmured, hovering beside Hannah. 'Mr Gifford didn't say when to expect him?'

'You know Giff, Mrs Edwards. Just carry on as normal and expect him when you see him. He's flown to France, apparently.'

'Aye. Didn't even have chance to get his head down. Though why he couldn't have left it till this morning, I'll never know.'

'Time, Mrs E. And money. And Giff's a workaholic.'

'Unlike some I could mention.'

'Present company excepted, of course?' A broad grin from Hannah, at their exchange of light banter. No undercurrents here, Stella observed with tangible relief. Normality. The first hint of normality. Or maybe, with worrying over Carly, Stella was simply overreacting, reading hidden meanings into every word or glance.

Leaving Hannah to her breakfast, Stella scraped back her chair, reached for James, allowed an idle thought to surface. 'I – er – thought I'd explore the village later. Give James an airing. It's a beautiful day for a walk,' she observed casually. And then, with some of Carly's comments in mind, added equally casually, 'Perhaps you'd like to join us?'

'In a walk?'

Stella flushed, held the younger woman's gaze without flinching and nodded. 'For a walk,' she repeated evenly, fingers crossed that she'd read things right.

Hannah's smile transformed her features. 'Why not?' she murmured, as if to herself. And then she nodded. 'Yes. I do believe a walk would be just the thing to blow away the cobwebs. Two o'clock suit? I'll look forward to it.'

An ally? Maybe, Stella allowed, settling James for a nap, but in the meantime she had work to do: a follow-up article she'd promised by nine o'clock on Tuesday morning, which luckily was almost finished but would normally go by E-mail. Stella's lips twisted. Normality. Chance would be a fine thing, given the set-up at Freshfields.

There was the semblance of normality while James dreamed the sleep of the innocent, leaving Stella free to concentrate on work – an engrossing hour on the laptop she never left home without. Since she couldn't risk it showing up on Alex Gifford's phone bill, she'd pop a paper copy in the post first thing tomorrow.

The last dot of an i, the cross of a t, and Stella let out a sigh of satisfaction. A cursory glance for errors and she was done.

So, next task; check on James, double check the house was quiet and then retreat to the safety of her bedroom, like an amateur detective in a low budget movie, Stella decided, vaguely amused. Using her mobile, she accessed her answer-machine, nervous fingers drumming an impatient tattoo on the bedside table.

Still no news from Carly. Thirty-six hours, she calculated swiftly, stifling her unease. But Carly was a grown woman who'd simply walked out on her job. Take that to the police and they'd doubtless smile and tell her she was overreacting. Give it a couple more days, a couple of weeks, and things might look different.

Stella smothered a sigh. Overreaction? Possibly. Probably, she hastily reassured herself, and, since there was nothing she could do but worry, why worry until she had to? Almost philosophical, she decided, smiling grimly. Smile. Loosen up. Call her cousin and attempt to sound insouciant.

'Stella! But I thought –'

'Sorry, Bethy, no time to explain.' Stella cut in lightly. 'I need help. Would you believe a baby book? Any chance of popping it in the post first thing tomorrow?'

'A *what* book? What on earth –? OK, OK,' she allowed, sensing Stella's impatience. 'Them that asks no questions can't be told no lies. But if you want me to pop it into the post, Stella Marshall, how about a teensy-weenie clue to your whereabouts?'

Stella told her. Her cousin's stunned reaction was vaguely alarming.

'Freshfields? You surely can't mean *that* Freshfields? Good heavens! Carly –'

'Isn't here,' Stella cut in. 'Nothing to worry about, I'm sure, but from what I can gather she walked out on Friday and she isn't coming back.'

'And let me guess? You're playing nursemaid? How on earth did you talk your way into that? No, don't stop to explain,' Beth entreated tersely, 'Just get the hell out of there – and fast. Please, Stella, promise you'll leave straight away.'

'Sorry, Bethy, no can do. There's a baby in desperate need of some tender loving care, and until Carly gets in touch I might as well stay put. Mary Poppins Mark II. Impressed, hey?'

'Not impressed, Stella,' Beth contradicted with a curious lack of emotion, 'just worried. Good grief, woman, you work in the business – surely you've heard? While you've been away one of the tabloids has been dishing the dirt on Chrissie Gifford's lovelife. And today's *Beacon* exclusive claims that whilst a drink and drugs cocktail *did* play a part, it wasn't so much the hand of God that led to her drowning as the hand of Alex Gifford.'

CHAPTER 4

Murder. An ugly word, an ugly deed. Gossip. Rumour. Innuendo. Nudge-nudge, wink-wink and have you heard . . . ? Gossip, slander, defamation and lies. Lies and dammed lies. According to Alex at least.

And Carly – oh, God, Carly! Missing. Too soon to overreact? Difficult not to, given the latest news. News? Stella scorned. Alex had been right in the first place. Gossip, slander, lies. No smoke without fire, came a voice inside her head – a voice she hastily stifled. Stay calm. Keep things normal. A baby to change and feed and then a stroll along leafy lanes to the village – a chatty Hannah beside her and every other sentence beginning with Giff.

Giff says . . . Giff does . . . Giff thinks . . .

Deserved praise, maybe, but to a watching Stella there was something vaguely disturbing about the girl's animation. 'He sounds a generous sort of guy?' she probed casually when Hannah paused for breath,

Hannah's smile spread. 'Only the best,' she acknowledged, blue eyes dancing. 'It was Giff's idea to set me up in business. After the accident. When everyone else offered sympathy and grapes, Giff put the money up. An interest-free loan repayable if and when. And I'll do it. I'm halfway there already,' she insisted fiercely.

Yes. Stella nodded her approval. She'd heard all about it from Carly – didn't doubt it for an instant. Thriving riding school and stables – achievement enough for a girl of twenty. For a girl with a disability caused by a fall from a horse nothing short of amazing. 'But doesn't it hurt to be surrounded by reminders?'

'Horses? Good heavens, no,' Hannah scoffed with a derisive toss of the head. 'I love it. It hurts that I can't ride any more, of course, but I'm luckier than most. And I have got Giff.'

Not quite, Stella amended, only silently, as another shiver of alarm ran the length of her spine.

'I don't suppose *you* ride?' Hannah enquired doubtfully. 'Giff can, but rarely has time, and James needs someone he can trust if he's to grow up loving horses. I tried persuading Carly, but she refused point-blank to go anywhere near the stables.'

'Understandable, I suppose, from a townie's point of view.' Stella swallowed a smile. Hannah wouldn't know it, but Carly was wary of animals big and small – legacy of a close encounter with the hoofed kind at an ill-fated Sunday school outing. 'But isn't James a bit young to be sitting in the saddle?'

Hannah almost snorted. 'Not sitting and riding – just watching, soaking up the smells, the noises, the atmosphere. But mention the word "horse" and Carly ran a mile.'

'A flighty piece, apparently?' Stella probed, slowing the pace and darting Hannah a smile of enquiry.

'No more than most. And she did stick around for a while.'

'Yes. And then she took off without a word to anyone. Doesn't that strike you as strange?'

Hannah shrugged, the halo of blonde waves glinting in the sun. 'I can't say that I blame her. Mrs E doesn't approve of single women under fifty, and Tamara's acid tongue is enough to make a saint scream. And though London's barely an hour away, it was forty minutes too far for Carly. There was something, though,' she tagged on thoughtfully.

'Oh?' Stella murmured with a shiver of excitement.

'She'd been seeing a chap from the village. Danny daVine, the local celebrity,' Hannah explained. 'An actor. Between shows and "resting" – and a girl on every stage if I know Danny. I wonder . . .' she mused, her narrowed gaze sliding across the park to the row of thatched cottages that bordered the green. 'I wonder if Danny daVine is up to receiving visitors.'

He was, curious black eyes switching from Hannah to Stella and back again, but his face closing up the moment Carly's name was mentioned.

'Sure I know her,' he conceded warily. 'We have a bit of fun. A meal in town, a drink, a show, a visit to the movies. Just the usual sort of thing and no strings attached. It isn't a crime as far as I know.' He shrugged, checked his watch. 'In fact, assuming she can get away, she's meeting me for a drink in the Feathers later.'

The knot of tension in the pit of Stella's stomach began to ease. Danny's defensive attitude was strangely reassuring. 'You mean you haven't heard? Carly's gone.'

'Gone?' he echoed absurdly. 'But she can't have gone. She'd have told me. She'd have –' He pulled himself up short, his face closing again. Twenty-five, twenty-six, Stella gauged, and every girl's dream.

'She'd have *what*, Danny?' Stella prompted softly.

He shrugged. 'Nothing. She'd have told me. I thought she'd have told me, that's all.'

'Only she didn't?'

'Not a word,' he conceded flatly. 'Not a flipping word.'

And, try though they did, not another word could they elicit.

'He's lying. Either that or he knows more than he's letting on.'

Stella ran a wary eye over the rustic bench that overlooked the pond, double checking it would take her weight before settling James on to her lap. 'Oh?' she murmured casually. 'And what makes you so sure?'

'Intuition,' Hannah explained, swinging the wheelchair nippily alongside. 'They've clearly had a row and Carly's issued an ultimatum. You mark my words. Now that he knows she's gone, he'll be hot on her heels as fast as he can pack. Either that or he doesn't give tuppence,' she pronounced, with an irrefutable heads-

I-win, tails-I-can't-lose logic that Stella hadn't the heart to challenge. 'Though whichever way you view it she'll have dented his pride. Now hang on a moment. What did I tell you —?'

As Hannah broke off, Stella turned her head, following the line of Hannah's gaze. Sure enough, Danny had appeared in the open doorway, overnight bag in one hand, car keys swinging in the other, his sense of urgency unmistakable.

'Bingo!' Hannah gleefully pronounced. 'Pity we can't hail a passing cab and follow,' she tossed out absurdly. 'Pity we can't – hey, what on earth –?'

'Won't be a jiffy,' Stella insisted, landing an uncomplaining James squarely on Hannah's lap before setting off across the grass. 'Wait. Please,' she called out urgently as Danny inserted his keys into the impressive Maserati parked in front of the cottage – not the sort of car Stella would have expected from an out of work thespian. 'Danny! Wait!'

He spun round, the gamut of expressions crossing his features; surprise, annoyance, wariness, most of all wariness. And, though he tossed the bag on to the passenger seat, he did stand and wait while Stella caught her breath.

'You're wasting your time,' he told her flatly, second-guessing what was coming. 'I don't know any more than you do.'

'Maybe,' Stella conceded with a smile of reassurance. 'And maybe not, hey, Danny? But, no,' she insisted as he made to interrupt, 'I don't expect you to tell me. But if you do track Carly down – if,' she repeated softly. 'Do me a favour and give her a message. Tell her Stella's home and she's worried. Ask her to phone. Please, Danny.' Hazel eyes softly pleaded. Black eyes brimmed with hurt. Hurt, Stella noted, storing that snippet away. 'Please.'

There was an interminable pause, the silence unnerving, just the soft rustle of the breeze in the trees, the occasional call of a bird, and then, from across the park, the distinctive wail of a baby.

Hurt, anger, pain – the flash of emotion was masked in a trice. 'Sure,' he murmured off-handedly. 'If I happen to see her. But since I sure as hell won't be going looking, don't hold your breath, lady.'

Dismissal. Cool. Indifferent. Hurt, Stella tried to reassure herself, slowly retracing her steps. He *does* know where to find her. And, fingers crossed, she willed herself to believe it.

Hannah's face was stony. 'Well, look who it isn't. Miss Amateur Detective herself,' she scoffed the moment Stella moved within earshot. 'Correct me if I'm wrong, but you're the nanny, not the sleuth,' she hissed, thrusting a wriggling, screaming James back into Stella's arms. 'And this child needs changing.'

'Yes.' Stella swallowed a smile. So she gathered. But it would keep. It would have to. 'Though not for long, hey, poppet?' she crooned, rocking James and instinctively making the sort of soft, soothing noises in the back of her throat that somehow worked miracles. Placing him back among the covers, she straightened, swung the pram around and nodded pleasantly at Hannah. 'Ready?'

It was an uncomfortable twenty minutes – the atmosphere strained, Stella's mind working overtime. Carly . . . James . . . Hannah's lightning change of mood. Not to mention the blatant unconcern. Not a word, not an enquiry, no hint of curiosity. Just a stony silence and the definite impression that Stella's concern for Carly was an absurd overreaction, not to mention none of her business. Which it wouldn't be, she supposed, in the normal run of things.

Careful, girl, she silently entreated herself as Hannah sped rudely away from her. An enquiry too many and it's exit one bogus nanny, with precious little to show for it bar that tenuous link with Danny. And, since Danny was the only lead she had, the longer she could stick around at Freshfields the better.

She paused to catch her breath at the top of the drive, tucked the paper she'd bought into the voluminous pockets of her bag. Oddly enough for a Sunday, there was a delivery van disappearing round the side of the house, and, catching a fleeting glimpse of Hannah just ahead of it, Stella ambled leisurely in the same direction. She was staff, and if the past twenty-four hours had taught her nothing else, at least now she knew her place. Be neither seen nor heard and definitely don't court the disapproval of the house guest.

But then that was only the theory. Rounding the final corner, she took one look at the trio of women blocking her way, their collective expressions grim, and wondered what on earth she'd done to provoke such hostility. Been rumbled, perhaps? But, since she didn't know for sure, she stayed calm, forced a smile, feeling her way.

'Deliveries on a Sunday?' she observed pleasantly. 'Sounds important. Someone's birthday?' she hazarded wildly, her gaze sliding from one cold set of eyes to another in search of a clue to this unlikely alliance. For if emotions between Mrs Edwards and Tamara normally ran high, right now they were united in hate. Tangible hate. Directed squarely at Stella. Coming up against the blank wall of their faces, Stella had the horrible feeling she was wasting her time. 'Yes? No?' she probed, damping down the panic. 'Ah, well . . .' She gave a shrug of resignation. 'Whatever the occasion, I'd say someone's in for a treat.'

Silence. An icy silence broken by the delivery man's cheery, tuneless whistle and the screech of metal as he raised the security grille.

And then Tamara broke ranks, stepped forward. 'My, my,' she drawled, chill green eyes flicking from Stella to the open side of the van and the impressive array of goods being speedily unloaded. 'You sure as hell didn't waste any time getting your claws into Alex.'

Vaguely amused, vaguely alarmed, Stella ignored her, attempting to push past, manoeuvre the pram into the glass-covered porch, and was brought up short by a grip on her arm.

Stella's turn to glower, to glance up and down, from diamond-hard eyes to the iron fingers that had tightened, were now digging cruelly into the soft skin of her inner arm.

Easy, girl, she silently told herself. You can't afford to blow it now. Think of Carly. Take a deep breath, count to ten and simply give as good as you get. Politely. She pulled free. 'Let go of me,' she insisted icily. 'And in future keep your talons, and your cheap and nasty comments, to yourself.'

'Or else?' Tamara challenged.

'Precisely. Or else,' Stella echoed grimly.

'Or else *what*?' Tamara scorned. 'You'll run and tell Alex? Run and tell – or kiss and tell? And you needn't bat those butter-wouldn't-melt eyes and think you can fool me. I know your sort and I know exactly what you're up to.'

'I doubt it,' Stella countered coldly, 'unless you happen to be clairvoyant. And, since it's clearly slipped your mind, I'm here to work. Nothing more, nothing less.'

'For now.'

'Meaning?'

A slow smile spread across a chalk-white face, the glossy red lips an obscene splash of colour. 'Use your imagination, my dear. You're an intelligent woman – apparently.'

'And you're determined to provoke me. Sorry, Miss Clayton, but it takes more than a thinly veiled insult to force a rise. It's the nature of the job,' Stella explained sweetly. 'Take the rough with the smooth and attempt to keep the peace. Delicacy, diplomacy and discretion.'

'You missed out devious and deceitful.'

Stella smiled. 'So I did. Put it down to tact,' she conceded lightly. 'But if the cap fits . . .'

A sharp intake of breath, a sudden stain of colour, and from somewhere near the door a low laugh.

Tamara's expression hardened. 'You know,' she hissed, that exquisite face twisted in fury, 'for a so-called intelligent woman you manage to miss the glaringly obvious. You're not welcome here. You're not wanted, and, like that flighty madam before you, you might as well pack up and leave before Alex arrives home.'

'And leave you holding the baby – literally, Miss Clayton? I think not,' Stella countered coolly. 'It's a job that doesn't appeal to you, I seem to recall. On the subject of which, I'm beginning to see why James goes through nannies faster than the proverbial dose of salts. A word of advice,' she murmured confidentially, 'if and when you land yourself a husband, buy him a set of ear muffs. The poor man will need them, coping with a tongue as sharp as yours.'

'And you'd know, of course, Miss Prim and Prissy Marshall. Experience, intuition, or sheer wishful thinking?' Tamara bit out.

'Take your pick,' Stella entreated, attempting to push past, bring the incident to a close before she said something she'd regret. She was aware that for all her resolutions she was swapping insults with her employer's fiancée for the second time in the space of twenty-four hours, and, though Alex wasn't here to witness it himself, it was only a matter of time before he heard all about it – in triplicate at that.

More words, insults, scorn and innuendo, and with the sound of World War Three ringing round the yard, was it any wonder James set up a protest?

James. Stella's mind cleared. Focusing on the baby, she abandoned the pram, hitched James securely over her shoulder and marched forwards, praying compassion, concern or sheer common sense would prevail. Only they didn't. Quick as a flash, Hannah moved her chair to block the open doorway while Tamara and Mrs Edwards stepped briskly into line beside her.

Pulling up short and logging the heady mix of anger, hate and spite, Stella finally acknowledged she was wasting her time.

'Fine,' she conceded tersely, rocking the sobbing baby over her shoulder. 'If you won't let me past, then I can't see to James. And since he clearly needs feeding – and changing – one of you will have to do the honours. Which begs the sixty-four-thousand-dollar question – who is it to be?'

'My thoughts precisely,' came another voice, vaguely amused, vaguely annoyed, and one hundred per cent male, Stella realized, swinging round, cheeks on fire at the thought of Alex listening, judging, finding Stella wanting. Though on second thoughts Alex Gifford's opinion really wasn't important. She'd done nothing wrong; why give him cause to believe it? And Stella raised her head, held his gaze, the jut of her chin unwittingly aggressive.

'Miss Marshall,' he acknowledged dryly. 'I do believe you've taken the words right out of my mouth.'

'I –'

'Alex –'

'Giff –'

'Mr Gifford, sir –'

An imperative wave of a hand and the silence was deafening. And, Alex being Alex, he switched his gaze from Stella to each of the women in turn and allowed the tension to rise.

Cool blue eyes came slowly back to Stella. The hint of admiration in their treacherous depths was surely sheer imagination. Or wishful thinking on Stella's part.

'There you have it, Miss Marshall,' he observed, saccharine-sweetly. 'Three willing volunteers. Take your pick. Since James is in your charge, I'd say the decision's all yours. I only hope for the child's sake you choose wisely.' He angled his head. 'Miss Marshall?'

'As you say,' she countered coolly, 'James is my charge, my responsibility. I'll take care of him. Unless . . .'

'Unless?' Cool, polite, that unnerving gaze fastened on hers, seeing to the centre of her soul.

'Unless you think my position's untenable?'

'I don't,' he conceded gravely. 'But I'd quite understand if you felt differently.'

Stella nodded. 'Fine. I'll see to James. If you'll excuse me?'

Another wave of the hand. 'Be my guest,' he conceded lazily, and, though lips and mouth curved into the semblance of a smile, the light didn't reach his eyes.

A long day – and as strange as it was long, given the generous array of gadgets that appeared in the nursery.

For despite his lack of sleep, not to mention flying to France and back, Alex Gifford had kept his word, had snapped his eloquently manicured fingers or waved a magic wand and, hey presto! You name it, Alex had thought of it. Hardly any need to make the two-floor trek to the basement, Stella supposed, lugging the black plastic sack down the final set of stairs. But if disposing of the rubbish wasn't strictly part of her brief, keeping the nursery clean and tidy was.

The kitchen door was open. Stella put her head round, caught a rustle of starch in the walk-in larder, and decided she had nothing to lose by observing the social niceties.

At Stella's light rap, the housekeeper spun round, the sudden surge of colour in her cheeks betraying her unease. 'Oh, it's you,' she murmured unnecessarily.

'I need to dispose of this,' Stella explained, holding out the bag.

'You should have phoned down,' came the crisp retort, part-statement, part-reprimand as Agnes Edwards struggled to regain her composure. 'Mandy could have fetched it. But she leaves at four on Sundays.'

'Exactly. And I know how busy you are. I'd have left it till morning,' Stella murmured pleasantly, 'had it been anything else but nappies.'

'Nappies? Yes. Well.' A sniff of disapproval. 'Seems a waste when there's a chest full of perfectly good terries up in the nursery. But mine not to reason why,' she conceded sourly.

'But think of all that washing,' Stella chided lightly.

'Not to mention buckets of soaking solution cluttering up the laundry. Less work for everyone this way.'

'Aye. Well . . .' She ran the palms of her hands over the sides of her apron in a give-away gesture of nerves. Another sign of nerves as she cleared her throat, raised her eyes, a wealth of embarrassment swimming in their depths.

Sensing what was coming next, Stella took the plunge. 'About this afternoon,' she began pleasantly. 'I guess it's apologies all round and no need to say another word. Least said, soonest mended,' she said brightly. 'So no hard feelings, hey?'

Agnes Edwards' chin snapped up. '*You're* apologizing to me? Oh, no, miss,' she countered awkwardly. 'Mr Gifford –'

'Expects you to make an apology?' Stella cut in mildly. She smiled, caught grudging admiration in the housekeeper's eyes and leaned forward confidentially. 'Well, fine. We'll simply take it as read. I'm happy, you're happy, he's happy. Incident closed. Agreed?'

The older woman nodded, a fleeting smile crossing her features, pulling the skin tight across surprisingly high cheekbones. Fifty-five, sixty at the most, Stella gauged, her journalistic mind switching to automatic. Long grey hair, scraped into an unflattering knot on the nape of her neck, bone structure excellent, but the whole effect marred by the etching of lines, the lemon-lips pout, that air of disapproval. For the woman of today in general? Stella mused. Or just flighty young misses who danced around Alex like moths around a candle? Carly. No, not Carly, she contradicted fiercely, shying away from the notion. Well-kept hands, she noted automatically, despite the job. Long, restless, ringless fingers. Ringless. Stella did a double take. Significant? Maybe not, but a woman of Mrs Edwards' generation wouldn't normally remove her wedding ring. Unless . . . Ah, yes, a courtesy title, then? Hardly important, Stella could allow, but she filed the snippet away as she made her escape, taking the first flight of stairs with a spring in her step that hadn't been there earlier.

One down, two to go – though she wouldn't mind betting the fiery Tamara wouldn't be quite so easily won round. Now hopefully Hannah –

'Stella –'

'Hannah! Good heavens.' The voice came out of nowhere and Stella visibly jumped, spun round, more unnerved than she'd care to admit by the silent approach of the wheelchair.

'Sorry.' Hannah's smile was disarming. 'I didn't mean to startle you. But of course, not knowing the lay-out of the house you wouldn't have been expecting me.'

'Expecting you?'

'My apartment. The purpose-built extension. Independence without the isolation,' Hannah explained without rancour. 'And a secret passage that connects with the house. And, yes,' she acknowledged, sensing Stella's confusion, 'I'm teasing. But there is a door behind me, if only you could see it.'

Stella strained her eyes. There had to be an opening

somewhere. How else could Hannah have caught her unawares? But for the life of her Stella couldn't make it out at all.

Hannah took pity. Swinging her wheelchair parallel to the wall, she pushed what appeared to be a knot in the grain of the wood, and sure enough a panel slid open as soundlessly and effortlessly as Hannah's own approach. 'Why not come through and see for yourself?' she invited. 'And allow to me apologize properly. I've been given my orders,' she explained with another disarming smile. 'But Giff's right, as usual.'

'Maybe,' Stella acknowledged pleasantly. 'But, since you weren't directly involved, an apology isn't required.'

'I was there,' Hannah pointed out wryly. 'It was enough for Giff. We were rude, dreadfully rude, and Giff was furious. He and Tamara have had a blazing row and she's stormed off in a huff. But if she thinks Giff's about to go hot-footing after her, she's in for a surprise. I'll lead the way, shall I?'

'I . . .' Stella shrugged. 'Yes, why not?' James was fast asleep, and sure to be safe for another ten minutes or so. Only bang on cue, of course, the unmistakable sound of a newly wakened baby drifted over the intercom. It was Stella's turn to smile. 'Duty calls,' she murmured brightly, apologetically. 'But another time, maybe?' And soon, she decided, halfway to being intrigued by the lay-out of a house that could have come straight out of a film set. Spacious rooms, secret doorways, and an open-plan, uncluttered design clearly created with a wheelchair in mind.

A nursery out of a film set too, thanks to Alex. Only she hadn't had time to thank him – would make a point of catching him alone as soon as possible. In the meanwhile, she'd settle James and allow some freshly perked coffee to set the seal on an anything but dull day. And if friendships had not exactly been forged with Hannah and Mrs Edwards, at least peace had been restored. Not so life with Tamara, but that would keep. With Tamara conspicuous by her absence, it would have to.

Absence. Word association. Carly. Access her answer-machine. Another waste of time, Stella was convinced, as she punched the code, nervous fingers tapping an impatient tattoo at the pause that seemed to last for ever and then, unbelievably, thankfully, the sound of Carly's voice:

'Stella. Heaven only knows when you're due home, and heaven only knows where you'll find me. But you're not to worry. I'm safe. Understand, Stella? I'm safe. And the moment I've sorted things out in my mind, I'll be in touch. Sorry, Stell, I've fouled things up, but I'm a big girl now and I'll sort it out my way. But I'm safe and that's the important thing.'

Safe? From what? Stella mused, cutting the connection and dropping the mobile into the pocket of her bag. From Danny daVine? Or from something in this house that was playing on her mind? Like what, for instance? Like murder, for instance, came the stark reply. Nonsense, she contradicted crisply. Lies, slander, defamation and downright absurdity. Chrissie Gifford. Verdict misadventure. A deadly cocktail of drink and drugs and water deep enough to drown in. An accident. Nothing more, nothing less. So why the unease, the festering shadows of doubt? Because the idea had been planted, of course. Insidious, sly, salacious, attention-grabbing headlines, designed to sell papers and make a lot of money and heaven help the lives they destroy along the way.

Only not Carly. Carly was safe, and in that case there was no real need for Stella to stick around. Just a ten-month-old child in need of some stability. Not her problem, she countered promptly, smothering pangs of guilt. But how to wriggle out of a job she'd no right taking in the first place? No contest. Simply turn her back and walk away, just like all those nannies before her – and far better to leave now before her cover was blown. Ah, yes, but strange though it seemed, in less than forty-eight hours she'd become absurdly attached to James. And as for his father – an icy trickle ran the length of her spine.

With a shiver of premonition, Stella swung round, watched in awful fascination as the handle of the door began to lever downwards, and as the door swung open with a soundless whoosh of air Stella backed away, eyes riveted on the gap.

Who on earth – or what on earth –?

'Alex!' she gasped as his familiar form stepped into the frame, tray in one hand, chilled bottle in the other, the expression on his face unreadable. 'Oh, Alex,' she breathed as her knees gave way. 'Did you have to scare me half to death?'

CHAPTER 5

'Caviar, madam? A bite-sized blini?'

'I –'

'Don't like it? Have never actually tried it? Or don't you believe in letting your hair down while on duty?' Alex teased, his very presence teasing, unnerving. Yet despite herself, Stella smiled, felt some of the tensions begin to drain away.

'Never tried it? Good heavens, no,' she trilled, popping a salty spoonful into her mouth. 'It's a staple food in my house. Morning, noon and night, and you've guessed it: caviar and bacon, caviar and chips, caviar and gravy, caviar and caviar. The permutations are endless. Red, black, Beluga, or common and garden fish roe. You name it, I've tried it. And as for caviar and ice cream –'

'I think you can spare me the finer details,' he drawled good-naturedly, pouring the wine – a well-chilled champagne, reason enough for Stella to feel uneasy. Champagne. A celebration? A simple thank-you for sticking the job more than twenty-four hours? Or an even more simple while-the-cat's-away-the-mouse-will-take-his-amusement-where-he-can ploy? she wondered warily, almost choking on her first sip of bubbles.

Bubbles. Champagne bubbles. Caviar bubbles. Worry bubbles in her mind. Because she was alone with a man, a devastating man. Difficult to relax – more difficult not to. Because Alex was in tormenting mode, laughing, teasing, talking, taking the strain and minute by minute, despite it all, putting Stella at her ease.

The champagne bubbles were going quickly to her head, allowing Stella's guard to drop. Dangerous. Even without the undercurrents of tension, the seeds of doubt surrounding Carly's disappearance, Stella needed to keep her wits. Easier said than done, she realized, for Alex had drained his glass, had placed it firmly down on the coffee table, had taken Stella's glass from between her trembling fingers and was cradling her hands in his.

'Stella,' he breathed almost smokily, 'look at me, Stella.'

And Stella did, raising her eyes from the hands that held hers, strong hands, lightly tanned, the tiny golden hairs on the backs catching facets of light from the table-lamp behind him, long, tapering fingers brushing the backs of hers, soothing, stirring. Strong hands. A man's hands. Capable of murder – no!

'No!' She pulled away, shrank back into the cushions, dropped her eyes, refusing to meet his gaze, to witness the hurt – or the naked contempt in his. Only Alex simply laughed, a low growl in the back of his throat, and then she caught the gurgle of wine as he refilled the glasses and realized Alex hadn't taken the hint, or taken the huff. She risked a glance through the veil of her lashes and discovered Alex was smiling, not mocking, just smiling, a quizzical expression in the depths of his eyes.

'Twenty-eight, twenty-nine?' he mused. 'And as nervous as a kitten. Now why, I wonder?'

'Not nerves,' she bit out. 'Just a simple matter of observing the proprieties.' And, angling her chin in defiance, she added with understated mildness, 'Sir.'

'Precisely.' Alex grinned. 'I'm the boss. I'm the one who issues the orders.'

'Like rule number one; thou shalt relax when so ordered. Two: thou shalt take drink with thy employer according to his whim. Three: thou shalt allow thy employer to walk all over you? Shall I go on?'

'And would you?'

'Would I what?' she stalled, his train of thought losing her.

'Allow your employer to walk all over you?'

Stella's turn to grin. 'What do you think?' she challenged, reaching for her glass.

'I don't think; I know,' he conceded lightly. 'Stella Marshall's made of granite. Leastwise,' he amended, blue eyes strangely thoughtful, 'that's the impression she'd like to give. A crisp outer shell that hides a –'

'Creamy soft centre?' she interrupted dryly. 'A Viennese truffle I'm not,' she conceded. 'But you'll work it out for yourself in time.'

'I'm glad to hear it. Time,' he explained, as Stella

raised an enquiring eyebrow. 'It's nice to know you're going to stick around.'

'Ah!'

'Ah, what?' he challenged softly. 'But, no, let me guess.' He folded his arms, didn't bother masking his contempt. 'You're chickening out, like all the rest. One hint of opposition and it's time to show a clean set of heels.'

'Hardly,' she bit out, the quick condemnation galling.

'No? So just how would you describe it?' he challenged, the edge to his tone barely perceptible but present nonetheless.

'All part and parcel of the job,' she reminded him mildly. 'I'm just the stand-in. Greenhavens will be in touch the moment a regulation nanny is available.' And if not the truth, the whole truth and nothing but the truth, then it was as much as she could give.

'Not good enough, I'm afraid,' Alex observed coolly.

'No?' Stella stalled. 'And why is that, precisely?'

'Because the agency has let me down. Again. And whilst once could be classed as careless, twice is unforgivable.'

'Fine. The answer's simple. Use another agency.'

'Another day, another agency – another flighty piece of baggage still wet behind the ears? Sounds just what James needs.'

'If you choose the right girl,' Stella insisted firmly, 'why not?'

'Girl.' He gave a disdainful snap of the fingers.

'Immature, inexperienced, and thoroughly unreliable, going on the evidence so far.'

'So you get what you pay for,' Stella couldn't resist needling. 'Don't sound so surprised.'

'Meaning?'

Stella shrugged. 'Meaning precisely that. Traditionally underpaid, overworked and ruthlessly exploited. It's a thankless task –'

'But *you* haven't suffered,' he interrupted slyly. 'A new car – a fast car, an expensive car – and as for your taste in clothes . . .'

But it wasn't the clothes Alex seemed to focus on. That appraising gaze missed nothing, not the single string of pearls – a priceless family heirloom if only Alex knew it – not the crisp cotton blouse that had somehow kept its shape despite the soaking James had ensured at bathtime, not even the soft pleats of a skirt that hadn't been bought in one of the more run-of-the-mill chain-stores, Oh, no. Alex's heated glance was far more devastating. It was a tangible caress of Stella's wayward body; the rapid rise and fall of breasts, the give-away thrust of nipples. Because Alex was touching. Touch. Nipples tightening, shamelessly thrusting. Because, heaven help her, she wanted him to touch.

Inspection over, Alex whistled under his breath. 'Classy,' he acknowledged locking his gaze on to hers. 'Definitely classy.'

'So I know the value of money,' Stella scorned. 'Classic clothes don't date, don't fall to pieces the first time they're washed, and they don't turn shabby with wear.'

'Exactly. You've lived. You're experienced. You've survived. Stability, maturity, reliability. In short, you're just what James needs.'

'A surrogate mother? Thanks, Mr Gifford, but no, thanks. It's a temporary arrangement – remember?'

'Not as far as I'm concerned. And, since an employer gets what he pays for, apparently, let's cut out all the bull and get straight down to basics. Name your price.'

'I beg your pardon?'

'Money. Cash. The stuff that pays the bills. Fast cars, classy clothes.'

'Not interested, Mr Gifford. The job suits me fine the way it is, and that's the way it's staying.'

'Like I said, why not name your price?'

'Money, Mr Gifford,' she chided mildly, 'isn't the be-all and end-all. I like moving around from commission to commission,' she added carefully. She hated the thought of lying, and whilst each and every word was the truth, she was achingly aware she was being evasive. Lying by omission. Nothing more, nothing less. Sly. Distasteful. A necessary evil. 'It's – what I know best,' she ended simply.

'Precisely. You walk in, you take over, you wave a magic wand. One day, two, a week, a month, a year. Time. Cunning little units,' he chided. 'Keep adding them together and who knows? You might even discover that you like it.'

'I doubt it,' Stella countered dryly. 'And if I were you, I sure as hell wouldn't bank on it.'

'No.' Surprisingly he smiled, reached for his glass, drained it, refilled it, then held out the bottle to Stella, who shook her head, continued to regard him warily.

An easy capitulation. Too easy, if she knew Alex Gifford. Only she didn't, and that was the way it was staying. So – with Carly safe and no real reason to stay, how to walk away without a backward glance? Easy. Phone the agency first thing tomorrow, she decided, visibly relaxing. And the moment her replacement walked in, Stella would walk out.

'Don't even think it,' he murmured softly.

'Th-think what?' Stella stalled, her sudden surge of colour a total give-away.

Alex smiled. Delightedly. 'Stella Marshall,' he purred, reaching for her hand, fingers closing round it, a single finger caressing the soft skin, sending currents of heat surging out from the point of contact. 'I do believe you're blushing. And furthermore,' he added smokily, raising her hand to his lips and dropping a light kiss into the open palm. 'I do believe it suits you. Coffee?' he suggested with a lightning change of mood. 'Time to put this highly expensive kitchen to the test. My treat,' he added, swinging up before Stella had chance to move. 'You sit right there and relax.'

Relax? Some hope, with her emotions in a churn. Rapid breathing, rapid pulse and butterflies chasing round her stomach. Ridiculous at her age, even more ridiculous given the length of their acquaintance. Yet how long does it take to fall in love? Love? Oh, no! Stella jerked upright, slurping wine over the rim of her glass and on to her skirt – hardly a problem, given the soaking James had already subjected it to. Only Alex would notice, and Alex would know. Nerves. At her age. Only he was wrong about the age. Thirty-two and footloose and fancy-free. Unlike Alex. Thirty-eight, she seemed to recall reading somewhere, and all male.

Devastatingly male. Tall, ruggedly good-looking, high cheekbones, an aquiline nose which, together with piercing blue eyes that missed little, could even be classed as cruel. Only not now. Because Alex was smiling, was humming lightly under his breath as he rummaged about the kitchen. His kitchen. His nursery. And yet he'd never once crossed the threshold, according to Carly, barely gave his baby son the time of day.

Stella frowned, annoyed she hadn't noticed the omission sooner. James. Fast asleep next door. Yet Alex Gifford hadn't once asked to take a peek.

High time Stella took a peek. Yes, there was a perfectly efficient listening device plugged into every room, but modern technology was no substitute for the human touch, the tender touch.

Touch. Poor little mite. Tiny fingers closed around Stella's finger, like the tendrils of a plant in search of some support. Silence. Semi-darkness. A clean, babypowder smell, an expensive aftershave aroma. Stella stiffened, for, silent as the night, Alex had joined her.

'Turn your back and walk away?' he challenged, not bothering to temper his derision. 'And who is Stella Marshall trying to kid? Face it, Stella, you're needed here. You're everything he needs. Stability, maturity. You're a breath of fresh air. Three months, Stella. Three days times thirty. Hardly a lifetime. Small, manageable units. You can stay. If you want to. And you want to –'

'No!' Stella swung away, Alex's lightning response forestalling her, and as iron fingers tightened their grip, she rode the waves of panic. 'Let go of me, Alex,' she insisted tersely.

'When I'm good and ready,' he growled. 'When you give me the answer I want. I want you to stay.'

'And what Alex Gifford wants, Alex Gifford buys – or takes?' she scorned.

'Hardly,' he bit out, almost shaking her. 'Unless this very stubborn lady is the exception that proves the rule. Why, Stella, why won't you stay? The child –'

'Has a name,' she hissed. 'A name his father rarely chooses to use. He's called James, Alex. James Gifford. Not such a terrible mouthful, surely?'

'He –'

'Needs a father and a mother, not a nursemaid,' she scorned. 'Tamara –'

'Doesn't know one end of a baby from another and isn't about to learn,' he derided. 'Hence the need for a nursemaid. What James needs now is you. Three weeks, three months –'

'And the next three months? And the next?' she challenged. 'More money, more pressure, more moral blackmail? Only it isn't going to happen,' she explained without emotion, pulling free and heading for the sitting room. 'I don't belong and I sure as hell won't be making plans to ship the rest of my wardrobe in. Do us all a favour, hey? Marry Tamara.'

'I'd rather marry you.'

She halted then, stopped dead in her tracks, the blood rushing into her ears and drowning out the sound of Alex moving across to stand behind her. Not touching, simply standing, and a rigid Stella was shockingly aware that if she leaned back his arms would close round her, that Alex would hold her, touch her, pull her against him. Man. All man. With a man's needs. Only she couldn't. Couldn't sleep with a man she didn't love, make love with a man she didn't love. Sex, she told herself. A physical coupling. Man and woman. Toby and Stella, Toby and Francine. Her best friend, she remembered – not wanting to remember, the image unendurable. Her best friend and her fiancée. Making love. All night long. The night before the wedding. Stella's wedding. No!

'Stella –'

'No! Don't. Don't touch me. Are you listening, Alex Gifford?' she demanded, silently cursing the shameful sting of tears. 'Don't touch me. Don't say another word. Just go. Leave me alone. Leave me alone, damn you.'

'To cry yourself stupid? Oh, no,' he contradicted in a voice that brooked no refusal. 'Like it or not, lady, I'm staying put.'

'It's your house, your prerogative,' she sniffed, rifling her pocket for a tissue.

'Here. Use this.'

'I don't –'

'Maybe not,' he agreed tersely, pushing a crisp square of linen between her rigid fingers, 'but that's an order, not a suggestion. And guess who gives the orders around here?'

'The mighty Alex Gifford?' she scorned. 'Thou shalt dry thy tears forthwith?' she challenged absurdly. 'Worry not, Mr Gifford, consider it done.' A careless sweep of her hand and there was nothing to show for her moment of weakness. 'There. All gone,' she insisted brightly. 'Happy now?'

'Hardly,' he bit out. 'But it's a start. Coffee,' he reminded her. 'And that, Miss Marshall, is –'

'An order, Mr Gifford? But of course. And, yes,' she conceded tersely, 'coffee would be lovely.'

Time. To pull herself together, to exercise some of the famed Marshall control. To show arrogant Alex Gifford she really was made of granite. Chipped granite, given the torrent of tears, but too late to worry about that now. Instead she'd simply prove the moment of weakness was past, never to return – in public at least. Public? An audience of one, she silently derided, but, oh, what an audience. Devastating.

And, more unnerved than she'd care to admit, she curled up on the sofa and drew her legs up under her body, the tight fold of arms across her chest an unwitting give-away.

And Alex noticed, Alex took the hint, taking the chair opposite and fastening his gaze on to Stella's. And Stella trembled, dropped her gaze to the cup she was cradling.

Coffee. Freshly perked. And, as Stella choked on her first scalding mouthful, clearly laced.

'Brandy,' he explained, patting the pocket of a carelessly discarded jacket. 'Given the air miles I manage in an average week, I never leave home without it. Purely medicinal, of course.'

'Oh, of course,' Stella echoed absurdly. Relax. Allow the brandy, and the champagne, to work a mellowing influence. Not so easy to relax with her emotions in a churn, but Stella had taken bigger knocks than this and survived.

Toby and Francine. Pain. More a dull ache, after nine lonely years. Lance the pain. Remember. Man and woman. Naked. Brazen. Or at least, Stella recalled, that had been Francine's reaction. Sex. Nothing more, nothing less. She'd simply been amusing herself with the nearest available male. Toby. Poor Toby. Taken for a ride, literally, by Francine, and then rejected so publicly by Stella.

Glancing up, she caught Alex's smile of amusement and stiffened. 'Something I did?' she queried tetchily. 'Or something I said?'

'Both,' he conceded lazily, enigmatically, and, resisting the urge to chivvy him along, Stella raised an enquiring eyebrow. 'Oh, nothing world-shatteringly important,' he reassured flippantly. 'Just your withering reaction to my suggestion.'

'Can't bear the thought of rejection, hey?'

'What rejection? Unless I'm growing deaf in my old age, a certain fiery lady didn't go so far as to turn me down.'

'No.' Stella swallowed a smile.

'Want to tell me about it?' Casual. Concern, not prurience, Stella realized, logging the expression in a set of velvet eyes, but she wasn't about to open her heart to a man – any man. Let alone this devastating man who'd managed to touch her very soul with a single careless remark.

She shook her head. 'Nothing to tell.'

'Liar.' Soft. Statement, not question. Too perceptive by far, Stella decided, dropping her gaze and focusing on the thin skin of cream forming on the rapidly cooling coffee. She swirled the coffee around the cup and watched the skin buckle and disintegrate. Swirls of hate – but, no, it had been a long and difficult day, and she was tired, too tired to cope with the demons of the past.

Stella moved, the rattle of spoon on saucer unnervingly loud, and, refusing point-blank to meet his gaze, she gathered the empty cups and glasses and stacked them on the tray before coming to her feet.

'Allow me –'

'I can manage,' she insisted tightly, snatching at the tray and almost toppling the expensive crystal flutes that Alex had thoughtfully provided.

On legs like jelly she moved quickly through to the kitchen, afraid Alex was watching every move, more afraid he wasn't. And he wasn't.

'Stella –'

A sharp hiss of indrawn breath – Stella's breath. Because Alex was standing behind her, not touching, simply standing, and the expensive tang of his aftershave caught in the back of her throat. Man and woman. Alone. Currents of heat were passing between them, and Stella's need was so exquisite she had to clench her fists in an effort to deny it.

Just how long does it take to fall in love? How could she possibly love a man she barely knew? Lust, not love, she told herself, seeing Francine and Toby in her mind's eye and beginning to understand the impulse that had driven them. Only Stella wasn't Francine, and this man wasn't Toby.

'Please, Alex,' she murmured in anguish.

'Please, Alex . . . what?' he queried, his breath a warm flutter on the back of Stella's neck, his fingers aflutter on the back of her neck. Fingers stroking, parting the luxuriant waves of hair. Fingers stroking, lips nuzzling.

Rigid as a statue, Stella closed her eyes, attempted to close her mind. It couldn't happen. Not in an instant. Not with a man she hadn't known existed just three short days ago, and, *yes*, she'd heard all about him from Carly – couldn't help but pick up the gossip. Playboy, with a string of beautiful women hanging on his arm, keeping his bed warm. Bed. Sex. Lust. Not love, she told herself, hating herself, hating Alex just as badly. For stirring up emotions she'd thought were long dead. Only she mustn't. Fall for Alex? Become another cold statistic? Yet another notch carved on his headboard? How many women? she couldn't help but wonder, twisting the knife-blade in her belly. And yet one woman, two, a dozen – it really didn't matter. *She* wanted him. Heaven help her, but she wanted this man to touch her, to kiss her, to take her.

Hands were sliding over her shoulders, urging her back against him. Hands were sliding down, slowly, over the swell of breasts that were screaming out for

Alex to touch, to cradle, to squeeze, and oh, God! His thumbs were playing havoc with her nipples, finger and thumb squeezing, teasing, and as the tremors began to ripple through her body Stella swayed back into the hard lines of his, and knew that she was lost.

'I want you,' Alex growled, hands sliding over the curve of her belly and urging her hard against him, the instinctive shimmy of Stella's hips triggering another throaty growl. 'And what Alex Gifford wants, Alex Gifford takes.'

CHAPTER 6

Madness. Man and woman, mouth to mouth, body to body, Alex's shirt carelessly discarded, Stella's blouse unbuttoned by nimble fingers that feathered a trail of devastation between her aching breasts, slid beneath the waistband of her skirt and into the dimple of her navel before sweeping back to the flimsy front fastening of her bra. And as Stella's full breasts spilled free it was Alex's turn to draw a sharp breath, Alex's turn to pause, to look, to savour, his eyes dropping from her face to her breasts, and back again, his whole expression smoky.

'Beautiful,' he breathed. 'Woman, you really are beautiful.'

Kneeling in reverence at her feet, glancing up, piercing blue eyes saw to the centre of her soul as Stella stood and trembled, half-naked and shameless, the buttons of the skirt mastered in a trice, allowing the skirt to drop unheeded to the floor, petticoat and tights just as easily disposed of.

Hands reaching up to touch, to hold, to take the weight of her aching breasts. Mouth closing round her, nuzzling, sucking, creating currents of heat that spread like lightning to each and every part of her. And with her legs turning to water Stella nudged the unwanted heap of skirt aside and sank down on to the rug. Man and woman, face to face, mouth to mouth.

'Beautiful, beautiful, beautiful,' Alex crooned, kissing, nibbling, nuzzling, biting. 'And I want you. Now. Here. Soon. Soon, woman, I promise,' he insisted thickly, hands ranging her body, creating havoc with every touch.

'Hush, sweetheart,' Stella soothed, pushing against him, skin to skin, breasts brushing the thick dark mass that covered a powerful chest, the sensation unbelievable.

Alex snatched her to him, holding her tight, almost squeezing the breath from her body, the low torrent of words passing Stella by and yet music to her ears. Love, not lust, she told herself. Whispered words, a lover's words. And kisses, touchings.

Easing Stella back on the rug, he paused to kneel beside her, to look, to savour, to enjoy, his gaze reverential, from head to toe and back again, an almost tangible caress that set the blood pounding in her ears. Hands and fingers followed the trail his eyes had blazed, a touch that wasn't a touch, Stella's body arching to make the connection that Alex denied. A hint of connection, a low laugh in the back of his throat, and on again, and down, soft, feather-light, stirring.

'Please, Alex,' she moaned as magic fingers glided the length of her legs, paused to tickle the sensitive spot behind each knee, resumed their upward journey, only slowly, inch by tantalizing inch. Nearer and nearer and nearer still to the centre of her emotions, the vee at the apex of her legs, the froth of lace that passed for panties shamelessly skimpy, shamelessly damp.

Another exquisite pause as Alex reached his goal. Stella's lids flew open, in anticipation not alarm, because she wanted him to touch, wanted this man with a need so exquisite that she couldn't bear to wait a single moment longer. And as she arched against the hovering hand, nudging Alex into action, Alex's growl of approval was music to her ears.

'Soon,' he insisted thickly, locking his gaze on to hers. 'Very soon, I promise.' And he nodded, and he stood, and he reached for the fastening of his trousers, drawing Stella's gaze. Logging the outline of his manhood as Alex disengaged the zipper, Stella felt the sudden thrill of fear, the thrill of anticipation, and flooded all over again.

'Oh God!' she murmured reverently as Alex peeled the fabric the length of his legs. Long legs, powerful, thigh muscles rippling, golden hairs gleaming in the soft glow of the lamplight. And Alex smiled, and Stella trembled. Anticipation, not fear. Because Alex would teach her body how to love.

Love, she told herself. Not lust. And never once in her wildest dreams had she imagined it would be like this.

Alex was kneeling beside her, naked but for the boxer shorts that seemed moulded to his body, concealing, revealing, the latent power awesome. Alex was kissing her, arching over her trembling body, holding himself aloof, denying Stella the contact she craved. Mouth to mouth, his tongue darting between her lips, into the moist recesses in a fervid exploration of her mouth, his lips gently nuzzling, teeth nibbling, that erotic tongue seeking hers, finding hers and sending shivers of heat swirling through her all over again.

Mouth moving down, slowly, exploring, tasting, devouring; tongue lapping at the hollow of her throat and down again, inch by tantalizing inch. Into the valley between her aching breasts – breasts that strained for Alex's touch, ached for the touch of skin on skin, and more, for Alex's mouth to devour them. Only Alex continued to deny her, skirting each rosy ripe breast with its dark straining bud, round and round, describing a figure of eight, one to the other and then onwards, drawing his tongue over the curve of her belly, darting into the dimple of her navel, another erotic swirl and then on again, so near, so far.

Unfair, her mind screamed as, sensing her frustration, he gave a low growl, bypassed completely the centre of her emotions, feathering her legs with his mouth, heightening the pleasure of pain as Stella writhed, trembled, fought the urge to plea, silently pleaded. Please, Alex. Oh, God, please, please, please, Alex.

And Alex glanced up, and Alex's smoky gaze locked with hers, and Alex smiled. Because Alex knew. He was taking Stella to the brink of heaven and then pulling back to leave her in torment.

'Now, Stella?' he queried smokily, pausing, hands sliding the length of her quivering thighs, his very touch scalding. 'Now, Stella?'

'Are you asking me – or telling me?' she countered saucily, flirting, teasing, paying him back in kind, although heaven help her, the wait was unendurable.

Blue eyes darkened, narrowed, sending fresh shivers of fear rippling through her body as Alex's hands tightened their grip, twin thumbs creating havoc with their rhythmic brushing of Stella's inner thighs.

'But I thought you knew,' he growled, eyes locking with hers and seeing to the centre of her soul. 'Alex Gifford doesn't ask; Alex Gifford takes. Any objections?'

'Like I said,' Stella purred, nerve-endings jangling, 'are you asking me, or telling me?'

'Just making sure you understand the rules,' he acknowledged huskily. 'Because I want you. I want you, and I'll take you, and I'll take you again and again and again, and still you'll be screaming out for more. And if you ask nicely – if,' he repeated thickly. 'I might finally give you what you crave. Understand?'

'And your needs, Alex?' Stella queried, the blood pounding in her ears, the tension unendurable. 'What happens to your needs when I finally say no?'

'No? No, no, no!' he growled, pulling her roughly into his arms and kissing her, lips bruising, punishing, pounding, persuading, coaxing, teasing, tasting, revering, easing . . .

Alex smiled a knowing smile, his eyes, the mirrors of the soul, locking with hers, smoky with love, heavy with need. Man to woman and back again, the message travelled between them. Love in Stella's mind, love in Alex's smouldering gaze – a gaze that travelled the lines of her body, slowly, reverently, in an almost tangible caress of a body primed for love, a body aching for the touch of skin on skin. Touch. Hands gliding the length of her thighs, nearer and nearer to the apex of her legs, the centre of her emotions. Pause. Exquisite pause. And then twin thumbs inched beneath the flimsy lace fabric and plunged into the heart of her.

'Say no, Stella,' he urged thickly. 'Say no, if you dare.'

'I – oh, God, Alex!' she moaned, writhing at the touch. 'Please, Alex. Please, please, please, Alex!'

'Ah, yes,' he growled. 'I do believe you're beginning to see things my way. Please, Alex. And the easiest way to please Alex is to tell him that you want him. Say it, Stella. Say it.'

'I want you. You know I want you. For pity's sake, Alex –'

A sudden cry, overloud on nerves as taut as fiddle strings, and as Stella broke off Alex's head snapped up in alarm. Alarm. Stella inwardly groaned. Baby alarm. James Gifford was stirring in his sleep, stirring, bleating, settling, leaving the lovers free to love. Love. Man and woman. Alex and Stella. Only Alex had loosened his hold with indecent haste, and, jerking away from her, reached for something out of Stella's line of vision under the chintz fringe of the armchair. Second-guessing what was coming, Stella went cold.

Not the *Sunday Beacon*, thank heavens. Even allowing for cold, professional interest, Stella would draw the line at reading that salacious rag that masqueraded as a news sheet. Not even one of the tabloids. But damning nonetheless, in Alex Gifford's eyes.

Cold eyes, switching from the paper folded open at the TV listings to Stella, chilled and practically naked on the rug, arms folded across her aching breasts. Heavy with condemnation, those eyes were raking the lines of her body, a body primed for love. Flicking back to the paper, which Alex deftly turned inside out. A cursory scan of the front page headlines and Alex homed in on the two column inches the *Beacon*'s claims had generated in one of the other more balanced members of the press.

'Well, madam?' he demanded icily.

'It's – not what it seems, Alex,' she pleaded softly. 'I –'

'You couldn't wait, could you, Stella? The first hint of scandal and you're scurrying off to the village to read all about it for yourself.'

'Hardly,' she countered mildly, as something vital died inside. Because Alex believed. And Alex was hurting. And Alex was hitting out at Stella. 'Think, Alex, think. If prurience was all-important I'd have bought the *Beacon* in the first place.'

'And walked bold as brass across my threshold? My house? My wife. My life. My private life at that? Oh, no. No.' He shook his head, raked her face with his frigid gaze. 'Not even you would have the nerve to go that far. Though on second thoughts,' he murmured coldly, eyes devoid of light, 'maybe you would. In fact, now that I come to think of it, who knows how far you'd be prepared to go purely out of interest? Sleep with the accused, perhaps?'

Stella's chin snapped up. 'Now you're being ridiculous. I –'

'Was enjoying each and every moment? But of course,' he acknowledged with bitter irony. 'After all, I'm a man of the world, and I don't make a habit of short-changing my women. And the same,' he tagged on frigidly, 'goes for murder.'

'I didn't –'

'Don't,' he entreated harshly. 'Don't lie. Don't pretend. Don't say another word. Believe me, madam, *this* speaks volumes.' Shaking the paper, almost thrusting it into her face, he tossed it aside and snatched at her shoulders, fingers biting deep, bruising, while eyes devoid of emotion raked the lines of her face.

'Alex!' Stella protested with a note of hysteria. 'Alex, you're hurting me.'

'Hurt you? Hurt you?' he demanded, releasing her abruptly. 'I wouldn't waste my time even thinking it. You know something, Stella?' he entreated, almost mildly. 'You disappoint me.'

'Because I'm human? Because I made an error of judgement – if I did make an error of judgement,' she tagged on flatly. 'Because, oddly enough, buying a Sunday paper wasn't a crime the last time I checked. Or because Alex Gifford snaps his fingers and expects everyone else to jump?' she enquired. 'Thou shalt not pay attention to slander, lies and defamation. Thou shalt not look, thou shalt not read, thou shalt not discuss. Because Alex Gifford has pronounced. Judge, jury and prosecution benches combined. Thou shalt not, full stop. And why is that, precisely? Unless,' she tagged on icily, 'unless you've something to hide?'

His face changed, the colour draining from his cheeks, the stark white lines flaring from nostrils to mouth more than eloquent proof of how badly she'd hurt him. Hurt him when she wanted to love him, comfort him, soothe him, bed him. Oh, yes, be honest at least. Shameless through and through, she wanted him. Only now she'd lost him. Not that he'd ever been hers to start with, she acknowledged as the pain scythed through her.

As if in a dream, or a slow, silent movie, Alex came to his feet, reached for the heap of clothes so carelessly discarded, and, ignoring the woman kneeling at his feet, poured himself back into the trousers, shrugged the shirt over powerful shoulders and with a long, contemptuous glance around the room that didn't choose to encompass the nearly naked Stella, he spun away.

Let him go, Stella decided, her stomach tying itself in knots. Don't plead, don't explain, don't apologize. Simply let him go.

'Alex?'

He halted at the door, didn't turn, didn't speak, simply stood and waited, his rigid spine unbending. Stella squeezed back the tears, dug her nails into her palms in an effort to stay in control while she searched her mind for the means to salve the pain.

'You can't walk away and pretend it doesn't exist, Alex,' she pointed out softly. 'You can't wave a magic wand and make everything smell of roses. Slander, lies, gossip and sheer speculation,' she reminded him. 'And the world will wonder, and the world will probe. But as long as *you* know the truth, the world doesn't have the power to hurt.'

'Not the world, Stella,' he countered coldly. 'The people I trust. The people I love. People like you. *You* believe it. And that's what I can't come to terms with. You believe.'

'Do I?' she murmured softly, and then she changed her mind, changed tack, closed her mind to the pain and prayed she wasn't about to push Alex Gifford so much as an inch too far. 'But, no, I guess you were right in the first place,' she taunted, angling her head in defiance as Alex spun round, disbelief shattering his features. 'Of course I believe,' she sneeringly conceded, inwardly flinching as Alex took half a step towards her. 'Because Alex Gifford says so,' she scorned. 'And when Alex Gifford pronounces,' she tagged on icily, 'then, yes, sir! It has to be true.' Raising a hand, she gave a disdainful snap of her fingers. 'Irrefutable. Indisputable. Infallible. But then, that's Alex Gifford, I guess. Arrogant as hell and too blind to see the wood for the trees.'

Unwilling to watch, to see the hate, the contempt, the disgust in his eyes, she dropped her gaze, squeezing back the tears. She felt the hot trickle on her cheeks and, though the soft click of the door told her she was alone, Stella choked back a sob. Pride. Like Alex, she had more than her fair share, and she wasn't about to let go, to indulge in a fit of the vapours. Because a man had taken her to the verge of making love? she wondered vaguely, audibly sniffing. Or because the same man despised her? Love and hate – facets of the same coin. And right now she hated him every bit as much as Alex hated her.

'Stella?'

Gulping, half-choking, colouring, her head snapped up in alarm. Because Alex hadn't moved, was leaning back against the closed door, watching her.

'Alex?' she retorted warily.

'I'm sorry.'

'Well, I'm not,' she railed as the anger surged. 'I've done nothing wrong and I'll be damned if I'll apologize, or walk around on glass because Alex Gifford's ego is in constant need of a feed. I'm here to work – nothing more, nothing less,' she railed, without thinking. 'And in future I'll thank you to remember it.'

'Stella Marshall,' he murmured gleefully, rugged features lightening in an instant. 'I do believe you've just talked your way into a job.'

Could she stay? A week, a month, three months? Knowing she loved him, wanted him, needed him? Knowing Alex was simply playing games. Hardly knowing Alex at all, in fact. Playboy. With his latest bright young thing cosily installed under the same roof. The same roof, the same bedroom, the same bed, no doubt. Tamara Clayton. Absent for now. And while the cat is away the mouse will play. And Alex had. With Stella.

Gullible Stella Marshall, who had reached the grand old age of thirty-two and had never come close to sleeping with a man. Gullible Stella Marshall, who hadn't had the sense to see what her best friend and her fiancée were getting up to behind her back. Gullible Stella Marshall, who could fall for man she barely knew hook, line and sinker. Alex Gifford. Playboy. And, despite the tragic death of his glamorous wife, he was still playing around, still feeding the scandal sheets. No smoke without fire, she told herself, hating herself. Because, heaven help her, she didn't want to believe it. Didn't believe it, couldn't believe it, wouldn't believe it. Yet, as Alex had taken pains to point out, she'd talked herself into staying.

A week, a month, three months? Stella's lips twisted bitterly. Three days was proving trial enough, and with Carly safe there was no real need for Stella to stay. So tempting to stay, to act out a role she was beginning to enjoy. Dangerous to stay. Too much pain, too many emotions. For Alex, for his son. For if impersonating a nanny wasn't exactly illegal, it was hardly something a man like Alex Gifford would condone. And as for her true occupation . . . Stella shivered. Given his reaction to the press as a whole, heaven help her. An innocent deception. But would Alex stop to see it that way?

A nightmare. Tossing and turning, dreaming, wanting, yearning, needing. Alex's face dissolved, a hooded figure taking its place. And she was suffocating. So hot. Couldn't breathe. Couldn't breathe with the weight of the world pressing down on her, smothering, stifling. And, struggle though she did to clear the fog from her mind, resistance was futile. She was pinned to the sheets and she was dying, suffocating. Couldn't breathe. Mustn't panic, mustn't simply drift away. Away. Push the weight away. A huge surge of effort and Stella was free, had jerked herself upright in the bed, her heart beating fit to burst. A nightmare. Long, deep gulps of air. Stifle the panic.

Panic because she wasn't alone. Someone was there in the darkness, silent, watching, breathing. Stella's ragged gasps were over-loud in the still night air. Panic. A nightmare. Too real to be a nightmare. Too old for nightmares.

Her eyes were adjusting to the darkness, picking out the now familiar objects of the room; the looming hulk of the wardrobe, the matching dresser and chest of drawers, the old-fashioned rocking chair tucked into the corner. And as her gaze moved on there came the faint rustle of air. Air. Because the door was swinging to when she'd made a point of propping it open with a heavy-based vase she'd discovered abandoned in the back of the wardrobe.

With slivers of ice trickling the length of her spine, Stella reached for the robe she'd draped across the rocking chair and, shrugging herself into it, padded silently to the door, kicking the discarded pillow out of the way in passing. A closed door. A locked door, she concluded, smothering the panic as the handle turned and the door swung open. Panic. Overreaction. Over-wrought nerves. Hardly surprising, given the emotional scene with Alex. Man and woman, touching, kissing, tasting, hurting. Only they'd salved the hurt, and Stella had committed herself to staying. For now.

The sitting room was empty, just as she'd expected. Stella glided to the door that led to the corridor, peered out into the gloom. Nothing. Not a rustle, not a shadow. She tiptoed into James to stand and watch the low rise and fall of the quilt. Normality. A ten-month-old baby, soft and ruffled from sleep. Sleep. She checked her wristwatch in the rosy glow of the nursery light. Three o'clock and she was wide awake. She needed a drink – a warm milky drink, she decided. She'd carry it back to bed, curl up with a book and will herself to relax.

Smiling, touching her fingers to her lips before pressing them gently against the sleeping child's forehead, she turned, tiptoeing out again, allowing the door to swing to under its own momentum. Standing and waiting for the soft click, she let her eyes idly flick across the sitting room. Not a thing was out of place – not even a crease in the rug she and Alex had come so close to making love on. Love. Fool, fool, fool, she told herself. But she was smiling. Because she was alive. For the first time in her life she was alive, and she wasn't about to spoil it with an old-fashioned dose of common sense.

A final glance around to reassure herself – of what? she wondered – and Stella turned, automatically glancing at the mirror on the wall as she patted her tousled hair into place.

Bitch.

Stella went cold, closed her eyes and opened them again, but, no, she wasn't dreaming. The word was scrawled across the mirror in lipstick – Stella's lipstick, at that, she realized as the nausea rose up to swamp her. Unbelieving, she sank down into the cushions of the settee, her mind refusing to function.

Carly. No wonder her sister had bolted if this was the treatment she'd endured. Bitch. A bitchy comment? Stella mused. A bitchy gesture, a female gesture, she reassured herself, willing herself to believe it. So, face it, Stella, someone you barely know hates you enough to tiptoe into your bedroom, place a pillow over your head and hold it in place until you begin to struggle and then glide soundlessly away, leaving that single word message as proof you haven't been dreaming.

And with Tamara away, and Hannah unable to cope with the stairs, that only left Mrs Edwards. Easy. Process of elimination. It had to be Mrs Edwards. Too easy, Stella decided at once. No one with a mind as devious as this would leave herself open to detection. Unless it was a double bluff. It could only be Mrs Edwards therefore it couldn't possibly be Mrs Edwards. Which didn't help at all, Stella realized, fetching a damp cloth and scrubbing at the word, cleaning away the evidence. Evidence? Stella shivered. She was beginning to sound like a court of law.

Law courts. Word association. Trial by jury. A

murder trial – oh, no. No! No! No! It couldn't be Alex. It was a bitchy, female gesture, she reassured herself. Only she didn't reassure herself at all. Because the stark fact was, whoever it turned out to be, whoever had had the temerity to walk bold as brass into her bedroom, place a pillow over her head, rummage through her make-up bag, and leave their calling card scrawled across the sitting room mirror, that someone was attempting to frighten her. But who? And, just as important, why?

Breakfast, and a sluggish Stella settled for orange juice and toast before sorting the full of beans James out. With a pleasant day in the offing, how to fill her time? Another walk to the village, perhaps, or a visit to the stables? See Hannah in her element? But first she would tidy the nursery, while James shuffled about on his bottom in his playpen.

Ten months. He'd be ready for crawling soon, Stella decided as he reached for a fluffy ball just out of reach, overreached, toppled sideways and, amazingly enough, landed like a gymnast, all fluid lines and gentle rolls. And then he struggled to push himself up off his face, ending up on all fours, his tiny face creased and red with concentration. Spotting the ball, only just out of reach, he seemed to weigh up the task, weigh up the distance as Stella silently urged him forwards. He was Rocking, working up a momentum, and Stella held her breath as James moved all right – only backwards, his delight at having moved at all tempered by being even further away from his goal. A delighted Stella laughed, took pity, rolled the ball back into reach and set about her task, fishing yesterday's baby clothes from the linen basket. An amazing amount of clothes for one little man – one little man who was clearly beginning to tire, she decided, recognizing the signs.

'Nap time. And no arguments,' she insisted, carrying him through to his cot. 'Just be thankful you're given the opportunity. What I'd give to change places for an hour or so.'

Twenty minutes later, and with James fast asleep, Stella popped down to the basement. She'd soon get the hang of the routine, but would need to feel her way carefully for a day or two – ask Mrs Edwards' advice, ensure she wasn't treading on any toes. And maybe coming face to face with her number one suspect would yield a few clues.

Only it wasn't Mrs Edwards she bumped into.

'Well, well, well, if it isn't Mary Poppins.'

Tamara, scantily clad in filmy nightdress and negligee, stepped across Stella's path as she rounded the newel post. 'Still here?' she queried absurdly. 'You haven't packed your bags and done a bunk like all the rest? No? No, of course you haven't. But you will. And, since it's only a matter of time, why not do yourself a favour and make it sooner rather than later?'

'And leave you – or Mrs Edwards – holding the baby? But it's a job that didn't appeal to either of you, I seem to recall. Like it or not, Miss Clayton, James needs a nanny.'

'Fine. The moment I'm in charge I'll choose one.'

'Fifty-five, fifteen stone and frumpish?'

'I beg your pardon?'

'The new nanny. I was hazarding a guess at her probable dimensions,' Stella retorted pleasantly. 'Can't have the master suffering any distractions.'

'I'm not sure I like what you're implying.'

'And I'm not sure I enjoy being bullied. You don't employ me yet, Miss Clayton, and the more you push, the more I'm likely to dig in my heels and stay.'

'But you're just the stand-in. As soon a girl becomes available –'

'Precisely. Girl. Young, inexperienced, and powerless to cope with the bullies of this world. At least I'm beginning to see why James has had more nannies than you've had hot dinners. Now if you'll excuse me –'

'And if I don't? If I decide I haven't finished our – cosy little chat?' Tamara drawled, putting out a hand, resting vivid red talons on Stella's arm.

'Why, then naturally I'll stay and listen,' Stella conceded coolly, glancing up, then down, then up again before adding almost as an afterthought, 'Ma'am.'

Tamara's exquisite features darkened. 'There's a fine line between respect and insolence,' she informed her. 'And I'm not sure you haven't just stepped over it.'

'Ah, yes,' Stella conceded pleasantly. 'But then, you *earn* respect, you don't command it.'

'You think you're so clever, don't you?'

'It's part and parcel of the job,' Stella replied carefully. 'A job I try to do despite the obstacles other people scatter at my feet in the hope of tripping me up. And since I do need a job, Miss Clayton, I can't afford to rock any boats.'

'Then you've a funny way of showing it. For a mere hired hand, you've managed to worm your way into Alex's affections in no time at all.'

Stella went cold. Gloves off for battle. Forget the thinly veiled insults, the innuendo, the throwaway snide remarks. Forget Alex's insistence on keeping the peace. Tamara wanted Stella out, and she wasn't about to beat around the bush.

'Meaning?'

'Meaning don't bother playing the sweet young thing; it isn't very becoming at your age,' she said saccharine-sweetly, patting Stella's arm. 'Meaning that vanload of equipment you managed to worm out of Alex in record quick time. Meaning dining with the family, mixing with the family. You're staff, and it wouldn't pay to forget it, and Alex –'

'Someone taking my name in vain, ladies?'

'Alex, darling!'

Tamara's ugly expression softened, changing like the wind as she spun round, launched herself into Alex's arms. A bemused Alex gently disengaged himself, yet made no effort to discourage Tamara from slipping her hand possessively into his. Tamara and Alex. Tamara's expression was heady with triumph. Tamara and Alex were watching Stella. Stella was achingly aware of fingers entwined with fingers, and, since Tamara was still in her nightwear, the implications were obvious.

Fool, fool, fool, she silently berated herself. For

hoping. For thinking Alex could care. For wanting a man who clearly belonged to another. Because while Stella had tossed and turned in her bed, her body primed for love, her body screaming out for this man's touch, it didn't take a genius to conclude that this man and this woman had been together making love.

Tears, at her age. How ridiculous – and with two sets of curious eyes fastened on hers, had she no pride? Stella swung away, Alex's hand on her arm pulling her up short. Skin on skin, the very touch was searing, and she wanted him. Even now she wanted him.

'Stella? What is it, Stella?' he entreated softly, as Stella fastened her gaze on the polished grain of the wood beneath her feet. And then a sigh, vaguely annoyed, vaguely amused. 'Don't tell me you two have been falling out again?'

'Good heavens, no,' Tamara interjected brightly. 'If you must know, darling, I was playing the dutiful fiancée and offering my apologies for yesterday's silly misunderstanding. And Miss Marshall, I assure you –'

She broke off as the thin wail of a newly wakened baby drifted across from the receiver plugged into the wall behind them. There was a listening device in most of the downstairs rooms and the transmitter in the nursery, where James's every murmur, every cry, could be detected loud and clear. And if it picked up the cry of a baby, what price the amplification of a love scene? Alex and Stella. Man and woman. And that heated scene that had started in the nursery.

Raising her eyes to Tamara, catching the grimace of hate that crossed her exquisite features, Stella couldn't shake the awful feeling that Tamara had been privy to each and every word.

'As I was saying,' Tamara breathed, the poison veiled, but present nonetheless, 'Miss Marshall and I understand one another completely.'

CHAPTER 7

'So you still haven't heard from Carly?'

'Just the message on the answer-machine. But I'm hardly likely to hear for a week or two. Assuming she's written, the letter's probably winging its way around Europe. Only . . .'

'Only, what?' Beth probed, grey eyes cloudy as she momentarily switched her gaze from two-year-old Connor, toddling round the tiny tots' playground, to Stella, perched on the bench beside her.

Stella shrugged. 'Danny daVine. I was so sure he knew where to find her, that he'd pass on my message at least. But there again,' she murmured brightly, 'since she'd already left a message confirming she was safe, Carly's probably convinced she's done her duty.'

'And you don't believe that any more than I do.'

Stella glanced across, caught a wealth of concern in her cousin's velvet eyes and swallowed hard. 'No,' she conceded, smiling despite herself. 'But to all intents and purposes I'm still roaming the continent. I can hardly blame Carly for failing to send me a revised itinerary.'

'Or landing you with the baby.'

'Hardly,' Stella demurred mildly. 'But since I was overdue a break . . .'

'Research?' Beth slipped in slyly. 'Given the current spate of headlines, you could make a killing with an exclusive inside story. Ouch.' Catching the pun, she winced, had the grace to look ashamed. 'But you know what I mean.'

'Yes, Beth. And, no, Beth.'

'No, Beth, what?'

'No, Beth, I've no intentions of exploiting a position of trust.'

'But you're a journalist.'

'So?'

'So journalists make a living by reporting, and face it, Stella, this story's red-hot.'

'Slander, lies, gossip and defamation,' Stella retorted, the edge to her tone barely perceptible. 'Beth Austin, I'm ashamed of you. You of all people ought to know better.'

'Because my marriage was rocked by a malicious pack of lies? You're right. I'm sorry. Only . . .'

'Only?' Stella probed, swallowing a smile.

'No smoke without fire,' Beth reminded her softly. 'And if the story in the *Beacon* turns out to be true –'

'Then Alex Gifford's guilty of murder. But if he's guilty – as *not* charged,' Stella said pointedly, 'then I'm Jack the Ripper's long-lost wife.'

'Don't be hurt, Stell. Believe me, I'm trying not to overreact. But I'm worried. First Carly and now you –'

'Incarcerated deep in the country with an axe-wielding madman, his Mrs Danvers look-alike and an assorted cast of hangers-on? Carly's safe. She gave up on the job. Nothing more, nothing less. And, having experienced the set-up for myself, I can hardly say that I blame her.'

'Ah!'

'Ah, what?'

'Ah, so there is a story there after all.'

'Human interest? Probably,' Stella acknowledged reluctantly. 'But, like I said, I'm paid to look after James, not tell tales out of school.'

'But once the job is over –'

'End of story.'

'So what's he like?'

'Who?' Stella snapped.

'Hunky Mr Gifford. And he is a hunk, judging from the pictures in the paper. Not that I've made a point of looking,' Beth added mildly.

'Oh, heaven forbid you'd be as nosy as the next nosy parker,' Stella drawled. 'But since I've only had the job a week, I'm hardly in a position to judge. Definitely hunky,' she acknowledged dryly. 'Even I don't go around with my eyes closed, Beth. But as for anything else –' She broke off, shrugged. 'Like I said, I've barely seen the guy. But he seems pretty well balanced for a psychopath.'

'Don't mock, Stell.'

'Don't probe, Beth. The guy's innocent until proven guilty, and there isn't even a charge in the offing.'

'And you're prickly as hell.'

'Just put it down to loyalty.'

'Or interest? An occupational hazard?' Beth probed carefully. 'Or do I detect an undercurrent?'

'Riddles, Beth?' Stella derided. 'This isn't like you. So whatever it is you're thinking, why not spit it out before it chokes you?'

'You won't like it, Stella Marshall.'

'Then don't say it, Bethy Austin.'

But she did. So Stella hit her. Playfully.

A long day; collecting her mail, no longer on a redirection notice, contacting her editor and requesting leave of absence.

'Indefinite? Stella Marshall, are you crazy? That last series from Spain pushed the circulation figures for the Tuesday edition through the roof. And we know from reader feedback it was your contribution. You can't do this to me.'

'Sorry, Nik. I just did. Give me a month,' she pleaded softly. 'I know it's more than I'm owed, but –'

'Precisely. No buts. Just get *your* butt in here first thing Monday morning.'

'No can do,' Stella retorted. 'Something's come up, something important. Family stuff,' she lied, only didn't lie, since Carly *was* still conspicuous by her absence. 'And until I've had time to sort it –'

'Consider yourself fired. Or unpaid. And if I were you, I'd polish those knees in readiness for crawling back. You owe me.'

'Bless you, Nik. You're an angel.'

'I'm a fool, Stella Marshall, but an old fool, and flattery will get you anywhere you want.'

Replaying the conversation in her mind, Stella smiled, slowed to make the right-hand turn into the private road that led to Freshfields, and was forced to brake hard as a distinctive white Élan shot up the drive and out of the gates. Tamara, she identified in the glare of the headlamps. Alone. And, though Stella's glimpse had been brief, it was enough to note that the woman's face was stony. A lovers' tiff? Stella mused, easing the car around the side of the house and into the space provided, between the wall and the neat row of privet hedge that provided a screen for the broad expanse of terrace.

To Stella's surprise, Agnes Edwards met her at the door. 'You're late.'

Stella's eyebrows arched. She double checked the time on the clock beyond the housekeeper's head. Ten o'clock. Which gave her two hours' leeway in her estimation.

'Problems?' she queried pleasantly, attempting to push past and foiled by a surprisingly nifty side-step. 'I thought I caught a glimpse of Tamara –'

'Don't ask me where she's off to. I might have been late passing on the message, but I've been rushed off my feet all day. And with Mandy going sick –'

'Oh?' Stella queried, vaguely alarmed. 'James –?'

'Is fine. No thanks to you or Tamara. Is it any wonder I forgot to mention that Mr Gifford had phoned?'

'And no prizes for guessing you've drawn the short straw? Thanks, Mrs E. It's nice to know someone's reliable. But now that I'm home, why not sit yourself down and relax, put your feet up?' she urged soothingly. And then, aware that if bridges needed mending there was nothing to lose by getting in first, 'Tell you what, why don't I slip upstairs and check on James, then pop back down and make us both a nice cup of tea? How does that sound?'

The stern features were vaguely unbending. 'Sounds like a bit of soft soap,' she sniffed. 'But that doesn't mean I can't be persuaded. Rushed off my feet, I've been . . .'

Stella left her chuntering away at no one in particular, taking the stairs in leaps and bounds. It was strangely quiet without the adults, and, though Stella had noted the glimmer of lights in Hannah's apartment, Hannah invariably kept herself to herself unless Alex was home.

All fine in the nursery, thanks to Mandy, but as for going sick . . . Stella smiled. A hot date, if she knew Mandy. And at seventeen who could blame her? Only, sensing the girl's potential, Stella was giving Mandy the chance to prove herself. Kitchen drudge to nanny – hardly the stairway to riches. But if things worked out the way Stella hoped, James would have all the stability he needed. But not if Mandy couldn't take the responsibility seriously, Stella mused, resolving to speak to Mandy first thing in the morning. In the meanwhile, there was that spot of soft soap she'd promised, and, since Mrs Edwards *had* kept an eye on James, no harm in piling it on thick. Chocolate biscuits. Nudging the packet off the shelf and allowing it to fall into her open palm, Stella grinned. Why not?

★ ★ ★

Midnight. The witching hour. Not a yawn, not a hint of tiredness, despite the long day. Time for a hot, milky drink, Stella decided, leaving her book to close under its own momentum and padding barefoot into the kitchen. The fridge was empty. Or as a good as, but, having airily told Mandy to help herself, Stella could hardly complain. Coffee, then? *Black* coffee – full of caffeine and sure to keep her awake. So, do without the drink or make the long trek down two sets of stairs? But, since she *was* wide awake, why not burn off some of that surplus energy and nip nimbly down to the basement?

All quiet. Not a sound, not a rustle, not a light. No, not quite, Stella amended, her gaze drawn to the pencil of light beneath the study door. Alex's study. Which meant Alex was home and he was working. At this hour! In need of a cup of coffee? she mused, pausing, hesitating, weighing all the options, yet deciding it was safer to simply pass by.

She was passing by as the door swung open, and she almost collided with a startled Alex. 'Stella! What on earth –?'

'I – er – coffee?' she stammered. 'I've run out milk, and then I saw your light . . .'

Alex's tired features dissolved in an instant. 'Woman, you must be psychic. Coffee sounds divine. But on one condition.'

'Oh?' Stella stalled, instantly wary.

'I get to make it; you get to drink it. Come in, why don't you?' he insisted, those piercing blue eyes locking with hers and dancing. 'Come in, sit down and make yourself at home. Unless, of course,' he added in an undertone, glancing left and right into the darkened hallway, 'you think the lemon-lipped Mrs Edwards wouldn't approve?'

Not to mention Tamara, Stella silently acknowledged, crossing the threshold as Alex melted away. The study. The one room in the house she hadn't been into, apart from the other bedrooms, and strangely male, strangely homely. Deep burgundy leather bucket chairs and matching two-seater sofa, a leather-bound desk strategically placed in the window bay to catch the best of the light. No light at this hour, Stella could see, and, since she clearly couldn't allow herself a peek at the papers strewn across it, she took Alex at his word and perched on one of the chairs.

Eyebrows were raised by Alex when he returned with the tray of coffee. Because Stella had opted for safety and given the settee a wide berth? Not so Alex, who flung himself down and stretched those long, muscular legs into the space between them. Very long legs, drawing Stella's gaze as Alex gave the coffee time to brew. Ankle to knee, knee to groin, thigh muscles rippling beneath the taut linen fabric as Alex shifted position slightly . . . Groin. Stella's eyes were drawn like magnets, her cheeks flaming as she logged the bulge she'd no right to focus on. And, tearing her gaze away, she raised her eyes, skimmed the powerful chest, the collar of the shirt carelessly unbuttoned – a careless invitation for fingers to dive into the mass of curls that Stella knew plunged from throat to navel. And on, until she reached his face, and guessed from the almost imperceptible twitch of generous lips that Alex was watching her, had been watching every move, and she had to brace herself to meet those piercing blue eyes.

'I —'

'Don't need to say a word,' he acknowledged softly. 'I know.'

Stella nodded, licked her dry lips. Yes. Impossible man.

'Coffee?' she murmured over-brightly, jumping up at once.

'Unless you'd rather opt for something more convivial. Wine? Brandy? You name it, I've probably got a bottle stashed away somewhere handy. Force of habit,' he explained, and, sensing he'd baffled Stella completely, carelessly added, 'Chrissie was a closet alcoholic.'

'Oh.'

'Just, oh? No gasp of horror, no feigned compassion, no murmurs of sympathy?'

'Should there be?' Stella queried evenly, pausing, coffee cup in one hand, cafetière in the other.

'Going by the usual response . . .' He gave a careless lift of powerful shoulders. 'Why not? The rest of the world can't get enough of it.'

'The *Sunday Beacon*?' she probed, sensing the pain behind the seeming insouciance.

'And the rest,' Alex scorned, scowling visibly. 'There's been a posse of reporters camped at the gates for days, Hannah's been pestered at the stables, and the phone's so hot I've arranged for a change of number first thing tomorrow. Gutter journalism,' he all but spat. 'No wonder Tamara's finding it a strain. If she were to walk out of here tonight and never came back, who could blame her?'

'You, perhaps,' Stella reminded him softly. 'But if she loves you –'

'Love me, love my money,' he scorned. 'Yet all the money in the world doesn't buy me peace and quiet. Trial by insinuation,' he said bitterly. 'But I suppose selling all those scandal-sheets must help make money for someone. Not to mention another posse of lawyers when I sue.'

'Good.'

'I beg your pardon?'

'Now you're hitting back instead of sitting there and wallowing. Man or mouse, Alex Gifford? Gossip, lies, defamation and lies, lies and more lies. And the onus of proof isn't even on you.'

'My, you are well primed, for the average nanny.'

'Average I ain't,' she bit out. Nanny she wasn't either, but she'd let that pass for now. 'And I'm simply well informed. Call it a legacy of staying abreast of the news, reading the papers – *quality* papers,' she emphasized grimly.

'A contradiction in terms – allegedly,' he spat. 'You can take it from me, there's no such thing.'

'And you'd know, of course. You've been there, seen that, done it, worked it. Read one or two as well, I bet, somewhere along the way,' she scorned. 'And that makes Alex Gifford an expert.'

'I don't read news; I make it,' he reminded her

coldly, sitting up and leaning forward. 'Whether I like it or not.'

'And because one unscrupulous rag prints poison, the responsible majority's condemned out of hand?'

'Got it in one. Take one rotten apple and –' He raised a hand, gave a derisory snap of the fingers.

'Oh, very fair,' Stella scorned. 'Don't weigh all the facts, or judge a case on merit, just make a blanket decision and stick to it come hell or high water. Tell me, though,' she invited saccharine-sweetly, 'how does that make you any better than Chas Fisher?'

'Chas *who*?' he queried with icy politeness, blue eyes pinpricks of hate.

Stella went cold. Chas Fisher. The *Beacon*'s acerbic editor. A flamboyant character both in and out of the business. But would your average nanny be expected to know that? Exposé time? Time to jump before she was rumbled and make a clean breast of it? Or stay cool, calm and collected and wait for Alex to work things out for himself. Not that it would take him long at this rate.

Stella forced a brittle smile. 'Chas Fisher. He's the editor of –'

'Thank you, Stella, but I know to my cost who that particular slimeball is. He's a slug – the lowest of the low. So low he could crawl under his own shadow without disturbing it. So, tell me – just to put my mind at rest, you understand – just what do you know about Fisher?'

'No more than you, I would imagine,' she retorted calmly, a lot more calmly than she felt, pushing the rapidly cooling cup of coffee towards him and taking the chair, perching on the edge again, instinctively poised for flight. 'But, since I am somewhat better read than your average nanny, naturally I've heard of him.'

'And?'

'And what?' she stalled, risking a glance through the veil of her lashes and wishing she hadn't bothered.

'Why, naturally,' he parodied cruelly, 'since you're "somewhat better read than the average nanny", I'd value your opinion.'

'Of Fisher? On hearsay?' she queried, deceptively mildly. 'Blacken the man's name on someone else's say-so? Oh, Alex,' she castigated softly, shaking her head. 'You of all people should know better than that.'

'Even though his reputation precedes him?'

'Even then,' she agreed, the faint rattle of cup in saucer a betrayal of overstretched nerves.

Silence. Not a word, not a sound, hardly a drawn breath. And Stella sat and inwardly squirmed, had to force herself to meet his gaze. Because Alex was boring holes in her head, was looking through her, not at her, his penetrating gaze all-seeing, all-knowing. And if he knew, then he was simply playing games with Stella, leading her on, giving her the rope to hang herself.

Stella winced. Strange how many thoughts seemed to lead to violent deeds. Murder. An ugly word, an ugly allegation. Precisely. An allegation. Chas Fisher's deliberate attempt to push up his circulation figures. And in refusing to condemn the man, Stella was giving Alex food for thought.

'Hearsay, Alex,' she repeated softly. 'Speculation, lies and defamation. I don't know Fisher, but I've heard enough to know he's not the sort of guy I'd care to confide in.'

'Unlike me, hey?'

'If you say so,' she teased as the atmosphere lightened, the awkward moment over – till the next time.

'So . . .' Alex smiled, reached for his coffee, winced when he found it was practically stone-cold and pushed the cup away in disgust. 'Fire away. I'm all ears. The Alex Gifford Consultation Agency is open for business.'

'Nothing to tell,' Stella insisted, and, taking a deep breath, risked another rebuke. 'Unlike a certain proud man not a million miles away across the coffee table.'

Alex's features hardened. 'I might have mellowed, but I haven't lost my mettle completely, Stella Marshall.'

'I didn't doubt it for an instant,' Stella riposted. 'It was an invitation to treat, not a decree. I'm here, I'm impartial, and I make a good listener. And I don't, repeat don't, have a direct line to Chas Fisher's desk.'

'Perish the thought,' Alex conceded, but he was smiling as he stretched, checked the time on his wristwatch, shot a glance of speculation at the desk, with its mountain of paperwork, and seemed to make a decision. 'Brandy, Stella? Or, since it's late, perhaps you'd rather go to bed?'

And how to answer that and keep a straight face?

Keep a straight face she didn't, and Alex smiled, and Stella's smile broadened.

'Brandy would be lovely,' she insisted. 'Beats cold coffee any day.'

'Not to mention that other Gifford speciality. A drop of the hard stuff,' he explained – only didn't explain, simply dribbled a trail of clues. 'Colourless. A distinctive odour of dill. Especially good for settling queasy tummies, so I've heard. Doubtless I've tried it myself in my dim and distant past, but never, I assure you, intentionally. Ten letters. Not a product of the grape, I believe, but the letter formation's close. Possible crossword clue: aquatic complaint. Water, pain, water –'

'Gripe?' Stella cut in dryly. 'But if I don't get that promised brandy soon, Alex Gifford, then gripe as in moan, complain, bend your shell-like till it aches is what I shall be doing. Very loud.'

Alex shook his head. 'Better not. You might wake the baby,' he warned.

The baby. Little James Gifford, tucked up safe and sound in bed. Bed. Stella's cheeks flamed, though luckily this time Alex had turned his back, was rummaging through a drawer in search of a key. He really had locked the brandy away in a cupboard!

Like the brandy, the atmosphere was mellow, and Stella snuggled down into the chair, swirled the amber liquid around the balloon of her glass and smiled inside. Glancing up, she found Alex's solemn gaze fastened on her face and felt the heat run through her. Man and woman. Alone. Not speaking, not touching, but with vibes of communication passing between them just the same. She wanted Alex. Alex wanted Stella.

Time, Stella acknowledged, with a thrill of anticipation. It was all a matter of time.

'Soon,' Alex murmured, uncannily reading her mind. 'Soon, I promise you.'

And Stella nodded. And Stella trembled. And she sipped her brandy and waited. And waited. And found the strain unendurable.

'I can't stay, Alex,' she blurted out baldly.

'Any particular reason why not?' he drawled, just a barely perceptible tightening of his mouth hinting at annoyance.

'You know why,' she half-stated, half-pleaded, aware that she'd hurt him, aware that he'd already suffered more than he deserved – first his wife's tragic death and now these horrible allegations.

'Tamara.' Statement, not question, Stella noted, and curiously flat.

She nodded. 'Partly,' she conceded, aware that if they were playing the truth game it would be Stella's turn to inflict the pain. For this ridiculous charade she'd no right starting in the first place. For keeping Alex in the dark. Lying by omission, she told herself. A betrayal of trust. And, given Alex's vehement reaction to anyone even remotely connected with the press, heaven help her if he stumbled on the truth. And so she'd have to go. Soon. She should never have stayed beyond the first weekend. The moment she'd known Carly was safe, Stella should have gone. Only she hadn't. Seven days. Seven days too many. Because she was snared. Alex and James. Father and son. And vulnerable Stella Marshall was caught fast. And she was surprised. Because she'd spent years building a wall around her heart, projecting a confidence that all of a sudden turned out to be nothing more substantial than fresh air.

'And the rest?' he queried politely.

'The rest?' Stella murmured absurdly.

'Your other reasons for leaving?' he reminded her, eyes fastened on hers, refusing to allow her to look away.

'I – family reasons, personal reasons,' she explained. Like worrying about Carly, loving Alex, loving James – not to mention the demands of her job, a job that Alex would despise. And he would despise Stella just as badly, she was beginning to see. Much better to go before Alex stumbled on the truth. Better to give him the truth herself, she realized, balking at the thought.

'You can't go, Stella, we need you here. You've turned the place around. In a few short days –'

'Exactly. Coincidence. I've done nothing apart from be here for James –'

'And now you're running out on him?'

Stella's head snapped up. 'Try some emotional blackmail, why don't you? It won't work, Alex,' she said tightly. 'It didn't work the last time; it won't work now. Face it, Alex, it's a temporary arrangement. I stepped in to cover the crisis, and crisis over, now it's time for me to leave.'

'Because you want to?'

'Because I want to,' she echoed, looking him in the face and lying. 'Got it in one. Because I want to.'

'Liar!'

Stella flushed. 'So I'm lying. So I love the job. So it's the best thing to happen to me since sliced bread. Everything's hunky-dory,' she conceded bitterly, hazel eyes cloudy. 'It couldn't be more perfect if I landed up in paradise. So how come I want out?'

'Commitment?' he mused, half to himself, as if turning the idea over in his mind. 'Here today, gone tomorrow and no strings attached. Here today, gone tomorrow and no time for emotion. Emotion. Raw emotion – like love, perhaps? That's it, isn't it, Stella?' he demanded frigidly. 'You're running scared. You're afraid. You're afraid someone's going to pierce that shell you've built around your heart and hurt you. But believe me, Stella, better the pain than the dull ache of unfulfilment.'

Love. In all its facets. And Alex had clearly loved his wife, clearly hadn't come to terms with her death. Incompatible with the stories circulating in the press, of course. And maybe Alex was right about that too. Maybe the job *was* the lowest of the low. Maybe Stella *was* every bit as low as the slug-like Fisher. Only it wasn't true, she told herself, willing herself to believe it. Like in every walk of life, there was the good, the bad and the indifferent. And Stella was good at her job. Stella was ashamed of her job, since she hadn't the guts to give Alex the truth. Food for thought. Just like the rest of the conversation.

'Tell me about him.'

'Wh-who?' Stella stammered, thoroughly confused.

'The man in your life. The man you're running away from. The man who's allowed you to run away. And believe me, Stella, whoever he is, he's a fool.'

'Why, thank you kindly, sir,' she said.

'A subtle way of telling me to mind my own business?' Alex grinned, folded his arms, leaned his head against the backrest and pinned dancing blue eyes on Stella. 'Fine. It was an invitation to treat, not a decree. I'm here, I freely admit to a vested interest, but, like you, I make a good listener.'

'And at the risk of repeating myself, there's nothing to tell. Not any more.'

'Ah.'

'Ah, what?' she bristled.

'Let me guess. A teenage romance? And the uncouth youth let you down?'

'And Alex's a poet and he doesn't know it. And Stella's not playing, relaying or saying,' Stella trilled lightly. She angled her head, met his gaze full on. 'There's nothing worth repeating, Alex, so why waste time on idle speculation?'

'Like I said, the offer's there if you'd care to take me up on it.'

'And bore you rigid? Thanks, Alex, but no, thanks.'

'He isn't important, then?'

'Not any more,' she conceded with an edge to her tone, yet amazingly enough she was giving him the truth.

'Good.'

'My turn now?' she challenged lightly.

'I –'

'Don't like the rules? But you *made* the rules,' she reminded him sweetly. 'Poke thy nose in where it's clearly not wanted.'

'Which got me nowhere precisely.'

'Can I help it if your killer instinct's all fizz and no bang?' she demanded, completely unthinking. Killer. Oh, God! 'Oh, Alex, I'm sorry.' Her hand flew to her mouth as the colour drained from his face. 'I didn't mean – I didn't –'

'You didn't. No offence meant; no offence taken,' he insisted, recovering fast and yet topping up the brandy without so much as a by her leave.

'Alex –'

'Leave it, Stella.'

'Pretend it doesn't exist, you mean? If that's the way you want to play it –'

'It isn't a game. This is my life we're talking about.'

'Only we're not. Talking,' she needled. 'Because the minute I come close, you freeze me out.'

'Shades of pot and kettle, I believe.'

'So we're quits. I don't trust you; you don't trust me.'

'Face it, Stella, I barely know you.'

'And you never will at this rate. I'm leaving, remember – soon. As soon as the agency sends round the replacement.'

'No!'

'Yes!'

'Why, damn you, why? Why can't you stay?'

'And why can't you simply accept that my mind's made up?'

'Because I want you to stay,' he all but bellowed.

'And what Alex Gifford wants he takes – or buys?' she spat, up on her feet and towering over him. 'Sorry, Mr Gifford, but not this time.'

'Because I refuse to open my heart to a perfect stranger?'

'So I'm perfect,' Stella bit out as the surge of anger vanished. 'Why not try me?'

'Tempting, woman, very tempting,' he acknowledged, a wry grin splitting his features. He spread his hands. 'See what I mean?' he entreated mildly. 'You can't go. You're good for the place, good for me. You're a breath of fresh air.'

'Here today, gone tomorrow,' she reminded him, slipping down into her seat.

'Oh, no, *that's* Mary Poppins' idea of commitment, not the Stella Marshall we know and love.'

'Love them and leave them,' she trilled, ignoring the stab of pain. Love. If only. Lots of if onlys. 'But you hit the nail on the head in the first place,' she said. 'You barely know me. Short of running a character check, who knows? I could be anyone straight off the streets.'

'Hardly,' he demurred. 'You were too well primed for that. And you did come from Greenhavens.'

'Indirectly,' she countered uneasily, hating the lies, the deception, intent on sticking as near to the truth as possible. 'Most of the time I'm freelance, remember.'

Alex's turn to swirl the brandy. 'A strange description for a nanny.'

'Must be all that journalese,' she demurred, playing

with fire, maybe, but if fate forced her hand, she'd come clean. Now. Risk everything. 'Putting ideas in my head.'

'Or reading too many papers – quality or otherwise,' Alex needled lightly.

'Oh, definitely quality,' Stella insisted. 'Of course,' she floated carefully, heart in mouth, 'there could be another explanation.'

'Oh?' Alex demurred, glancing up, suddenly alert.

'Perhaps I'm not a nanny after all,' she tossed out defiantly. 'Perhaps it's just a cover.'

'Undercover agent? Police plant? The *Sunday Beacon*'s secret weapon?' Alex all but snorted. 'When all I have to do is lift up the phone and have one of my staff run a check through the computer?'

'But of course,' Stella scathingly allowed. 'How could I have forgotten? You're a man with influence. In which case, Alex, I'm only surprised you didn't do exactly that days ago.'

'And what makes you so sure that I didn't?'

He knows, Stella decided, forcing herself to meet that gaze unblinkingly. A curiously frank gaze, all-knowing, all-seeing. And Alex Gifford was no fool. He ran a multi-million pound organization. He didn't trip up on basics and forget to vet his staff, from the all-important right-hand man – or woman – to the humblest member of the Gifford empire – messenger boy, gofer, cleaner, nanny for his son. Nanny. And Carly's background details would easily lead to Stella – wouldn't need to lead to Stella, since she was here, bold as brass, a journalist masquerading as a nanny.

Only he couldn't know. Somehow – incredible though it seemed – running a check on someone as vital as his baby son's nanny just hadn't crossed his mind. Or maybe Alex simply didn't care who looked after James as long as she kept the child out of his hair. The child. Alex's curious way of referring to his son. And Carly was right. He really didn't care. And since it had been obvious to Stella herself from the moment she walked in, why should the knowledge hurt?

'So surprise me,' she invited with all the composure she could muster. 'Age, height, weight, colour of hair, dress size? Shouldn't be difficult, since I'm sitting as large as life in front of you,' she scorned. 'In which case, what couldn't you know from pure observation? Education?' she clipped. 'Qualifications, previous occupation,' she itemized, ticking them off on her fingers. 'Hobbies, secret vices, favourite food, favourite book, preferred daily paper, perhaps?' she entreated saccharine-sweetly. 'Family commitments, status: single, married, divorced –'

'Widowed?' Alex cut in, the edge to his tone barely perceptible but present nonetheless. Widowed. Alex's current status, and a subtle reminder to Stella that she was overstepping the mark. Well, tough. Alex had set the ball rolling; Alex could live with the consequences. Consequences. Blurt out the truth and hurt Alex. And Alex was hurting. Because, contrary to public opinion, Alex had loved his wife.

Stella's spurt of annoyance withered and died. An overreaction in any case, since Alex hadn't run that computer check – yet.

'Yes. No,' she murmured absurdly, and then she risked a glance from beneath her lashes, saw the pain, the contempt, the hate in his eyes, and wished she hadn't bothered. 'I'm sorry.'

'For what?'

'For hitting out,' she explained, eyes silently pleading. 'For forgetting that oft-quoted Marshall maxim – put thy brain into gear before opening thy mouth.'

'You're treading on glass again.'

'Meaning?'

'Meaning, my ego isn't so fragile that it has to be wrapped in cotton wool,' he chided softly. 'Now a little TLC on certain other parts of me . . .'

Stella's cheeks flamed.

'No prizes for guessing what's going through *your* mind, Stella Marshall,' he tossed out gleefully.

'Wishful thinking, Alex Gifford?'

'Could be,' he freely acknowledged. 'But it's a cloudless night. I might just wish upon a star and persuade the gods it's my turn.'

Time passed. Mellow. No controversial subjects. Almost as if they sensed that time was too precious to waste in pointless niggles. Because Stella would go.

'You'll be back,' Alex insisted matter-of-factly, uncannily reading her mind. But at least he had accepted Stella would be leaving.

'So sure, Alex?' she chided softly. 'Isn't there a saying about pride going before a fall?'

'Not this time, Stella Marshall. You belong. I know it; you know it.' He shrugged. 'I might not like it, but I'll wait.'

And coming from a man who bought – or took – what he wanted, when he wanted, his being prepared to wait for anything was nothing short of miraculous. But then, once Alex knew the truth, the whole truth and nothing but the truth, Stella acknowledged grimly, that was precisely what she'd need. A miracle.

Always assuming they *were* on the same wavelength. Nanny or lover? Nanny or mistress? Stella mused, Tamara's exquisite features swimming into focus. And in a house this size, and given the nature of Tamara's job, how easy to combine the roles. Impossible thought. The stab of pain so sharp Stella choked on the brandy, spluttered, fumbled in a pocket for a tissue and had one of those crisp squares of linen thrust between her fingers. Because fast as the wind Alex had moved, had come to kneel before her.

With nerve-endings dancing, tingling with fear – and the shameful thrill of desire rippling through her – Stella dropped her watery gaze, attempted to focus on the monogram, the cursive capital A, embroidered in white and standing out like a cameo on one corner of the handkerchief, saw Alex's long, tapering fingers slide to cover hers, and knew she had a battle on her hands. Give in to the needs of her body – allow Alex to take her, wake her, woo her, love her, knowing she was deceiving him – an innocent deception maybe, but a deception nonetheless.

Or give him the truth, once and for all?

CHAPTER 8

'Stella.'

Soft. Soft as the breeze, a whisper, a caress – just like that touch of skin on skin. And Stella's resolve didn't stand a chance. Because she wanted him. And, in the absence of Tamara, Alex wanted her. Brutal, but true. Irrelevant, too. She forced herself to swallow. Alex wanted Stella; Stella wanted Alex. Man and woman, way past the age of consent, and old enough to know that life was strewn with decisions. The right decisions – and the wrong ones. But Stella had a choice. She might want Alex, but she didn't have to indulge the want like a love-sick adolescent.

She closed her eyes, praying for the strength to deny him, to deny them both.

'Stella –'

'No, Alex.'

'I want you –'

'Tamara –'

'Doesn't count.'

'Out of sight, out of mind, hey?' Stella needled, irrationally hurt and attempting to pull free.

Only Alex simply tightened his grip, allowing twin thumbs to trace erotic circles on the insides of her wrists, send shivers of heat rippling through her treacherous body.

'Sometimes,' Alex conceded thickly. 'But not always, Stella, I promise you. You –'

'I'm the exception that proves the rule, I suppose?' she couldn't help but sneer, and, catching him unawares, she pushed against the hands that held her, pushing him away, using the precious seconds it gave her to scramble to her feet, move safely out of range.

'No, Stella.'

'Exactly. No,' she repeated, standing her ground, folding her arms and angling her head in defiance. 'Not now, not here, not ever,' she insisted. 'We don't belong. And *you*,' she underlined coldly, 'are engaged to be married.'

'Ah, yes, marriage,' he mused. 'A lifelong commitment. Love, honour and cherish. Till death – or the law courts – do us part. And which of those scenarios is likely to apply to Tamara?'

'Your business – and Tamara's, presumably,' Stella bit out, hazel eyes shooting venom.

'Fine.' A racing pulse at his temple drew Stella's gaze. 'I'll discuss it with Tamara, and soon. In the meantime –'

'The hired hand is strictly off limits.'

'So prove it.'

'I beg your pardon?'

'Prove you're off limits, prove you're immune. Walk out of here now, Stella Marshall, and sleep the sleep of the innocent – or toss and turn for the rest of the night. All night, Stella,' he repeated slyly. 'Alone. In bed. When you'd rather be with me.'

'Arrogant as always, hey, Alex? Worry not, I'll sleep all right. Alone. Goodnight, Alex, sweet dreams,' she murmured, walking with slow, unhurried footsteps to the door, irrationally hurt that he made no effort to stop her. And then she reached the door and understood.

Spinning round, she pinned her frigid gaze on Alex and waited for him to make the next move.

Like a magician producing a rabbit from a hat, he held out the key. 'Is this what you're looking for?'

Stella nodded, licked her dry lips, braced herself for the unnerving proximity when Alex crossed to the door. Only Alex didn't. He simply stood and waited. And Stella waited. And the tension grew till Stella felt fit to burst.

'Alex –'

'Stella?'

'Stop playing games, Alex.'

'Stop denying that you want me, Stella.'

'So I want you,' she conceded flippantly. 'I'm human. I breathe. I have needs. Being human, and blessed with the double-edged sword of choice, I don't have to indulge those needs. My decision.'

'Like I said, prove it.'

'I just did. I was walking away, in case you hadn't noticed. But someone – *you*,' she reminded him tightly, 'have had the nerve to lock the door. What's the matter?' she jeered, the fold of arms across her chest a give-away gesture of protection. 'Afraid you're losing your touch? Afraid the Alex Gifford charm is losing its appeal?'

'Afraid you'll singe if you come too close to the flame, Stella? You're running scared, Stella Marshall, and it shows.'

'I'm simply applying the rules of common sense,' she hissed. 'One of us needs to.'

'Why?'

'Why? *Why*?' she repeated incredulously. 'Isn't it obvious? Because it's wrong. Because it's unfair on Tamara. Because we barely know one another. Because people generally don't hop into bed on a week or so's acquaintance. Because you're the boss and I'm –'

'The hired hand?' he queried incredulously, as if that was the be-all and end-all of Stella's objection.

'Not for much longer,' Stella bit out. 'Five more days, Alex. Five days at the most.'

'Good.'

'*Good*?' she queried, the disappointment hitting like a blow to the belly. 'And this from the man who wanted me to stay?'

Alex shrugged. 'So you walk out of one door and in through another. Exit Stella Marshall, nanny. Enter Stella Marshall –'

'Plaything, mistress, lover?'

'Oh, definitely lover,' he agreed, lips twitching at the corners.

Stella saw red. 'Well, it isn't going to happen. Are you listening, Alex? I'll go, and I'm never walking back. And, given that famed Alex Gifford philosophy

– out of sight equals out of mind – I doubt I'll even be missed.'

'Depends how long it takes to walk from one door to another. But I guess I can wait.'

'For ever,' Stella bit out. 'And even then I wouldn't hold your breath. Now, will you please unlock that door so that I can go to bed?'

'Bed . . .'

'Alone. By myself. As in nobody with me. Understand?'

'Perfectly. So, if you've really made up your mind, why not simply fetch the key and open the door yourself?'

Why not indeed? Stella mused, half taking a step towards him, her chin snapping up in alarm as Alex dropped the key casually into the pocket of his shirt.

Cloudy hazel eyes locked with dancing blue ones.

'Like I said,' he repeated softly, his expression unfathomable, 'if you want it, come and get it.'

'I –' Stella broke off, licked her dry lips, covered the panic with a show of sheer bravado. 'Fine,' she said, marching across, open palm uppermost. 'Thank you, Alex, I'd like the key.'

'Help yourself,' he invited, his smile spreading as he spread his hands.

Stella counted to three and screamed. Only silently. And raised her eyes to his and knew she wasting her time. Alex was playing games. Alex was enjoying himself immensely. And Alex could keep the give and take going for the rest of the night. Only Stella was tired, and, unlike Alex, she'd be up at the crack of dawn.

'Let me go, Alex?' she asked simply. 'James –'

'Isn't crying, or we'd hear him. See.' He waved an airy hand to the socket on the skirting board. 'No need to panic.'

'I'm not panicking, damn you, I'm flagging. I'm tired. And if I'm to do the job I'm paid to do –'

'OK, OK.' He held up his hands in surrender. 'You win, lady – this time.'

A lazy stroll to the door as Stella stood and watched, hardly daring to believe such an easy capitulation. Key in lock, teeth engaging, soundlessly turning, and Alex smiled, stood to one side, gave another airy wave of invitation. 'After you,' he urged politely.

Stella bit her lip. She'd far rather Alex went first, but wouldn't dream of giving him the satisfaction of knowing. So, bracing herself, she covered the half-dozen paces needed to carry her to the open door, and, with the scent of freedom in her nostrils, resisted the urge to bolt.

Ten seconds, eight, six, and on the point of drawing level, Alex stepped nimbly into the frame.

Stella's chin snapped up. 'But you promised.'

'Did I?' he queried softly. And then he shook his head. 'I don't think so.'

'But you said –'

'You win? And so you did, Stella. That time. That was then and this is now.'

'All of ten seconds later? You are joking?'

'Am I?' Soft, teasing, eyes as blue as cornflowers dancing in the breeze. 'Your move, Stella,' he reminded her.

'How can I possibly move anywhere,' she ground out in anguish, 'when you're blocking the way?'

'An invitation to treat?' he suggested. 'How about the lady pays a forfeit?'

'How about the male masquerading as a gentleman goes to hell?' she bit out.

Alex shook his head. 'Insults not allowed,' he insisted blandly.

'So who's insulting?' Stella riposted, and, sensing Alex would keep her there all night if it helped break down her resistance, enquired warily, 'What sort of forfeit?'

' "One kiss, my bonny sweetheart, I'm after a prize tonight –" '

'No!'

'No? Fine. Since you don't like my terms, why not save us both some time and make me an offer?'

Stella licked her lips. 'An offer?'

Alex nodded. 'An offer. Cross my heart and hope to die, all reasonable offers considered.'

Considered, weighed, judged, found wanting and ultimately discarded if Stella knew Alex. So she might as well grit her teeth, smile sweetly, offer her mouth and get the forfeit over and done with.

'One kiss,' she warned. 'And one kiss only.'

'Fine. So before I claim my prize, answer me a question.'

'One kiss, one question?' Stella shrugged. 'Sure, why not?'

'How long is a piece of string?'

'A piece of –? How on earth do I know?' she snapped, nerves in shreds.

'Since you're about to find out . . .' Alex smiled, hands reaching out, closing round Stella's shoulders as she braced herself. One kiss. Only Alex wasn't about to rush things. Touch. Not part of the bargain, Stella railed, only silently, closing her eyes and praying for strength. She had to be strong. She had to resist. Allow Alex to kiss her, maybe, but she didn't have to respond, didn't have to return the kiss.

Interminable wait. Nerve-endings tingling. Alex's hands on her shoulders burning through the fabric of her blouse, scalding, searing, twin thumbs describing erotic circles.

Relax, Alex silently urged. A feather-light touch both soothing and stirring. And Stella was losing the battle – had never really stood a chance of holding out. Because, shameless through and through, she wanted him.

Kiss. Mouth to mouth. Little more than a hint of a connection, and yet Alex didn't make the mistake of drawing away, simply breathed, and touched, and traced the outline of her lips with his tongue.

Arms clamped rigid to her sides, Stella shivered, closed her mind to the exquisite waves of pleasure and knew she had to be strong.

Strong. Fingers clenched, lips belatedly closed against him, repelling invaders. Only Alex simply laughed, little more than a growl in the back of his throat, and as Stella gasped he seized his chance, invading her mouth with his tongue, and, oh, heaven help her but she wanted him. She recalled, too late, that she mustn't make it easy for Alex, and gave an echoing mew of protest.

Another gasp as Alex's hands slid the length of her spine and over the swell of her buttocks, urging her against him, the body to body contact shocking because Alex was moving against her, hips swaying, pelvis gently grinding, his need as urgent as Stella's. Man and woman. The currents of heat surging out from every point of contact.

Madness, Stella screamed, dredging the depths of control and refusing to melt against him. So easy to melt against him, to join in the love-dance, match the sway and thrust of hips with frantic undulations of her own. Only she mustn't. One kiss. Nothing more, nothing less. Because Alex didn't belong, never would belong. And if the man was inside her head already, tearing her apart, destroying her peace of mind, think how much worse it would be once Stella tasted the manna of love. Love! she silently derided. Lust. Sex. A physical need. A biological craving. A coupling. Body to body. Not body and soul, body and mind.

Only Stella was losing the battle. Because she loved him, because she wanted him, needed him, craved him. A craving, she insisted, legs turning to jelly. How could she possibly *love* a man she barely knew – a man with the shadow of death hanging over him? Death by misadventure. A lethal cocktail of drink, drugs and a private swimming pool. A tragic accident. And Stella had to believe it. Because she loved him.

'Alex. Please, Alex.' The words were lost beneath the onslaught of his lips, yet if his mouth was creating havoc, the erotic fingers sliding beneath the hem of her blouse were blazing a trail of devastation. Skin on skin. Scorching, caressing, climbing higher and higher, skirting Stella's aching breasts and then doubling back, snapping the catch at the front of the wisp of lace to allow cupped palms to take the weight the moment her breasts spilled free, giving idle thumbs access to thrusting nipples.

Shameless. Stella wanted Alex and Alex had his proof.

'How long is a peace of string?' he murmured in anguish, his lips nuzzling at the corners of her mouth. 'Not nearly long enough,' he growled. 'Not nearly long enough. Hell, woman, but I want you.'

Want. Stella froze. No commitment, no wild declarations of love, just the truth as Alex saw it. Want. He wanted her, therefore he'd take her. Because that's how the Alex Giffords of the world operated.

'Alex –'

A door slammed in the distance. Stella's head snapped up in alarm, Alex's flash of annoyance giving way to vague amusement at Stella's audible gasp.

'Relax. It's only –'

'Tamara!' Stella breathed, gauging the distance to the stairs and bolting, her heart thumping nineteen to the dozen.

Escape.

Standing over the sleeping baby, watching the gentle rise and fall of the quilt. Five minutes, ten, twenty, and still her pulse refused to calm. She needed a drink. A stiff one. She would settle for that soothing malted milk if only she could summon the nerve to creep down to the basement. Another ten minutes, she decided, wriggling out of her clothes and standing naked in front of the mirror, scanning her still quivering flesh for signs of Alex's brand.

Full breasts, tightening again at the thought of Alex's hands, his idle thumbs tweaking the straining nipples. Shameless – or shameful? Because she wanted a man to look, to taste, to touch? Because she wanted a man full stop? No. No shame, she told herself. She wasn't a tramp. She loved Alex, she wanted Alex, and if Alex were to walk through that door and climb into her bed this instant, she'd be curled up beside him so fast her feet would barely touch the ground. Only he wouldn't. Because Tamara was home now, and Alex would be indulging the needs of his body with the woman in his bed. Brutal, but true.

Squeezing back the tears, Stella shrugged her still tingling body into nightgown and robe, and moved with wooden footsteps to the door, wincing at the squeal of hinges. Silence. She paused, stepping out into the corridor and leaning back against the carefully closed door, adjusting her eyes to the darkness before setting off on soundless feet the interminable length of the corridor, wondering, not for the first time, at the isolation of the nursery wing.

Yet another pause at the head of the stairs. Her eyes checked for lights, ears straining for any hint that the house hadn't settled – that Alex and Tamara hadn't settled, she tagged on bitterly, imagining, hating, aching, replaying the scene over and over in her mind's eye.

Drawing level with Alex's study and spotting the telltale pencil of light, Stella pulled up in alarm. Silence. Not a whisper, not a sound. No murmur of voices, no rustle of papers. Which meant Alex had been in such a hurry to reach Tamara's bed that he'd forgotten to turn the light out. Turn the light out herself? Risk being caught in Alex's inner sanctum? Oh, no. Before she could change her mind, Stella set off again, padding softly down the final set of stairs to the basement.

It was darker here, and Stella pulled up on the threshold, waiting for the objects of the kitchen to climb out of the inky darkness and identify themselves. Fridge. The splash of light as she opened the door was unnerving, blinding, and, clutching the precious carton of milk, Stella paused again, needing time to readjust to the blackness.

Back on the ground floor, Stella spun round in alarm when a draught of air caught the hem of her robe. The back door, she realized. Tamara's point of entry, since the cars were parked at the rear of the house. So, had Tamara forgotten to close and lock the door behind her, or had someone, Tamara perhaps, gone out again? Unlikely, Stella conceded, opening the door a crack and peering out. All clear. Four cars clearly shadowed against the hedge. Which meant the occupants of the house were safely tucked up in bed. Bed. Stella's cheeks flamed. Did all her thoughts have to lead to bed? Bed with Alex. Stella and Alex. Alex and Tamara. Unbearable thought.

Loath to turn the key and risk locking someone out, and yet equally loath to go wandering the gardens at this time of night, Stella stood and waited. The clock in the hall chimed the hour. Three o'clock. Time for bed. Alone. When she knew she wouldn't sleep. Might just as well hang on a couple of minutes. Five minutes, she gauged, and, fingers crossed, she turned the key, slid home the bolt and set off for the nursery, where another finger of light pulled her up short.

The door was open. The door she'd taken such pains to close. The door she distinctly remembered leaning back against. Tiny hairs on the back of her neck began to prickle as an icy hand touched her heart. Because someone – surely not the anything but doting father? she silently scorned – had paid a visit to the nursery.

The sitting room was empty, the soft glow of the lamp reassuringly normal, simply reassuring. Kitchen. Illuminated, empty, mug and packet of malted milk at the ready alongside the microwave.

And yet someone *had* been there; Stella would stake her life on it. And then she caught a sound – music, no, not music, a nursery rhyme, the refrain slowing, like an old-fashioned gramophone winding down. 'Brahms' Lullaby' – the mobile above James's cot, she identified.

Heart in mouth, she tiptoed across and pushed open the bedroom door, her eyes automatically swivelling to the cot. Empty. Stella closed her eyes briefly, found the cot still empty when she raised her leaden lids again, and stifled the panic with a huge effort of will.

Catching another sound, the soft whimper of a child in sleep, she spun round, the relief unbelievable. He was safe. Fast asleep on the floor of his playpen, but safe and sound and securely wrapped in his quilt.

Only who? And why?

Her legs like jelly, Stella sank down to her knees, leaned her arms on the top edge of the playpen and resisted the urge to place her head in her hands and cry. Tears of relief? Tears of fear? For James? For herself? she mused. And yet it didn't make sense. Tamara? She'd barely been in the house thirty minutes, and Tamara wouldn't waste time on these sorts of games. Unless it really was that warning. Hands off, he's mine, and don't think I don't know what you're getting up to the moment my back's turned? Doubtful, Stella conceded, her mind moving leaden-like on to Alex.

Alex wouldn't, Stella scorned. He might not dote on James but he wouldn't wish him any harm – probably didn't give him a second thought from one day's end to the next.

Mrs Edwards, then? Not as prickly inside as she'd have the world believe, but desperate to keep up appearances. Not openly malicious, unless Tamara happened to be in view. No, not Mrs Edwards. Clearly not Hannah. So, no obvious motive, no obvious perpetrator. Only someone *had* moved James out of his cot, and frightened Stella half to death in the process. Yet why the surprise? she silently berated herself. It wasn't the first time. A pillow over her face, a low laugh as Stella struggled with her nightmare – a living nightmare. And that warning scrawled across the mirror. Bitch. Unnerving for Stella. More than enough to frighten away a string of impressionable young girls.

So, she'd have to tell Alex. She didn't really relish his reaction: Been drinking, Stella? A brandy too many? Not the gripe-water, surely, my dear?

And who could blame him? The whole thing was absurd. Only Stella was beginning to make sense of it all. No wonder James had had more nannies than Stella had had hot dinners. 'It's this house,' Carly had insisted. It had given her the creeps, seemed to be closing in on her. She'd sensed evil lurking in corners. And, though she'd lasted longer than most, she'd finally bolted – or had been frightened into bolting. And now it was time to try the same tactics with Stella. Only Stella wasn't some slip of a girl, easily driven away.

So, first thing tomorrow she'd face the derision of Alex and –

A sudden commotion, a hammering of fists on a door – the front door, Stella identified, up on her feet in an instant and heading for the landing. What on earth were they trying to do? Wake the dead? she derided, wincing at the phrase and blending back into the shadows as a tousled Tamara glided from her bedroom to hover, waif-like, at the top of the stairs.

There was a sudden flood of light as Alex, fully dressed and weary, emerged from the study, strode the length of the hall and threw open the door, allowing the nocturnal visitors to spill through.

An unearthly enactment. Voices, incongruously indistinct, given the row they'd already made. Alex's shrug of resignation. Tamara tripping down the stairs, baby-doll nightdress transparent against the light.

'Alex . . . ?' She was pausing for effect halfway down the stairs, and, sure enough, the five men below glanced up and froze. A single, hesitant step lower. A tremulous hand fluttering to her throat. 'What is it, darling? Alex –' She broke off, looking from one to the other, that little-girl-lost expression not fooling Stella for an instant. But then, Stella wasn't male and susceptible to the charms of a beautiful woman.

A rapid exchange of words, and then one of the men stepped forward. 'CID, miss. Nothing to worry about, miss. Just a few routine questions –'

'At this time of night?' Tamara breathed, eyelashes aflutter. 'But surely, Inspector, it could wait until tomorrow. I can assure –'

'Leave it, Tamara,' Alex cut in wearily. 'I've done nothing wrong, so we might as well get it over and done with. Go back to bed,' he instructed. 'I promise I'll be home first thing tomorrow. But if not –' He broke off, shrugged, smiled.

Though the light didn't reach his eyes, Stella noticed from her vantage point, wishing she could help, but powerless to help, to offer any moral support. But with Alex's eyes, like the detectives', fastened on Tamara, he was oblivious to Stella's silent presence a dozen steps above.

'If not . . .' he repeated, angling his head, his gaze slipping past Tamara and unerringly finding Stella, despite the cloak of darkness. And though the message was simple enough, the words carefully chosen for everyone to hear, the meaning behind them was for Stella and Stella alone. 'If not, I need you there to take care of things for me. I need to know that you'll be waiting when I come home.'

CHAPTER 9

'You're crazy.'

'Not crazy, Beth, just concerned.'

'You and me both, Stella. *I'm* concerned – about you.'

'Well, you needn't be. I'm a big girl now, and you can take it from me, it takes a lot to scare Stella Marshall.'

'Like what, for instance? Like your younger sister upping and leaving at the drop of a hat? Like a houseful of misfits clearly at each other's throats? Or death by misadventure, perhaps – not to mention the hand of Alex Gifford,' she tagged on bitterly.

'Don't, Bethy. If you don't know the set-up, you can't possibly understand –'

'So enlighten me. Tell me why you're hell-bent on staying. Tell me why Carly clearly had more sense. In fact,' she added frantically, 'tell me precisely what you've done to track Carly down.'

'Nothing. Like me, Carly's old enough to take care of herself. And she's safe, Beth.'

'Really? And how can you possibly be so sure?'

'She's my sister. If Carly was in danger, don't you think I'd know? And she did phone –'

'A week ago.'

'Precisely. *After* she left Freshfields. She's safe.'

'If you say so.'

'I do.'

'And if she's not?'

'Then I'll face that eventuality when it happens. If it happens.'

'I'm coming over.'

'You can't.'

'Just try stopping me.'

'Why, Bethy?'

'To see for myself what's keeping you there. Not that I really need to. It's as plain as the nose on my face. Stella Marshall's besotted.'

'Now you're being ridiculous.'

'Am I? So prove it. Invite me down.'

'You just invited yourself – remember?'

'So I did. How does Friday suit?'

'It doesn't, but I don't suppose that's going to stop you.'

'Got it in one. Expect me when you see me. Oh, yes, and in the meantime, Stella Marshall, make sure you take care. Losing one cousin might be overlooked, losing two is nothing short of careless. You take care, do you hear?'

'Yes, Bethy, no, Bethy, three bags full, Bethy. Oh, and Bethy?'

'Yes, Stella Marshall?

'If you happen to bump into any of the family, you will –'

'Be sunshine and light and the soul of discretion? What do you think?'

Stella cut the connection, decided the battery was fading and plugged the mobile phone into the charger. The joys of modern technology. One of those double-edged swords, if she didn't want to be found, but Carly *would* get in touch, the moment Danny daVine passed on Stella's message. If Danny remembered. If Danny had intended tracking Carly down in the first place.

With an icy trickle running down her spine, Stella smothered the thought. Because if Danny really didn't lead her to Carly – and soon – Stella would be forced to report her as missing. Exit one bogus nanny, fast. The thought of facing Alex and giving him the truth was more than she could stand.

The truth. That Stella had deceived him all along. That a young woman in his employ was missing, presumed – *what*, exactly? Because that was how the police would view it. And the questions and the interrogations and the late-night hammerings on the door would start again. 'Helping the police with their enquiries'. An innocuous phrase that covered a wealth of sins. Murder? Manslaughter? Death by misadventure? A tragic accident, Stella stubbornly insisted. Verdict, misadventure. And Carly *had* been in touch, would get in touch the moment Danny gave her the message. If Danny bothered to find her.

'Penny for *those* thoughts, Stella Marshall.'

'Alex!' Stella glanced up, a flood of guilty colour swamping her cheeks. Guilt, when she'd one nothing wrong, for heaven's sake. Just spent the past ten minutes on the phone – her own phone at that – to a member of her family. Ah, yes, but with the great man himself the subject under discussion, the great man might just take exception to the gossip. Not gossip, Stella amended. And Alex Gifford hadn't been the subject, the whole subject and nothing but the subject. Carly. Beth had been worried and Carly's name had been mentioned more than once. So if Alex *had* been listening in . . .

It was his house, his prerogative, and yet, with those generous lips twitching, Alex's mood clearly wasn't one of annoyance.

'Lost your way?' she bit out, overstretched nerves forcing her on to the defensive. 'Took a wrong turn at the top of the stairs?'

'Meaning?' Cool, the lazy smile vanishing in a trice.

'Meaning, this is the nursery, in case you've forgotten. There isn't a secret stairway leading down to the adult Gifford residence. It's a dead end. And there's nobody here but the hired hand and the shamefully neglected son and heir.'

'Neglected?' Cold, dangerous. And it was patently untrue, since James wanted for nothing that money could buy. Money – when all a small child really needs is food in his belly and the security of being warm, dry and loved. Love. Some chance for James when the nearest he came to that was the hired hand. The bogus hired hand. And the soon to be ex-hired hand if Stella didn't curb an over-sharp tongue.

As Stella licked her dry lips, Alex took a menacing step closer.

'Neglected?' he repeated in a voice devoid of emotion. 'And what, pray, does that mean?'

'Nothing,' Stella bit out, the fold of her arms across her chest unwittingly defensive. 'I wasn't thinking. I didn't mean –'

'Oh, but you did, Stella,' Alex contradicted coldly. 'Unthinking, maybe, but you meant every word. James and the hired hand are feeling neglected. Ignored. Overlooked. Disregarded. Avoided. Ostracized. Shunned. And, since James is too young to voice an opinion, I guess it's the hired hand who's feeling peeved. Now why, I wonder?'

'Then wonder no longer. I'm not. Not for me, at least. James –'

'Wants for nothing.'

Sharp blue eyes pointedly swept the room – an expensively furnished sitting room for a nanny, no second-hand furnishings here, no making do with cast-offs from the rest of the house. A self-contained wing with no expense spared; sitting room, kitchen, bedroom, baby's room. Everything that money could buy and more. For a woefully neglected baby. Ignored, overlooked, disregarded, avoided. By his father at least. Poor motherless mite.

Stella's spurt of anger tempered. Motherless. And avoided by his father. Because Alex had loved his wife and couldn't bear to live with the reminder. Chrissie Gifford's son. Alex's son too, and Alex *would* come to terms with it in time. Or leastways, Stella amended, swallowing hard, that was what she was hoping.

Those cold blue eyes came back to Stella. 'Enlighten me. Tell me what I'm missing?'

'As if you'd listen.'

'I'm here, aren't I?'

'Like I said, lost your way?'

'Since I'm clearly not welcome, you tell me.'

'But of course you're welcome,' Stella snapped, annoyed with Alex, more annoyed with herself for snapping in the first place. 'It's your house, remember? You live here. And visiting the nursery isn't compulsory.'

'More like highly recommended. Thou shalt visit the nursery or face the wrath of Stella.' Surprisingly he grinned. 'No contest. Why else do you think I'm here?'

'Why else indeed?' Stella drawled, and, sensing a subtle change in atmosphere, waved Alex to a chair. 'Coffee?'

'Thank you, Stella. Coffee is just what I need. I don't suppose you've a drop of the hard stuff to go in it?'

'Gripe-water? At this hour of the day?' she teased in turn. 'Certainly not.'

'The mood I'm in, Stella, believe me, a long, hard slug of gripe-water wouldn't go amiss.'

'Problems?' she probed, moving through the archway and flicking the switch on the kettle.

'No more than usual,' he conceded, tugging at his tie and snapping the top two buttons of his shirt, the dishevelled result strangely appealing.

'Police?' Stella hazarded, pausing, spoon in one hand, open jar of coffee in the other. 'Let me guess, in the interests of their ongoing enquiries, they'd like you to visit the station again? At your convenience, of course.'

'Word perfect. Only past tense. I've spent the morning fielding yet another barrage of highly personal questions, and I guess you caught me on the raw. I shouldn't have overreacted.'

'And I shouldn't poke my nose in where it's clearly not wanted. I'm sorry. I'm your son's nanny, not your keeper, and I've no right to judge.'

'Guilty as charged, I'm afraid. Woeful neglect of the child, at least. Perhaps m'lady would care to put the accused out of his misery and pass sentence?'

'Don't mock, Alex,' Stella entreated, aware that he was hurting, that the flippant words didn't even come close to masking the pain.

'Don't tell the truth, you mean? You can't run with the hare and hunt with hounds,' he chided lightly. 'And you're right, as usual. Only –'

'You can't look at James without seeing his mother? I know –'

'I doubt it,' he bit out, that haunted expression in his eyes again.

'Alex –'

'Leave it, Stella. You've more than made your point. Stella one, Alex nil. Now quit while you're ahead.'

Yes, sir! she muttered, only silently, not wanting to provoke Alex's usual electric response to that particular retort.

She took the chair opposite, logged the pain in his eyes, the sharp set of his mouth, the taut stretch of skin across the high cheekbones, the general air of weariness. Hardly surprising, Stella, conceded, given the morning he must have endured.

He glanced up suddenly, caught Stella's open scrutiny and winced. 'Guilty as charged, huh?' he repeated.

'You mean blatant neglect of your son?' she allowed with deliberate misunderstanding. 'Worry not, Alex, he's a normal, healthy ten-month-old, and you've all the time in the world to make up for a few missed months.'

'Thanks. On both counts.'

Stella raised an enquiring eyebrow.

'For believing I'll be around to witness the growing up. For sticking around yourself despite your reservations. The other night –'

'I could hardly pack up and leave the moment you were frogmarched out of the house,' she reminded him softly. 'I'm here –'

'For as long as James needs you.'

'No, Alex. James needs stability –'

'And let me guess, Mary Poppins Mark II doesn't want to provide it?'

'Unfair, Alex. Stella Marshall Mark I has a life of her own.'

'So tell me about it.'

'I beg your pardon?'

'This life of yours. Family?'

'Why, yes, as it happens. Parents long gone, I'm

afraid, but I've a younger sister, and a cousin or two –'

'Sister, huh? As pretty as you?'

'Who knows?' Stella scorned. 'Since beauty's in the eye of the beholder and is generally a matter of taste. But, yes, I'd say she was attractive.'

'And does this youthful beauty have a name?'

'As it's a pretty normal accessory in this day and age,' Stella retorted sharply, 'she certainly does,'

'Angela? Belinda? Christine? Delilah –'

'Elspeth, Frankie, Gertrude. Hilda, Ingrid, Jane,' Stella parodied, catching his drift at once. 'New game?' she enquired saccharine-sweetly. 'Why didn't you say? H, I, J – which takes us neatly up to K. Katy, Laura, Milly-Molly-Mandy –'

'Thirteen down, thirteen to go. Unless you'd like to give a guy a clue?'

'How about N for No? Or NOP? For a certain Nosy Old Parker is wasting his time fishing?'

'Old? Me? I can assure you, Miss Marshall, at thirty-eight I'm in my prime. And I'm not, repeat not, being nosy. Just interested.'

'Why?'

'What do you mean, why?'

'Why the interest?'

'Just fostering that all-important employer-employee relationship, I suppose.'

'As you always do?'

Alex grinned. 'No, not always. But I do try to take an interest in my staff.'

'From your trusty right hand to your baby son's nanny, with several hundred others in between?' she queried, making a calculated guess at the number on his payroll. 'Perhaps I should be flattered.'

'Perhaps you should at that. Only you're not?'

Stella's turn to grin. 'I'm afraid not.'

'And you're not about to open your heart and confide either.'

'Pot and kettle, Mr Gifford? We've travelled this road before, I believe.'

'And let me guess, you're freezing me out?'

'Hardly freezing, just keeping you politely in your place.'

'Thank heavens for small mercies,' he drawled. 'And remind me never to cross you. I should hate that iron fist in its velvet glove to catch me unawares.'

Stella smiled, changed the subject, introduced Beth and Connor and their visit.

'Family, Stella? Kith and kin? But aren't you forgetting that Marshall obsession for keeping private things private?'

'Hardly,' she demurred. 'Like you, I prefer to screen out the prurient. But, if subjected to the third degree –'

'You close up like a clam. Let's hope you never get yourself arrested,' he murmured dryly. 'Since even silence counts against you these days. Allegedly.'

'I'll take that as a yes, then?' Stella probed, preferring to stick to a subject she felt happy with.

'Sure, why not? Any particular day in mind?'

'Beth mentioned Friday.'

'Friday? Even better. Hannah's having open house at the stables – the place will be buzzing.'

'And you don't mind?'

'About your cousin? Good heavens, no.'

'I – was thinking more along the lines of a gross invasion of privacy. Given the latest glare of publicity, there are bound to be the ghouls, the grims and the downright nosy.'

'Not to mention the Press.'

'I – er – yes. Inevitable, I suppose.'

'Just one of life's minor irritations,' he drawled with heavy irony. 'I'm almost sorry I won't be around to provide my share of copy.'

'Oh?' Stella mused.

'All work and no play . . .' he explained, spreading his hands. 'And I have been putting the hours in lately.'

'So you work for a living, like all the rest,' Stella scorned. 'I don't suppose you complain when the money rolls in.'

'In my line of work, it's a case of if, rather than when,' he reminded her coolly. 'It's a risky business, wine production. One bad year can ruin a lifetime's work – not to mention a worldwide reputation.'

'So why not diversify? Why risk all your eggs – or should that be vines – in one basket?'

'Why, thank you, Stella. Do you know, that thought had never struck me.'

'Ah! The words "grandmother", "eggs", "suck" and "teach" spring to mind?'

'They certainly do. Which is why I've been somewhat overdoing things lately. Not so much intent on making millions, as making sure I stay afloat when the next blight occurs – not to mention the possibility of spending time as a guest of Her Majesty.'

'Her Maj –? Ah, yes. I see what you mean.'

'You think that it's likely, then?'

'I don't,' Stella replied without emotion. 'But it's clearly crossed your mind?'

'Having spent more hours than I care to recall assisting with enquiries, believe me, it doesn't pay to take anything for granted these days.'

'But you're innocent.'

'Are you asking me – or telling me?'

'Does it matter?'

'Your opinion? Curiously enough, Stella, yes.'

'Then I'm telling you.'

'Official verdict? Woman's intuition? Or simple gut response?'

'Any – or all,' she conceded. 'Personal observation for a start.'

'On less than a fortnight's acquaintance? You're either very trusting or exceedingly naïve.'

'Or a good judge of character.'

'Yes. You're good with words too. Beauty and brains, a pretty potent combination.'

'I'm glad you're impressed.'

'Oh, definitely impressed,' he agreed solemnly. 'Your turn now.'

'For what?'

'To hand out the compliments.'

'One good turn deserves another, huh? Sure, why not?' Her gaze swept over him, assessing, appraising, enjoying, tip to toe and back again, from laughing blue eyes in a rugged face – the strain of the past few days just beginning to tell in the tracery of lines fanning from the corners of his eyes, the corners of his mouth – down over the powerful barrel of his chest and the crisp white shirt, almost, but not quite, concealing the mass of hair simply made for fingers – Stella's fingers – to scrunch, and on again. Dark, expensively tailored trousers encasing legs that seemed never to end – only they did. At a groin Stella stubbornly refused to focus on, instead simply skimming, moving steadily back to lock her gaze defiantly on to his. 'Youngish, richish, ruggedly good-looking,' she conceded. 'Not to mention good with words.' She shrugged. 'A heady combination, I'd say.'

'But?'

'Did I say there was a but?'

'You didn't need to. You're prepared to walk away, and *that*, Miss Stella Marshall, speaks volumes.'

Yes. She loved him. She didn't want to hurt him. She hadn't even told him what was preying on her mind because she couldn't bear to add to his problems. But Alex was entitled to know. Someone in this house was determined to drive Stella away. Or maybe it was more than that. Maybe, she mused, the motive was much more basic.

She cast her mind back, recalled the day she'd arrived and that heated conversation she'd been privy to. A row about James – or his absent nanny – and a very telling phrase that had stuck in her mind. A snivelling brat who belonged in an orphanage on Mars. A throw-away comment, Stella had assumed at the time. But maybe not so much an off-the-cuff remark as a slip of the tongue. Maybe Tamara Clayton wanted James out of the way. Only why? Jealousy? Stella mused. Surely not. Surely a grown woman couldn't be jealous of a ten-month-old child? Ah, yes, but James was the child of another woman – and not just any woman, she conceded, turning the idea over. Alex's wife. Alex's late wife. And James was living proof of it, a lasting reminder of Alex's love for another woman.

Jealousy? An irrational emotion at the best of times, but for someone to go to the lengths of scaring off a succession of nannies in the hope of banishing the baby had to be nothing short of madness. Madness. Insanity. Irrational behaviour. Tamara? Cold and calculating, maybe, but underhand, sly, malicious? Not Tamara's style at all. Besides which, Tamara was no fool. She might resent James, but she'd have sense enough to realize that in a set-up like this a permanent nanny would grow attached to James, would grow protective, possessive of her charge. And the baby would grow to depend on the only stable person in his world – his nanny.

Stella openly scowled. No, not Tamara. James was no threat to her. Which left Stella where, precisely? Back at square one. But if Stella was determined to leave, and soon, she was equally determined to leave James with the sort of stability even Alex accepted was sorely needed.

She glanced across, caught the thinly veiled amusement on Alex's handsome face and bristled. 'So I'm prepared to walk away,' she said coolly. 'Why the surprise? It was always a temporary arrangement. I'm a stop-gap, nothing more, nothing less. But if it helps, I'd say the perfect solution's right here in this house already.'

'Mrs Edwards –'

'Has enough to do, and would doubtless run a mile at the thought.'

'Ditto Tamara. You surely didn't mean Tamara?' he enquired politely, leaning forward.

'Heaven forbid,' Stella conceded grimly. 'And don't assume that only leaves Hannah.'

'If you say so,' he riposted, lips twitching at Stella's snappy tone.

Stella flushed but didn't reply, simply waited for Alex to work it out for himself.

'One of the grooms?' he hazarded, clearly teasing. 'A stable girl or two? The gardener's wife, perhaps? A bit long in the tooth, but the mother of a healthy brood, so I believe, and if they've long fled the nest, the instinct's never lost. You can't mean that sour-faced Mrs Mop who whizzes through the house like a dose of salts, dustpan in one hand, vacuum cleaner hose in the other, and woe betide the inconsiderate person who dares even to look at a newly plumped cushion let alone sit on it?' he scorned. 'And since that neatly disposes of the female contingents, that, Miss Marshall, only leaves you. Had a change of mind?'

'If and when I did,' she said sweetly, 'you'd be the first to know.'

'Only you won't.'

Stella smiled. 'Got it in one. It's a –'

'Temporary arrangement?' he interrupted dryly. He folded his arms, leaned back, continued to regard her with that insufferable air that seemed to hint that if Stella was being stubborn, it was only a matter of time before Alex Gifford wore her down. 'Yes, Stella,' he conceded, the expression on his face giving the lie to his words. 'Even I'm beginning to get that message. Pay-rise?' he tagged on hopefully. 'Double it, treble it – name your price, in fact.'

'Since we haven't agreed present terms,' Stella reminded him tartly, 'double or treble nothing still makes nothing.'

'Why?'

'Don't tell me you missed out on school?' she scorned with deliberate misunderstanding. 'What, never learned the joys of chanting your tables? Once nothing is nothing,' she said, features impassive. 'Two nothings are nothing, three nothings are nothing, four –'

'Thank you, Stella,' he interrupted dryly. 'We'll treat that one with the contempt it deserves. So?'

'So?'

'So why haven't we agreed terms?' he asked patiently. 'Why doesn't the agency –?'

'It doesn't employ me, remember?' she bit out, reaching shifting sands and instantly wary.

'So it doesn't,' he mused thoughtfully. 'But it does take a cut?'

'For making the introduction in the first place? What do you think?' She stalled, hating the thought of looking him in the eye and telling an outright lie.

'Five per cent?' he hazarded, those sharp blue eyes fastened on hers. 'Although ten per cent seems reasonable, and, let me guess, ten per cent of nothing is –'

'Got it in one. It's time to name my price, I believe?'

'For *staying*, Stella,' he solemnly underlined. 'Which presumably means you're having second thoughts.'

'Wouldn't you like to believe that?' she scorned.

'Fine.' Only it wasn't. Alex was annoyed, and the set of the mouth betrayed him. 'Normal rates it is, then.'

'Plus ten per cent,' she carefully reminded him, making a mental note to donate the lot to charity. Easier to live with the deception that way. No thirty pieces of silver, no guilty conscience for taking money she'd have earned, rightly enough, but under false pretences. An innocent deception. Risking a glance at Alex's glowering face, she fervently hoped that if and when the truth leaked out, Alex would see things that way.

He nodded. 'But of course. Heaven forbid you'd be out of pocket.'

'And would you?' she enquired politely. 'Would the hard-headed businessman accept less than his worth, or allow someone to underbid for a consignment of wine?'

'The "hard-headed businessman", like the hard-headed nanny,' he sneered, 'wouldn't dream of underselling himself. I know my worth.'

'As I know mine. And all the money in the world,' she said tersely, 'wouldn't be enough to buy me.'

'Not even for James?'

Stella flushed. 'Unfair. Unfair on me, unfair on James, and, talking of James –'

Bang on cue came a lusty wail from his bedroom.

'Duty calls,' Stella murmured, up on her feet in an instant, seizing the diversion like a lifeline. 'But do feel free to make another coffee.'

Or run a mile. Spend five minutes with your son? Heaven forbid, she silently berated, allowing the door to swing to under its own momentum and heading straight for the cot and the damp and tousled baby.

Definitely damp, she discovered, cradling James over one shoulder and making soft, soothing noises in the back of her throat as she moved across to draw the curtains, allowing fingers of sunlight into the room.

'Hungry?' she crooned, holding him close. 'Or, since it's barely twelve, maybe you need a drink? Though on second thoughts, let's deal with that soggy nappy first.'

She was humming lightly as she skirted the playpen, reached for the changing mat she still didn't trust herself to use on the dizzy heights of the purpose-built cabinet.

'No chance of this little man wriggling over the edge and on to the floor,' she conceded, sinking to her knees. And, heady from the newly discovered joy of crawling forwards, wriggle he definitely would.

She placed him on the terry-lined mat, whipped the sodden nappy off, baby-wiped and dusted the relevant nooks and crannies, and was reaching for an unopened packet of nappies when she thought she caught the sound of the telephone. Mrs Edwards, at a guess, enquiring if Stella and James would be eating in the nursery. And, since Alex had clearly run that mile, Stella supposed she'd better answer it.

Swinging James back on to her shoulder, she was up in an instant, had barely managed to reach the door when Alex put his head round.

'Phone. Greenhavens. After their ten per cent, at a guess. Or does the hard-headed nanny beat them down to seven point five?'

'Since you took the call, I'm surprised you didn't enquire,' she snapped.

'And come between a nanny and her conscience?' Alex shook his head. 'Oh, no. And, since I know to the penny what the going rate should be, I doubt you'd dare to overchar— Hey!' He broke off as Stella swept past, thrust the wriggling James into his arms in passing. 'You can't –'

'I just did,' she retorted, completely unrepentant. 'And if I were you I'd get a clean nappy in place fast. Heaven forbid Gifford junior should christen his doting papa. You will excuse me, won't you?' she trilled. 'I shouldn't be more than a moment.'

'Better hadn't be more than a moment,' he warned her, but Stella ignored him, pulled the door firmly shut behind her and took a deep breath before reaching for the handset.

'Stella Marshall speaking. Sorry to keep you.'

'Not at all. It was good of you to leave your name and number. We'd been wondering what was happening at Freshfields.'

I'll bet, Stella mused, only silently, choosing instead to fill Helene Whiting in on the current state of play – more a holding exercise really, don't call us, we'll call you the moment we have something definite to report. Like a resident nanny – a permanent resident nanny, if Stella could bring Alex round to seeing things her way. Talking of which, time to see how father and son were bonding.

She pulled up on the threshold, didn't really believe what she was seeing. Alex, on hands and knees, attempting, gingerly, to restrain James with one hand whilst struggling with the intricacies of a disposable nappy in the other, and so engrossed in the task that he hadn't noticed Stella's silent reappearance.

'Now, whoa, there,' he murmured as James twisted over on to his tummy, launched himself into movement. Still on hands and knees, Alex dived forward, caught the gurgling baby around the middle and swung him, laughing, over his shoulder. 'Don't you know a guy can get himself arrested wandering the streets in a state of undress?' he chided lightly. 'Nappy time. And if the effort half kills me, I'll make sure the dratted thing stays in place this time.'

This time? Ah! Catching sight of a couple of unused nappies, clearly discarded in disgust when the sticky tapes became unsticky due to the rigours of over-handling, Stella understood. And, since practice makes perfect, who was she to interfere?

Only before Alex could lower the baby on to the changing mat, James decided he'd already waited long enough. And his aim was perfect.

'What the –? Oh, hell!'

Stella laughed.

Alex's chin snapped up. 'Not funny, Stella,' he bit out, the expression on his face a curious mix of shock, horror and indignation.

'No, Alex?' she queried, attempting to stifle her amusement and failing miserably.

'No, Stella. You could have warned me. Here, you take the little wretch while I do something about this shirt before the stain sets. I'll use your bathroom, if I may?'

'Make yourself at home,' she derided. 'Not that there's any need, with a bathroom of your own barely a dozen yards or so along the hallway.'

'Maybe so,' he conceded tightly. 'But, at the risk of seeming picky, I tend to draw the line at wandering the house in soiled clothing.' He wrinkled his nose in disgust. 'Good heavens, woman, I reek. What on earth do you feed him on?'

But as he didn't wait to find out Stella didn't get to explain. But she might, if Alex stuck around long enough.

He was less than ten minutes, by which time Stella had dried and dusted the culprit, refilled the kettle, and settled down in the rocking chair to give James his well-earned drink. She raised an enquiring eyebrow as Alex reappeared, freshly rinsed shirt in hand, naked chest unnerving.

'Drying machine?' he queried tartly. 'Since I ordered mod-cons by the dozen less than a fortnight ago, I assume that won't be a problem?'

Stella waved an airy hand. 'Help yourself,' she murmured. 'And while you're there, be an angel and make a girl a coffee. White, two sugars and not too strong.'

'Anything else while I'm at it?' he enquired through gritted teeth.

'James's lunch?' she tossed out wickedly. 'There's a dish of –'

'Oh, no. Coffee, yes. Baby food, no. And that, Stella Marshall, is final. Understand?'

Yes, sir! Only Stella didn't say it – this time. Next time, she vowed, she'd give Alex Gifford a taste of his own medicine.

'So, madam, you were saying?' Alex sat cross-legged on the floor while Stella and James continued to rock gently backwards and forwards on the only piece of furniture designed for adult seating. Alex, with that naked chest drawing Stella's gaze despite massive efforts to avert her eyes. Alex, strangely at home, strangely vulnerable in his state of half-dress. And appealing. And deceptively dangerous.

Because Stella was mellowing, was weakening, wanted for all the world to change her mind and stay. Only she mustn't. Because she loved Alex. Because Alex didn't need another woman in his life. Because Alex was still grieving for his wife and, despite all Tamara's efforts to entice him to the altar, Alex was simply playing around. With Tamara. With Stella, too, if she hadn't the sense to see it. Only she had. And she wouldn't play. So she'd leave. Simple. Devastating. But sooner rather than later, and most definitely before Alex discovered her true occupation . . .

'I was saying?' she probed warily.

'Food, baby, diet of. That unlovely aroma that rained down on me – and literally at that. I was wondering what you were feeding the poor child on.'

The 'poor child', having finished his drink – little more than an ounce since Stella would be feeding him soon – gave an appreciative burp before twisting his head to gaze up at Stella, who smiled, rose automatically, and placed him flat on his back in the safety of the playpen, where he promptly rolled over and pushed himself up on to all fours.

'Feed him on? Just the usual,' she explained. 'Bacon and eggs for breakfast, roast beef and vegetables for lunch and something light for tea. Cheese soufflé, perhaps, or, by way of a change, lightly poached haddock.'

'Curiously mushed and pulped and commercially sealed in convenient single serving jars, I suppose?' Alex drawled. 'And heaven only knows what else goes into them.'

'Sometimes,' Stella conceded coolly. 'The jars are handy to have in as a standby, and as for their contents they're nutritionally balanced – full of vitamins and minerals, and everything and more a healthy tot like James would need. Only not very often. Because James eats like you and I. Normal food – salt-free, sugar-free, lightly puréed, maybe, but most definitely not homogenous mush.'

'Salt-free? So that's why the food's been tasting strange just lately. The Marshall effect.'

'If you like,' Stella agreed. 'It seemed a waste cooking separate meals up here in the nursery. And, since Mrs Edwards was happy to oblige . . .'

'Happy? Agnes Edwards? Good God, woman, if I manage to coax a smile it's a miracle. Oblige? Put herself out? Undo years of conditioning with pans of over-boiled greens and the salt pot? I'm impressed.'

'Some of us are born sweet, some have sweetness thrust upon them. Others need a little persuasion,' Stella preened. 'The woman's lonely.'

'And prickly as hell. Tamara – Ah, yes–' He broke off, gave a rueful grin. 'Tamara. Oil and water. Point made. And just to underline it, Mrs E has a soft spot for Hannah.'

'Hardly surprising, since Hannah's part of the family.'

'And Tamara isn't?'

'Not at the moment,' Stella carefully conceded, holding his gaze.

Pause. Not a long pause, but enough for that prickle of alarm to travel the length of Stella's spine, to allow that ever-present fear to paralyze her mind. *Engagement*. Alex and Stella had an announcement scheduled for the end of the summer. According to Tamara. And this was Alex's chance to confirm it.

'Hmm,' he mused, studiously non-committal. 'You're right, as usual. Which leaves you – where, I wonder?'

'Out of the frame, Alex. And soon.'

'How soon?'

'As soon as I'm sure James is properly taken care of.

A permanent nanny, carefully chosen to fit in with James and everyone else at Freshfields.'

'Good,' he retorted grimly. 'I'll schedule the interviews for the year two thousand and ten.'

Stella ignored the sarcasm. 'No need. As I was saying, the perfect solution's right here already.'

'It certainly is. I'm looking at her.'

'And I'm out of the running.'

'But why? Why, Stella? Damn it all, woman, you're perfect.'

Practically perfect in every way – more shades of Mary Poppins. Only Alex was wrong. Because Stella was living a lie, and the longer she stayed, the harder it would be to leave. She was leaving herself wide open to being taken by the scruff of the neck and forcibly ejected. The anger wouldn't hurt – Alex's fury that she'd deceived him, that she belonged to that openly reviled profession – and neither would the shame of being shown the door. Or if they did, they'd be way down the scale of Stella's emotions. No, she acknowledged, swallowing hard, watching Alex, loving Alex, wanting Alex. What she couldn't bear to live with was the hurt. Alex's hurt. An innocent betrayal. Only Alex wouldn't see it that way. And Alex would be hurt. And Alex would hate.

In need if a diversion, she dropped to her knees beside the playpen, putting its width between herself and Alex. And Alex noticed. And Alex moved. And Stella was trapped. Because Alex was gripping her shoulders with fingers that bit. And Alex's eyes were swirling with emotion.

Desperate to avoid the mesmeric gaze, Stella was twisting her head, first one way, then the other. Only Alex slid a hand from shoulder to chin – yet another grip of iron. And when Stella closed her eyes, determined to avoid looking into his, not to allow Alex to gaze into hers and see to the centre of her soul, Alex simply laughed, dipped his head, and kissed her.

CHAPTER 10

'Very impressive.'

'The house?' Stella queried dryly. 'Or the grounds?'

'Neither – or both. The subject under discussion, as well you know, Stella Marshall, is the dynamic owner himself.'

'I'm glad you approve.'

'Oh but I don't. I was simply making an observation. The man's dynamite and I quite understand why you're smitten.'

'Observation?' Stella queried sharply. 'Or, given the length of your acquaintance, mere wishful thinking, Beth Austin?'

'Are you crazy? With his reputation? He's –'

'Innocent in the eyes of the law,' Stella interrupted sharply. 'And as far as I'm concerned, that's good enough for me.'

'And the rest?' Beth probed, grey eyes fleetingly cloudy. 'The string of beautiful women. The wild parties, late nights, the whiff of scandal on the club scene. Booze, drugs, women. You name it, Alex Gifford's name is never far away. And as for murder –'

'No, Beth,' Stella whispered, gazing frantically round to check they couldn't be overheard. 'Not here. Not ever as far as I'm concerned. Now, will you please drop the subject once and for all and judge the man on merit?'

'As you have?'

'As I have,' Stella agreed grimly. 'And believe me, Beth, I've seen enough to know that the man beneath the image wouldn't hurt so much as a fly. Arrogant, yes. Imperious, high-handed, overbearing on occasion, but not, repeat not, the out and out villain he's painted.'

'And you love him.'

Statement, not question, Stella noted automatically, and, glancing at the woman beside her, seeing the doubt, the concern, the almost tangible fear, Stella swallowed hard and gave her cousin the truth.

'I love him.'

'And?'

Stella shrugged, the off-hand gesture not really convincing. 'And nothing. He's engaged, or as good as, and if he does settle down it won't be with me.'

'So you admit the man's a philanderer?'

'Past tense, Beth. Assuming you can believe what's written in the Press.'

'And you should know.'

'Hardly,' Stella demurred. 'I cover news, not gossip. And I've nothing else to go on but three weeks' observation.'

Beth's turn to sigh, to recommence pushing Connor's buggy, with a subdued Stella matching her step for step as they ambled across the yard. Open day at the stables. And, since the stables were an integral part of the Gifford estate, the ghouls, the grims and the downright nosy had duly put in an appearance. Not to mention the unmentionables. Reporters. Drifting in and out in search of a fresh angle on yesterday's news. Because that was all it was now. History. Time to make someone else's life a misery. Not that Alex had allowed them to dictate terms in the first place. Hence his change of mind.

'Stopping over in town?' he'd echoed, waylaying Stella and Beth as they'd emerged from the house, Connor and James fast asleep in their respective buggies. 'What, and miss out on a chance to make the acquaintance of such a charming lady?'

And he'd taken Beth's hand, raised it to his lips and kissed it, gazing into her eyes with such quizzical intensity that a watching Stella could only stand and seethe. And suppress other emotions she'd rather not admit to. A touch of the green-eyed monster, she'd identified absurdly, drifting towards the yard and waiting for Beth to take the hint and follow. Now had it been Tamara she could have understood it. But Beth? Older than Stella, and definitely attractive, but a one-man woman if ever Stella had met one. And yet as fast as Alex had appeared, he'd melted away, back to the side of a glowering Tamara.

'Come and meet Hannah,' Stella urged, checking the time on her wristwatch. 'She said she'd take a break about eleven.'

'You mean, in there, actually in the stables?' Beth stalled, pulling up short.

Stella nodded. 'Since that's the whole point of open day, of course I mean the stables. And since you chose to invite yourself,' she pointedly reminded her, 'you can hardly complain.' An impish grin split her features. 'But I was almost forgetting. Where horses are concerned, you and Carilyn could be sisters instead of cousins.'

'Cari –? Ah! I see what you mean.' Beth lowered her voice, glanced around, an exaggerated surreptitious gesture that didn't impress Stella one iota. 'Stables have ears and all that sort of thing.'

'They certainly do,' Stella acknowledged crisply. 'In sets of two, I believe, and firmly attached to the beasts. Horses. With ears. And teeth. Horrid yellow gnashers that bite.'

'Precisely. And legs with hooves that kick. Which settles it. I'm staying outside.'

'Fine, I'll have Hannah bring her latest acquisition out to meet you. Four legs. Definitely equine. The requisite number of ears, teeth and hooves in all the right places and in full working order. Nay, lass,' she teased, catching the look of pure horror that crossed her cousin's face, 'you needn't retreat behind the nearest haystack. He's a pony; he's no more than this high,' she explained, holding the flat of her hand out at chest height. 'And he's the sweetest little chap you could ever hope to meet.'

'Nay, lass,' Beth parodied tartly. 'As in, no, I couldn't possibly want to meet him. But I don't suppose that's going to stop you.'

It didn't.

'Isn't he lovely?' Hannah, beaming, was clearly in her element, stroking the flank of the perfectly proportioned dappled grey trotted out by a shy young stable girl. 'He's a Connemara. Gentle and placid and thoroughly reliable. Just perfect for the small ones. And I'm no fool. If I can hook them at three or four, they're smitten for life.'

'Just like you, in fact,' Stella added, completely unthinking, so comfortable with Hannah that she rarely saw beyond the girl to the wheelchair. And the reason for the chair. At Beth's muffled gasp, Stella put her hand to her mouth. 'Oh, Hannah. I'm sorry. I wasn't –'

'Thinking?' Hannah supplied, smiling, easing away the awkward moment. 'Good. Because that's how I like it. It's a disability, not a handicap, and thanks to Giff I've a successful business to prove it.'

'Giff?' Beth queried lightly. 'Oh, you mean Alex.'

Hannah nodded. 'After the accident he refused to let me wallow in self-pity. He goaded and coaxed till I was ready to scream or tear my hair out, and he gave me back a reason for living. I'd given up,' she explained without a trace of self-pity now. 'Only Giff wouldn't let me. And when he dangled the carrot of the riding school –'

'You couldn't look a gift horse in the mouth, I suppose?' Beth mused wickedly.

Hannah grinned. 'Got it in one. And it worked. And it's mine, all mine, and no one can ever take it away from me. But why not come through and see for yourself?'

Beth was instantly wary. 'I –'

'Wouldn't miss it for the world, hey, Beth?' Stella urged silkily. 'Why not follow Marbles to the tiny tots arena? Who knows? Connor might just turn out to be a natural.'

'Heaven forbid,' Beth muttered an undertone. And though she smiled at Hannah, and set off across the paddock at a very wary distance, the glance she shot at Stella would have pickled a tub full of onions.

Stella grinned, watched them out of sight, adjusted the parasol to shade James's face from the sun, and froze.

'Got you!'

A pair of hands slid round her waist.

'Alex! Are you mad?' Stella hissed, attempting to wriggle free and succeeding in making things worse instead of better. 'Tamara –'

'Recalled a prior engagement. And, since she does model clothes for a living –' He broke off, shrugged, grinned – a disarming smile that didn't fool Stella for a minute. 'But knowing Tam, I'd say the idea of sharing centre stage with a stable full of horses simply didn't appeal.'

'A legacy of those enormous green eyes,' Stella bit out, the casual use of the nickname an exquisite stab of pain. 'Seeing all, imagining more and positively glowering at every passable female under the age of forty.'

'Oh, definitely passable,' he growled, tugging her even closer. Stella's grip on James's pushchair loosened. 'Passable, kissable, touchable –'

'No, Alex!' Stella hissed, frantic eyes searching the

yard, unbelievably thankfully empty, for the moment at least. A moment of madness. Just long enough for Alex to nudge aside her hair and nibble the nape of her neck. Tiny, devastating kisses. Kissing, touching, wanting, needing – 'No!' Stella groaned in anguish. 'No! No! No!' And with a super-human effort, she broke free. 'Don't!' she pleaded, the breath leaving her body as she stumbled, lost her balance, collided with the wall behind. 'Don't touch, don't look, don't kiss. Ever. Stella Marshall is strictly off limits – to you and any other predatory male with time on his hands and mauling in his mind. Understand, Alex? You *don't*.'

Handsome features hardened. 'Don't worry, Stella, I know when to take a hint. I don't need to force my attentions where they're clearly not appreciated. There's never any need,' he sneeringly conceded, 'because if and when I need a woman –'

'You click those arrogant Gifford fingers and half a dozen come running? Yes, Alex,' she acknowledged tightly, 'I know. Slander, lies and defamation notwithstanding, society page news can give a fascinating glimpse of how the other half lives.'

'You're wrong.' A rapidly beating pulse at his temple drew Stella's gaze.

'Am I?'

'Very wrong. I haven't made that sort of news in years.'

'Quite the reformed character,' she sneered, eyes pools of hate as they locked with his. 'In which case, Alex, why try it on with me?'

'I wasn't –'

'Mauling?'

'Your definition or mine?' he bit out. 'Touching, kissing, stroking —'

'A rose by any other name,' she jeered.

'If you insist,' he acknowledged tersely. 'But I didn't notice any prissy protestations the other day.'

'That was —'

'Different?' he queried silkily. 'Enjoyable? Or are you going to look me in the eye and lie through your teeth?'

Lie? When she was living a lie, here, now, masquerading as a nanny. Lie, when she'd kissed him, allowed Alex to kiss her, and more. Touch, taste, savour . . . She closed her eyes, blocking out the present as the memory flooded back to haunt her . . .

A kiss. Man and woman. A moment of magic. Because Alex had only to touch his lips to hers and Stella was lost, her mouth opening like the petals of a flower. A kiss. Breathtakingly brief, little more than a whisper of breath, but enough to set the currents surging.

And Stella's gasp of pleasure — and pain — as Alex pulled away had been matched by Alex's hiss of indrawn breath. Pause. Man and woman. Alone. The atmosphere electric. Blue eyes gazing into hers and seeing to the centre of her soul. Blue eyes full of hope, wonder, a smouldering intensity. Because Alex wanted Stella, and, shamelessly shameless, Stella wanted Alex.

'Alex . . .'

'Hush,' he'd said thickly. 'You know, and I know,

and knowledge is truth. Words, Stella. We're beyond the need for words.'

'So kiss me,' she'd entreated hoarsely, raising her face and offering her mouth. 'So kiss me.'

And he had, another searing touch. A gasp of pain as he jerked his head away, those piercing eyes raking her face in, a frantic search for *what*, she couldn't say, but, satisfied, he'd nodded, tightened his grip, the audible groan of anguish as he'd pulled her against him music to her ears.

Music in her ears as Alex nibbled at her earlobes, lapped at the folds of skin, nuzzling the nooks and crannies while crooning a love song, the hands on her body picking out the refrain, a perfect harmonization.

Body tingling, nerve-endings jingling, jangling, dancing, Stella raised her arms to run her fingers through the soft spikes of his hair, cupped his head in her hands and urged his mouth on to hers.

Shameless. Pushing against him. Aching breasts brushing against a powerful chest. And Alex's throaty growl stoking the heats of desire.

'Stella, Stella, Stella,' he'd crooned over and over as his mouth devoured her, lips to lips, lips to eyelid, a trail of devastation across her fevered brow and down to nibble at the corner of her mouth. Yet another growl of pleasure as she parted her lips, an eloquent invitation for his tongue to slide through, to explore the secret, sensitive, sensitized interior. A frantic sweep, corner to corner, and across the tingling layer of skin inside her lower lip. Stella's turn to moan, to kiss, to suck, to gasp afresh as Alex pulled away.

'No!'

'No!' he'd thundered in agreement, but he was smiling, touching, caressing, reassuring, his hands sliding from her shoulders to her waist to tug the folds of her blouse free of the waistband of her skirt, to slip his hands beneath the fabric to the scalded skin beneath.

Skin to skin, and upwards, snapping the poppers – thank heaven for poppers, Stella's mind sang as Alex blazed his trail nearer and nearer to her straining, aching breasts, the swollen nipples standing out against the lace of her bra.

'Woman,' he breathed, pulling the last folds of her blouse apart before pushing the offending garment over her shoulders, allowing him to feast his eyes on the swell of breast, the dark areola beneath the creamy lace. 'Oh, woman, you really are amazing.'

Stella laughed. 'My turn,' she insisted, itching to start at the waistband of his trousers and work down, but curbing the impulse with a massive surge of will as she raised a hand, swirled a lazy thumb across the knot of his Adam's apple with its faint rasp of stubble.

Down, slowly, frustrating Alex, frustrating herself just as badly, but the spring of curl beneath her fingers was fitting consolation, and Stella smiled inside, the lights dancing in her eyes as she raised her lids to find his gaze locked on to hers, the rawness of emotion knocking the breath from her body.

'Alex –'

'Hush.' He shook his head, placed a finger on her lip. 'No need for words,' he reminded her huskily.

And he smiled, nodded, nudged her hand back into motion, a hand that trembled as she reached the point where the taper of curls disappeared into tailored dark linen. And Stella paused, such an exquisite pause, allowed her hand to hover as she raised her eyes again, saw the need, the ache, the want in his eyes, and trembled deep inside. And touched him. And shivered. And felt the shuddering response beneath her fingers and shivered all over again.

Alex groaned, thrust against her outstretched hand. The heat of him, the hardness created explosions in Stella's mind and body, the thrill of fear effectively blocking out the room and everything in it. She wanted him. Every nerve, every pore, each and every fibre of her body was crying out for Alex to take her in his arms, to place her down on the floor, to cover her body with his own and take her. And take her again. And again and again and again. And then to sleep, arms and legs entwined, and wake refreshed and start to love all over again. Love, she told herself in wonder. Because she was a woman, alone with a man, and for the first time in her life she knew how it felt to need a man so badly that it hurt.

'Alex –'

'Soon,' he told her smokily, locking his smouldering gaze on to hers. 'But first I want to touch, and taste, and feast my eyes. And then, my love . . .' He smiled, nodded, reached out a lazy hand to snap the catch at the front of her bra, and, as Stella's aching, straining breasts spilled free, he switched his gaze from face to breasts and back again. 'A feast fit for a king,' he conceded thickly. 'Beautiful,' he breathed. 'These are beautiful,' he insisted, taking the weight of her breasts in the palms of his hands. 'But you – you are simply unbelievable. And I want you. Understand, Stella, I'm going to take you. Here. Soon. But first I shall touch, taste and feast my eyes.'

Touch. An idle thumb flicking against a nipple. Nipples swelling, thrusting, demanding that he touch, taste, savour. And Alex did, dipping his head, a fleeting touch of mouth on skin, a tantalizing pause as he drew back, allowed his tongue to swirl across the aching bud before his teeth closed round, the pressure almost sheer imagination. Almost. And Stella gasped, and Alex smiled, banished the momentary stab of fear with another languid probe of tongue and exchanged the gentle vice of teeth for the tender tug of lips.

And tug they did – an exquisite sensation that pulsed from breast to belly and back again, and Stella was moaning, undulating gently to the rhythm of the tugging, the sucking, the occasional nip of teeth. Mouth to breast, fingers to breast, an adroit switch of mouth from breast to breast, sucking, nibbling, biting, sucking, inciting, exciting, driving Stella crazy with desire.

'Alex! Please, Alex! Oh, God, Alex!' she moaned as he buried his head in the valley between her breasts.

Another moan. An unwelcome intrusion. A strange, gurgling sound coming from somewhere close by, vaguely impinging, vaguely alarming, yet nothing like as distracting as having Alex's hands pushing her breasts together to deepen the valley, allowing him to lap at the slopes, to climb the slopes inch by tantalizing inch, to circle first one rigid bud then the other, denying her, inciting her, denying her again, before pulling her close and fastening a greedy mouth on the shamelessly thrusting nipple.

Unbelievable. Undeniable. Unstoppable, she acknowledged as Alex placed her gently down upon the rug. And she smiled, and she opened her arms, and she caught a movement out of the corner of her eye and froze. A baby. A happy, gurgling baby in his playpen, paying scant attention to the games of the grown-ups, but a baby nonetheless. And as the realization hit her she saw the same shock reflected in Alex's widening eyes and was forced to stifle a giggle.

'Bad timing, huh?' he acknowledged wryly, stooping to kiss her, to offer a hand to tug her to her feet. Face to face, hips to hips, he refused to release her, instead simply stood, simply glanced down, the expression in eyes unfathomable. 'Bad timing – this time,' he conceded. 'But never again, I promise you. Next time, Stella –'

'Hush,' she insisted, placing a finger on his lips. 'We're beyond the need for words, remember?'

Alex nodded, drew the finger into his mouth and bit. Gently . . .

'You never did reveal your sister's name,' Alex chided softly as Stella dragged her mind back to the present, amazed to discover that nothing had changed, that the yard was thankfully deserted, the hypnotic drone of bees and the vague murmur of voices belying their isolation.

'I wasn't –'

'Recalling every touch, every kiss, each and every heated moment?' He raised a sceptical eyebrow. 'Don't lie, Stella,' he entreated mildly. 'We're beyond the need for words – remember?'

Oh, yes, Stella remembered. And Alex had followed every thought, every tiny nuance of expression. And, since they clearly were beyond the need for words, this time at least, she'd be wasting her breath voicing her denials.

She shrugged. 'So we are,' she agreed pleasantly, mustering the remnants of composure and tightening her grip on James's buggy, knuckles straining white. 'So you won't need reminding that as from now Stella Marshall's strictly off limits.'

'Better late than never, huh?' Another shrug, another raised brow. 'If you say so.'

'I do. But there again, I say a lot of things that Alex Gifford chooses to ignore.'

'All part and parcel of the charm,' he conceded lightly.

'Or the arrogance.'

The smile tightened. 'Sure. Why not? Nobody's totally perfect, and if that's my only failing I've precious little to apologize for. Now you, on the other hand . . .'

An appraising glance, top to toe and back again, only slowly, forcing Stella to suppress the urge to bolt, to grit her teeth and seem blithely unconcerned when Alex homed in on the rapid rise and fall of breasts that in less than three weeks he'd managed to become almost as intimately acquainted with as Stella herself. And, sure enough, the nipples tightened of their own accord, would be clearly outlined against the fabric of her blouse.

The lazy gaze ambled back to her face. Alex nodded. 'Practically perfect,' he conceded. 'So, having established that, where were we? Ah, yes? N for no, I seem to recall. Or NOP for Nosy Old Parker. And whilst mildly curious I'll happily own to, nosy and old I strongly refute. But I'm not the subject under discussion. You are. Or rather, your strangely nameless sister. Q?' he queried, furrowing his brow. 'Queenie? Roberta? Selina? Teresa? No? Not even a teensy-weenie clue?' he entreated, spreading his smile along with his hands. 'Unfair, Stella Marshall. Unsporting. Uncompromising –'

'Understandable?' she queried waspishly.

'*U*nimpressionable, apparently. *V*ery *W*ary, *X*-ceptional, *Y*oung and most definitely at the *Z*enith of life. Impressed?'

'Not unless I'm suffering from the proverbial loose screw. Talking of which –'

'Doubly unfair, Stella Marshall. Is it my fault I'm besotted?'

'Piqued, peeved and put out, you mean. All those lashings of Gifford charm and still I'm unimpressed.'

'Allegedly.'

'Why, no. You've agreed on this already. Unimpressionable,' she reminded him. 'Very Wary, *X*-ceptional – spelling not your strong point, Alex?' she needled lightly, leaning forward confidentially. 'Public schools these days have such a lot to answer for. Poor at maths, hopeless at spelling. I wonder if there's anything you're good at – but, no, on second thoughts, I really don't want to know.'

'You will.'

'Like I said, arrogant as always.'

'So, like the proverbial Persian carpet, there's an inbuilt flaw. Some are born perfect, some have perfection thrust upon them, and –'

'Some are too arrogant to care? Yes, Alex, we've tested that theory already' she reminded him sweetly. 'Which neatly proves my point. A lesser ego wouldn't own to any imperfection. But not Alex Gifford,' she scorned. 'Oh, no. Trust arrogant Alex Gifford to make a virtue out of a fault.'

'Have you quite finished?' Cold, polite, the expression on his face unreadable, but the message was loud and clear. She'd overstepped the mark and he was miffed.

'As it happens,' she reminded him tersely, 'I didn't want to start this conversation in the first place. But, yes, Alex,' she conceded tightly, 'I've finished. Yet even if I hadn't,' she tagged on coldly, 'I don't suppose it would make a penny farthing's worth of difference. *You've* had enough, therefore end of conversation. Arrogant?' she challenged, eyes raining scorn. 'The word doesn't even come close.'

'Why, thank you, Stella. Coming from anyone else, I'd be inclined to take offence. Coming from you, I'll take it as a –'

'Compliment? Yes, Alex,' she acknowledged bitterly. 'Somehow I didn't doubt it for a minute.'

He swung away, surprisingly enough allowing Stella the last word. Or maybe, with an ego as high as the sky, he simply didn't care. Well, fine, that made two of them. And better open animosity than the sort of intimate interludes Alex clearly had in mind. In which case she'd be foolish to slam shut a door whilst leaving an open window to beckon, to goad, to tantalize. Carly. Why make an issue of a name? Only she had. Guilt, she acknowledged. The thought of looking him in the eye and lying. Only she wouldn't be lying. Simply stretching the truth a little. But better to close the subject once and for all, before Alex recommenced his game of cat and mouse.

Stella took a deep breath, tightened her grip on the sleeping James's pushchair and half took a step forwards.

'Alex.'

He paused, spun – slowly – on his heels, raised a lazy eyebrow. 'Stella?'

'I thought you were curious to know my sister's name.'

'So I was. But that was then and this is now,' he carelessly conceded. 'Besides, there's no need – not any more.'

'You mean arrogant Alex Gifford is seeing things my way for once? My, my,' Stella derided, 'miracles never cease to amaze me.'

'Not miracles, Stella,' he contradicted mildly. 'Something much more down to earth. Believe it or not, I've just recalled an alternative source of information.'

'Oh?' Stella queried, a prickle of alarm running the length of her spine.

'Oh? Is that all you can find to say?' he mocked, folding his arms and surveying her from under hooded lids. 'Stuck for words, Stella, or back to playing games?' he asked silkily. 'So, is that oh as in: oh-oh, I'm worried; Alex clearly has an ace up his sleeve and it's time to resort to that Marshall speciality the alphabetic method of evasion?' he queried absurdly. 'Or oh as in: oh, really, Stella Marshall's mildly curious – only mildly, mind?'

Stella gritted her teeth and forced a smile. 'How about: oh, why don't you stop wasting time?' she needled lightly. 'And when it comes to being evasive, Alex Gifford, I'm looking at an expert.'

'Why, thank you, Stella. I knew you'd see things my way eventually. Want to test the theory again some time? In bed, perhaps? Your bed or mine? All you have to do –'

'Alex!' she warned, aware of voices growing louder, desperately afraid she was wasting her time, that it was only a matter of time before Alex wore down her resistance. Bed. Her bed or Alex's or the rug in the nursery. It was all the same to him. In which case, Beth's assessment of Alex had been right in the first place. Philanderer. Womanizer. And while Tamara's away, Alex will play. Insatiable. Alex was a man, all man, and, despite her resolutions, Stella was a woman giving all the right signals: I'm here, take me. Take me, pleasure me, use me.

And if that was what Alex believed, who could

blame him? Because besotted Stella Marshall hadn't managed even a token resistance. Only she wouldn't give it. Wouldn't, mustn't, couldn't. Pride. Scant comfort in the dark hours, but better a void than the pain of knowing she was just another notch on Alex's bed-head. And, since she didn't know what she was missing . . . Stella inwardly winced. Oh, didn't she? Well, maybe she didn't, but she sure as hell suspected. Heaven on earth with Alex. And then hell on earth without him.

'Words, Stella,' he reminded her, catching the scent of panic, vague amusement swirling in the depths of his eyes. 'And, since I know perfectly well what's running through your mind, I can bide my time – let the subject drop, switch to something innocuous if it makes you feel secure. Small talk. This and that. Something and nothing. Isn't it a glorious day?' he improvised absurdly. 'But I was almost forgetting that other intriguing subject, the doting sister's evasion. And since the doting sister refuses to be drawn,' he gleefully conceded, 'I'll simply turn the famed Gifford charm on the doting sister's cousin.'

'Beth –'

'Won't even suspect that I'm fishing, Stella. Watch me. I'll simply steer the subject my way over dinner.'

'Dinner?'

'Yes. You know. An evening meal – in this part of the world at least. Later than high tea, a mite earlier than supper. Seven o'clockish. Though the time is normally set to suit the host. So, seven o'clock it is, and plenty of time to get Connor and James ready for bed.'

'I think you'll find Beth would rather take Connor home.'

'And I think you'll find not. And, since I took the precaution of asking while her prickly cousin was safely out of earshot, I think you'll find that Beth's looking forward to joining us all for dinner. Nothing too formal, since she didn't think to bring a change of clothes, but dinner all the same. Impressed, huh? Or peeved you've boxed yourself into a corner, perhaps? Because, irrelevant though the issue is, if you'd given me what I wanted in the first place, Stella –' He broke off, shrugged, smiled, spread his hands. 'Like I said, you'll learn – the hard way. Because what Alex Gifford wants, Alex Gifford simply bides his time and takes.'

CHAPTER 11

'So tell me, Beth, what do you think of the place so far?'

Alex – smiling broadly, topping up glasses. Mineral water for Stella and Beth, because Beth was driving and Stella was determined to keep her wits. For, with Tamara conspicuous by her absence, Alex's need for a woman in his bed had to be all-engrossing. Only not Stella. Decision time. Departure time. Turn her back and walk away. Tomorrow, or the next day, or Monday at the latest. No dithering, no regrets, no dangerous second thoughts. She had to go. Now. And the sooner she broached the subject of Mandy, the sooner she could make it. But, come hell or high water, by Monday at the latest Stella was leaving.

'The house?' Beth queried, wrinkling her brow and smiling. 'Or the grounds?'

'Why not the whole caboodle?' he entreated pleasantly. 'I assume Stella made time to show you round.'

'Worry not, Alex,' Stella reassured him sweetly. 'As guided tours go it was sadly lacking in commentary, but the walk was pleasant enough, and barely a blade of grass was overlooked for praise. It was – most impressive.'

'But?'

'Did I say but?'

'You didn't need to. As always, it came across loud and clear all by itself. Stella Marshall doesn't approve. Deny it if you dare.'

'Since my opinion surely doesn't count for *that* much,' Stella scorned, snapping her fingers, 'why should I waste my breath saying anything?'

'Manners?' he challenged silkily. 'Since I'm the host and you're –'

'Working my notice? You do recall I'm working my notice?' she queried, using the buffering presence of Hannah and Beth as a subtle reminder to Alex that he was wasting time playing games with Stella. Word games. Love games. Any games.

'Sure.' Alex's derision spoke volumes. 'A week, a month, three months. Assuming you can turn your back and walk away from a child who needs you.'

'Try three days, Alex,' she suggested baldly.

'You can't.'

'Correction. I not only can, but will.'

'And James –'

'Needs someone who's going to be around for a while. Someone who knows her way around the village, isn't afraid to face out the gossips. Someone young and willing to learn.'

'Sounds perfect. A perfect paragon. Too perfect to be true,' he scorned.

'But if she exists?'

The bread between his fingers was reduced to a heap of crumbs on his plate. 'I thought she did. Past tense, since she's hell-bent on leaving.'

'Leaving, yes. Walking out, abandoning James, no. He'll be well taken care of.'

'He's well taken care of now. He's happy, I'm happy, you're –'

'A stop-gap. Nothing more, nothing less,' she reminded him less heatedly, holding his gaze, praying he'd accept the decision once and for all, that he wouldn't cause a scene in public, that he'd listen, consider and weigh all the options. And Stella simply wasn't an option.

'Ah, yes,' he scorned. 'So you are. A temporary arrangement. Because that's the way Stella Marshall likes to operate. Love them and leave them. No strings, no ties, no commitment. Right, Stella?'

'Wrong, Alex, But, since you refuse point-blank to believe it –'

'The sooner you go the better?' he interrupted savagely. He bared his teeth in a mocking semblance of a smile. 'I rest my case.'

'Giff . . .' A mild interception. Hannah's voice. Hannah's blue eyes fleetingly cloudy, her hand on Alex's arm, her lightly tanned skin standing out against the steel-grey fabric of the jacket.

And Alex seemed to shake his head, banish the shadows with a dazzling smile that was meant for Hannah and Hannah alone. And Stella saw. And Stella felt the stirrings of alarm. Because Alex had smiled at his sister-in-law? she forced herself to ask.

An innocent gesture, surely, and all the more reason for Stella to go. To be jealous of Tamara was one thing; to resent Hannah's place in Alex's life was nothing short of madness.

Long, tapering fingers closed around Hannah's, and as Stella looked on in silent misery Alex raised the hand to his lips, dropped a light kiss into the open palm and cast an apologetic glance around the table.

'Hannah's right, as usual. I've been unforgivably rude.'

'All part and parcel of the strain you've been subjected to,' Beth said mildly, her own smile spreading. 'And losing my gem of a cousin sounds the last straw?'

'A gem indeed,' Alex conceded, his gaze passing from Beth to Stella and refusing to allow her to look away. 'Flawless, I believe, and overdue an apology. Would it help if I went down on my knees and grovelled?'

'It would help if you'd listen,' Stella told him softly. 'If you'd hear me out and keep an open mind.'

'Since you've chosen your moment to perfection, I guess I haven't much choice, hey, Stella?'

'All's fair in love, war and the world of work,' she retorted as the atmosphere lightened. She reached for her glass, the Paris goblet with its chilled white wine – and an excellent wine at that, judging from the single sip she'd rationed herself to. Only, nerves all a-jangle, right now she needed a drink with a kick. 'To the future?' she proposed, glancing from one to the other. From Beth's familiar face, vaguely worried despite the bright smile, to Hannah, basking in the glow of Alex's approval, of that innocent gesture of affection Stella had yet to come to terms with, and finally on to Alex. Who knew. It was written loud and clear in those sharp blue eyes. Stella was running scared. In a one to one situation Alex would wear her down, and so Stella had taken the coward's way out and broached the subject in public, forcing Alex to capitulate. For now.

Alex nodded. 'To the future, and whatever it may bring,' he acknowledged with a faint trace of mockery. 'So, Miss Practically Perfect in Every Way – and too clever by half at times. Isn't it time you came clean?'

'C-came clean?' Stella stalled, a surge of guilty colour flooding her cheeks.

'But of course. Nanny. Future tense. Unless this is some elaborate hoax on your part, you're about to wave a magic wand and conjure up the perfect specimen.'

'Hardly,' Stella demurred. 'But I've a hunch I could be right.'

'Fine.' Alex spread his hands. 'I'm all ears. Fire away.'

Stella did.

'Mandy?' he breathed incredulously. 'As in Mandy Shaw, product of the local comprehensive and heaven help James if he mislays one of his toes?' he derided. 'You *are* joking?'

'Do I look like I'm joking?' she countered mildly.

'It was – wishful thinking on my part,' he scorned. 'And if Mandy's three sheets to the wind, the complaint is clearly catching. The idea's absurd.'

'I don't agree.'

'You wouldn't. It isn't your child you're proposing to abandon to her care.'

'Maybe not, but I am,' Beth interjected mildly. And as Alex gave another snort of derision she raised a hand, commanding silence. 'Listen.'

' "Rockaby baby on the tree-top. When the wind blows, the cradle will rock . . ." '

Slightly out of tune and tinny, given the distortion of the intercom, but the age-old rhyme was still recognizable.

'Let me guess,' Alex drawled incredulously. 'Miss Mandy Shaw, no less. Putting James and Connor to bed.'

'But since sir is clearly unbelieving,' Beth acknowledged mildly, 'why not come along with me and see for yourself?'

'I –'

'I think it's a wonderful idea,' Hannah supplied dryly. 'If I could wave a magic wand and whisk myself upstairs, I'd insist on coming with you.'

And argue with that Alex couldn't.

'So, you really are going?' Hannah, her blue eyes strangely cloudy as they locked with Stella's.

Stella nodded. 'I must. I shouldn't have stayed this long.'

'And the longer you stay the harder it is to tear yourself away?'

'It's – too easy to let emotions take over,' Stella acknowledged frankly. 'And James is an absolute treasure. But at least I can be sure he'll be well looked after.'

'Mandy?' Hannah's turn to nod. 'Kind of obvious when you think of it. Only we didn't. Crazy, huh?'

'It's generally the case,' Stella reassured her lightly. 'And hardly surprising, given the upheavals. It – can't have been easy for anyone?' she probed carefully.

Hannah's eyes swam with tears. 'Giff took it hard,' she acknowledged tightly. 'He blamed himself – still does, if the truth's known. He found her, you know, and he's convinced she was still breathing when he pulled her out of the water. But by the time the ambulance arrived it was too late. Of course, if Chrissie hadn't been drinking she might have stood a chance. As it was . . .' A shrug, a smile of reassurance that didn't fool Stella for an instant. For if Alex had lost his wife, Hannah had lost a sister.

'I know it's scant consolation,' Stella acknowledged softly, 'but you and Alex have James – and, just as importantly, you have each other.'

'Till death – or Tamara – do us part?' Hannah scorned, features fleetingly ugly. 'But you're right, of course. We have James. And as for Tamara –'

'Taking my name in vain?' came a lazy voice from the archway, the edge to her tone barely perceptible.

'Speak of the devil?' Hannah countered coldly, completely unfazed by Tamara's appearance out of nowhere.

Green eyes flashed their derision. 'Where's Alex?' she bit out, switching her gaze from Hannah to Stella and back again.

'Would you believe, playing happy families in the nursery?' Hannah supplied dryly.

'While the nanny of the year lets her hair down?' Tamara jeered with an appraising glance at Stella. 'Been drinking, Hannah? Over-indulging in the wine, perhaps? A family failing, so I've heard. Like sister, like –'

'Bitch!'

'If the cap fits,' Tamara drawled, taking a menacing step forward. 'As I was saying, like sister, like sister. Only here's one little sister who won't, repeat won't, be getting her claws into Alex. Understand?' Bending, placing her palms on the table, she brought her dark head close in to Hannah's, her whole expression ugly. 'He's mine,' Tamara hissed. 'And you can take it from me, Alex is all man. It takes a woman, a real woman to hold him. Understand?'

'A real woman not a wreck, you mean? A real woman not a cripple –'

'Hannah –'

'It's OK, Stella,' Hannah reassured her swiftly. 'It really doesn't hurt any more. And Tamara's perfectly right. Giff needs a woman – a real woman,' she conceded sweetly. 'And as far as I'm concerned, the sooner he finds her the better.'

'You know, coming from anyone else,' Tamara acknowledged softly, viciously, as Stella inwardly flinched, 'I'd be sorely tempted to scratch their eyes out. Coming from you, I'm naturally forced to make allowances. This time.' She stretched, shot a dismissive glance at Stella, a dart of pure poison at Hannah, spun on her heels and sashayed towards the stairs, the tap of stiletto heels over-loud in the silence.

Stiletto heels. The same stiletto heels she'd presumably been wearing when she'd arrived, Stella mused, frowning. But she'd arrived silently. Appearing out of nowhere. Sly. Underhand. Given to creeping around the house in the dark hours, perhaps? Only, tucked up in bed with Alex, of course she wouldn't need to.

'Doesn't it bother you? Seeing Tamara in your sister's place, I mean?' Stella probed as the echo of footsteps died away.

'Good Lord, no,' Hannah derided, her scowl banished in a trice. 'Giff's had more women than I've had hot dinners. Tamara won't hold him any more than Chrissie did. And if she's lasted longer than most,' she scornfully conceded, 'she's simply holding on by the curve of her claws. Talons. A girl's best friend, judging by Tamara. Dig deep, hold tight and viciously repel all rivals.'

'She finds you a threat?'

'Don't sound so surprised,' Hannah chided lightly. 'I'm young, and at the risk of sounding smug I believe I'm reasonably attractive, and deep down inside, where it counts, I'm all woman. And even if I'm forced to spend my days confined to this chair,' she added without rancour, 'I'm more gainfully employed than Tamara could ever be, strutting along a catwalk. And though my legs refuse to work, there's precious little wrong with the rest of me.'

'No.' Stella smiled. 'You certainly give as good as you take, and that's for sure. Alex –'

'Sees what he wants to see,' Hannah cut in as the

sound of voices drifted down the stairwell. 'And that's the way I'd like it to stay.'

'Of course.' Stella gave her a smile of reassurance. Hannah didn't want to rock any boats – wouldn't need to rock any boats if nature took its course. Because Tamara was just another woman to keep Alex's bed warm. As Stella would be. Assuming she was foolish enough to fall for the age-old patter.

'Ah, Mrs Edwards. Perfect timing as always,' Alex pronounced, arriving at the archway with Beth on his arm as the housekeeper appeared from the opposite direction.

'I was wondering whether to set another place, sir? For Miss Clayton. I know you said she wouldn't be dining, but I'm sure I heard her car . . .'

'Better safe than sorry? Good thinking,' he acknowledged warmly. 'But make it snappy, hey? I'm hungry enough to eat a horse.'

'Don't even think it,' Hannah warned, but she was smiling, teasing, the angry scene with Tamara clearly forgotten.

Dinner went on, minus Tamara, and for once Agnes Edwards really had excelled herself. Seafood parcels – succulent mussels and cockles in a featherlight puff of pastry with a rich creamy sauce hinting at the flavour of leeks – followed by a roast rack of lamb with a peppery herb crust and seasonal vegetables cooked to perfection. No watery greens, no sea of greasy gravy, just fresh food, beautifully cooked, beautifully served, and as for the dessert . . .

'Bread and butter pudding or walnut ice cream.

Home-made, of course,' Mrs Edwards added tartly, thin cheeks glowing from the praise Alex had spread as thickly as newly churned butter.

'But of course,' Alex echoed with his most winning smile. 'Bread and butter pudding sounds divine. *With* the ice cream. And if there's a chance of seconds –'

'Pudding and ice cream both count as seconds,' she retorted sharply. And, though she gave an audible sniff, there was a definite smile of approval playing about the corners of her mouth.

'Amazing,' Alex conceded, beaming round the table. 'Yet another of Stella's magic wands, I suppose. And while Mandy does seem an adequate replacement, I'm inclined to wonder how we'll feel when this paragon of virtue drives off into the sunset.'

'Deprived. Apparently.' Tamara – sliding into a vacant chair and pushing the unused set of cutlery carelessly to one side as she reached for a glass, pointedly held it out for Alex to fill. Without a word, she raised it to her lips, drained it in one, and held it out for a refill.

Eyebrows disappearing into his hairline, Alex complied. 'Glad you could join us,' he murmured pleasantly.

'Had I known we were dining unfashionably early,' she needled, 'naturally I'd have made the effort to be here.'

'No problem.' Alex smiled, turned to find his housekeeper hovering and allowed the smile to broaden. 'I'm sure Mrs Edwards has been kind enough to keep something warm.'

'Try rat on toast,' Hannah murmured, and Stella choked on her sip of wine. Another sip of wine. Because, nerves in shreds, she needed a drink – needed to stay sober just as badly.

Tamara glared at Hannah from her lofty position on Alex's right. Lady of the house. And if Stella could make the connection, Hannah wouldn't be far behind. And it would hurt. Because Tamara was taking her sister's place, and because Hannah was human enough to want Alex's full attention? As a brother? Stella mused, setting a chain of thought into motion and resenting the images it raised, the relentless play in her mind. Or something else? Like what, for instance? Like lover, maybe, or husband?

All woman. Young, attractive and strangely vulnerable. And why not? Stella asked herself. Why shouldn't Hannah dream? Pipe-dreams, she scorned. Just like Stella's. Love Alex, maybe. But be loved by Alex? When, as Hannah was quick to point out, there wasn't a woman born who could hold him? Womanizer. Playboy. Darling of the gossip sheets. Until the death of his wife, that was. And then the gossip had turned to condemnation. Murder. An ugly deed, an ugly word. And the finger of suspicion stubbornly refused to go away.

No!

Stella visibly started. Womanizer, yes, she told herself, willing herself to believe it. But anything else was nothing short of lunacy.

'Wine, Beth? No? Fine. I know you'll be driving home soon. Stella? Not even half a glass?' Alex chided, eyes heavy with challenge. Because Stella had braced herself to meet his gaze, and sure enough Alex was aware of her unease. 'Hannah? Tamara?'

'On an empty stomach?' Tamara drawled, her exquisite features fleetingly ugly. 'What do you think?'

'Hungry, my love? Like I said, Mrs Edwards –'

'Will have binned it or burned it or doubtless smothered it in gravy by now.' Tamara forced a smile. 'Don't worry, darling, I'll make do with cheese and biscuits. You know me, I simply hate to make a fuss. And it's such a lovely evening – too lovely to niggle, too lovely to sit indoors. Let's have coffee on the terrace.'

On the terrace, with its canopied swing chair – a double-seated chair. No prizes for guessing who managed to manoeuvre Alex to sit beside her. Tamara, dressed for dinner, the slinky black sheath fitting like a glove and in stark contrast to Hannah's habitual blouse and trousers, to the casual attire Beth and Stella had donned for a ramble round stable and gardens.

More an estate than a garden, Stella corrected automatically, since everything as far as the eye could see presumably belonged to Alex. Formal gardens in the foreground, kitchen garden tucked around the corner, orchard and lawns stretching down to the discreetly planted line of trees that marked the southern edge of the Gifford estate. Not to mention the unmentionable, the fully equipped leisure wing with fitness room, sauna and swimming pool – drained and out of bounds since the accident. It was another world to Stella, and all the more amazing in that Alex had shunned the sort of sophisticated security system that would have kept the rat pack of reporters at bay indefinitely.

'A waste of time,' he explained, when Stella raised the subject. 'Too many comings and goings. The riding school, the stables, visitors, staff and inmates –'

'And which of those quaint descriptions would you apply to me?' Tamara enquired archly. ' "Inmates"? You make the place sound like a prison.'

' "Stone walls do not a prison make," ' Alex quoted lightly.

'How very poetic,' Tamara drawled, wrinkling her pert little nose. And then, with a pointed glance at Stella, tucked between Beth and Hannah on a surprisingly comfortable wickerwork chair, 'All from the Miss Stella Marshall school of philosophy, I presume? Such a moderating influence. I'm almost sorry to hear you're leaving,' she conceded flippantly. 'The place simply won't be the same without you. And, correct me I'm wrong, but *who* did I hear you nominate to fill the vacant throne? Surely not that pathetic little kitchen drudge? Alex, darling, I really must object.'

'Overruled, I'm afraid,' he murmured pleasantly. 'Mandy's the obvious replacement, as I'm sure you'll discover for yourself in time.'

'And if she isn't?' she murmured confidentially, sliding her fingers with their vivid red talons beneath the hand Alex had rested lightly on the cushions between them. 'If she goes the way of all the other flighty young things –'

'She won't,' he interrupted lightly, his hand closing round hers to give a reassuring squeeze. 'Young she may be, flighty she isn't. And, yes, I know there's a lovesick swain loitering in the background. He's unemployed, but as honest as the day is long, from what I've heard, and he sounds the ideal replacement for Tommy Haig.'

'Gardener? Are you mad? He probably doesn't know a blade of grass from an ornamental lily.'

'Then he'll learn. And with Cooper in charge, he won't go far wrong.'

'My, my, marvellous Miss Marshall really has pulled out all the stops.' Tamara smiled – leastways, the curl of lips exposed a flash of white teeth that would have done a basking shark proud. And, leaning forward, she dropped her voice, donned an air of confidentiality that didn't fool Stella for an instant. 'Take it from me, you're wasted as a nanny, my dear. With talents like that you should be setting up in business. I can almost see the name in lights above the door. "The Marshall Domestic Consultancy",' she mocked. ' "Problems with staff? Not any more. Come to Marshalls. Nothing too small or too big. All grades and categories covered. Butler, baker, butcher-boy – oh, yes, and our especial speciality, replacements for runaway nannies –"'

'Talking of which,' Alex interrupted, the edge to his tone a thinly veiled warning, 'Carly's returned the Mini.'

The glass of red wine held in Stella's rigid fingers

slipped from her grasp and shattered noisily at her feet, liberally splashing her legs.

'I –'

'Don't move!' Alex commanded, up on his feet in an instant. 'You'll only tread glass into the house and give the mellowing Mrs Edwards an excuse to revert to type. I'll be back in a jiffy.'

He was as good as his word. With dustpan, brush and snatch of terry cloths, Alex cleared away the debris, practically kneeling at Stella's feet to wipe away the spreading stain of wine that was thankfully confined to her legs. Bare legs. The soft, rhythmic stroke of Alex's hands – not skin to skin, exactly, but more than enough to unnerve an already thoroughly unnerved Stella, whose cheeks were soon glowing to match the wine in the replacement glass he pressed between her fingers.

'All done,' he murmured, smiling up at her, blue eyes locking with hers and seeing to the centre of her soul. And they were alone. Man and woman. And the message passed between them. Love. Given, received, acknowledged, returned. And Stella smiled, and Alex's smile deepened. And somewhere close at hand a woman pointedly yawned.

'You were saying?' Tamara prompted stonily.

'I was saying?' he queried pleasantly, regaining his place beside her.

'The errant nanny,' Tamara needled. 'Don't tell me she's actually had the nerve to show her face?'

'Hardly,' he demurred. 'But she has had the decency to post the car keys. Along with directions to its whereabouts. I'll have someone pick it up first thing tomorrow.'

'Somewhere close at hand, I hope?' Beth probed politely, while Stella's grip on her glass threatened to snap the slender stem and recreate chaos.

'Close enough,' Alex conceded lightly. 'For a car park in central London, that is.'

'So the girl's safe?' Stella spoke, careful to focus her gaze on the swirl of liquid in her glass.

'Safe? I didn't doubt it for an instant,' Alex retorted sharply. 'Did you?'

'It – crossed my mind,' she conceded awkwardly, forced to raise her lids, look Alex in the eye, forced to witness the pain in cloudy blue depths. Because Alex's mind was attuned to Stella's. No need for words, she acknowledged bitterly. For with fresh speculation in the Press, not to mention visits from the local CID, the unspeakable was screaming loud and clear between them. Wife, accidental drowning – or something more sinister? The wife's child's nanny, missing presumed – what?

'Nineteen? Twenty?' Stella stalled. 'And suddenly not around. In this day and age, you can't be too careful, don't you think?'

'I was the girl's employer, not her keeper,' he reminded her coolly, impatient fingers tugging at his tie and snapping the topmost buttons of his shirt. The strangely casual result tugged at Stella's heartstrings. 'And if her family had been worried, they'd no doubt have made enquiries.'

'First stop Freshfields? Always assuming they

knew, of course. Always assuming you'd even bothered to let them know?'

'Like I said, I was her employer, not her keeper. And she is a fully fledged adult. Her life, her decision, her lack of responsibility.'

'And now she's safe and sound so we can all stop worrying? Not that "worry" is the word that springs to mind,' Stella heard herself needling – a ridiculous overreaction in any case, since Carly had been 'missing' for barely three days before calling.

'I don't think –'

'No,' Stella snapped bitterly. 'That's painfully obvious. But suppose –'

'It had been Carilyn?' Beth interrupted mildly, placing a warning hand on Stella's arm. 'That's it, isn't it, Stella?' she half probed, half reminded, grey eyes full of silent messages that Stella was dangerously close to giving herself away. And why create waves when she'd be leaving shortly in any case? 'You're imagining how you'd feel if Carilyn was missing and no one bothered to let you know?'

'Carilyn?' Tamara, vaguely amused by the spat that had blown up out of nowhere, was only vaguely curious as to why.

'My sister,' Stella supplied flatly. 'And Beth's right. I'd be worried sick.'

'And in the absence of parents,' Alex murmured softly, eyes narrowing thoughtfully, 'you'd have every right to be annoyed. Like Beth, I think I'm beginning to see. And you're perfectly right, as always,' he conceded. 'I should have made my own enquiries.'

'Only you didn't?'

'Just a trace on the car,' he conceded frankly. 'And even that proved fruitless. I can only assume the girl went to ground for some reasons of her own.'

'Probably pregnant,' Tamara tossed in maliciously. 'And deserted by the father – assuming she could pin it on one in particular.'

Stella saw red. 'Carly –'

'Wasn't the sort to sleep around,' Hannah interrupted mildly, pointedly turning her gaze on Tamara. 'Unlike some I could mention.'

'Meaning?'

Hannah smiled, spread her hands. 'It was – just an observation,' she conceded, her expression curiously bland. 'No offence intended. But if the cap –'

'Not a good idea,' Alex cut in smoothly. 'The car's recoverable, the girl's safe, the subject's closed.'

'And the reason Carly left in the first place?' Stella probed politely.

'Irrelevant, wouldn't you say? Since Mandy's all set to step into her shoes? And, at the risk of starting World War III, I'd say Tamara's assessment probably hit the nail on the head in the first place. Now, can we please drop the subject once and for all?'

'Time I was leaving in any case,' Beth conceded wryly, coming to her feet and darting another pointed glance at Stella in the process. 'I'll pop up and collect Connor and then I'd better head for home.'

'And we'll see you next month.' Hannah nodded at Beth, baffling Stella completely. 'Always assuming you've overcome your fear of horses?'

'Ah! You noticed?' Beth smiled broadly, tucked a stray lock of hair behind an ear. 'And I thought I'd hidden it well.'

'So you had,' Hannah reassured her, deftly swinging her chair round to lead the way inside. 'But the moment I mentioned the loan of a hat and tackle, you went a whiter shade of pale.'

'But, phobia notwithstanding, you'll be joining us again?' Alex was as puzzled as Stella, eyebrow raised in enquiry.

'If you don't mind?' Beth murmured pleasantly. 'Hannah's been kind enough to offer the use of the stables for the day. Oh, not for me,' she added hastily, 'I –'

'Beth helps out with a disabled children's group,' Hannah cut in. 'And she happened to mention a sponsor had let them down. And since I knew you wouldn't mind . . .'

'Nothing to mind about. What happens at the stables is squarely down to you. I'm only surprised you didn't hit on the idea sooner.'

'It's – crossed my mind,' Hannah conceded, clearly steering the conversation around to something else that was eating away at her. 'Of course,' she added carefully, 'to make the day really special, we could always throw open the swimming pool.'

'I –'

'Don't say no. Please, Giff. Don't say no without giving it some thought at least. Please, Giff. Pretty please,' she pleaded, fastening her gaze on to his and treating Alex to a very winning smile. 'Because seeing

222

a disabled child in water is seeing the child and the child alone – seeing the child competing as an equal. And that's important. I know.'

'I –'

'You don't even have to be here,' Hannah interrupted softly. 'You simply have to say the word. Your house, your pool, your decision.'

'And if I say no?'

'*If* – not when?' Hannah pointed out, a hint of a smile playing about the corners of her mouth. 'Believe me, Giff, that small word speaks volumes.'

CHAPTER 12

The nightmare again. A pillow over her face, a mocking peal of laughter. Struggling, pushing, fighting. Jerking wide awake, heart thumping nineteen to the dozen. A nightmare. A bad dream, Stella reassured herself, eyes adjusting to the gloom, the familiar objects of a room clearly empty save for Stella herself. No place to hide. No shady corners, no window bay or niche – nothing beyond the simple cloak of darkness. Yet Stella was reminded of a poem she'd learned at school: ' "Is there anybody there?" said the traveller, knocking on the moonlit door.' And, whilst no answer was the stern reply, a host of creatures had been listening. Listening, watching, waiting.

The tiny hairs on the back of Stella's neck began to rise like the hackles of a cat. Listening. Watching. Waiting. No place to hide, she reminded herself, and yet the sudden splash of light from the bedside lamp was still unnervingly reassuring.

She glanced round the neat and tidy room – not a thing out place since she'd barely a thing to put in it: wardrobe to dressing table, to chair, to window, to door – firmly closed because she'd taken to sleeping with it closed – heavy book propped against it lest an unknown, unwanted visitor should feel the need to call unexpectedly. Sure enough the book hadn't been moved and the door was firmly shut. No place to hide. And yet Stella was unnerved, was allowing the tensions of the house – and Alex – to unnerve her.

A sudden noise. An icy trickle the length of her spine. And then the relief. James. Crying out, stirring, settling, whimpering, and, since the night was warm, doubtless in need of drink.

Without bothering to don the cotton robe draped handy at the foot of the bed, Stella padded silently through to James's bedroom, pausing on the threshold, half convinced she was imagining things. But no. Intense blue eyes returned her gaze unblinkingly.

'Hello, little man. Couldn't sleep, hey? You and me both,' she ruefully conceded as James wrestled himself into a sitting position, smiling a gummy smile before pulling himself up by the rails. 'Thirsty, too, I'll bet.' Lifting him out, she automatically checked his nappy. Damp. And it would be damper still before the night was over, so she'd change him first, then sit in the chair and rock him, soothe him – soothe herself more with the normality of the routine. Drink, nappy, cuddle, sleep. Only James wasn't the least bit sleepy, and so Stella smiled, allowed the baby his head as he pushed himself upright on her lap, his heady flash of triumph infectious.

'Determined to walk, huh?' Stella probed, laughing. 'Well, maybe you are at that. Only not tonight, my adventurous one. Tonight I'm going to allow ten minutes of freedom exactly, and then it's beddybyes. For both of us. Are you listening, James Gifford? It's back to bed and sleep. But first,' she insisted, standing, swinging James on to her hip and sashaying into the kitchen, 'I'm entitled to a drink myself, wouldn't you say?'

Ten minutes. Cradling a glass of water as she rocked back and forth in the chair, she watched James's surprisingly fast progress around the floor of his bedroom. He'd be eleven months old in a week or so, and a few weeks later would reach a milestone; his first birthday. And Stella wouldn't be around to witness the celebrations. Celebrations? A party with jelly and cakes and balloons and a doting papa laden down with presents? Or the doting stepmother elect, all sweetness and light as she lit the candle on the cake.

A knife-blade twisted. Because the idea was absurd? Stella probed. Another day, another milestone, another example of Alex's indifference? Or because she couldn't bear the thought of Tamara queening it at Freshfields, monopolizing the father whilst continuing to ignore the son? Poor James. Poor little rich boy. A bit like Alex himself, in fact. Everything that money could buy bar that elusive, all-important commodity: love.

Only Stella loved James, and, absurd though it seemed, given the brevity of their acquaintance, Stella loved Alex. Arrogant Alex Gifford. A man of many facets, she was beginning to see. Hard-working, highly successful, given the public standing of a multi-million pound organization, and clearly possessed of all the right attributes; an iron fist in a velvet glove, the ability to crack the whip and drive his workforce hard balanced by an ability to arbitrate, mediate, persuade and cajole until any lingering opposition was swept aside. Because what Alex Gifford wanted, Alex Gifford was determined to have. Stella – no. Not Stella, she told herself, willing herself to believe it. Because in three days' time Stella would be gone. Unbearable thought. She closed her mind to the bleakness that lay ahead, burying the pain beneath the normality of the routine.

Catch James, change James, cuddle James. Smile, blow him a kiss goodnight and then stand out of sight, waiting, listening, hoping he'd settle, because a string of disturbed nights was beginning to take its toll on Stella and she needed to be strong to face Alex, to hold out against Alex. Stella was leaving. On Monday. No arguments. A temporary arrangement was coming to an end. And if life for Alex Gifford went on pretty much as before, who was Stella to voice her disapproval? She'd tried. She'd gone above and beyond the line of duty. She'd done what she could to bring father and son closer together, and if she hadn't been successful, it wasn't for the want of trying.

Tired. Like James, she was flagging, ready for sleep. Dimming the light, she padded silently back to her room, automatically checking the mirror for messages in passing and smiling despite it all. She pulled up on the threshold. And went cold – oh, so cold.

'Oh, hell.'

Hell indeed. A perfectly made bed, but chaos all around. Stella's clothes pulled from their hangers and strewn across the floor – skirts, blouses, panties and bras. Someone, heaven alone knew who, had been rummaging through her underclothes. The very thought was enough to make her flesh creep. She felt unclean. Like the victim of a burglary. It was a gross invasion of privacy – an imposition, a violation. And Stella wanted to cry, to crawl beneath the duvet, bury her head in the pillow and cry. Because someone in this house was determined to drive her away.

Not Hannah, she realized instinctively. Because Hannah was aware of Stella's plans, knew that Stella would be leaving on Monday. And not Hannah for the glaringly obvious reason of mobility. And yet surely Tamara was equally aware that Stella was leaving? Mrs Edwards, then, continuing to harbour some strange resentment despite the apparent truce? She was still blissfully unaware of the latest turn of events; it might even make sense. Only nothing made sense, not any more.

Closing her mind, blinking back the tears, she swept the flimsy garments into a heap and piled them back into the drawers, draping dresses, skirts and blouses over the back of the chair. Time enough to sort it out in the morning. To pack, Stella told herself grimly, reaching for a scrap of lace peeping out from beneath the valance. No, correction, two scraps of – A handkerchief? A handkerchief. Stella's fingers curled round it automatically. A large square of white with its telltale signature – that distinctive letter A in the corner.

'No!' Stunned, Stella sank down on the bed, the newly made bed, when she distinctly remembered pushing the duvet to one side before padding through to James. Newly made. With a brand new negligee spread across the pillow, its flimsy edges disappearing beneath the duvet. Stella's negligee. Valencienne lace and an impulse buy at the end of her last commission. Unworn. Unwearable. Because someone had coolly and calmly taken a pair of scissors and cut it from neckline to hem before carefully rearranging it. Which begged the fifty-thousand-dollar-question – who, and why?

Why, why, why? she asked herself, her mind automatically filtering out the most damning piece of evidence. Not Alex. Please God, not Alex, she silently intoned over and over as she hugged herself, rocked herself. Like the message on the mirror, it was a bitchy gesture, a female gesture. It couldn't be Alex. It *wouldn't* be Alex. It was Alex who wanted her stay, she reassured herself. And he was hardly likely to accomplish that by this sort of intimidation. Presumably the same sort of intimidation suffered by Carly and a string of nannies before her. No, not Alex, she insisted. This was the work of a devious mind, a warped mind. A mind capable of murder? an unwanted voice insisted on asking. No! No! No!

So. Time to talk to Alex. Tomorrow. Time for Alex to put a stop to this ridiculous state of affairs once and for all.

* * *

She bearded the lion in his den.

'We need to talk.'

'Had a change of mind, Stella? Having second thoughts?'

'You know I haven't. But I can't leave –'

'Oh, but you can, Stella,' he interrupted silkily. 'Bright and early Monday morning. You're going. Walking out. Leaving. Your life, your decision. End of discussion. Talk? Pray, what is there left to say at this late stage?' he demanded frigidly, swinging the chair round to face her fully. 'The size of your pay-off?'

'Don't be ridiculous. The normal rates apply, as well you know.'

'Plus the agency's cut. Ten per cent, I believe?' he reminded her slyly, producing chequebook and pen from an inside pocket and tossing both on to the desk with a gesture of disdain. 'And, since this particular arrangement is unusual, we might as well settle it here and now. Tell me, Stella,' he entreated coldly, snatching the pen to scrawl her name before signing his own with a flourish, 'that's ten per cent of what, precisely?'

Stella licked her lips, searched the fog of her mind for a realistic figure. Pay-day. And with a sleepless night behind her, she was functioning automatically, unthinkingly. Shower and dress. Feed James, bath James, play with James. Sit and watch as James flagged, struggled to stay awake, finally slept the sleep of the innocent. And then, leaving an eager-faced Mandy to hold the fort, Stella had forced herself the length of the corridor and down the stairs, her heart growing colder by the moment.

Because she was afraid. It was time to talk, not to mention pray that Alex would listen. The house was poison. There was evil lurking in corners and it was high time Alex was told. Hannah? Tamara? Agnes Edwards? Or, the unthinkable, the unmentionable, the unbearable – Alex. No! Stella closed her mind. Not Alex. She loved Alex. She trusted Alex. It couldn't be Alex. And running through her head, over and over, a relentless refrain: verdict misadventure, death by drowning, accidental drowning, verdict misadventure, misadventure, murder, murder.

Murder!

No! Stella squeezed back the tears, dug fingernails into the palms of her hand in an effort to stay in control. Not Alex. She had to believe it. Please God, how she wanted to believe it. 'I –'

'Come now,' he rasped, ice-blue eyes oozing scorn. 'Don't be coy. A labourer is worthy of her hire, don't forget, and the normal rates of pay won't have slipped Stella Marshall's razor-sharp mind. Name a figure, Stella. Or double it, treble it – times it by ten if it makes you feel better,' he tossed out absurdly. 'But you decide. Name your price and name it now.'

'I can't.'

Expressive eyebrows rose. 'Can't? Now there's a surprise. Stella Marshall admitting to a failing. Beginning to feel the strain?' he demanded, leaning forward, the sneering curl of lips completely at odds with the air of confidentiality. 'Can't stand the pace, hey? Another week, another baby, another job well done. And it's off with the old and on with the new and never so much as a backward glance. So hectic, so demanding, so exacting,' he scorned. 'But dear me, I was almost forgetting. *You* set the pace. Here today, gone tomorrow. Tend them and leave them, and out of sight means out of mind. Your decision, Stella,' he reminded her grimly. 'Not mine. Your life, your decision, your responsibility. Like I said, name your price. No? Fine.'

He nodded, swung back to the desk, completed the cheque in a trice and was up on his feet before Stella had time to react, closing in on her, menacing, unnerving.

Reaching for her hand, he thrust the cheque between her clenched fingers, and, second-guessing her reaction, iron fingers closed around hers. 'Take it,' he insisted tersely, his vicious gaze wounding. 'You'll take it and you'll use it, and the moment it's cleared by the bank is the moment we're all square. Understand, Stella? I won't owe you, and you won't owe me so much as another thought. No unfinished business, Stella. It's a job well done and now it's over and done with. All you have to do is prove it. Proof. My proof – and yours. Understand?'

Stella glanced down, did a double take and wished she hadn't bothered. 'I can't take this. It's – it's obscene.'

'I don't agree. It's my assessment of your worth and you can take it from me; Alex Gifford is a man who likes value for money.'

'You're mad. Carly –'

'Don't worry, Stella, Carly was paid the going rate.

But that was then and this is now,' he slipped in slyly. 'And a man must move with the times. Another week, another nanny, another rate of pay. Only fair, wouldn't you say?'

'So Carly's loss is Mandy's gain?'

'I beg your pardon?'

'Mandy. Carly's replacement. And a *permanent* replacement at that. Understand?'

'Perfectly, Stella. You're calling my bluff. Pay Mandy a small fortune or else.' He barred his teeth in mocking semblance of a smile. 'Tell me, though – just out of idle curiosity, of course. Pay Mandy or else *what*, precisely?'

'I'd say that's between you and your conscience – always assuming you have one.'

'Indeed. And supposing I haven't? Supposing I lie through my teeth and say what you want to hear? Would you know, would you even care?'

'I wouldn't need to. *You'd* know, and that's what really matters.'

'And if I give my word?'

'Then I'll believe you.'

A pause, intense blue eyes locking with hers, searching hers, seeing to the centre of her soul, and Stella held her breath, aware of a subtle change in atmosphere. Because the anger had burnt itself out and Stella's simply stated faith was balm to a battered ego. Stella believed. Little enough to believe in, maybe, but it was enough.

'Thank you.'

'For what?'

'You know what.'

'Yes.' She dropped her gaze, attempting to close her mind, block out the message he was silently conveying, denying Alex, denying herself just as badly.

'Stella.' Soft. Less a word than a caress, stirring the blood in her veins. 'Look at me, Stella. Please, Stella.'

Words caressing, fingers caressing. Idle thumbs tracing erotic circles on the inside of her wrists. And Stella was losing the battle, had to break away, had to get away before Alex broke down her resistance. She wanted him; Alex wanted her. And whilst Stella was short on practice, this man was an expert. And so he'd take her. Take her, pleasure her, teach her body how to love. And Stella would be snared. She loved him, she wanted him, she needed him — a bitter-sweet craving she could never hope to salve without a long-term commitment. Love. Man and woman. Alex and Stella. Toby and Stella. Toby and Francine. No.

'No!' She pushed him away and stepped backwards, seeing the hurt, the pain, the sheer incredulity etched in granite features. Because Alex Gifford was a man of the world and Alex Gifford wasn't programmed for denial. He wanted, therefore he'd take. Simple. Only Stella wasn't playing.

'Fine.' Terse. Anger simmering beneath the surface. Hurt pride, Stella insisted, achingly aware that with the right word from Alex — or the wrong one — Stella would succumb. 'Have it your own way,' he chillingly conceded, the pulse beating a rapid tattoo at his temple drawing her gaze, giving Stella's churning mind something to focus on. 'Turn your back and walk away,' he scorned, eyes nuggets of ice in the mask of his face. 'First James, now me,' he rasped. 'Walk away and don't look back. And to think,' he tagged on bitterly, 'to think you had the nerve to lecture *me* on the subject of conscience.'

'My conscience is clear.'

'And mine isn't? Is that what your implying?'

'No, Alex, I was simply stating a fact.'

'Liar.'

'I never lie.'

'You want me.'

A lightning change of subject, but the challenge was unmistakable. Because even if Stella couldn't speak a lie, she was horribly afraid she was living one.

'So I want you,' she conceded lightly. 'I don't have to indulge each and every whim that crosses my mind.'

'Whim? *Whim?*' he all but bellowed, his head snapping up at the unintended insult. And to Stella's amazement he threw back his head and laughed. 'Why, thank you, Stella Marshall,' he drawled. 'Queen of the understated put-down. Remind me never to cross you when you're really in the mood for a fight.'

'Unlikely, since I'm leaving.'

'So you are. Monday morning, bright and early. So I guess this is the cue for goodbye. Goodbye, Stella,' he barked, rugged features impassive. 'It's been – quite something to have known you. A pleasure. A privilege. A real education in fact. But now it's good-bye. And, since I'm cutting it fine for the airport . . .' He shrugged, swung away, a calculated gesture of dismissal as he rummaged through the drawers of his desk. Keys, passport, wad of notes and traveller's cheques. Italian lire, Stella noted automatically. So it really was goodbye. And it hurt. Because Alex had dismissed her. Back turned, attention diverted. Out of sight, out of mind, to quote his oft-used phrase.

'But – you can't leave now,' Stella wailed absurdly. 'We need to talk.'

'You may need to talk. My needs, I assure you, are much more basic.'

'Sex?'

'Biological, mechanical, functional?' He paused, angled his head, fixed her with a faintly mocking stare. 'No, Stella,' he contradicted mildly. 'Not sex. Man and woman making love. Love, Stella,' he repeated, straightening, pausing, allowing his gaze to cross the room and touch her. 'Kissing, touching, tasting, caressing, exploring. Pleasure given and received.'

'Sex.'

'Not in my book. I make love. I enjoy. But perhaps the men your life haven't my finesse?' He shrugged, smiled, held out his palms in casual invitation. 'Why not give it a try? Who knows? You might just discover what you're missing.'

'I doubt it.'

'Ah, yes, Stella, but therein lies the rub. Doubt.' Another smile, another shrug. 'Face it, Stella, you don't know for sure. Your problem, not mine. But never let it be said I didn't try to warn you.' He raised a hand to his temple in jaunty salute. 'Goodbye, Stella. See you around some time. Maybe.'

'You're leaving?'

'And let me guess, you're missing me already?'

'Hardly.'

'But you will. Give it time. You'll see.'

'Alex Gifford —'

'Stella Marshall?'

'Oh, man, but you're impossible,' she bit out, impatient fingers pushing a stray lock of hair from her forehead. 'Arrogant, pig-headed, downright impossible. And will you please stop looking at your watch when I'm trying to talk?'

'Past tense, Stella. Time to split. *Ciao, signorina. Arrivederci* and goodbye.'

'Alex —'

'More talk? I should be so lucky all of a sudden.'

'It's important, Alex.

'Not so important that it won't keep.'

'Your opinion or mine?' she snapped. 'Well, fine. Don't say I didn't warn you. And since James's welfare is clearly unimportant —'

'Unfair, Stella. The child wants for nothing.'

'That, Alex Gifford, is a matter of opinion.'

'So stick around,' he slipped in slyly. 'Give the child what he needs, since you're such an expert. Only you won't.'

'You know I can't.'

'Can't — or daren't?' he rasped.

'Irrelevant,' she clipped. 'And you know full well I hadn't planned to stay.'

'Precisely. I rest my case. James's welfare is unimportant.'

'My, my, progress indeed,' Stella scorned, just the twin spots of colour in her cheeks betraying her annoyance.

'Meaning?'

'James. You're not as indifferent as you'd have the world believe. 'The child,' she emphasized grimly, 'has a name, and the child has needs. I'm just relieved to note your acknowledgement of both.'

'And on that happy note,' he growled, the warning muted but present nonetheless, 'I really must fly. Literally. If you'll excuse me.'

'But –'

'No buts. No long drawn-out goodbyes. No second thoughts. Like you,' he pointedly needled, an Arctic smile crossing his features, 'I'm going, and, furthermore, I'm going now. The difference is, I'm coming back. Enjoy the rest of your life, my dear, and always remember that precious Stella Marshall maxim; Thou shalt not get involved. Safer that way. Boring – but safe.'

A grim nod, a final glance around the room and he snapped shut the briefcase, setting the lock with a careless flick, long, tapering fingers closing round the handle. For Alex was ready to leave, was running late, by his own admission, was clearly cutting it fine, judging from the impatient glance at his wristwatch, the almost imperceptible tightening of lips as he swept past. But if Alex had dismissed Stella, Stella was determined to make one last stand.

'Alex –'

'Too late. You had your chance and you've blown it.'

'But James –'

'Wants for nothing. Ditto his new nursemaid.'

'Everything that money can buy?' she scorned, bringing up the rear and resisting the urge to clutch at his coat-tails. 'So I've noticed. But it's more than that. There's – something wrong.'

'With James?' He stopped dead in his tracks, a distracted Stella careering full pelt into him.

'No. Not James,' she gasped, the breath leaving her body at the shock of connection. 'The house. There's something wrong.'

'The house?' he mouthed incredulously. 'You can't be serious? OK, OK,' he soothed impatiently, catching her expression. 'So drop me a line. Pick up the phone. The Hotel Hermitage in Rome,' he carelessly informed her. 'Who knows? You might even hit lucky and catch me in.'

'Alex –'

'Alex! Darling!' A heady cloud of perfume drifted past Stella as the younger woman tripped lightly down the final flight of stairs and launched herself into his arms.

'Tam! What on earth –'

'Such wonderful news,' she trilled, her upturned face silent invitation for a kiss. 'Just wait until you –' No time to wait as Alex dipped his head, mouth to mouth, lips to lips, the careless intimacy driving the breath from Stella's body all over again. And, frozen in time, Stella could only stand and watch, and wait, and grow oh, so cold.

A lifetime later Alex raised his head, his gaze

reaching out to Stella, a curious mix of pain and defiance shadowing his eyes.

Not so Tamara. Sensing Alex's preoccupation, she spun round, couldn't resist a heady flash of triumph. 'Goodness, you look dreadful,' she informed Stella gleefully, threading her fingers through Alex's and pointedly pulling him close. 'Don't tell me you're missing us already?'

'Hardly,' Stella clipped, caught between the devil and the deep blue sea, the need to walk away, close her eyes, close her mind, tempered by some vestige of pride. Pride. Defiance. Indifference. Show Alex – and the world – she really didn't care. Only she was lying. And, catching Alex's narrowed gaze, she was horribly afraid that Alex knew she was.

Nerves as taut as fiddle strings, she swung away, Tamara's low laugh triggering a trickle of tears. Not that Alex would notice. He was too caught up in Tamara for that.

'Darling.' The casual endearment drifted back to Stella as leaden feet took her closer to the kitchen and safety. 'You'll never believe it. Such wonderful news,' Tamara breathed. 'The break I've been waiting for. GG phoned. You remember GG – GG Jay, the advertising ace . . .' A torrent of words, snatches of words that Stella's reeling mind hadn't the strength – or the inclination – to unscramble. But the final note of woe was strangely incongruous and halted Stella in her tracks. 'Oh, but, Alex, you haven't time to listen now. Oh, darling –'

'Nonsense, sweetheart.' A husky interruption, the

very tone a velvet caress. 'Of course I've time,' Alex reassured her smokily. 'For you, Tam, I've all the time in the world.'

'But your plane –'

'Miss one, catch the next,' he airily informed her. 'This is more important than boring old business. And believe me, Tam, I can't wait to hear all about it in triplicate.'

And because Stella was listening, watching, waiting, hating herself for the weakness but unable to tear herself away – or maybe because her presence simply didn't impinge – Alex drew the younger woman into his arms, tucked a tender finger beneath her chin and tilted that exquisitely sculpted head for a kiss that seemed to last for ever.

CHAPTER 13

'A fashion shoot? In Tunisia? Tamara!' Hannah, her voice and eyes oozing scorn, swung herself through the double doorway and into the airy brightness of the lounge – the smaller of the reception rooms, though no less impressive, a legacy of Alex's mother, who'd gutted the interior more than thirty years ago, Stella had been amazed to discover. Lots of light and space and uncluttered lines that had clearly proved a Godsend to Hannah. Hannah laughed, a high-pitched sound that grated on Stella's ears. 'Fashion shoot? If the truth's known,' she scathingly pronounced, 'she's probably little more than a glorified tea girl.'

'Aye, well.' The housekeeper's smile was sly as she brought up the rear. 'That's not what I heard. Over the moon, she was, and as for Mr Gifford, he clean forgot that he'd a plane to catch.'

'You mean Giff hasn't gone?' Casual, too causal by far, Stella decided, a prickle of alarm running the length of her spine. 'Pity. I've promised to join pushy Terri Clarke in that ostentatious heap she calls a home. South Ridings! Talk about pretension. Heaven only knows how I talked my way into that one. A house party! Tedious conversation, lukewarm food and miles and miles of draughty corridors.' Hannah smothered a yawn. 'Still, I suppose I could always rustle up a migraine.'

'And waste those lovely clothes you've bought? You go, lovey,' the housekeeper urged. 'There's nothing to keep you here, and it might just be good for business. Rumour has it Jen and Johnny Rogers are dropping by for dinner.'

'Lord Rogers, Master of the Hunt?'

'The one and only.'

'Oh, goodie. We can talk horses. Who knows where it might lead to? But if Giff's home for dinner –' Breaking off, she caught the older woman's rueful shake of the head. 'Ah! He won't be home for dinner?'

'Drove her ladyship to the airport and caught a later plane. Mind you, the way they were carrying on, I'm surprised they managed to point the car in the right direction. If I hadn't seen it for myself, I wouldn't have believed it. Talk about besotted.'

A moue of distaste marred a heart-shaped face. 'Yuk! How disgusting. How surprising. I thought Giff had more sense these days.'

'You and me both, lovey, you and me both. Still there's no accounting for taste.'

'Or lack of it. South Ridings. Hmm, I wonder . . .' Hannah's voice trailed off, and, glancing across, Stella caught the expression in a set of innocent blue eyes and felt a shiver of apprehension. 'I don't suppose, Stella, you'd care to keep me company at the Clarkes?'

Stella closed her book. Not that she'd been reading. Thinking, brooding, giving Mandy space in the nursery, yes. Reading, no. But at least she'd been alone. 'But I haven't been invited,' she demurred, the very thought anathema. The country set. Horsy women and parlour games and polite conversation with plum-voiced men dressed to the nines and drinking. Heaven forbid. Give her a quiet night in with a book any time.

'Oh, that wouldn't matter,' Hannah airily pronounced. 'Terri Clarke owes me. I'm sure I could swing it. Who knows? It might even be fun.'

'I doubt it,' Stella murmured dryly. 'And besides, I'm needed here to look after James.'

'Mandy –'

'Will move her things in on Monday. In the meantime, she is entitled to an evening off.'

'And you're not?'

'I – haven't done too badly,' Stella reminded her, the concern unexpected and touching. Or maybe Stella's imminent departure had triggered a spurt of generosity. 'And James –'

'He won't wake, won't stir – sure as eggs is eggs he won't miss you when you've gone. Anyway, Mrs Edwards would do the honours just this once, wouldn't you Mrs E?' Another winning smile, shining eyes reminiscent of cornflowers dancing in the breeze.

The housekeeper's smile was tinged with relief. 'Not tonight, lovey. I've promised my sister I'd stay. She's nervous in the house alone, and with Jack away on business . . .'

'South Ridings, here I come. Alone. Talking of which –' She broke off, paused, and another prickle of alarm ran the length of Stella's spine as she raised her head, met Hannah's gaze full on. The curiously bland expression in the younger woman's eyes was thoroughly unnerving. And then Hannah smiled. Slyly. 'It looks like you and James will have the house all to yourselves, hey, Stella.'

Alone. In a house the size of a small mansion. A house that could give her the creeps when it was bustling with people. Yet better alone, Stella decided, wandering aimlessly round the nursery, bereft of occupation. No laundry, no tidying up, no nursery meals to plan. Because an eager-faced Mandy had everything under control. To all intents and purposes, Stella was redundant. And she was alone. Apart from James. And the demons of her mind were closing in on her.

'Damn, damn and damn you, Alex Gifford,' she railed vehemently, pacing up and down the sitting room. 'Why couldn't you listen? Five minutes. That's all I needed. Five minutes to explain, but, no, spend five minutes with the hired hand discussing your son, indirectly or otherwise? Heaven forbid when you've a plane to catch. "Miss one, catch the next,"' she scorned. 'And that's what you did in the end. Thanks to Tamara. As for me –'

She broke off, sure she'd caught a noise, strained her ears, caught nothing but the creaks and sighs of an old house settling and decided she was overreacting. She needed a drink. But, short of stealing down to the kitchen and raiding the pantry for the cooking sherry, she would have to do without. The demon drink. Contributory factor in Chrissie Gifford's death. And, despite a dozen or more wineries dotted about the globe, Alex had never eschewed the habit of keeping all things vaguely alcoholic under lock and key. Only Chrissie, presumably, had had a source he hadn't been aware of. Or a supplier. Supplier of booze, supplier of drugs. Poor Alex. Life must have been hell for both of them.

Another sound broke the silence. The sound of an empty stomach rumbling. Time to eat. Humming lightly to herself, she pottered about the kitchen, inspecting cupboards and fridge. Precious little to choose from. Two lonely-looking eggs, but vegetables aplenty, so Hobson's would have to do. Omelette. Spanish. Dice the veg and put the pan on to heat, whisk the eggs into a froth. Knob of butter, dash of salt and pepper and –

Somewhere in the distance a door slammed. Stella froze. Just the wind, she reassured herself, aware the evening breeze had stiffened. But she opened the door to the hallway, and she stood and she listened and she waited. Nothing. Just a screaming, sighing silence.

Only partly reassured, she propped the door ajar before switching her attention back to the stove, and, damn and blast, while she'd been standing having hysterics, she'd let the butter burn!

Start again. Drain the dregs on to kitchen paper, wash and size the pan, turn the heat up on the grill and she was ready – edgy but ready, she acknowledged wryly, reaching for the basin as the grandfather clock at the foot of the stairs began to chime the hour, the sound echoed eerily through the stairwell. The grandfather clock. The same clock that Stella recalled patting in passing. A temperamental clock. That had stopped. That occasionally responded to a gentle tap by coughing into life. Only it hadn't. Then. Oh, God.

The basin she'd been clutching slipped through rigid fingers, shattering at her feet, spraying her legs with the sticky goo of beaten egg. So bang went her supper. Not that she was hungry. Just a bundle of nerves. And sticky. Even stickier by the time she'd mopped up the mess. And the smell of raw egg was insidiously clawing.

Soak in the bath. Long, hot and fragrant. The background sound of the radio masked the silence, soothing. Next problem; shrug a bathrobe over her shoulders or get dressed? Hardly worth the effort of dressing, since she'd soon be going to bed. Alone. All alone in a house that gave her the creeps, had given Carly the creeps.

The phone rang – the melodious trill of her mobile. Nik, taking Stella at her word and wasting no time phoning through a commission, no doubt. Only she was wrong.

'Carly – thank heavens. I've been worried sick.'

'Not half as worried as I was when Danny passed on your message. Listen, Stell, you've got to get away – tonight. Please, Stell, promise you won't stay a single moment longer than it takes to pack. You've got to get away. Now. Tonight. Before something awful happens. Please, Stell, promise you'll leave –'

'Bright and early Monday morning,' Stella cut in mildly. 'I can't leave tonight, love. You've got to understand, I can't leave James alone. We're alone. We're perfectly safe.'

'You and me both, hey, Stella? But *you* don't understand. Things started happening. They happened to me and they'll happen to you. Please, Stella. Leave. Now. Tonight.'

'James –'

'Bring James with you.'

'And have Alex sue me for kidnap on top of misrepresentation, impersonation, and a dozen other charges a man with clout could doubtless conjure out of nowhere? Oh, no. James and I are staying put.'

'Stella –'

'Listen, Carly –'

'No, Stella,' she interrupted wildly. 'You listen. You've got to get away. *Now*. Don't you understand?' she railed on a note of rising hysteria. 'If it happened to me, it will happen to you. Why on earth do you think I bolted, Stell? I loved that job; I loved that baby. But I had to get away, I had to escape. I just couldn't stand it any longer. Oh, Stell, Stell, Stell,' she murmured in anguish. 'It was awful. I was so afraid, and when Danny didn't believe me, I was convinced I was going mad. Only I wasn't. I was perfectly sane. Which means everything I thought was over-active imagination was real. Believe me, Stell, someone in that house was trying to kill me. Now do you see?'

★ ★ ★

Alex's problem, not Stella's she told herself grimly, but first he had to be told – wouldn't need telling if he'd spared the hired hand another five minutes. Only he hadn't. Which meant Stella would have to phone. Tomorrow, she promised herself. She'd work out the difference in time and give arrogant Alex Gifford an early-morning call. And if Stella's revelations caused a freshly baked croissant to stick in his throat, then tough.

Until then she was safe; she was alone. Alone in the house. Stella and James. No Alex, no Hannah, no Tamara, no brooding Mrs Edwards. No problem. She was alone. She was perfectly safe. But it had taken thirty frantic minutes to calm Carly down, convince her sister that the danger – if there had been a danger – was past. Stella was leaving. The need to frighten her away like the string of nannies before her was past. Ah, yes, a sly voice reminded her. But if that was the case, how to explain away last night's little visit? Just a not too subtle reminder, Stella reassured herself. Leave. Or else. It was the 'or else' that was worrying her. And the reason she chose to get dressed. Ludicrous, really. Bathrobe or dress; it would be all the same to a killer. Only she wasn't in any danger, of course. But that didn't stop her shutting out the rest of the house and wedging a thin block of wood under the door.

Footsteps. Not her imagination this time. Like the slam of a door thirty seconds earlier, and, since the air had calmed, she couldn't even blame the wind. Stella stifled the panic, chivvied herself for overreacting, kicked away the wedge with the tip of her toe and opened the door a fraction, peering out into the gloom. Footsteps. Echoing eerily through the stairwell. Strange how noises magnified at night. An empty house. An open-plan house. Huge, empty spaces and an expanse of parquet flooring. And footsteps. Crossing the hall, into the lounge and out again, receding, returning as Stella followed their progress in her mind's eye.

A single set of footsteps, reaching the foot of the stairs. And pausing. Then taking the stairs in leaps and bounds. Twenty seconds to cross the landing, heading for the bedrooms; Tamara's, the guest room, Alex's and – oh, God! The nocturnal visitor was heading this way. Twenty seconds, fifteen, ten. Stella's fingers tightened their grip on the first heavy object that came to hand. Don't panic. Mustn't panic. Ridiculous to panic. Because if someone really was hell-bent on scaring her – or worse – he or she would hardly broadcast their approach. They'd creep in. In the dead of night. While Stella slept. As they had done before. Which meant –

'Alex!'

'The one and only,' he grinned, his familiar, powerful form following his disembodied head through the door. 'Who else were you expecting, Stella? No, don't tell me, judging from your face I'd say Lucifer himself? Am I right or am right?'

'But – you're in Italy,' she breathed incredulously, backing away, putting space between them – nothing like enough space between them in a room this size. 'The wine fair –'

'Slight change of plan, my love. Like planes, wine conventions are ten a penny. Miss one, catch the next,' he reminded her airily. 'Believe me, this is much more important.'

'What is?'

'You. James. That gourmet meal I promised. Surely you can't have forgotten?'

'But that was then and this is now,' Stella said, the panic back with a vengeance. Because she was alone. With Alex. And she was afraid. Because she loved him. And if Alex had cancelled plans for Italy there had to be a reason. Stella. Alone. No Tamara, no Hannah, no tight-lipped Mrs Edwards. Just Alex and Stella – alone. And Alex had never made any secret of his motives. He wanted her.

'Now, then,' he mused, depositing an assortment of bags on the worktop and casting an appraising glance around the kitchen. 'First things first – something for the flowers, I think. Ah!' Blue eyes danced, logging the heavy-based vase Stella was clutching to her chest in an effort to instill some control. 'Stella, I do believe you're psychic. Roses. You do like roses?' he enquired absurdly, when Stella didn't speak, made not the slightest effort to relinquish her unconventional, totally inadequate weapon. And then, crossing to prise the vase from between rigid fingers, he went on, 'Don't tell me, madam prefers white, and she's too polite to say. I'm sorry.'

'Sorry? *Sorry?*' she railed, nerves in shreds, the sleepless nights, Alex, the vibes of the house beginning to take their toll. 'Alex Gifford, is that all you can say? Have you no soul, have you no compassion? Have you any idea what you've put me through these past ten minutes? Sneaking in here in the dead of night –'

'Seven-fifty-nine, to be precise,' he cut in mildly, his gaze flicking to the clock on the wall and back again. 'And forgive me for stating the obvious, but my own home at that.'

'But you weren't supposed to be here. You weren't coming back,' she bit out, the spicy tang of aftershave catching the back of her throat and triggering waves of emotion. Because he was here. And he was close. And Stella was achingly aware of everything about him. ' "*Ciao, signorina*"?,' she pointedly reminded him. ' "*Arrivederci* and goodbye"?'

'But if that's your only objection –'

'It isn't.'

'No, I can see that's it's not. Exit stage left, then.' Features impassive, he swung away, placing the vase on the sideboard in passing.

'But –' More panic, rivers of ice running in her veins. 'Where are you going?'

'Going, Stella? Why, surely it's obvious. I'm going back downstairs to the car and heading east – southeast, to be precise, since I'm supposed to be in Rome. And I'll drive and drive and drive, and the moment I feel you've had time to reconsider your position, I'll pull into a lay-by and phone. I'll phone, I'll apologize – for walking away this morning,' he explained softly, 'for fouling things up just now. And then I'll ask, which is what I should have done in the first place. Stella Marshall, would you do me the honour of joining me for dinner? Nothing special, you understand. Just a little something I've been planning all my life. Let me see, five minutes should cover it. Stella? Aw, Stella, sweetheart . . .' He was running his fingers through the crop of his hair, and the reproach in his tone was the final undoing for Stella. 'Please, sweetheart, please don't cry.'

Moving forward, he pulled a rigid Stella into his arms, holding, rocking, soothing, stroking, waiting. Until Stella's slender body was no longer racked with sobs. And then he slid an exquisitely tender finger beneath her chin, tilted back her head, locked his bottomless gaze on to to hers and smiled. And Stella smiled. And Alex kissed her.

'Asparagus. My favourite. And Hollandaise sauce with lashings of melted butter. Alex Gifford,' she beamed tremulously across the narrow width of the table, 'you must be psychic.'

'Just hopeful,' he demurred modestly, shaking out a napkin – an expensive, embossed Damask, that Stella could be sure hadn't been gathering dust on the shelves in the nursery. 'Still travelling hopefully, in fact. It would be nice to think that I'd arrived,' he explained as Stella raised an enquiring eyebrow. 'But I'm not about to make the mistake of taking anything for granted. Not this time.'

'No.' Stella swallowed a smile. Ditto Stella. She was sharing a meal with man, a dynamic man, and she wouldn't look beyond it. No anticipation, no wishful thinking. She'd simply take what Alex was offering and rejoice. And if that meant nothing more than sharing his bed, sharing his body for a priceless moment in time, then Stella would be content. For now.

'Oh!'

'Something wrong, my lady?' A light enquiry as Alex poured the wine, a deliciously crisp white from one of the Gifford estates. And, coming on top of a generous slug of brandy, was it any wonder Stella had mellowed?

'Good for shock,' Alex had insisted – a lifetime ago now, it seemed – having pressed the balloon into her hand, standing and watching as Stella took tentative sips and grimaced. 'Although, strangely enough, I don't recall having quite that effect on a woman before.'

No. Stella had smiled, leaving Alex in blissful ignorance. Time enough later for the problems of the world to impinge. Not to mention those closer to home at Freshfields. Like Stella's reason for being there, her innocent deception. And, despite her resolution, an icy finger had touched her heart.

Seeing the shadow in her eyes, Alex had smiled, dipped his head to kiss her again, forcing Stella to banish the thought. Later. And, please God, Alex would give her time to explain, would find it in his heart to forgive.

But now, in the meanwhile, logging the generous, though single delicate arrangement of asparagus set down between the flickering candles, the scarcity of cutlery that didn't seem to fit, Stella's mouth formed a perfect O.

'Fingers,' Alex explained, only didn't explain, sensing her dilemma.

'Fingers?'

'Uh-huh. Fingers. I feed you; you feed me. Simple. Watch.'

And Stella did, following each and every move that he made, the sun-bronzed arm that stretched across the table, shirt pushed back at the elbow, golden hairs glinting in the flicker of light as Alex's fingers hovered, pondered, weighed and rejected before closing round the first slender spear which he then dipped into the dish of creamy yellow sauce, ensuring a generous coating before gliding over to Stella.

And Stella opened her mouth, accepted the morsel and swallowed.

'My turn now. Or yours, depending how you view it.'

'Yours,' Stella agreed, aware of salt trickles of butter around her mouth and not the least bit self-conscious.

Erotic. As Alex had intended. A feast for lovers. Only they weren't. Yet. And, conscious it was only a matter of time, Stella trembled, and smiled, and glowed, and gave and received in turn.

The last spear went to Alex. 'Ambrosia,' he breathed as Stella brushed against his mouth. 'The food of the gods.' And as Stella made to pull away he parted his lips, took a single finger into his mouth and bit. Gently.

Deliciously erotic.

Taking her cue from Alex, who stood to clear away,

Stella reached for her napkin, caught his nod of disapproval and paused.

'No?' she queried smokily, gazing up through the veil of her lashes.

'Definitely no,' he agreed solemnly.

'Then how –?'

'Watch me,' he entreated thickly, moving round the table to her side. 'Look, no hands.' And he dipped his head and kissed her, and lapped, and drove the breath from her body at every point of contact.

Delightfully erotic.

No need for words as Alex's feast unfolded; bite-sized pieces of tenderloin pork in a sherry-cream sauce on a bed of wild rice, easily disposed off without benefit of a knife. Just glances, and smiles, his hand resting on the table, the upturned palm an open invitation for Stella to slide her own into the hollow, to tremble afresh at the contact, the heat, the blood-churning swirl of a lazy thumb. Unbearably erotic, fanning the flames that were spreading upwards and outwards to each and every part of her.

'Unfair,' she breathed when Alex broke off, leaned across to kiss the tingling palm.

'Madam wants more?'

'Much more,' she agreed solemnly. 'But patience is a virtue, so I'm told. Madam can wait.' A bitter-sweet denial – for both of them.

Alex nodded, rose, tugged her to her feet, kissed her upturned nose before leading her across to the sofa. 'If madam will sit,' he invited, 'sir will be pleased to serve the next course.' He returned a moment later with a covered bowl, fresh napkins and a knife.

'Fruit!' Stella exclaimed as Alex knelt at her feet, whisked away the cover.

'Disappointed, my love?'

'Never disappointed,' she reassured him, love in her eyes, her heart in her eyes as she leaned across to kiss the tip of his nose. She turned the kiss into a gentle nip of teeth and laughed aloud at Alex's howl of protest.

'Unfair,' he growled, but he was smiling. He spread one of the napkins over her lap and held out the bowl in silent invitation.

Decisions, decisions. So much to choose from – so much she barely recognized. Juicy purple figs and spicy pink-fleshed mangoes, pomegranate, persimmon, passion fruit, pear. The cocktail of texture and flavour was a heady combination, the touch of finger to lips a more potent elixir still. And Stella ate, and she waited, and she trembled.

'All gone,' she exclaimed, popping the last slice of mango into Alex's juice-stained mouth.

'Not quite,' he contradicted, and, like a magician producing a rabbit from a hat, whisked another tiny brown-skinned offering from somewhere out of sight.

'But – what is it?' she enquired, pert nose wrinkled in puzzlement. 'An apple – no. And yet . . .'

'Close, very close,' he acknowledged, a half-smile playing about the corners of his mouth. 'But not close enough, I'm afraid.' Taking the knife, he sliced it open, placed the two halves with their strange eye-shaped contents on to Stella's plate and raised an enquiring eyebrow. 'Guess.'

'Clue?' she prompted, more in hope than anticipation.

Alex shook his head. 'Guess.'

'But I can't guess. It's nothing I've ever seen before – nothing I've heard described. Unless it's Italian?' she ventured at last.

'Not this one,' he laughingly informed her. 'Harrods food hall. Late this afternoon. Though I suppose it could have been shipped in from anywhere.'

'Huh! Some help you are. Well?'

He cradled one of the halves in the palm of his hand. 'Eaten half-rotten, would you believe –'

'Yuk!' An instinctive recoil. Yet the fruit looked appealing enough, even seemed fragrant.

'Somewhat out of fashion these days,' Alex revealed, 'but a source of bawdy jokes in several Elizabethan plays.' He shot her a strange, assessing glance. 'How good's your Shakespeare?'

'Schoolgirlish,' Stella owned. '*Twelfth Night, Macbeth, Romeo and Jul* –'

'Warm. Definitely warmer. But maybe schools shy away from the ribald when it comes to the humour of The Bard?'

'Yours didn't – apparently,' Stella pointed out tartly.

'Ah, yes, but I went to a boys' school, not a genteel ladies' academy.'

'Local comp,' Stella sniped good-naturedly. 'And a mixed comp at that.'

'Which probably explains it.'

'Explains what?'

'This yawning gap in an otherwise well-informed mind. I almost hate to say it, Stella, but set against this, my own academic failings seem trifling. Still . . .' He gave an exaggerated sigh, an equally exaggerated shake of the head. 'At least you learned to chant your tables. Not to mention the intricacies of spelling.'

'I learned how to scream, shout and kick too,' she warned, the gleam in her eye unmistakable.

Alex took the hint. 'It's called a medlar.'

'Yes?'

'Yes.'

'Yes, Alex,' she obligingly repeated. 'The name is vaguely familiar. And?'

'Ah, yes, the and. Want to try some?' He offered the fruit in the cup of his hands, Stella's vehement shake of the head provoking a throaty chuckle. 'No? No. Probably wise, my love. Probably very wise. But it's something I've always wanted to try, and now seems, well . . .' He paused, inhaled the fragrance, shot another searing glance at Stella and smiled. 'Omen-like,' he murmured enigmatically. 'Definitively an omen.' Raising his hands like a grail, Alex tasted his fill.

'Well?' Stella needled when he finally glanced up again.

'A foretaste, Stella. A mere foretaste of things to come.' And, having succeeded in baffling her completely, he leaned across to put her out of her misery, nibbling at her earlobe in passing. 'It's supposed to resemble the female form,' he growled. 'Though which particular part, I really couldn't say. Except – well . . .' Pause, kiss, nibble again. 'Use your imagination, Stella.'

Stella did. Glancing down at the remaining piece of fruit, she caught Alex's meaning precisely, turned a beautiful shade of red at the thought of things to come and was forced to bury her head in her hands.

'I'll check on James.'

'*We'll* check on James.'

Unnerving. Tiptoeing in to stand and watch, stand and listen to the rhythmic draw of breath. Hand in hand, Alex and Stella, man and woman, drawing an eventful evening to a close. Only Stella knew better. And Alex knew that she knew. And Alex, being Alex, was stoking the heat of desire. A glance, a touch, a warm flutter of breath as Alex explored mouth and throat, nuzzled the hollow in the crook of her arm, allowed exploring thumbs the merest hint of contact with her straining breasts, rigid nipples. And it was wonderful. And the wait was unendurable. Time. Alex was still travelling hopefully, wasn't about to risk unforeseen delays to his plans. But with James freshly changed and watered, and sleeping the sleep of the innocent, Stella knew that, far from being over, the night had barely begun.

'Stella.' He drew her out of the nursery, halting on the threshold of the bedroom and cupping her face in his hands. Drinking his fill, tasting his fill, Alex let his solemn gaze reach to the centre of her soul. 'Oh,

Stella,' he breathed, kissing nose, mouth and eyelids, nose, mouth, and mouth all over again. 'Oh, Stella, you won't believe how much I want you. I want you, Stella,' he insisted thickly, taking her hand and tugging her forward. 'I want you, I need you and I've already waited long enough. And now it's time. I'm going to take you – again and again and again,' he growled. 'And maybe, just maybe, you'll begin to understand how much I want you.'

CHAPTER 14

They slept. An hour, Stella guessed, opening her eyes to the dawn and checking the time on the bedside clock. Six-forty-five. And with Mandy expected at nine, precious little time left to savour her love.

Love . . . Kissing, touching, tasting. Not a hint of shyness as Alex had snapped the buttons of her dress, the simple button-through shift she'd donned all those hours ago in a laughable attempt to ward off the demons.

No demons here, just twinges of conscience – for things past, not to come, she realized, riding the waves of nausea. Because Stella had deceived him. An innocent deception, but she'd lied just the same. Lying by omission. And, though her motives were faultless, Alex would be hurt.

'Stella, oh, Stella!' Reverential. Alex's heated gaze was a tangible caress as he took a step back, feasted his eyes. And, naked but for the skimpiest veil of bra and pants, Stella had trembled, and smiled, and waited.

Touch. Hands sliding into the curve of her waist

and triggering shock waves, lazy thumbs swirling across the flat plain of her belly as Stella arched back from the pivot of her waist, an unconscious offer of breasts that an anguished Alex couldn't resist. Snapping the catch with a deft flick of fingers, he dropped to his knees, pulled her against him and buried his head in her breasts.

'Stella, Stella, Stella,' he moaned, nuzzling, nibbling, touching, tasting. Mouth, hands, fingers. Circling breasts, kneading the creamy fullness and moving almost imperceptibly nearer to the rigid buds at the centre which were screaming out for Alex's hands, Alex's mouth.

'Alex, please,' Stella breathed in turn. 'Please, Alex, please, please, please,' she implored, with deplorable lack of shame.

And Alex laughed, a sensuous growl in the back of his throat, but instead of taking pity he pulled away, leaned back on his heels and hungrily devoured her with his gaze.

'Alex –'

'Soon, my little tigress,' he soothed, eyes breathing fire. 'Very soon, I promise.'

Not nearly soon enough, Stella contradicted silently, tersely, but she couldn't deny the compensations, the sight of a powerful chest as an impatient Alex tugged his shirt over his head in a single, fluid movement that bypassed completely the inconvenience of buttons. Naked. Sun-bronzed. The thick mass of hair simply irresistible as Stella gave instinct its head, reached across to touch, to scrunch, to brush against an inviting pink tip barely showing through the curls.

'No!' Alex insisted, his vice-like grip on her wrist exquisitely frustrating.

'Yes!' Stella contradicted, bringing her free hand swiftly into play. Playing games, love games. Touch, tease, tantalize. Man and woman both, minds in perfect harmony, heightening the tension. Enough, no more. To rouse, to excite, to incite, to deny, to rouse again, to take to the very brink and then –

'Soon?' she saucily challenged, jerking away as Alex made to tug her closer. 'And pray, sir, how soon is soon, precisely?'

Alex laughed. 'As soon as I can catch you, my little minx. I'll kiss you, I'll touch you, I'll –'

'Taste me?' she prompted, seeing again in her mind's eye Alex's sensuous enjoyment of the medlar.

Eyes glowed like molten sapphires. 'Oh, yes, Stella,' he insisted, inching back into range. And he nodded, and he dropped his gaze, reached out to slide a single, searing finger along the inside of her quivering thigh and he smiled. And halted at the brink. And Stella stood and trembled, hardly knowing when to breathe.

'Alex –'

'Oh, yes, Stella,' he repeated, sliding beneath the hem of her panties to plunge into the heart of her, driving the breath from her body. 'I'll kiss you, I'll touch you, I'll taste you – I'll take you. But first –'

Oh, God, first! Disposing of her panties by the simple expedient of rending the lace as if it were paper, seconds later he was plundering the curls, fingers and thumbs, fingers and fingers, exploring, caressing, probing, searching, seeking, homing in on the tiny ridge of pleasure. Such exquisite pleasure. And as Stella gasped, Alex smiled a knowing smile. Because Alex knew. He was taking Stella to the very brink, the outer limits of pleasure – and pain – until she reached the point of no return, enough, but no more, his ultimate denial stoking the rages of desire.

'You can't –'

'Oh, but I can,' he countered thickly. 'Though heaven help me,' he added in anguish, 'the effort's almost more than I can take.'

'So take me,' she implored, rocking shamelessly backwards and forwards against his hand. 'Please, Alex. For pity's sake, Alex –'

'For Alex's sake, Stella,' he growled, up on his feet in an instant and sweeping her into his arms before striding across to the bed. 'For Alex's sake – and yours.'

Placing her gently down among the covers, arching over her, he kissed mouth, temples, nose, chin, the hollow in her throat where a pulse raced. Pause, to pleasure, and on again, shoulder to shoulder, and then back to the central pathway that would lead Alex and Stella both to the brink of heaven. Into the valley between her breasts, Stella's straining breasts an erotic distraction. Circle, nuzzle, suckle the rigid buds at the centre, all the time not touching, denying Stella the contact of skin on skin, save for lips, mouth and tongue, creating havoc where they touched, creating havoc where they didn't.

And Stella was moaning, writhing, silently screaming, had clamped rigid arms to her sides in an effort to stay in control, was thrillingly aware she was losing the battle!

'*Al-ex!*' she cried as an exploring tongue slid into the dimple of her navel, swirled across the pucker of skin to move onwards, downwards, blazing a delicious trail of destruction. And Alex laughed, his breath a warm flutter on over-sensitized skin, the gurgle of laughter an erotic reverberation.

And still he refused to touch her, except with his mouth, arched away when Stella reached for him. A moan of protest from Stella, a matching growl from Alex, who chose to take pity. He was up on his feet in an instant, the hand at the waistband of his trousers drawing Stella's gaze to the swelling at his groin and – oh, God! She'd known he was magnificent clothed; naked and proud the sense of power was awesome. Alex was awesome. A thrill of fear rippled through her, yet Stella caught the expression in intense blue eyes and knew she had nothing to fear. Alex loved her. Alex wanted her. Alex would teach her body how to love.

'Now, Stella?' he crooned, kneeling astride, still not touching. 'Now – or later?'

'Now – and later,' she smokily reminded him. 'And again and again and again – remember?'

'Peckish, huh?' he queried dryly. 'Which reminds me.' Shifting position, he blazed another trail of destruction, from the tip of her toe to the back of her knee – not a single inch neglected. One leg pleasured, then time to switch track, blaze a parallel trail the length of another, upwards, slowly, tantalizingly slowly. He was kissing, lapping, nuzzling, higher, relentlessly upwards, ankle to knee, knee to creamy thigh, and still Alex hadn't had nearly enough of her. A frantic Stella was writhing at every touch, every pause, every flutter of breath.

Breathing. Forgetting to breathe. Lying rigid among the covers as Alex drew nearer and nearer – now a playful nip of teeth, now a sensuous lap of tongue. So near, so far. Such excruciating pain and pleasure both. And his first sip of nectar a trigger for the shock waves.

'Oh, my love, my love, my wonderful love,' she crooned in anguish, writhing, arching, pulsing, living. Stella was alive, truly alive, giving pleasure to a man, receiving homage in return, because Alex was tasting from the honeypot of love. Yet if Stella's need of Alex grew more urgent by the second, Alex's own need of Stella was ruthlessly suppressed. Until the tremors racking her body began to spiral out of control, and then, only then, did Alex allow that rigid self-control to snap.

Aeons later – well, a whole twenty minutes, at a guess, just time enough for racing hearts to calm he spoke. 'Hungry, my love?'

'For you? Ravenous,' she declared, shameless to the end.

Alex simply laughed, dipped his head to kiss her, padded naked from the room to raid the fridge. More fruit, a platter of pâté and cheese and crisp French bread with the perfect accompaniment – well-chilled champagne.

'A picnic! At this time of night.' Like a child, Stella clapped her hands in delight. 'Oh, but think of the mess, think of the crumbs, think of the indigestion –'

'Think of the fun,' Alex growled, popping grapes into her mouth to stifle her protest. 'Besides, the night's still young, and a man needs to keep his strength up. And as for the woman . . .'

'Yes, Alex?' she enquired, smiling archly. 'About the woman?'

'Just a hunch, a spot of male intuition,' he allowed, features impassive. 'Correct me if I'm wrong, Stella, but I had the distinct impression a certain little lady couldn't wait to get her hands on my body.'

'Who said anything about hands?' Stella purred, kneeling in front of him. And, hands on hips, she leaned forward, brushing his chest with her breasts.

'Stella –'

'My turn,' she reminded him smokily, maintaining the contact with shameless undulations. 'And look, no hands!'

'Woman –'

'All woman,' she agreed. 'And I'm going to kiss you, taste you, pleasure you, without benefit of hands. And *you*, Alex Gifford, will simply have to take it like a man. Understand?'

'I hope so,' he growled, eyes dancing as he lay back upon the pillow, placed his hands behind his head. 'I really do hope so.'

Stella's turn to smile. And kiss him. And punish

him. Mouth to chin, the rasp of stubble strangely erotic, over the stone of his Adam's apple, a rain of tiny kisses along his jawline, and then down over the barrel of his chest. Nuzzling the curls, she parted the hair with her tongue, homing in on an inviting pink bud, and Alex's groan of anguish was music to her ears. And onwards, to lap and nuzzle, lap and nibble, lap and lap again, now a feather of kisses, now a flutter of kisses, a sensuous slurp of kisses over the angles and plains of a powerful body. All man, she told herself, the thrill of pleasure shocking. Her man. And, whatever the future held, he'd always be her man. Because Stella would remember and Stella would savour, and Stella would be proud to have loved him.

Love, love, love, she crooned in her head, circling his navel with her tongue before darting into the creases. And, though Alex lay rigid beneath her, she felt the tension ripple through his body and smiled. All man. Muscles hard as granite, a will as hard as granite. But Stella would break him. Oh, yes, before Stella was finished she'd have Alex Gifford begging for mercy. No hands. Just a lazy flick of tongue, a nuzzle of lips, so near so far. Continuing to deny him, enflame him, deny him all over again. And then, on the point of making the contact he craved, pulling away.

'Oh, no, you don't,' he growled. And quick as a flash he'd snared her, pulling her down on top of him, powerful arms encircling, restraining, pinning – pinning her beneath him as he deftly switched position, cleverly turned the tables. And he sat astride her, the weight on her thighs barely registering, the lazy thumbs at her breasts driving the breath from her body all over again.

'My turn?' she enquired smokily. 'My turn to what?'

'To lie there and take it like a woman,' he growled. 'A touch that isn't a touch, a kiss that isn't a kiss. Let's see how cool, calm and collected Stella Marshall enjoys having the tables turned.'

'You'll crack first,' she warned, completely unrepentant.

'We'll see,' he retorted thickly. 'We'll see.'

Stella did.

Aeons and aeons later.

'Oh, Alex! Oh, yes, Alex. Oh, God, Alex.' She writhed, arching against him. 'Yes, yes, yes!'

'I win.'

'I sure as hell didn't lose,' she replied, nestling down, wriggling her bottom into the curve of his belly, snug as a set of love spoons.

A snatch of sleep. And now Alex stirring in his sleep – in more ways than one, Stella realized delightedly, giving nature a helping hand by shimmying against him.

'You, madam, are shameless. Insatiable . . .'

'Fact, Alex Gifford, or sheer wishful thinking on your part?'

'Both,' he growled, nibbling her earlobe. 'Not that I'm complaining, you understand?'

'No, but *I* shall, if a guy doesn't give a girl what she's craving, and soon.'

'Hungry, huh?'

'Just a teeny-weenie bit peckish,' she allowed. 'How about you?'

'Could be,' he conceded wryly, like Stella, aware of the iron press of his manhood at the small of her back. 'Nothing a plateful of bacon and eggs couldn't put right in a trice.'

'Stodge,' Stella chided. 'Bad for the waistline.'

'Protein,' he riposted. 'And good for the libido. The lady wants I should put it to the test?'

'No can do,' Stella countered mournfully. 'No bacon, no eggs, no early-morning practice.'

'Who mentioned practice? What I had in mind was another polished performance between the sheets.'

'And under the sheets, and on the sheets –'

'The rug in front of the fire?' he probed.

'Bedroom, kitchen, bathroom and then back to bed –'

'To sleep, woman,' he groaned in anguish. 'Have you no pity? Have you no compassion? A guy needs a break –'

'Like I need a hole in the head. Love first, sleep later,' she insisted pertly. 'If you're lucky . . .'

'Luck, Stella,' he growled, flipping her on to her back and running the heel of his palm over the curve of her belly, 'simply doesn't feature in the Alex Gifford scheme of things.' Blue eyes were fastened on hers, a wealth of emotion in their bottomless pools. 'Now you, on the other hand . . .'

She would have to give him the truth. Today. Before Mandy arrived. Two more precious hours of love with her beloved. And then it would be over. A temporary arrangement would come to an end and then it would be over. No Alex, no love, no life. Just a long and lonely existence.

Breakfast, a newly nervous Stella reducing the sweet, warm bread to an untidy heap of crumbs on her plate. Croissants. Courtesy of Alex, who had clearly thought of everything. Another feast for lovers. Past tense, Stella amended, blinking back the tears. Because the moment she gave him the truth was the moment she destroyed them both.

'Not hungry, my love? Isn't the food to madam's taste?'

'Fishing, Alex? Double checking your performance wasn't lacking?'

'Just a mite concerned that you're not eating.'

'Alex –'

'Telephone. Let's ignore it. Though on second thoughts,' he gleefully conceded. 'It might even be Mandy calling in sick. Do you want to take it or shall I?'

Stella shook her head. With her luck it would prove to be Tamara, checking up on Alex having drawn a blank in Rome. She was suddenly so sure it was Tamara that she couldn't bear to stay and listen, and so the moment he palmed the receiver she padded through to James. A sleeping James – though not for much longer, Stella realized, aware that he was stirring. Another five minutes, ten at the most, and he'd be wide awake, demanding food and attention.

Reaching out, she trailed a single finger across his

damp brow and made her silent goodbyes. Because she was leaving. Today, she realized instinctively. Only first and foremost she had to face Alex with the truth.

The moment she opened the door, she knew. Someone – Tamara at a guess – had got to him first.

'Why, Stella? Tell me why?' he enquired without turning. 'Why did you lie?'

'I didn't –'

'Lie through your teeth? Walk into my house unannounced and uninvited and make yourself at home? No, of course not,' he conceded with a curious lack of emotion. 'I was almost forgetting. It's open house at Freshfields any day of the week. What with that posse of reporters camped at the gates – a clever distraction that, by the way – to near daily visits from the law, what's an impostor or two between friends? Toss in the butcher, the baker, the candlestick-maker and the place is almost cosy. I guess it's all those comings and goings,' he scorned. 'The riding school, the stables, visitors, staff and inmates. And then the icing on the cake. You. Mary Poppins Mark II. Miss Practically Perfect In Every Way – and simply too good to be true, hey, Stella,' he needled. 'Since it's all a sham?'

'I –'

'You lied. End of discussion. Understand, Stella?' he bit, snapping his head round to pin her with a blood-chilling gaze. 'The end. It's over. You, me, this ridiculous charade. You're rumbled. Now pack your precious world exclusive, along with your doubtless shabby bags,' he snapped, 'and get out. Get out of my life and stay out.'

'Alex –'

'No.'

'I can explain –'

'I'll bet. If I'm stupid enough to listen. Which I'm not. Not interested, you see?' he scorned, twisting fully round to face her, leaning back against the counter, the grim fold of arms across his chest belying the carelessly casual pose. 'Because you, your lies, and your cheating, scheming behaviour are simply not important.'

'Please, Alex –'

'Not even pretty please, Stella. Just go. And do me a favour, hey? Slam the front door behind you – hard. Proof that you've gone,' he explained unnecessarily. 'Proof that the latch has dropped. After all, I should hate for any Tom, Dick or Harry to drift in unannounced.'

Stella blinked back the tears. Too easy to cry, she told herself. To give in to the pain. This was Alex's reaction. Hurt. Hit out. Salve the pain with bitter words. Stella would cry, of course. Only not now. Because after today she'd have all the time in world for tears.

Silence. Just the blood pounding in her ears. The noise filling her head but not her mind. How to reach him? Give him the truth? Dear God, surely he would listen to the truth, would believe? She wouldn't ask for forgiveness. Just a tacit understanding of her motives. And yet logging the pain, the hurt, the contempt in a set of frigid eyes, the hatred and pain oozing from every pore of his body, she knew she was wasting her time.

She'd lied. Oh, not with words; she could allow that. But look him in the eye and spout so much as a single glib evasion? Good heavens, no, nothing so venial. No, she acknowledged bitterly. She'd been living a lie, acting a lie, she'd deceived him – bad enough when taken in isolation. Set it alongside that other heinous offence, her means of making a living, and Stella was doomed. Alex had trusted Stella and Stella had let him down – and how.

The thin wail of a baby broke the silence. Stella visibly started, took a half-step towards the bedroom door, but Alex's voice sliced across to halt her.

'Leave it.'

'James –'

'Needs a nursemaid. Correct me if I'm wrong, Miss Marshall, but *you* don't qualify.'

'Maybe not. But I have looked after James –'

'Past tense, Miss Marshall. For if ignorance was bliss, the knowledge that you've lied and cheated your way into my home puts a whole new slant on things. I don't owe you, you don't owe me, and that's the way I'd like it to stay.'

'Fine. So we're quits. So my services are surplus to requirements. You're a grown man, you're entitled to make whatever decision you like. But James –'

'Will be perfectly fine till Mandy arrives. Thirty minutes,' he reminded her, pointedly checking his watch. 'You've thirty minutes, precisely to dress, pack and leave.'

Dress. Inwardly she flinched at the contempt he didn't bother to mask as his vicious gaze travelled over her body – decently clad in the bathrobe, thank goodness, but the body beneath was almost as familiar to Alex as to Stella herself. From face to breasts – breasts bruised and tingling from the touch of mouth and fingers – down to pause at the juncture of her legs, a slow and deliberate perusal, a calculated insult as the gaze climbed up again, homed in on the give-away jut of nipples beneath the flimsy fabric. Because, shameless through and through, Stella wanted Alex. And Alex saw. And Alex's sneering curl of lips spoke volumes.

Squirming, crying inside, dying inside, Stella resisted the urge to tug the edges of the robe together, to knot the belt more securely.

'But James needs feeding, damn you,' she bit out, the tilt of her chin unwittingly aggressive. 'Five minutes, Alex. He doesn't understand. He's a baby. Damn it all, Alex, he's your son.'

'Yet another fine misconception,' he sneered. 'It's just not your day, is it?'

'Meaning?

'James. He isn't – never has been, never will be – my son. Fact. Incontrovertible truth. Surprised? My dear, you do surprise me. But, no . . .' Another pause, another sneering curl of lips. 'You'll have trawled enough gutters in the name of human interest. Miss out on a juicy little morsel like this?' he scorned. 'Our award-winning journalist? Surely not. Come now, Stella,' he entreated saccharine-sweetly. 'Don't be coy, be honest – for once in your life at least.'

'So Chrissie played around,' Stella observed coolly, prepared to understand, though not excuse much of Alex's behaviour where James was concerned. 'It's not the exclusive prerogative of the female of the species.'

Alex's head snapped up. 'Ouch. Guilty as charged,' he allowed. 'And, now that I come to think of it, a risky occupation in this day and age. Sex. Fun while it lasts of course, but –'

'Yes, but,' Stella cut in. 'Worry not, Alex. We've already established that Father of the Year you'll never be. If I did fall pregnant –'

'Difficult to *fall*, surely, my dear, from the dizzy heights of the gutter?'

'Do you have to be so revolting?'

'It isn't compulsory. But for you, Stella,' he jeered, 'anything. And just between you, me and that gutter you're so fond of, the perils of falling pregnant are heavily outweighed by other . . .' Another pause, another sneer, a theatrical lowering of tone as he leaned towards her. 'Let's say, other considerations,' he murmured confidentially. 'Sex,' he underlined softly. 'And unprotected sex at that.'

'I'm not sure that I like what you're implying.'

'You don't have to. You don't even have to stay and listen.' He gave a pointed glance at the clock on the wall behind her. 'Eight thirty-five,' he stated. 'Exit, one bogus nanny, before I call the police.'

'Only you won't.'

'I don't have to. You're leaving. You quit, remember? Another day, another baby, another sordid little story.'

'No news is bad news,' Stella informed him grimly. 'Don't flatter yourself, Alex. There's been nothing here to interest me.'

'Liar!' he almost bellowed. ' "The inside story. The story you've all been waiting for. Another world exclusive from the pen of Stella Marshall",' he supplied, word-perfectly. 'Freshfields today, Bosnia tomorrow –'

'My, someone has been busy,' Stella derided coolly. 'Tamara –'

'Not Tamara. As far as Tamara's concerned, I was spending the night in Rome. God knows, I only wish that I had,' he tagged on bitterly.

'But of course,' Stella derided. 'Remorse. It's the morning after the night before and time to repent of that age-old human failing. Temptation. The inability to resist thereof. Adam and Eve. Alex and Stella. Only someone – you,' she pointedly needled, 'changed the rules of the game.'

'Meaning?'

'Temptation. Seduction. Forbidden fruit – a nice little touch that, by the way. Correct me if I'm wrong, Alex, but didn't that particular wily female set out to trap her man?'

'I don't see –'

'The connection? But of course not. You're a man. Blame,' she clipped. 'It's a simple matter of blame. Damned if I do, damned if I don't. Alex Gifford arrives unannounced and uninvited and talks his way into my bed. My fault.'

'I didn't notice any objections.'

'I rest my case. The lady consents, the lady condones, the lady carries the blame.'

'Now you're being paranoid.'

'Realistic, reviled, resigned. But I don't, repeat, don't regret a single thing that happened last night. I did nothing to be ashamed of.'

'Meaning I did?'

'Who knows?' Stella derided. 'Who cares? Tamara, I suppose, if you're foolish enough to tell her. But, no – kiss and tell, kiss and beg forgiveness, kiss and risk the wrath of a cheated woman when blissful ignorance serves a better purpose? Well, rest assured. I won't tell if you don't.'

'Promises, promises. And this from the woman who wouldn't recognize a lie if the devil incarnate swore black was white to her face.'

'I don't lie.'

Alex spread his hands. 'See what I mean? You don't even know you're doing it. But then, you're a journalist. Lying's a way of life.'

Yes. Stella's anger died. She was a journalist, a writer, a purveyor of words. Words. The complexity of language. A simple little word like 'lie'. Lie as a noun: false statement made to deceive, an intentional violation of the truth. Not guilty, she acknowledged bitterly. Because lie as a verb: imitate, disguise, misrepresent – that covered her actions exactly. She didn't lie, she *was* that lie.

'I'm sorry.'

'So you damn well should be. Assuming you're telling the truth for once.'

'Alex –'

'Forget it. I really don't want to know. I don't care. You've got what you came for, Stella. Let's just leave it at that, hey? Goodbye, Stella. See you in court, maybe.'

'Meaning?'

'That Stella Marshall exclusive. Print and be damned. Or break the habit of a lifetime – have the *Beacon* print the truth for once.' He smiled evilly. 'Now there's a dilemma. The truth, the whole truth and nothing but the truth – or a circulation-busting pack of lies? But I was forgetting. You've done better than most. Last night's fiasco,' he reminded her bitterly. 'And quite a coup for Stella Marshall. Just think of the headlines: "My Night Of Passion With The Accused", perhaps. Or "Baby James, The Inside Story". Tell me, Stella, just between you, me and that gutter, of course, what's it to be?'

'Neither. I don't work for Fisher. Never have, never will. And for your information, *mister*, when Stella Marshall needs a story, Stella Marshall goes for news. News,' she emphasized grimly. 'Not kiss and tell.'

'Precisely. News. Alex Gifford.'

'Ah, yes, but is that Alex Gifford, playboy? Alex Gifford, entrepreneur? Or Alex Gifford, rat of the year?'

'A rose by any other name,' he mocked. 'And you missed out the obvious.'

'Meaning?'

'Come now, Stella, don't be coy. You don't have to pretend, not with me. The real reason you're here.

The story the world's been waiting for. Was Chrissie Gifford alone that day? Drinking alone, swimming alone, dying alone. The hand of God,' he reminded her, the words an uncanny echo of Beth's terse quote from that *Sunday Beacon* exclusive, a lifetime ago now, it seemed. 'Or the hand of Alex Gifford?'

'You know,' Stella told him, leaning forward confidentially, 'with your gift for words, you're the one who should be writing copy.'

'I'd rather sell my soul to the devil,' he scorned. 'Body and soul both – hey, Stella?' he added tersely. 'Since I was foolish enough to spend the night with you.'

'Just one of the perils of playing around.'

'You're right. It pays to be choosy. I'll bear it in mind – next time. And, furthermore, I'll double check the lady's credentials before she crosses my threshold.'

'Maybe so, but would a lady worthy of the name be tempted?'

'You were.'

'Yes.' A ghost of a smile from Stella at the backhanded compliment. Slut to lady in the space of ten minutes.

'Only you're not, of course.'

'I beg your pardon?'

'Lady. Now lady of the night . . .'

'Only one. Last night,' she hissed, catching his drift at once. 'And I don't, repeat, don't make a habit of sleeping around.'

'I should hope not. Sell yourself short when the highest bidder is there for the fleecing? Talking of which, how much are you looking for, precisely?'

'From you? Not even the time of day,' she spat.

'Like I said, see you in court.'

'Arrogant as always, hey, Alex?' she needled. 'But maybe you know something I don't.'

'And what the hell is that supposed to mean?'

'Court. Trial by jury. Twelve good men and true. Ah, yes,' she jeered as he blanched beneath the sun tan. 'Touched a chord, did I?'

Alex swore. Softly, viciously. 'Get out,' he bit, snapping forward before she could react, vicious fingers snatching at her shoulders, shaking her. 'Get out before I throw you out,' he spat, the flare of white lines from the base of his nostrils sending a chill to Stella's heart. 'Are you listening, madam? Get out and stay out.'

'Alex! Please, Alex.' She was protesting, struggling to be free. Only the more she squirmed, the deeper the fingers bit, and as for the expression in his eyes – no! Don't even think it. He wouldn't. He couldn't. He hadn't. She loved him, for heaven's sake. She loved him, she wanted him, she needed him, and Alex wanted her. Proof. He'd pulled her against him and Alex was reacting. And Stella was weakening. God help her, she wanted him. Only not like this.

'No! No,' she gasped, because she was choking. She couldn't breathe. Alex had pulled her against him and he was naked, the skimpy pair of boxers no barrier at all. 'Please, Alex! No, no, no!' she railed, closing her eyes, attempting to close her mind as Alex relaxed his hold, slid one hand into the small of her back, slid the other to her throat.

The hand at her throat closed round, the pressure pure imagination, she told herself, swaying dizzily against him as her knees gave way.

'Stella. Look at me, Stella,' he insisted in a tone that brooked no refusal. And Stella opened her eyes, saw her own eyes reflected in the mirrors of his, and wanted to curl up and die. Because she was afraid. And the scent of fear was unmistakable. Alex saw. Alex knew. Which meant –

'No, Alex.' Soft. Pleading. Pleading for Alex to meet her gaze. Because the shutters had dropped into place and he was looking through her, not at her, she realized as her released her. 'Please, Alex.'

He swung away. 'I'd better get dressed,' he murmured wearily, running his fingers through the crop of his hair. 'Mandy's due any minute. Though heaven knows,' he added with a wry flash of humour, 'what's a scandal or two between nannies? But I was forgetting. Nanny. Present company excepted. You lied.'

'I didn't lie, Alex.'

'No, Stella? So tell me,' he entreated coldly, 'just to put the record straight. How would you describe your actions of the past three weeks? Honest? Altruistic? Above board and legal? Ethical? Honorable? Moral? Legitimate?' he bit out. 'Or lying, scheming, underhand, sly, deceitful, cunning, dishonest, dissembling, fake? Shall I go on?'

'Why bother?' Stella demurred in a voice devoid of emotion. 'Guilty as charged. On all counts. I won't even bother with a plea of mitigation –'

'Because you can't. Because, despite your reasons

for turning up here, the moment you saw your chance you reverted to form. Once a journalist, always a journalist. Pity. You had the makings of a human being once.'

'Unkind, Alex. Unfair. I didn't set out to hurt –'

'So who's hurting?' he jeered. 'Angry and annoyed, yes – because I should have known, should have seen, should have checked you out in the first place. Only I didn't. And that, my dear, is a lesson well learned. Never again.'

A smile that wasn't a smile, another glance that cut straight through her, and Stella was dismissed – could only stand and watch as Alex gathered his scattered clothes together, didn't want to watch as he poured himself back into shirt and trousers. And, since to all intents and purposes she'd ceased to exist, she took the hint, moved with wooden footsteps to the bedroom. Bed. The unmistakable scent of love in the air. Sex, she silently contradicted, rubbing salt into the wound and crying inside, dying inside.

And with the sound of an angry James bellowing through the intercom, she stripped and remade the bed, packed the rest of her clothes, washed and dressed without conscious thought. Five minutes. Another two minutes to put the sheets in to wash and she'd be gone. She prayed she could slip out unnoticed. No Mandy, no Alex, no James. No looking back. And then she remembered. James. Which settled it. She had to talk to Alex, whether he liked it or not.

'Carly?' he queried as Stella hovered on the threshold of the nursery, amazed to find a ravenous James devouring his bottle snug in the crook of Alex's arm. 'Ah, yes. The previous incumbent. A flighty piece, apparently. Though maybe the concerned older sister knows better?'

Stella's head snapped up. 'You knew? All this time and you didn't say a word? And to think,' she tossed out bitterly, 'you had the nerve to snipe at me for being evasive.'

Only Alex shook his head, smiled the smile that wasn't a smile, and waited for Stella's racing mind to work things out for herself.

The phone call. Not Tamara. Which meant –

'Yes, Stella. The caring employer finally bowed to pressure and made a few enquiries. Carly Kendal. Missing presumed what, exactly? And, surprise, surprise, guess who's listed as next as kin? And before you ask, it doesn't make a penny's worth of difference. Not to me. You lied. The end.' A pugnacious jut of the chin, another evil smile. 'As they say in the movies, time to roll the credits, my dear, and don't forget to slam the door behind you when you leave. Goodbye, Stella. And if I never see or hear from you again, ever, it will still be a lifetime too soon. Only I was almost forgetting. This isn't so much goodbye as see you in court.'

CHAPTER 15

'Married? But, Carly, you've barely known him five minutes.'

'Five months, Stell. And I love him. When I walked out of Freshfields I thought I'd lost him for ever. Only I hadn't. Danny came to find me. Don't you see?' Carly pleaded, tawny eyes fleetingly cloudy. 'He even missed auditioning for a part he'd set his heart on because he cared about me. I love him. Please, Stell. Please say you're pleased. Pretty please.'

Stella froze. Pretty please. Shades of Alex that last dreadful night. Nine weeks, she calculated swiftly, and each and every one a lifetime. Nine weeks, three days, seven hours precisely. And Alex had denied her. No explanation, no excuses, no room for mercy. Unfair. But then, life generally was, she was beginning to think, hurting inside but prepared to understand, to forgive. Because she loved him. Because Alex had been hurt – and not only by Stella. Because despite the shell of indifference he really did care about James. Or leastways, she amended, the image of James cocooned in Alex's arms a glimmer of light in the whole sordid mess, that was what she wanted to believe.

'Stella?'

Stella shook her head, banished the shadow with a massive surge of will and flashed her sister a reassuring smile.

An answering smile came from Carly, who sprang from her chair to throw her arms around Stella's neck, half smothering her in the process.

'Carly!'

'Say you're pleased,' she trilled, obligingly releasing her. 'Say you'll be my bridesmaid. Nothing fancy, you understand, because every penny's needed for a deposit on the flat. We thought we'd keep it simple. Beth's offered to make my outfit, Connor can be pageboy and Simon will give me away.'

'It sounds like everything's settled?'

Carly nodded, crossing to the sideboard to rummage through a pile of glossy brochures. Wedding brochures, Stella noted, smothering a smile. Nothing fancy? Who was Carly trying to kid? Even allowing for family and close friends only, the tally of guests would be sure to top thirty. But if a girl couldn't make a splash on her wedding day, life would be pretty grim. And, though Carly wouldn't dream of asking, Stella would insist on footing the bill. Yes, why not? It would be Stella's wedding gift to Carly and Danny.

'So,' Stella prompted brightly, 'when's it to be?'

'Thursday the fourteenth,' Carly explained, leaning back against the sideboard as if in need of some support.

'Thursday the fourteenth of what?' Stella probed, hoping the enquiry sounded suitably casual. Because Thursday the fourteenth of this month was a scant fortnight away, and an awful suspicion was beginning to dawn. A ridiculous notion, since Stella knew her sister. Carly wouldn't. Only Carly didn't answer, seemed to be looking anywhere but at Stella, and Stella didn't need to focus on Carly's newly rounded waistline to confirm her suspicions. She took a deep breath. 'Bridesmaid it is, then,' she conceded lightly. 'You know I wouldn't miss it for the world. And the same, Carly Kendal,' she needled mildly, 'goes for the christening.'

Carly had the grace to blush, unconsciously patting her stomach. 'Ah! You know? Of course you do, you're Stella.' Her smile was uncertain. 'You don't mind?'

Mind? When there but for the grace of God went Stella! 'Of course I don't mind,' she reassured her softly. 'As long as you're happy –'

'Happy? I'm over the moon. And Danny's over the moon, and Mrs Fielding's over the moon at the thought of being a granny –'

'Mrs who?' Stella cut in, smiling despite it all. Carly's youthful exuberance was infectious.

'Danny's mother,' Carly explained, coming to kneel beside her. 'Oh, Stella, you didn't think I'd be –'

'Mrs Carly daVine?' Stella grinned, reached out to push a stray lock of hair from Carly's eyes. 'Why not? It's certainly different. Sort of heavenly. You know, heavenly, divine . . .'

'Ridiculously twee? No chance. Besides, even if

Danny does land that part he's hankering for, we'll need something to fall back on when he's "resting". As it happens, he thinks he might have found it.'

'Oh?' Stella murmured, beginning to think she'd been living on Mars for the past few weeks, and wondering how much more had simply passed her by. Work, work and more work. No time for idle thoughts as she'd focused her mind on the task in hand; the emergence of the Third World and the changing role of women. Precious little change as far as Stella was concerned. Her hard-hitting series on the daily grind, the hand-to-mouth existence, the appalling depths of poverty and entrenched male stereotypes across a broad swathe of Asia had created waves, enhanced Stella's standing in the media.

Chequebook journalism? Gutter press? Eat your heart out, Alex Gifford, she silently derided. You ain't seen nothing yet. Only Alex wouldn't have noticed, of course. Wouldn't notice, wouldn't care. Unlike Stella, who poured heart and soul into the job in an effort to dull the pain.

'Stella? Stella Marshall, I do believe you're miles away. Anywhere I know?' Carly enquired as Stella blinked back the tears. Tears! For a man! When she hadn't cried about a man since Toby betrayed her with Francine. Nine years, Stella realized. Another time, another place, another wedding. 'Oh, Stella,' Carly murmured with an amazing flash of insight. 'You're thinking about Toby. Oh, darling, I'm sorry.'

'Well, I'm not,' Stella murmured briskly, giving her the truth. Because Toby wasn't important, hadn't been important for years. And Francine had done them both a favour. Marriage to Toby? She'd have been bored out of her mind. Why, she hadn't even loved him, she finally realized. she'd simply been in love with the idea. Unlike Alex – no! Stella closed her mind, focused her gaze on Carly's upturned face. 'No regrets,' she insisted on a lighter note. 'Promise.'

'Hmm,' Carly murmured doubtfully.

'Hmm, yourself,' Stella echoed, provoking a smile. 'You can take it from me, the thought of being Mrs Toby Jugg for the rest of my life simply didn't appeal.'

'Stella, he wasn't – oh, you're teasing?'

'Only a teensy-weenie little bit,' Stella conceded. 'But enough about me. You were saying? Something about Danny, I believe, and the prospects of a full-time job?'

Not exactly, Stella conceded, when Carly had finished explaining. But, in the precarious world of show biz, probably the next best thing.

It was a glorious day, the late summer sun having broken through the clouds as the bridal cars arrived. Stella, Beth and Connor in the first, and a radiant Carly with Simon beside her in the second – Beth's handsome husband pleased as punch at the honour of giving the bride away. There was a surprising amount of interest in such a low-key wedding, Stella was intrigued to discover, the knot of young girls at the gates and the flurry of cameramen providing food for thought. Danny was young, talented, undoubtedly good-looking – and his celebrity status was clearly more established than Stella had suspected. For the first time in months she began to relax. Carly was happy, and Danny's long-term prospects were secure – thanks to the new venture, the Heaven-Help-U Theatre Company, a tongue-in-cheek play on his stage name. Though he hadn't landed the coveted role, he had picked up one of the other leads in a brand-new West End production. And just time to squeeze in a honeymoon before rehearsals began in earnest. A week in Spain, Carly had explained. The loan of a villa courtesy of a friend of a friend.

'It's been quite a day,' Stella observed in the afternoon lull, that quiet hour, born of a surfeit of first-class food and free-flowing wine, before the influx of bright young things invited for the evening breathed fresh life into the jaded. 'And, though I'm naturally biased where Carly's concerned, I must say I thought she looked wonderful.'

'Divine, surely,' Beth put in dryly – almost as dry as the wine in the glass she was cradling. 'And definitely blooming, unlike her normally vivacious sister.'

'Don't nag, Bethy, I'm fine.'

'Fine. Fine, I'll allow. But a stone and a half lighter and a whiter shade of pale doesn't qualify in my book. Damn it all, Stella, you've spent weeks and weeks living in the tropics. Anyone else would flaunt a tan, but does the Stella Marshall we know and love? Sun tan? Chance would be a fine thing,' she derided. 'Not even a solitary freckle,' Beth scorned. 'Unless –?'

Grey eyes narrowed suddenly, switching from Stella to Carly and back again, and, watching Beth,

Stella held her breath, could almost follow the workings of her mind. Stella was pale, listless, losing weight. Unlike Carly, who'd passed the early-morning sickness stage. And, whilst not beyond the realms of possibility . . .

No. Beth's almost imperceptible shake of the head spoke volumes. Stella wouldn't. Stella hadn't. And, though Beth wouldn't know it, the fact that Stella wasn't pregnant was in no way down to Stella. Just luck. Beginner's luck? she scorned silently, bitterly. And damn Alex Gifford for his vile insinuations.

Logging Beth's tangible disappointment, Stella swallowed the pain, forced an enquiring smile. 'Unless what?' she prompted, eyes wide and innocent.

'Unless you're sickening for something?' Beth retorted tetchily. 'A legacy of foreign climes. Malaria, typhoid, rabies?' she suggested absurdly. 'Common or garden flu, perhaps? No? No, of course not,' she berated. 'Not even a touch of heatstroke. And you needn't bat those luminous brown eyes and think you can fool me. Something's eating away at you.'

'Work. Carly. Arrangements for the wedding. And what a waste of time that's proving to be. Carly's radiant.'

'She's in love. You ought to try it some time. Who knows? It might even suit you.'

'But there again,' Stella retorted, not in the least put out by the spat of ill-humour, 'it might just make me tetchy. Talking of which, what's your excuse?'

'Pregnancy. Failure of,' Beth clipped out. 'A baby

sister for Connor. We've been trying for months, and when I was late –'

'Oh, Bethy, Bethy, I'm sorry.' Reaching across to hug her, hold her, she sensed her cousin's disappointment. 'Why didn't you say?'

'How could I say? It's Carly's special day. I could hardly stand up in church and make an unhappy announcement, now, could I?' she sniffed. And then she caught her husband's eye over the sea of heads and visibly brightened. 'Not that I'm complaining. We're luckier than most. We do have Connor, and, according to Simon, every cloud has a silver lining. Though I must confess, right at this moment I'm having trouble seeing it myself.'

Stella smiled, leaned forward, lowered her voice. 'Maybe so, Beth,' she agreed, features impassive. 'But just think of all that practice.'

Beth did. And turned the prettiest shade of pink imaginable.

'I still don't understand why Carly bolted,' Stella murmured ten minutes later, the conversation having swung full circle. 'So I was out of reach,' she conceded, reaching for the peanuts and absent-mindedly popping a generous handful into her mouth. 'But the flat was standing empty and Carly had a key. Why not simply go to ground at my place, or turn to you?'

'Pride,' Beth insisted. 'Panic. The thought of looking you in the eye and confessing she was pregnant.'

'But I'm her sister, not some Victorian martinet. I'd have understood.'

'Understood, yes. Offered a shoulder to cry on as

well, no doubt. But what Carly needed most was space. Think, Stella, think,' Beth chided lightly. 'Danny, events at Freshfields, the baby. She'd fouled things up, and it was suddenly all too much for her. Carly wasn't thinking straight. And you should know.'

'Me?'

'Carly managed three months at Freshfields. You found three weeks a strain. Heaven knows how Mandy's coping with the same practical joker on the loose.'

'I'm surprised you didn't make a point of asking. Your day at the stables,' Stella prompted, sensing Beth's confusion. 'You know, the treat for the children. Rides on Marbles, fun in the pool –' She broke off, her face hardening. 'Let me guess. Hannah – or Alex – withdrew the offer?'

'As a matter of fact, no,' Beth countered mildly. 'But there simply weren't enough helpers, so Hannah suggested leaving it a while and joining forces with the annual village fête. More fun for everyone that way. I wonder . . .'

A sudden narrowing of Beth's eyes made the hairs on the back of Stella's neck prickle out a warning. Eyeing her cousin warily, she took a generous sip of wine, allowed the bubbles to sit on her tongue. And waited.

'If you're likely to be around for a week or two,' Beth murmured casually – too casually by far, 'why not come along and lend a hand?'

Stella choked. 'I – yes! I mean, no! I'm not – *when* did you say it was?' she stammered absurdly.

Beth told her, and Stella's relief was almost tangible.

'Sorry, Beth. You know I'd love to help. But duty calls,' she burbled brightly. 'India . . . Bangladesh . . . Pakistan . . . Who knows where I'm likely to be next?'

'Hmm. I suppose so.' Beth nodded, looking anything but convinced. 'But it was only a thought, and you're right. I'll be seeing Mandy myself soon enough. In the meantime –'

'Well, if that's all that's worrying you,' Stella cut in, almost tripping over her tongue in her haste to change the subject, 'let me put your mind at rest. As it happens, Carly spoke to Mandy in the week, when she phoned to thank her for the present. Everything's hunky-dory at Freshfields. James has been walking for weeks now, Mrs Edwards is sweetness and light, Hannah's engrossed with the stables, and as for Tamara, well –' an eloquent shrug of the shoulders '– on the odd occasion she condescends to visit, Tamara's like a dog with two tails. Fame clearly suits her.'

'And Alex?'

'Who knows?' Stella scorned, silently cursing the give-away surge of colour. 'Who cares?'

'Ah.'

'Ah, what?' Stella bit out.

'Just, ah. I guess that serves to explain things,' Beth murmured vaguely, waylaying a passing waiter and swapping her empty glass for a full one. And with that Stella had to be content.

The room began to fill. It was a function room in a plusher part of London than Stella had envisaged when she'd offered to foot the bill, and, suddenly in need of some fresh air, she wandered through the open terrace windows into the gardens beyond.

She checked her watch. Nine o'clock. And, whilst the bride and groom were set to slip away at midnight, the young hoards still arriving would no doubt dance till dawn. Not to mention eat, drink and be merry, Stella amended, not really minding that the guest list had burgeoned. Besides, the drinks tab had been taken care of already, thanks to Danny's network of friends and friends of friends.

'And what's my lovely sister-in-law doing hiding away in the shadows?'

'Danny! You shouldn't be looking for me. Carly –'

'Was wondering where you'd got to. She's doing her broody hen bit and fretting,' he explained enigmatically. 'So I've been charged with the honour of tracking you down.'

'Hardly an honour,' Stella teased as Danny slid into the chair opposite.

'Hardly tracking either,' he allowed, grinning broadly and raising a lazy hand to attract a waiter's attention.

Easy enough to attract attention when you're twenty-six and stunningly good-looking, Stella could allow, but the lighting was subdued, the terrace practically empty, and, minor celebrity or no, Danny would be lucky to elicit a response.

But there again, thanks to his training, Danny would doubtless exude a presence – as the discreet cough of the waiter at his elbow served to underline. A bit like Alex, she found herself musing as the man across the table slipped out of focus. Alex. An icy trickle ran down her spine, a shiver of premonition. Alex. She could almost see him, smell him, touch him. Wishful thinking? she silently berated. Or the ramblings of the certifiably insane?

'Drink, Stella?' Danny prompted, cutting into dangerous thoughts. 'Wine? Red, white, dry, rosé or sparkling? You name it, we've probably got it – thanks to Gi – er, thanks to my new partner in crime.'

'Oh?' Stella murmured politely.

'Heaven-Help-U,' he explained. 'Much as I'd like to take the credit, it wasn't my idea.'

'No?' Stella smiled. 'But you have managed to raise what you need?'

'Thanks to you.'

'Me? Oh no.' Stella shook her head. 'I simply –'

'Came up with the deposit for the flat and convinced a doting mother her son was a good investment. Until then she'd been proud, but wary of seeing good money thrown after bad.'

'I'm not sure that I follow?' Stella probed, wrinkling her nose.

'My inheritance. When Dad died I came into quite a sum, and between you, me and the gatepost, apart from the car, I've precious little left to show for it.'

'Better the gatepost than the gutter, I suppose,' Stella observed absent-mindedly, vaguely wondering why. And then it hit her. Alex. Her cheeks flamed.

Sensing her confusion, Danny laughed. 'Your turn to lose me,' he conceded lightly. 'Private joke, huh?'

'Something like that,' Stella conceded. 'It would –

lose a lot in translation,' she stalled. 'So, young man, you've come to confess your dissolute past and beg my forgiveness, have you?' she challenged mock severely.

'Do I need to?'

'No, Danny. You don't have to explain – about anything. Not to me. Now Carly, on the other hand –'

'Worships the ground I walk on, and I will not, repeat, not be letting her down.'

'Good.'

'So, since we both want what's best for Carly, why not come back inside and show her how pleased you are?'

'Don't I look pleased?'

'You look happy enough to me,' he admitted wryly. 'But then, I don't know you as well as Carly.'

'And Carly's not convinced?'

'She's – worried that all work and no play is her sister's way of masking disappointment.'

'Then she's wrong,' Stella insisted, looking him squarely in the eye and giving him the truth. 'Next to Carly, I'm the happiest and proudest woman in the world.'

'Yeah.' Danny's black velvet eyes crinkled at the corners. 'She said you were kind of special.' He took her hand, drew her arm though his. 'Miss Marshall, would you do me the honour of the next dance?'

And the next and the next and the next, and then a laughing Stella gave way to a beaming Carly, but her relief at sitting down was short-lived.

'Simon! Show mercy, for pity's sake. I'm too old for tripping the light fantastic. And as for modern music –'

'Just stand and shimmy your hips,' he instructed, raising a hand to Beth in passing. Carly and Beth were watching Stella and wondering, waiting. Waiting for what? Stella mused with a shiver of apprehension. And then the lights dimmed, the music changing to a slow, smoochy number, and as Simon melted away in search of his wife Stella airily kissed her fingers in blessing and swung round, convinced she'd stepped into a nightmare when strong arms reached out to pull her close.

'My dance, I believe.'

'But I –'

'You don't need to say a word, Stella,' Alex insisted gravely, eyes locking with hers and seeing to the centre of her soul. 'All you have to do is follow the lead given by the music and smooch.'

'I'd rather shuffle my way around a bear pit,' she hissed, but she was wasting her time. Alex wasn't listening. Worse than that. In tugging her even closer he was giving the distinct impression that he'd missed her. And how!

A nightmare. Wanting him, touching him, holding him. Feeling taut muscles ripple beneath her fingers, powerful thighs brush against hers. Closing her eyes as her knees turned to jelly, Stella swayed against him. Easier that way, she reassured herself. Because she didn't have to look, couldn't bear to look, to read what she wanted to see in those treacherous, swirling depths.

Fool, fool, fool, she silently berated as Alex slid his

hands over the curve of her bottom, moulding her to him. Man and woman, alone on a dance floor. The man's lips nuzzling the woman's fevered temple; the woman's heart thumping wildly in her breast. Love – lust! she told herself, the tug in her belly a bitter-sweet reflex. Sex. Pure and simple. Biological, functional, mechanical. Good sex, she could allow that – if she was stupid enough to allow it. Only she wouldn't. She'd tried that already and it hurt. It hurt like hell. So, never again. Not with Alex, not with any man. And if Alex needed a good lay, Alex could find another little lady to oblige. Tamara – ah, yes, Tamara. Of course. Stella should have known. While the cat's away, the rat will play. Only not, repeat, not with Stella.

Safety in numbers, she decided relaxing imperceptibly, and yet, feeling a sudden draught on her arms, her eyes snapped open in alarm. They were alone. Round one to Alex. Totally caught up in her private rantings and ravings, she'd simply followed his lead as they shuffled aimlessly around the dance floor. Aimless, my foot, she silently scorned. Because, too clever by half, Alex had steered them towards the open doorway and the terrace beyond.

Logging the candlelit table, the chilled champagne, the crystal flutes on a crisp damask cloth, not to mention the single red rose in the silver bud vase, Stella could almost be impressed. Almost.

Without a word, Alex released her, crossed to pour the wine, his eyes fastened on hers. Space – physically at least. Her chance to escape, Stella acknowledged. Only she wouldn't. Scuttle away like some frightened rabbit? No chance. She'd stay, she'd hold her own, she'd keep him at a distance.

'Why, Alex?' she demanded coldly, folding her arms and ignoring the glass that he proffered. 'Why are you here? This is my sister's wedding –'

'And when the invitation landed on my mat, naturally enough I couldn't turn it down. But if you're wondering why I'm late –'

'I wasn't. I was wondering how you'd had the nerve to show your face at all. Carly –'

'Knew I couldn't make the service. A prior engagement,' he explained, only didn't explain, and when Stella didn't relent, didn't blink, barely seemed to draw breath, he placed the untouched glass on the table and moved back within range. Touching range. And he did.

'Don't –'

'Precisely. Take your own advice, Stella. Don't. Don't judge, don't condemn, don't reject the hand of friendship.'

'Friendship? Ha!' she sneered, achingly aware of his hands on her arms, skin against skin, of the currents of heat swirling outwards and inwards. 'And how do you make that out? Friends have things in common, Mr Gifford. They're generally well acquainted, for a start. They're warm and loyal, understanding and forgiving. They share things. The good and the bad, the rough and the smooth. Friends don't condemn out of hand.'

'So I was wrong. I'm man enough to own it. And just for the record, I didn't condemn –'

' "Once a journalist, always a journalist",' she

reminded him bitterly. 'And you can take it from me, eleven and a half weeks on, nothing's changed.'

'Eleven and a half weeks precisely, Stella?' he probed absurdly.

'Yes! No! How the hell do I know?' she snapped, stepping into the trap with her eyes wide open. Because Alex knew. Eleven and a half weeks precisely. Not a carelessly rounded three months.

She twisted free, flounced across to the table for the drink he'd earlier poured and raised the glass with a flourish. 'To friends old and new?' she scorned, eyes nuggets of ice.

'Present company included, Stella?'

'What do you think, Alex?'

'I don't think, *I know*. Acquainted? Why, yes, as it happens. Leastways,' he smilingly amended, his expression fleetingly tender, 'we've whiled away the odd hour. Things in common? Like Carly and James and Freshfields. And as for sharing –'

'Thank you, Alex. I think I get the picture.'

'Friends it is, then?'

'Not even friend of a friend of a friend,' she jeered. 'But that doesn't mean we can't be –'

'Lovers?' he slipped in slyly.

' "Civil" was the word that sprang to mind.'

'Progress indeed,' he allowed, smiling, moving to top up his glass. And, since Stella had managed to drain hers without conscious thought, he angled the bottle, raised an enquiring eyebrow.

Flustered, flummoxed and thoroughly unnerved, Stella thrust her glass rudely towards him. Alex took it. And placed it down on the table along with the bottle. And coiled his fingers around her wrist and reeled her towards him.

'No –'

'Yes!' he contradicted tersely. And then he kissed her.

'Alex –'

'Hmm?' he murmured, coming up for air. 'Does madam have a problem?'

'I –'

'Don't like it?' he challenged, cupping her face in his hands and gazing down at her, a wealth of emotion swirling in his eyes. Dipping his head, he kissed the tip of her nose, nuzzled her nose with his own, and then plundered her mouth with devastating thoroughness. 'Liar,' he growled against her ear. But he was smiling as he released her, still smiling as he led her across to a chair, putting the narrow width of the table between them.

Heaven alone knew why, but he was giving her space – and, irrational through and through, Stella was piqued. Or annoyed that Alex managed to stay in control. Easy to stay in control when your emotions aren't involved, she told herself waspishly.

He was looking tired, she decided, gazing across through the veil of her lashes. Well, snap, that made two of them. What with pushing herself hard and sleepless nights, was it any wonder she'd no appetite? Not that it had anything to do with the devastating man now openly regarding her.

'You've lost weight.'

Accusation rather than question, she noted, hoping the flickering shadows of light would hide the sudden flush of colour.

'Like it?' she trilled, up on her feet in an instant, treating him to a twirl on the spot, and glad she'd blown the rest of her savings on the dusky pink two-piece that wouldn't fester at the back of the wardrobe when life went back to normal. If it ever went back to normal. And, since she'd left the bolero jacket inside, the fitted lace bodice hugged the curves. Lots of curves to hug, she realized as Alex's eyes darkened, despite the sleeker, slimline Stella.

'The dress?' he queried dryly. 'Or the bod –'

'Thank you, Alex, a simple yes or no will suffice.'

'Then, yes, Stella. On both counts.'

'Oh!' More blushes. The sudden need to fiddle with the strap of her shoe. Yet even as she straightened she was shockingly aware of his eyes openly devouring her.

They were bottomless pools in a rugged face, the play of shadow and light sharpening the angles and planes and giving Alex a lean and hungry look that tugged at Stella's heartstrings. Vulnerable – no! Champagne on top of wine had clearly gone to her head. Devastating, she could allow, because Alex was all man, would manage to make an impact in crumpled jeans and tee-shirt. But to hanker for the sensitive side of him was nothing short of madness. Besides, the expensive steel-grey suit and carelessly knotted tie served as a powerful reminder – the apparent contradiction was a deliberate signal, if she knew Alex.

Confidence. Supreme confidence. Arrogance, more like, she told herself, scowling visibly.

Alex mistook the gesture. 'You're cold? Perhaps we should go inside?'

'And smooch the night away, hey, Alex?' she needled.

'If you like.'

'I don't, but that needn't stop you having a good time. You don't have to stay and make small talk on my account.'

'I wasn't planning to. Believe me, Stella, what I had in mind relied on other, more tactile methods of communication.'

Stella's cheeks flamed. Impossible man! Damned if she did and damned if she didn't. So, small talk it would be, and an openly nervous Stella chattered away with barely a pause for Alex's dry replies:

'The stables?'

'Yes, Stella, Marbles has proved the hit of the season.'

'And Hannah?'

'She's working hard, as always – too hard on occasion. A bit like you, in fact,' he mused, eyes narrowing thoughtfully. 'Almost as if she has something to prove.'

Ignoring remarks she felt she couldn't cope with, Stella's tongue ran on.

'The harvest? Why, Stella, I didn't realize you took an interest? But disappointing, as it happens. All that late frost, you know. Luckily for me, I don't have all my grapes in one basket. In fact, I've been branching out of late – taking advantage of certain shall we say, heaven-sent opportunities. You'll be reassured to know that not all the Gifford baskets are devoted to grapes these days.'

And, when Stella finally ran out of steam: 'Don't worry, Stella,' he drawled, that velvet voice threaded with amusement. 'Everything's fine at Freshfields.'

Yes. So she'd gathered. According to Carly, Mandy had taken to the job like a duck to water, and as for ghoulies and ghosties and things going bump in the night, Alex had been true to his word. Just another facet of this devastating man. Because when Stella had turned back to face him, that terrible Sunday morning, instead of the derision she'd braced herself to take Alex had stunned her. He'd listened, he'd believed, he'd given his word.

'It won't happen again, Stella,' he'd reassured her grimly. 'But how I wish to God someone – Carly – *you*,' he'd added in anguish, running his fingers through the crop of his hair, 'had had the sense to tell me sooner.'

'The sense – or the nerve?' she'd sneered, stung on to the defensive. 'Face it, Alex, if Carly had come running with a tale like that you'd have laughed her all the way to the madhouse.'

'A moot point, Stella, since from all accounts she was living in Bedlam. But, despite how it seemed, Carly was never in any danger.'

'And Mandy?' she'd probed.

'Like I said, it won't happen again. You have my word.'

And, curiously enough, with that Stella had been satisfied.

Less satisfied now, however. Because he'd kissed her, touched her, roused her. He was back to playing games. Love games, man and woman, Stella and Alex, Alex and Tamara. Ah, yes, Tamara. Out of sight, out of mind? Stella wondered grimly. Or a simple matter of forgetting to practise what he preached? The man was practically engaged; it was high time he acknowledged it. She told him so.

'All in good time,' he drawled, with another flash of amusement. 'After all, marriage is a solemn step. It doesn't pay to rush into it. And with my track record . . .'

Yes. The case was closed, Stella had recently been pleased to discover. The original verdict would stand. Not that she'd ever doubted it. And yet for one dreadful moment she'd been afraid, had allowed that fear to show. Hardly surprising Alex had despised her – despised her still if the truth were known. Yes, why not? It might just be the lever she needed to keep him at a distance.

'I was wrong, Stella,' he began solemnly, unnervingly forestalling her. 'I misjudged you.'

'Not half as badly as I misjudged you. Leave it, Alex. It's over. It was over and done with weeks ago – eleven and a half weeks ago precisely,' she underlined bitterly. 'Subject closed.'

'I hurt you –'

'You noticed? But, no, as it happens,' she scorned. 'Hurt implies a degree of involvement, emotional involvement, and in my line of work that's an encumbrance. So, no involvement, no pain.'

'You're lying.'

'The story of my life?' she sneered. 'Once a liar, always a liar, hey, Alex?'

'I didn't mean –'

'I *know* what you meant,' she bit out. 'And I know where this is leading. Sex. Good sex. Mind-blowing sex. Kiss and make up and let's carry on where we left off all those weeks ago. Forget the insults and the snide insinuations. Let's climb into bed and pretend it never happened. Only it did. You said it. I was it. Irrefutable.'

'For God's sake, Stella –'

'Not even for Alex's sake, Alex,' she hissed. 'You're wasting your time. I simply don't want to know.'

'Damn it all, woman, you're not being fair. Can't you see I'm trying to apologize?'

'For what? Speaking the truth as you saw it? Well, for your information, Alex Gifford, nothing's changed. I'm me. Stella Marshall. The same Stella Marshall I've always been. You didn't approve then, and I sure as hell don't care what you think of me now. Once a journalist, always a journalist,' she reminded him. 'And just because I haven't seen fit to publish and be damned – yet,' she hissed, 'doesn't mean you can relax. And on that you have my word.'

It was Simon who came to find them, and for this Stella was grateful.

'The happy couple are ready to leave,' he explained, his quizzical gaze passing from Stella to Alex and back again, the atmosphere so thick he could have cut it with a knife. 'And Beth was wondering where you'd got to.'

I'll bet, Stella railed, only silently.

Leaving the two men to make their own acquaintance, she swept back inside. Catching Carly's worried gaze alongside Beth's very knowing one, she flashed a smile of reassurance at the first, an eyeful of daggers at the second, and prayed her lipstick would hold up to close inspection.

'And you, Beth Austin,' she hissed in passing, 'ought to have more sense.'

'Carly's wedding; Carly's guest list,' Beth countered sweetly, following her drift exactly. 'Of course, if he hadn't wanted to come in the first place –'

'Fiddlesticks,' Stella bit out, allowing the crush of people to carry her to the door.

Tears, hugs, kisses. And stepping nimbly out of the path of the bridal bouquet – tossed at random, to be sure, but still heading unerringly towards her by some perverse quirk of fate. Always the bridesmaid, never the bride, she reassured herself bitterly. And with the chauffeur-driven car disappearing into the night, Stella used the cover provided by the noisy surge of people to step off the kerb and hail a passing cab.

CHAPTER 16

'You left.'

'Ten out of ten for observation, Beth.'

'You went home. Alone.'

'I live alone, remember? And it isn't a crime as far as I know.'

'But you left without saying goodbye. Alex –'

'Isn't used to rejection? Yes, Beth, so I'd imagine. But since he wasn't, repeat, wasn't teamed up with me, I don't see the problem. And if Carly had to invite the great man himself,' she tagged on huffily, 'she should have had the manners to include Tamara.'

'She did.'

'And?'

'Fishing, Stell?'

'Just mildly curious, Beth Austin. But let me guess. The call of fame was simply irresistible?'

'As a matter of fact, no. From what I can gather, she's recovering in hospital. Just a minor operation, apparently.'

'Oh.'

'Yes, oh.'

Stella had the grace to look ashamed, her spat of ill-humour more bluff than bluster. 'Sorry, Bethy. I thought you and Carly were scheming. I guess I'm growing paranoid.'

'It comes of living alone,' Beth slipped in slyly. 'And spending too much time in the middle of nowhere with nothing but a laptop for company. Where did you say you were off to next?'

'Haven't a clue. Nik's stalling me. In the meantime, I'm standing in for Teresa Tyler on the local desk.'

'Births, weddings and discreet family announcements? Sounds right up your street.'

'Wouldn't you like to believe it?'

'Does it hurt for a girl to hope?'

'A girl – or her scheming older cousin?'

'Ouch. Coming from anyone else, Stella Marshall, I'd be forced to take offence. As it is –'

'You're guilty on both counts. *Scheming*, Beth. And at your age you ought to know better.'

'Age has nothing to do with it. Is it my fault I'm incurably romantic?'

'Is it my fault I'm immune?'

'Ah, yes. But are you, though?'

'Wouldn't you like to know, Beth Austin?'

'I'd certainly enjoy being a fly on the wall once in a while,' she conceded wistfully. She nudged the lid off the box of chocolate biscuits, allowed her fingers to hover, clearly having trouble making up her mind. 'Simon says you quarrelled.'

'Why on earth would I quarrel with Simon? He's

the most mild-mannered man I know. He'd have to be, being married to you.'

'Don't be obtuse, Stella Marshall, it really doesn't become you. Alex –'

'Is engaged – or as good as. And he's not, repeat, not playing fast and loose with me.'

'Just hoping to?'

'Irrelevant. I'm immune – remember?'

'You're certainly playing hard to get.'

'Wrong, Bethy. I'm not playing – ever. And most definitely not with Alex.'

'Oh, goodie, it's serious, then?'

Stella counted to ten. Then screamed. Loudly.

'You'll wake Connor.'

'I'll scream fit to wake the dead if you don't stop provoking me.'

'Fine. Subject closed. May I be struck dumb if the name of Alex Gifford ever crosses my lips again,' Beth conceded huffily, dunking a chocolate cookie and losing half her biscuit. 'Although it did cross my mind that you'd want to thank him.'

'What on earth for? Employer of the Year he'll never be. Carly –'

'Needed a reference – a first-class reference. How else do you think she landed that cushy little number at Eastlands?'

Eastlands. Chelsea's exclusive day crèche for the rich and famous. And, once Carly's baby was born, all the attendant staff perks. Courtesy of Alex.

Stella slumped down into her seat, pulled her rapidly cooling coffee towards her and absent-mindedly heaped in the sugar. A first-class reference. Wonders never ceased to amaze her, though heaven alone knew why, unless – ah, yes. A belated pricking of conscience, huh? Better late than never, she supposed sourly. Like tracking Carly down in the first place. Because until Stella had openly niggled, he hadn't seen the need. But as for being grateful . . .

'No, Beth,' she contradicted starkly, swallowing a lukewarm mouthful of what appeared to be syrup. 'I don't want to thank him. Carly went through hell at Freshfields, so if Alex Gifford's had the decency to pull a few strings, then fine. As far as I'm concerned, he's simply wiped the slate clean. Now, can we please change the subject once and for all?'

Irritating start notwithstanding, it was a pleasant afternoon. Stella and Connor gathered windfall apples from the garden while Beth turned her hand to the pastry – just one of those domestic skills Stella had never had time to acquire.

'Too late now,' she acknowledged without rancour, layering slices of apple over perfectly rolled circles while Connor scattered liberal spoonfuls of sugar, his shiny face furrowed in concentration.

'It's never to late to learn,' Beth countered cheerfully. 'Why not stay over one weekend and I'll teach you? It's bound to come in handy when you're –'

'Stuck in the middle of nowhere with just a laptop for company?' Stella cut in dryly.

'I was about to say married.'

'Really? But haven't you heard?' Stella probed, features carefully neutral. 'Goodness, Beth Austin, you do surprise me.' With a pointed glance at Connor, Stella dropped her voice, leaned forward confidentially. 'The attributes of the perfect wife,' she explained, ticking them off on her fingers. 'Cook in the kitchen, maid in the parlour and whore in the bedroom. So if I'm ever inclined to try,' she conceded solemnly, 'I'll simply hire the first two and take care of the third myself.'

'Stella Marshall!' Beth scalded playfully. 'Now I've heard everything.' And then she paused, folded her floury arms across a liberally floured chest, and regarded Stella through very narrowed eyes. 'Or have I?'

But on that Stella staunchly refused to be drawn.

A mellow hour later, reaching the door, carrying the still warm pie like a delicate piece of china, Stella paused. There was something eating away at the back of her mind. Something she couldn't put her finger on.

Her thoughtful gaze travelled the lines of the kitchen, all cheerful yellows and warm, scrubbed pine, from the impressive array of cupboards to the focal point of the room, the enormous table in the centre, where Connor, safely harnessed in his booster chair, was busy colouring in, jumbo box of crayons propped against the fruit bowl. No exotic reminders here of a certain unforgettable night, Stella noted automatically. Just apples, bananas, grapes. Grapes. Along with flowers, the hospital visitor's ubiquitous offering. But of course. And, whilst not really any of her business, it wouldn't hurt to ask. Only polite really, since she knew the girl.

'Beth?'

'Hmm?'

'About Tamara. The – er – operation you mentioned?' she murmured awkwardly. 'I take it everything went OK?'

'Guilty conscience needling, Stell?'

'Not exactly. Only – now that I come to think of it, Alex was looking strained . . .'

'Hardly surprising,' Beth agreed solemnly as Stella held her breath, pressed rigid fingers into golden crisp pastry, the soft ooze of apple barely impinging. 'They're tricky things, ingrowing toenails.'

Too late to wake Connor, so wake the dead would have to do.

It didn't help one jot.

Neither did phoning work and tracking down her strangely elusive editor.

Paris? For a fashion show? Sure she was hearing things, Stella pulled the receiver away from her ear and switched hands, eyed the familiar wedge of plastic as if it was a smouldering stick of explosive. Fashion show? Oh, no! Not on top of a month's worth of births, weddings and discreet family announcements. It was unfair. It was crazy. It was unthinkable, unspeakable, undo-able.

'Damn it all, Nik,' she barked into the handset. 'You can't. I cover news, remember? News. N-E-W-S. Civil wars, guerrilla warfare, kidnap, rape and pillage. Human and moral issues,' she bit. 'Female circumcision, *yes*. Anorexic coat-hangers, *no*. N – O.

Are you listening, Nik? I am not, repeat, not spending four boring days crouched beneath a catwalk.'

'Sorry, Stell. The decision's out of my hands. No more roving commissions until further notice, by order of the management.'

'But you *are* the management,' she ground out huffily. 'You're the boss. So why not simply write yourself a memo countermanding orders?'

'Not any longer. There's been a buy-out.'

'Since when?'

'Midnight on Thursday.'

'*Last* Thursday?' she challenged incredulously. 'So what happened to Friday through Wednesday's news?' Midnight on Thursday. While she'd been letting her hair down at her sister's wedding, allowing Alex Gifford back within singeing range, someone with more money than sense, at a guess, had been signing Stella's life away. Not that he had need to. The way Stella was behaving lately she could manage that herself. Alex Gifford. Fool, fool, fool, she berated, breathing fire and brimstone down the phone line.

'Aw, come on, Stell,' Nik entreated mildly when Stella finally ran out steam. 'Things have been dicey for months. You must have heard the rumours?'

'Rumours, yes. It's part and parcel of the job,' she reminded him sweetly. 'But facts? As it happens, Nik, no. Not from the horse's mouth, at least.'

'So a guy has trouble getting a word in edgeways?' he sniped good-humouredly. 'And you must admit you have been overdoing things lately.'

Stella counted to ten. Slowly. While she'd been

'overdoing things', her normally reliable boss had sold the whole caboodle down the river. His business, his prerogative. But Stella didn't have to like it.

'So do yourself a favour, take a break,' he suggested mildly when Stella put the thought into words. 'Paris. Please, Stella. Pretty please,' he wheedled persuasively. 'After all, as long as you're writing copy, you have the means to pay the bills.'

Bills. Wedding cars and flowers and champagne flowing like water. Because Stella couldn't forgive herself for letting Carly down. Because she had. Stella simply hadn't been there when her sister had needed her most. She'd been too busy working. The story of her life, she was beginning to think. And once Stella had learned of Danny's plan, she'd reached another momentous decision. The deposit for the flat. After all, Danny needed every penny to invest in the new business.

'OK, Nik,' she conceded ungraciously, running her fingers through the tangle of her hair. 'You win. Paris it is – this time.'

Paris. Little time to sample the local colour with the autumn collections creating a stir, but, conscious that all work and no play was her way of masking the pain, Stella was careful to build time for herself into each of the days. Four days and then it would be back to births, marriages and discreet family announcements, she supposed sourly, beginning to suspect she was losing her nose for news.

Because Press coverage of Carly and Danny's big

day had uncovered another fascinating fact. The honeymoon. A villa in Spain, Carly had blithely informed her, courtesy of a friend of a friend – the self-same friend who'd been kind enough to supply the air tickets. Alex Gifford. All in all, quite a conscience needling. For Carly, Stella wondered, and her three months of hell at Freshfields? Or for Stella? Not that it really mattered. As she'd been quick to remind Beth, Alex had simply wiped the slate clean.

As she would wipe her mind clean as she wandered the tree-lined boulevards. Eiffel Tower Tuesday, Notre Dame Wednesday, the Louvre on Thursday, which left the breathtaking steps of Sacré Coeur and the pavements of Montmartre for Friday. Home on Saturday, Carly and Danny's on Sunday – lunch. And that should be interesting, given Carly's novice status as a housewife, then back to the grind on Monday. Monday's child is what? Stella mused, but, try though she would, the childhood rhyme eluded her.

So, time to brush the cobwebs away and head back to the crowded auditorium, those steaming marquees. Not that she had need to. She'd already done everything Nik had asked of her, and more. Only Stella was looking for more. News. A new angle. New fabrics, new colours, new designs, new, surprisingly *un*anorexic models. Well, some of them at least. But as for news . . . Unless she delved a bit deeper. A behind the scenes peep at *haute couture*, poached designs, sweatshops, drugs and sex – there was sure to be drugs and sex somewhere, she argued, assuming she had the time to delve. Only she hadn't, of course. No more roving commissions until further notice, whenever that might be. So, in the meanwhile, make a case for herself and take just enough back to whet Nik Watson's jaded appetite.

Plenty to whet Stella's appetite, and, since she was hungry for once, she'd grab a snack at one of the pavement cafés and wander the banks of the Seine . . . in the rain . . . Warm rain, admittedly, but wet, definitely wet. Ah, well, she consoled herself, closing her bedroom window and reaching a momentous decision. What the hell? Room bill excepted, her expenses claim was practically blank. Hungry? Why, she could eat a horse – and literally at that, in this part of the world. So in that case she was dining in style – downstairs in that sumptuous restaurant she'd caught a glimpse of *en route* to the breakfast room.

In leggings and baggy jumper? she mused, eyeing her reflection in the full-length mirror. Or, conscious that she was covering a fashion show after all, that filmy calf-length skirt and over-blouse she'd tucked into her case on the off chance? Though the off chance of what had never quite crystallized.

Very sleek, sophisticated almost, thanks to the trailing scarf she'd draped around her neck, she was humming lightly under her breath as she stepped from the lift and joined the pre-theatre diners heading for the restaurant. A leisurely amble across the marble-tiled foyer – not quite the Ritz, but definitely a cut above the usual, thanks to the short notice – and heaven help Nik if he dared to complain.

'*Madame*, your scarf.' Pulling up short, she retrieved the wisp of chiffon from the bellhop's outstretched hand, pausing to knot it more securely. Vaguely distracted, Stella reached the open double doors just a fraction ahead of the man approaching from the opposite direction.

'*Madame, monsieur*? Table for two?'

'Good heavens, no,' Stella blurted, and, belatedly aware she must have sounded rude, swung round, raised her face, her smile of apology freezing on her lips. 'You!'

A lazy smile, a mocking bow. 'Nothing wrong with your memory, I see. Manners, yes. Memory no. The wedding?' Alex supplied, sensing that he'd lost her. 'And the Stella Marshall disappearing act?'

'You noticed? My, things are looking up,' she couldn't help but sneer. 'Let's hope you have the nous to take the hint at the last. But, just in case, I'll say it loud and clear. Goodbye, Alex. Over and out.'

With a defiant toss of the head, she set off behind the steward, never dreaming that Alex would follow, and pulled up in alarm when she reached the table. A table set for two. In an alcove. Screened from the rest of the room by a strategic bank of plants. Cosy. Too cosy by far. And the steward was waiting politely for Stella to take the chair that he proffered.

An awful thought crossed her mind. Alex wouldn't. Alex *would*. Ah, yes, but even Alex couldn't have known she was staying at the Monceau. Waves of relief. She matched those cool blue eyes with a chill in her own, held his gaze, not a blink, not a breath, not an outward sign of the turmoil raging.

'I –'

'Prefer to eat alone?' Alex challenged softly. 'Now, why doesn't that surprise me?'

Stella surprised him. Smiling sweetly, she sat.

Five long and silent minutes later, and the leather-bound menu proved a welcome diversion – page after page of classic French cuisine, complete with butter-rich sauces and no concession to the dietary squeamish. Only the soft rustle of pages broke the silence. And if Alex wasn't in the mood for small talk, that was fine by Stella. She was here to eat, not exchange pleasantries about the weather or life in general, or Alex Gifford's life in particular. Though, judging by the evidence just across the table, life was treating him well. There was no sign of the strain she'd noticed at the wedding, so life for Alex – and Tamara, presumably – was looking good. And on the subject of Tamara – Stella took a deep breath, took the plunge.

'Why, thank you, Stella,' he murmured solemnly in response to her terse enquiry. 'You'll be pleased to know she's fully recovered. I'll pass on your good wishes when I see her, shall I?'

'She isn't here, then? In Paris, I mean? The fashion show?' Stella blurted awkwardly, silently cursing the give-away surge of colour to her cheeks.

'Good heavens, no. Haven't you heard? She's been snapped up by GG Jay, the advertising ace. The world's Tamara's oyster these days. If my memory serves me right, she's flying to Japan on Monday.'

Japan? An oyster indeed. Lucky Tamara. A dream of a career break and a man like Alex. All man, Stella could acknowledge, risking another glance through the veil of her lashes and suppressing a stab of pain. Another time, another place, another suit. Savile Row? she wondered idly. Or the Avenue Montaigne? Not that it really mattered, given the impact of the lightweight navy blue wool, perfectly offset by the crisp white shirt and navy striped tie.

Yet for once in her life Stella didn't feel at a disadvantage. Admittedly her own filmy outfit would never grace a catwalk, but it didn't look out of place even in these elegant surroundings. And on the subject of surroundings, she was almost sorry they were sitting in an alcove. Think of the envious glances she'd have drawn with a man like Alex dancing attention. Only he wasn't. Engrossed in the wine list, he might have been alone on a desert island for all the notice he was taking of Stella, and, irrational or otherwise, the knowledge was galling.

'Not a single grey hair,' Alex mocked as, too late, Stella realized she'd been staring, that Alex had clearly clocked the fact minutes ago and was amused by her frank appraisal. 'Understandable, I suppose, since I'm barely a day older since when we last met. No – correction.' Another smile, a theatrical glance at his wristwatch. 'It's been eleven days, nineteen hours, forty-two minutes precisely since you scuttled like a frightened rabbit into the night.'

'I simply called a cab and went home. It had been a long day and I was tired.'

'Too tired to say goodnight to an old friend?'

'Friend you ain't, mister,' she bit out.

'Old I ain't either,' he tossed out mildly. 'Just in case you were thinking it.'

She wasn't. But it wouldn't hurt to let him stew.

Exquisite hors d'oeuvres were duly followed by *potages*, the unhurried pace of the meal matched by the murmur of conversation. A bevy of waiters arrived with the main course, the silver-domed lids removed with a synchronized flourish to expose the delights beneath. Noisettes of lamb with artichoke hearts and *duxelle* mushrooms for Stella; *filet* of turbot with Bresse Blue for Alex. And, whilst Turbot Farci Charies Rigoucot sounded much more exotic than turbot and cheese, Alex's meal, like Stella's, was no less than a work of art. Beautifully cooked, beautifully presented. It was surely a crime to break up the picture by stealing even a tiny forkful. Only they did. And another and another and another.

It was a mellowing experience; good food, good wine, good company – devastating company as far as Stella was concerned. But, in light of the unspoken truce, at least she could relax, enjoy the gentle ebb and flow of words. So when the spat did erupt it was all the more surprising that an idle remark from Stella turned out to be the trigger.

'Stay at the Ritz? Good heavens, no,' Alex demurred, parrying her dig about 'roughing it' at the Monceau. 'Exclusive though it might be, there's no guarantee of peace. Money, fame or notoriety – it's all the same to the newshounds. The attentions of the Press,' he explained, as if talking to an imbecile. 'Despite tough laws governing privacy over here, there's generally someone loitering on the off chance. I find it pays to avoid them.'

'Bully for you,' Stella needled, not so mellow that she didn't recognize an insult when it was wafted beneath her nose.

'Mind you,' Alex mused, the expression in his eyes curiously bland, 'that's only the theory. How else would you explain what went wrong this time?'

Stella's head snapped up. 'You rat.'

'I have my moments,' he conceded mildly. 'As we all do, Stella.'

Unimpressed, Stella visibly bristled. Her napkin landed in a heap on the table as she scraped back her chair and stumbled to her feet, eyes shooting flames. 'I don't have to sit and listen to this.'

'Indeed you don't,' he agreed solemnly. 'The alternatives are legion. You could flounce out of here in a flurry of indignation. You could toss the contents of that glass in my face – though at three hundred francs a bottle,' he slipped in absurdly, 'I really do hope that you don't. Failing that, you could do what you're best at. Stay and fight back.'

'Why?'

'Why, what?'

'Why should I stay? Why should I argue?'

He sat back in his chair, folded his arms, clearly amused by Stella's reaction. 'I like it when you argue,' he explained absurdly. 'It brings you alive. Not the only trigger by any means,' he conceded absurdly, 'but a safer option in public, don't you think?' A nod, a heated glance, an almost tangible caress of Stella's trembling body. And a definite lingering on agitated breasts with their give-away thrust of nipples. Blue eyes were swirling with emotion as they came back to lock with hers. 'But if you'd rather . . .'

'I think not,' Stella bit out, cheeks on fire at the image he'd concocted. Kissing, touching, tasting, making love. Love, she derided as the knife-blade twisted. As if. She angled her head. 'You insulted me.'

'Did I?'

'You said –'

'Yes, Stella?' he queried mildly. 'What did I say precisely?'

'You know what you said. You know what you implied.'

'And the cap fitted, huh?'

'No –'

'But you can't have it all ways, Stella. If the insult doesn't apply,' he pointed out with maddening insouciance, 'you can hardly take the hump. Logic. Irrefutable. I win.'

'The skirmish but not the battle,' she warned. 'And with a tongue as sharp as yours, Alex Gifford, it wouldn't do to be careless. Heaven forbid you slip and cut your own throat.'

'Why, thank you, Stella, it's nice to know you care. And, since one kind word deserves another, allow me to make amends. The remark was uncalled for. I apologize.'

'Don't bother. You were right in the first place. Once a journalist, always a journalist – *maybe*,' she rasped. 'But I've nothing to be ashamed of.'

'Good.'

'I beg your pardon?'

'You're you. Stella Marshall. The same Stella Marshall you've always been. Determined, hard-working, caring, loving, considerate, gutsy, loyal, protective –'

'Lying, scheming, cheating – your opinion, not mine,' she spat. 'And I –'

Catching Alex's broad smile, the shake of his head, the gleeful admonition, she broke off, realized where her words had been leading her and flushed. Because clever Alex had baited his trap, and Stella had jumped without looking.

'Another cap that didn't fit, hey, Stella?' he murmured softly as, stunned, she sat down again. Taking pity, he reached across the table to capture her hand, tugging it towards him. Cradling the hand like a fragile piece of porcelain, he turned it over oh, so gently, and, dipping his head, nuzzled the inside of her wrist.

The rest of the meal was a haze. Dessert – pear and crême patissière tart for Stella; rum and chocolate bavarois for Alex – followed by cheese – wonderfully ripe wedges of Brie, baby Camemberts and creamy Pont La Veque served as only the French could, on delicate plates garnished with wisps of frisée and rocket leaves, and eaten with knife and fork – and then coffee – tiny fragrant cups that yielded but a mouthful, the generous cafetière luckily yielding lots of refills.

Because Stella was growing more nervous by the second. And she was spinning out the meal. Cheese, coffee, rich mint chocolates, tiny nibbles, tiny sips. And Alex simply smiled, allowed Stella to chatter aimlessly on and on.

A scraping back of chairs. An interminable walk the length of the restaurant. Side by side, sure enough, but careful not to touch. No need to touch, with currents of electricity bridging the gap.

An awkward pause in the foyer, and a frantic Stella surreptitiously wiped damp palms on her skirt, looking anywhere but at Alex.

'I'll see you to your room.'

'Thank you, Alex, but I'm a big girl now. I'm hardly likely to come to any harm in a place like this.'

'Maybe not, but –'

'No buts, no arguments. You don't even need to walk me to the lifts,' she demurred brusquely, upping her pace and fervently praying he'd take the hint.

He didn't, matching her step for step across the chequered marble floor.

Arriving at the lifts as two sets of doors slid soundlessly open, she turned, smiled, waved an airy hand. 'Well, there you have it. Lifts are like buses; they prefer to travel in packs. His and hers. How convenient. Goodnight Alex,' she pointedly needled, stepping forward. 'See you at breakfast.' Maybe.

Second floor. Thirty seconds. Barely time to acknowledge her face in the bronze-tinted mirrors before the doors swung open. Two paces forward and she pulled up. 'Alex!'

'Stella?'

'Are you following me?'

'Are *you* following me?' he countered absurdly.

'Don't be ridiculous –'

'Precisely. Going my way? But why didn't you say, my dear?' Grinning, he proffered an arm with a theatrical flourish. 'Allow me.'

'Thank you, but –'

'No?' A maddening twitch of generous lips. 'No, of course not.'

Stella stomped ahead, nerve-endings tingling, and had to fight the urge to break into a run. A dozen paces and she'd be safe, she calculated swiftly. She could dive into her room and slam the door. Ah, yes, but then Alex would know precisely which room was Stella's. Pretend to trip, fiddle with the strap of her shoe and stall, allowing Alex to pass her? she mused. Not that Alex would be likely to leave her in a heap on the floor. And anyway, if Alex was really determined to track her down, all he had to do was call Reception.

Too late now in any case. She reached her door and halted, breathed a huge sigh of relief as Alex strolled past. And inserted his key in the lock next door.

Stella's face was stony. 'You *are* following me.'

'No, Stella, *you* are following me. My room's further along the corridor, see?' he explained, spreading his hands. 'Stands to reason. I'm four paces ahead, you're lagging behind. Which means –'

'Thank you, Alex,' she ground out huffily. 'I know precisely what it means.' It meant lying in bed knowing Alex would be sleeping soundly just the other side of the wall. It meant tossing and turning all night – again – with the focus of her thoughts almost within touching distance. And Stella wouldn't sleep. Because she wanted him and the need refused to go away.

'Stella?'

She angled her head, met his gaze full-on, prayed none of the inner turmoil would show in her eyes. 'Alex?'

'A wee nightcap, Stella? After all, it's barely eleven, and the Stella Marshall disappearing trick isn't due for another hour.'

'I —'

'Can't trust yourself alone in a bedroom with a guy like me, hey? Understandable, I suppose,' he conceded solemnly. 'But if it helps to put your mind at rest, there's a perfectly respectable sitting room, with *single* chairs would you believe? And if *that* doesn't sway you, we'll simply leave the door wide open. See?' The door swung open on its hinges as Alex finished speaking, and he smiled, waved a hand, inviting her inside.

'I —'

'You'd prefer to take brandy in the corridor?' he enquired incredulously. 'Well, if that's what it takes to have the pleasure of your company, Stella, consider it done.'

CHAPTER 17

Brandy. Far too large a measure in Stella's estimation, but too late to object now. Too late to wish she'd called his bluff and opted for safety and the corridor. Besides, knowing Alex, he'd have done precisely that – set up table and chairs smack bang outside his bedroom door. Sitting room door, she amended absent-mindedly. And all in all quite impressive – wall to wall opulence and plush, inviting chairs. A plush, inviting sofa too, but she was giving *that* a very wide berth. As for the bedroom, barely a peep as she was passing on her way to the bathroom, but enough to confirm her worst fears. Double bed. Enormous double bed. Bed, with Alex. Only she mustn't.

She glanced up suddenly, and immediately wished she hadn't. Alex was watching her, the expression in his eyes unfathomable, and Stella flushed, forced herself not to look away. Not that she really wanted to. She wanted to feast her eyes, had to content herself with what she hoped was a casual appraisal. Casual. Alex's appearance was too casual by far, the dishevelled result of the carelessly discarded jacket and tie hinting at an intimacy Stella knew she'd be powerless to resist if Alex set the train of events in motion. A look, a touch, a kiss and Stella would be lost.

She cradled the glass, swirled the golden liquid round and round the balloon and racked her brains for some safe, innocuous topic of conversation. Damn Alex Gifford for sitting there in silence, so cool, calm and collected, while Stella's nerves frazzled every bit as much as they had at the wedding.

Wedding. Carly. Belated thanks? When as far as Stella was concerned he'd simply wiped the slate clean? Maybe so, she allowed, but it did seem churlish not even to acknowledge it.

'The reference was the least I could do,' he lazily demurred when Stella summoned the nerve to mention it. 'And Carly was good at her job, as was her immediate successor. Caring must run in the family.'

Stella flushed. 'We simply aim to please,' she countered primly. 'Despite our motives.'

'Motives?'

'My real reason for being there. But, believe it or not, James was a bonus.'

'Yes.'

'He's a beautiful little boy, Alex.'

'Did I speak? Did I say a word?'

'You don't have to. James isn't yours. End of story,' she tossed out bitterly.

'He isn't your child either,' he countered mildly. 'But that didn't stop you loving him.'

'I –'

'Simply did the job I paid you for? No, Stella,' he

contradicted firmly. 'A temporary arrangement it may have been, but you went way beyond that. I owe you. We all do. And as for James . . .'

'James?' Stella probed carefully, the hairs on the back of her neck prickling out a warning.

'When he's old enough to understand, his doting papa will tell him all about Miss Practically Perfect In Every Way, who breezed into his life out of nowhere and proceeded to transform it.'

'Oh!'

'Just, oh?' he queried provokingly.

'Yes, Alex, just oh,' she snapped. But she was smiling, as Alex was, because Alex's easy words had put her mind at rest.

Easy enough now to mention his wedding gift to Carly. Not a squaring of the conscience, Stella decided. Just a nice gesture from a pretty nice guy . . . a devastating guy . . . A guy whose hungry gaze was fastened on hers, she couldn't help but notice, and the swirls of emotion in the depths of his eyes were more than enough to set her pulse rate soaring . . . A guy who wasn't hers –, never had been, never would be, she tagged on bitterly.

So, time to leave, head for her own room and safety. Only first there was another pang of guilt eating away at her. That dreadful moment when she'd all but accused him of killing his wife. And, *yes*, she'd simply been hitting out, paying Alex back for a catalogue of insults. But he'd apologized, and more. And he'd been toweringly angry. And if the cap didn't fit . . . Which meant Stella's throwaway comment didn't matter to

Alex either. Not really. A huge weight lifted from her shoulders. Even so, it wouldn't stop her mentioning it in passing – just a casual comment on her way to the door, perhaps.

She abandoned the brandy, came lazily to her feet. Long and slow. No overreaction, no outward signs of panic. She sashayed across the thick pile of the carpet with the soft folds of her skirt swirling round her legs. And if she was shockingly aware of Alex, just a pace or two behind, no need to betray the fact. Nice and easy. So near, so far. Reach for the handle, half turn towards him, say the words she'd been practising over and over in her head.

'Hmm,' he mused when she'd finished speaking. 'As apologies go, I *suppose* it was adequate.'

'Adequate, my foot,' she bit out, sensing he was teasing, that the teasing was dangerous – every bit as dangerous as the man himself, invading her personal body space and far too close for comfort. 'If *monsieur* doesn't like it, *monsieur* knows what he can do with it.'

'As a matter of fact, he doesn't,' he conceded lightly. 'So maybe *mademoiselle* would care to enlighten me?'

Mademoiselle wouldn't. *Mademoiselle* was leaving. Now.

'Not so fast –'

'No, Alex –'

'*Yes*, Stella,' he insisted, his hand on the door, both hands on the door, as Stella twisted round, backed herself against it, unconsciously pinning herself between the splayed fingers. So near, so far. Because he wasn't touching Stella by any means, he was simply there, the burning intensity of his gaze pinning her fast. And she wanted him. And she could see him, was inhaling the unique body scent, could reach out and touch . . .

Touch. Just a whisper, the merest hint of connection, a single thumb brushing against her cheek. And Stella closed her eyes, denying him, denying them both. Because she loved him. And she wanted him. And Alex didn't belong to Stella. And the ecstasy of giving herself tonight would be more than matched by the hell of waking up tomorrow knowing she was expendable. He wanted her, he'd take her, and then he'd toss her aside with barely a second thought.

Not true, her mind screamed. Sex. Mind-blowing sex. He'd remember, all right, and he'd know that Stella was available. A night here, an afternoon there – whenever Tamara happened to let him off the leash. Tamara. Stella could almost feel it in her heart to feel sorry for her. Because at least Stella knew. Alex didn't pretend. Alex played around. Alex was brutally honest with Stella. There had been no rash promises the first time; he sure as hell wouldn't be making any this time. Sex. Nothing more, nothing less. Only there wasn't going to be a this time.

'Stella.'

'Let me go, Alex.'

'Don't fight it, Stella.'

'Don't make it any harder than it is, Alex. Let me go.'

'If that's what you want?'

She swallowed hard, nodded, felt the sudden well of

tears and clamped her lids together even tighter, her rigid control at breaking point.

'Say it, Stella,' Alex commanded harshly. 'Look at me, Stella.'

'No!'

'Yes!'

'No!'

'Because you can't. Because you daren't. Because you want me –'

'No! No, no, no!' she wailed in anguish.

'Oh, but yes!' he insisted. 'Look me in the eye and lie, damn you.'

'No –'

'Fine. Don't look, don't speak, don't even blink, if it makes you feel better, but don't say I didn't warn you. Just stand there and continue to deny me,' he rasped. 'Because the moment you react, I'm going to take you. Understand, Stella?' he queried harshly. 'The moment you respond, you're mine. And now I'm going to prove it. I'm going to touch you. Just once. And look, no hands!'

'*Alex!*' Her lids flew open, pupils dilated, and the shock of connection thrilled her.

'No hands,' he repeated, grinding his hips against her, the heat and the hardness driving the breath from her body.

And Stella was moving against him, wanted him, needed him, had felt herself flood at the first awesome thrust. Only Alex laughed, an ugly sound that echoed horribly inside Stella's head, would come back to haunt her in the dark hours. Because, having proved his point with brutal eloquence, Alex pulled away, froze the blood in her veins with the expression in his eyes.

Folding his arms, he angled his head, pinned her back against the door again. 'But I was forgetting. You don't want me. You didn't react. Only you did, of course.'

'Alex –'

'No, Stella!' he roared, cutting her off with an imperative slice of the arm. 'You lied – again. You *said* you didn't want me.'

'I want you.'

'I *know* you want me.'

'Take me, Alex.'

'No, Stella.'

'Please, Alex.'

'Not even pretty please, Stella.'

'But you *said* you'd take me. You said –'

'So I lied. So we're quits. You lied to me; I lied to you.'

'And now you don't want me?'

He dropped his gaze, looked her up and down – an insolent appraisal of her body, a body that tightened with every passing second, the ache in her belly unendurable. Because Stella wanted him. And Alex lingered on the rigid thrust of nipples beneath the filmy blouse, and, having drunk his fill, snapped his frigid gaze back to lock with Stella's. 'I don't want you.'

'So who's lying now?' she challenged softly. Because she wasn't hurting any more. Not for herself at least.

Because she understood. She'd hurt him. She'd denied him. She'd lied. The story of her life, she was beginning to think, not for the first time.

'Like I said, it simply makes us quits.'

'Fine. You had your chance, now it's my turn.'

'Stella –'

'No! My turn.' She snapped the buttons of her blouse with fingers that shook, shaking out the folds, watching Alex watching her, the contempt in his eyes almost more than she could take. Shrugging the blouse over her shoulders, she allowed it to drop, then reached round behind to tug at the zipper of her skirt, the resultant thrust of breasts not missed by the man now regarding her with undisguised disgust. All man, Stella told herself, allowing her gaze to drop to his groin, to log the effect she was having on his body. Oh, yes, all man. And he wanted her. And Stella wanted him – so badly that the shame of openly begging simply didn't matter any more. She wanted him.

A shimmy of hips and the skirt concertinaed around her ankles. A deft kick of a toe, and skirt and blouse were gone.

Silence. The atmosphere was so thick she could have cut it with a knife. Man and woman. Alone. Woman half-naked and shameless. Woman snapping the catch of her bra, allowing full breasts to spill free. Woman smiling inside at the man's hiss of indrawn breath. And still Alex didn't move, simply dropped his gaze, feasted his hungry gaze on the rigid pink buds at the centre of Stella's aching breasts.

Stella smiled. In her mind. Because man and woman were engaged in silent battle, and she wasn't about to risk losing all with anything so innocuous as a blink of an eyelid. She wanted him. Dear God, she had to prove to Alex just how much she wanted him.

So, with just those shamefully skimpy, shamefully damp panties to dispose of, Stella took her time, slid her hands up to her breasts, cupped her breasts, allowed idle thumbs to brush against her nipples, over the swell and down . . . Over the flat plains of her belly, into the curve of her hips, splayed fingers sliding beneath the waistband of her panties . . . and pausing.

An eternity passed. Alex's smouldering eyes flicked to Stella's. He wanted her. Stella wanted Alex. It was only a matter of time. Another eternity passed. Stella sighed, broke the impasse, pushed the flimsy lace panties down over her hips and stepped shamelessly out of them.

Angling her head in defiance, she waited. And waited. And Alex waited. And Stella openly smiled, brought her hands up to her breasts and made silent offering to the man whose own need of Stella was growing more urgent by the second. 'No?' she queried smokily.

Alex shook his head.

So Stella smiled, trailed her hands once more down over the plains of her belly to the lush triangle of hair at the apex of her legs. And paused again. Splaying her fingers, she brought her thumbs together as if in prayer, before swirling her palms down over the tangle of curls to part her thighs, allowing the thumbs to hover at the very edge, to threaten to plunge –

'No!' With the roar of a wounded animal Alex had moved, had ripped the shirt from his back, disposed of trousers and boxers and was pinning her to the door, kissing her, tasting her, driving her insane with the touch of skin on skin.

All man, she told herself, smiling inside.

'Stella, Stella, Stella,' he crooned in anguish. 'I want you. I want you so badly that it hurts. I want you, my love. *Now*, Stella,' he groaned, thrusting hard, making the connection that she craved. 'Oh, Stella, Stella, Stella,' he breathed, his hands cupping her buttocks, all but lifting her from the floor. 'I want you *now*.'

Stella's heart soared. Just as well, she silently concluded, given her own palpable need. And if not quite that sumptuous double bed she'd envisaged, she was more than happy to forgo it. All feathers and softness, the bed was redundant. For Alex was hard, wonderfully hard, his normally rigid control hanging by a thread. Because he wanted Stella every bit as badly as she wanted him, and oh, God, how she wanted him . . . revelled in the touch, the taste, the smell of him.

Taste. She was kissing Alex, mouth to mouth, lips to lips, was pushing her tongue into the steamy recesses of his mouth, sweeping across his sensitive inner lip, provoking a shudder that seemed to travel the length of his body. Smiling, she took pity, easing the tension but a fraction as she nuzzled the corners of his mouth, rained tiny kisses across his jawline, the rasp of stubble another erotic sensation. Nibbling at his shoulder, she inhaled the very essence of him, slid her arms around him, kneading the glistening flesh, the corresponding ripple of muscles sending her heart soaring skywards and beyond. She wanted him, she needed him, she needed him *now*, and the thought of having to wait a single moment longer was simply unendurable.

'Stella, please, Stella,' he implored as she ground herself against him. 'No, Stella! Oh, my love, I can't – oh hell! Oh, Stella. Oh, my love!' One last juddering thrust and Alex was spent, had slumped against Stella, who was rammed against the door, a silent torrent of tears pouring down her cheeks. Because she loved him. And, in his own way, Alex loved Stella.

'I'm sorry.'

'I'm sorry, too. Sorry I hurt you –'

He placed a tender finger on her lips. 'Hush. My bed, my apology. I was revolting.'

'Magnificently revolting. Well, magnificent, full stop,' she amended playfully. 'Again, Alex?'

'No, *mademoiselle*. Certainly not. Or leastways,' he added, kissing her, hugging her fiercely, 'never, ever in anger. Never again. I'm ashamed.'

'You should be proud.'

'That I hurt you, denied you, goaded you beyond endurance?'

'Ah, you noticed? And I thought I'd taken it like a lady, been cool, calm, collected and discreet.'

'Very discreet,' he breathed, 'for a wanton.'

'Guilty as charged,' she mournfully allowed. 'Shocking.'

'Positively shameless, I'd say.'

'You would? Oh, good, I should hate you to gain the wrong impression.'

'I love you.'

Yes. Stella smiled and cried, both in her mind. She guessed he did at that. After all, love was a complex emotion. The love of a mother for her child, a child for its parents, brother for sister, man for woman, men and women the world over, battling against the odds to help their fellow human beings. So many facets. And Stella loved Alex – passionately, unconditionally – which was why she would never dream of making any demands. So, definitely shameless. She'd take whatever Alex was offering and be grateful. No demands, no wild, impassioned pleas, no unreasonable behaviour. She was Alex's for as long as he wanted, and as for Tamara –

No. Stella closed her mind. She wouldn't ask, she wouldn't probe, she wouldn't resent. Hurt, yes. Sob her heart out in the dark hours alone, where no one would ever know, yes. Because Alex must never know just how badly she needed him.

'I love you,' he said again, and he fastened his smouldering gaze on to hers and nodded. 'I love you.'

Stella smiled. 'Thank you.' It was enough. It was more than she expected. Alex loved her. Was it Alex's fault he loved Tamara more?

So little time, so much love, so much loving. Now tender and gentle, now more urgent – though not so urgent that Alex lost control. Never again, he'd promised her. Never again was what he meant. Love. Man and woman giving love, receiving love, living and breathing love. And in the scant hour before dawn, they finally slept.

Alex woke first, and Stella opened her eyes to find him propped up on an elbow, gazing down at her, a wealth of emotion in his eyes.

'I love you,' he breathed. And then he proved it. He took her. Gently.

Aching with love, Stella snuggled down into the pillows while Alex showered and planned the rest of her life. She smiled. No more roving commissions, Nik had told her; no more roving commissions she'd happily comply with. Because, permanently based in London, she'd be on hand for Alex. She'd be on hand for Carly too, and the idea of soon being a real live aunty was decidedly appealing.

And, on the subject of babies, Stella needed to ensure she didn't upset the balance of her life with Alex. No demands, no unreasonable behaviour. Besides, it wouldn't be fair to bring a child into the world without benefit of a father. Not that Alex would deny his son – and it would be a son, she decided, smothering the stab of pain. Only she mustn't. It wouldn't be fair to any of them, but most of all it wouldn't be fair on a child. So she'd take care of that side of things the moment they landed in London.

A rap at the door put an end to her musings. Room service. Breakfast. Piping hot coffee, orange juice, freshly baked croissants and morning paper.

'Give me five minutes,' Alex called out through the steam of the bathroom.

At the sight of food, Stella's tummy gave an audible rumble, and she pulled up her chair, draped Alex's crumpled shirt around her shoulders – less for the sake of modesty than the need to inhale his unique body scent – and poured herself a glass of juice.

The Times, she noted idly, reaching for the paper. How terribly English. How typically English, she conceded, vaguely amused. The eccentricities of the Englishman abroad and craving news of home.

Yet, in the light of Alex's sneering contempt of all things journalistic, Stella's amusement was tinged with alarm. A premonition? she was later to wonder. Even so, it didn't serve to prepare her for the bombshell.

No world crises, no political sleaze, no celebrity marriage in trouble. No news was certainly bad news from a professional point of view, she silently acknowledged, flicking through the pages. So, in the light of her own recently negotiated role – albeit fiercely resisted – the births, marriages and discreet family announcements page would serve to fill an idle moment.

'Oh, God.' Stella closed her eyes, squeezing back the tears. 'No. Please, God, no.' But it was still there when she steeled herself to look again. In black and white. Irrefutable.

Mr AW Gifford and Miss TA Clayton. The engagement is announced . . .

'No. No, no, no.' Unable to sit, she began to pace up

and down, up and down, aimlessly pacing, a wild animal in a cage. She didn't want to believe it. He loved Stella. Ah, yes, but he loved Tamara more. She'd always known that Tamara came first. And the engagement had been planned for months – bang on cue at the end of the summer, according to Tamara, with the wedding itself not far behind.

Stella pushed her fist into her mouth in an effort to stay in control. Take whatever Alex was offering and be grateful? she silently scorned, sitting down suddenly, hugging herself, rocking herself backwards and forwards. Don't rock any boats? No demands, no impassioned pleas? Well, maybe she'd even believed it at the time, but, no. She couldn't do it. She loved him. Heaven help her, she loved him, and all the time they'd been making love Alex had known that his engagement to Tamara was on the verge of being made public. Of course Alex had known, she concluded bitterly. Why else would he swallow his bile and request a morning paper? As he had done. Proof.

The room swam dizzily. Stella rode the waves of nausea, driving her fingernails into her palms in an effort to stay in control. Oh, Alex. Oh, my love. Only you're not my love. Never have been, never will be. And I'm sorry, but I can't spend the rest of my life lapping up the crumbs. I thought I could, she silently conceded, wiping away a tear. But I was wrong. It was all or nothing, and I should have had the sense to see it all along.

So – she had to be strong. She had to deny him, look him in the eye and lie as she'd never lied before. Only this time she had to convince Alex she was giving him the truth. It was over and it was finished – for good.

There was a sudden silence as the background sound of running water ceased. Stella's head snapped up. Panic. Face Alex and be strong? Face Alex and pretend she didn't love him? Face Alex and lie?

She couldn't do it. Instead, she did the only thing she could do. She bolted.

Thirty seconds to slip into skirt and blouse, tuck bra and panties between rigid fingers. Another thirty seconds to reach the safety of her room. Only she wasn't safe, would never be safe with Alex next door, she realized hysterically, scrambling into leggings and jumper and ramming the rest of her things into the overnight bag.

No time to wait for the lift. Take the stairs in leaps and bounds. Reach the normality of the hotel lobby and then pause for breath, stifle the panic and think – *think*, Stella, think. No time to think. Too much time to think in the interminable wait at Reception. Key. Check out. Room bill. Restaurant bill –

'Oh, no, you don't.' A hand reached over her shoulder to snatch the chit from beneath her trembling fingers and Stella prayed for the ground to open up and swallow her. 'Dinner was my treat, Stella,' Alex insisted frigidly, spinning her round to face him. 'As were the rest of the night's events. My treat, my pleasure,' he underlined tersely. 'So perhaps you wouldn't mind explaining what the hell is going on?'

Stella did. Succinctly.

'Leaving! Just like that?'

'Just like that,' she echoed, seeing the pain, the disbelief etched in the well-loved features and closing her mind to the hurt, the torment, the sheer incredulity streaming from each and every pore of him.

'Why?'

'What do you mean, why? It was a temporary arrangement, Alex. Surely you understood that? You have your life, I have mine, and that's the way it's staying.'

'But last night –'

'We made love? Yes,' she conceded coolly, 'I did notice.'

'But you can't just walk away, damn you –'

'Just watch me,' she sneered, reaching for the bag which she'd dropped at her feet.

Alex snatched at her arm, wrapping iron fingers around her wrist. 'No!'

'Yes, Alex,' she contradicted tersely, the currents spreading out from the point of contact filling her with heat, filling her with dread. 'My life, my decision. And my life, I can assure you, is mapped out already. Men, and all the attendant complications, I can well do without.'

'And sex, Stella? Good sex, mind-blowing sex – your words, not mine,' he hissed as Stella's head snapped up.

'You're not the only man with a passable technique,' she sneered, hurting him, hurting herself more, but desperate to keep him at arm's length.

'You little –'

'Bitch? Why, yes, Alex,' she cut in tersely. 'I do

believe we established that some time ago. A case of once a bitch –'

'Always a bitch? Lady, you said it,' he rasped. 'I *believed* in you.'

'Then more fool you, Alex Gifford.'

'Why, Stella? Why are you doing this?'

'I don't have to explain myself to you,' she pointed out coolly. 'I don't have to explain myself to any man.'

'Shouldn't that be plural, Stella? *Men*,' he emphasized nastily, the fingers on her wrist biting deep. 'How many men? Tell me, Stella,' he entreated frigidly, tugging her close, his eyes pools of hate as they locked with hers. 'Just for the record, of course, how many men does it take to teach a tramp like you the tricks of the trade?'

Stella blanched, the scythe of pain almost unendurable. 'Only one,' she conceded thickly, swallowing hard, suppressing the tears with a massive surge of will. 'But you can take it from me, he was quite a guy.'

'All man, hey, Stella?' Alex jeered.

'As it happens, yes, Alex.'

'And you love him?'

'Love? Who knows? Who cares?' she tossed out flippantly. 'But, yes, Alex. Since you've asked, I'll tell you. I love him. I've loved him almost from the day we met.'

'And this – man,' he sneeringly entreated, 'has he made you what you are today?'

'I didn't notice any complaints from the last guy I shared a bed with. In fact,' she conceded silkily, 'I'd say he enjoyed each and every moment – hey, Alex?'

'And you didn't. Is that what you're saying?'

'Hardly. Even I can't fake that sort of performance,' she reminded him.

'Precisely. Performance. And what a performance. And all for the price of a slap-up meal. A bargain.'

'But don't forget the cost of the wine, Alex,' Stella slipped in slyly, dying inside but damned if she'd let it show. Not now. Not ever again. 'Three hundred francs a bottle,' she scoffed. 'Times two. But silly me, I was almost forgetting. Maths isn't your strong point.'

'It doesn't need to be. I know when to cut my losses –'

'Oh, no!' Stella pulled free of his vice-like grip, the sudden surge of anger helping to keep the tears at bay. 'Enough!' she insisted with an imperative slice of her arm. 'I don't have to stand and listen to your insults, your vile insinuations,' she hissed, eyes pools of hate in a chalk-white face. 'And just to put the record straight, who's walking out on whom?'

He gave a derisory snap of fingers. 'So you're walking. You'll be back. You can't get enough of me.'

'If and when I need a man,' she witheringly informed him, 'I promise I'll bear you in mind. Only do yourself a favour – don't hold your breath.'

'Don't call me, I'll call you, hey?' he jeered, looking her up and down, from face to breasts, lingering on her breasts, those rigid nipples jutting through the fabric of her sweater, and down, in an insolent appraisal that seemed to reach out to touch her before embarking on the long, lazy climb back to her face. 'Lady,' he conceded with a derisive curl of lip, 'if I thought it was worth three lousy francs for a five-minute tumble, I'd be waiting. Only it isn't. I know.'

'Then I'll just have to keep on practising, hey, Alex?' she jeered, cold, so cold her heart could be made of ice. Only it wasn't. Because ice would mask the pain, such terrible pain, she conceded wearily, wondering how long it would take for the pain to go away. 'Only not, repeat, not,' she emphasized tersely, 'with you. This little lady's just upped her price, and sorry to disappoint you, mister, but that puts you way down the league – so far down you've dropped off the bottom. Goodbye, Alex, and thanks for the slap-up meal. As evenings go,' she conceded tightly, 'it was pretty entertaining on occasion.'

With a curt nod of dismissal, she swung away, swung her bag over her shoulder. She was amazed to discover they weren't alone, and that when it came to entertainment half of Paris had been lapping up the show. And quite a show at that, for if the words required translation, not so the flood of raw emotion. Not that Stella cared any more, and, raising her head, she jutted her chin in defiance and began the interminable walk across the chequered marble floor.

'That's right, Stella,' Alex goaded, his voice slicing across to halt her. 'Walk away. Walk every step of the way back to England and safety,' he scorned. 'But you can't escape. You'll never escape. You want me. Last night you were insatiable, and you can take it from me – a need like that doesn't disappear in a shower of rain.

A temporary arrangement?' he queried nastily as Stella half turned to face him, seeing his face, hearing his voice as if through a smothering wad of cotton wool. 'And who the hell are you trying to kid? You want me, all right. And sooner or later,' he insisted tersely, 'you'll be forced to admit it. See you next week, my dear.'

'I beg your pardon?'

'Saturday week. Ten a.m. sharp. Lady Rogers is opening the fête – the village fête – and with Freshfields taking central stage. It's high time we cashed in on some positive publicity.' He waved an expansive arm. 'The feature's all yours. A Stella Marshall exclusive.'

'Thanks, but no, thanks,' she retorted evenly. 'I'd rather starve in a garret than darken your door.'

'You might have to.'

'Meaning?'

'The feature. You haven't any choice. Nik Watson owes me, and I do believe it's time to call in that favour.'

'And surprise, surprise, Stella Marshall does as she's told or she's out of a job? Well, fine. You hit the nail on the head in the first place,' she bit out. 'As jobs go, this really is the lowest of the low at times; it probably comes of covering the antics of slimeballs like you,' she informed him confidentially. 'Only not any more. I've had enough. No feature, no job, no problem. Suits me.'

'And Beth? And that host of disabled children?' he tossed out slyly. 'Turn your back on me, by all means,

Stella, but can you really live with your conscience if you let them down?'

Let them down? What on earth was he wittering on about? 'How can I possibly let them down when I won't even be there?' she demanded incredulously.

Alex smiled, a muted flash of triumph that made Stella's blood run cold. 'Simple, Stella. No feature, no fête, no funding for the kids.'

'You wouldn't.'

'Wouldn't I?'

'But – You're crazy. You can't. You can't punish a bunch of innocent kids just to hit back at me,' she spat, choking back the tears. 'It's obscene. It's crazy. It's immoral. You can't pull out now, damn you. Think of the kids. Think of the disappointment. Grab the headlines by all means, Alex,' she conceded icily. 'But you'll need to find another mug to cover it. Another day, another story, another rat-pack of reporters,' she scorned with a derisive snap of the fingers. 'And, since reporters are twelve a penny these days, take a tip from soon to be ex-reporter Stella Marshall and hire yourself a dozen.'

'But I don't want a dozen, Stella,' he stunned her by conceding. 'I want you.'

CHAPTER 18

Want. And what Alex Gifford wanted, Alex Gifford bought – or took – or bullied for. So Stella would cover the fête, by order of the management. Because that was another fascinating fact she'd uncovered quite by chance when she'd reported in to work on Monday morning. The buy-out that Nik had been curiously loath to expand on. Stella should have known.

If you can't beat 'em, join 'em, hey, Alex? she'd silently scorned, raising a lukewarm cup of coffee in bitter, mocking tribute. But he'd need to make the most of it. As from midnight on Saturday evening, Stella Marshall, journalist, would cease to ply her trade. Work for Alex? She'd rather work in hell.

Hell. Days of hell. Of loving Alex, hating Alex, loathing Alex. But most of all loving Alex. Because the insults and the vile remarks didn't matter. She'd hurt him. She'd taken him to the brink of heaven, then landed him in hell. And Alex was simply paying her back. Only it didn't matter. The cap didn't fit, she consoled herself. But it was scant consolation in the dark hours.

Saturday. Another day of hell? Glorious blue skies and laughing children. The evocative aroma of hot dogs and candy floss and sticky toffee apples. For the annual village fête was in full swing: coconut shies and bran tubs, shove-a-penny and hoop-la stalls and guess the weight of the piglet – though heaven only knows why anyone would want to take that particular prize home!

Stella smiled despite herself, paused to watch the frown of concentration on a small child's face as he carefully recorded his answer on the scorecard and dropped it into the box. In unlikely the event of a tie, the boldly printed notice at the side proclaimed, the winning ticket would be *brawn* from a hat. Stella did a double take, then decided the pun was deliberate.

'Go on, be a devil,' drawled a familiar voice at her elbow. And, though deep down inside she'd been expecting it, dreading it, the absence of Alex's distinctive XJ8 and Tamara's equally impressive Élan when she'd pulled into yard all those hours ago had allowed the foolish hope that Alex would have the decency to stay away. His house, his share of the glory, she scathingly acknowledged, and, bracing herself for the contempt he surely wouldn't choose to mask, she spun round to face him.

Only Alex was smiling, was holding out a card in silent invitation. 'Guess the weight of the piglet,' he reminded her, and, when Stella didn't blink, didn't move, didn't react, he reached into a pocket and dropped a handful of coins into the collection jar.

'Worth fifty pence of well-earned money any day of the week. All in a good cause, of course.'

'The Saint Alex, "Let's Show the World How Wrong it's Been Show"?' she couldn't help but sneer.

'If you like,' he conceded mildly – too mildly to Stella's mind, given all that had passed between them. 'But, since it's the kids who benefit most, why take a snipe at me? Here –' He thrust the card into her hand. 'Swallow your bile for the next thirty seconds and guess the weight of the pig.'

Stella did, handing the card back to Alex instead of dropping it in the box.

'Thirteen stones?' he queried incredulously, and then his face darkened as the penny dropped. 'Unkind, Stella,' he murmured coldly. 'Not to mention a good half-stone out, despite your passing acquaintance with the body in question. I did hope you'd have the decency to call a truce,' he rasped. 'For the sake of the kids, if nothing else. But I should have known I was wasting my time.'

'Wrong, Alex,' she retorted sweetly. 'I'm happy to call a truce for an hour or so any day of the week. But I just couldn't resist putting one of those famed Gifford theories to the test. Does the cap fit?'

'And does it?'

'Oh, no. You're not dipping out of that one. *You* tell me.'

'Fine. Over a sandwich and pint in the Feathers.'

'Why?'

'Because that gives me time to put another Gifford

theory to the test. Something to do with the heart, absence and the means to make it fonder.'

'A whole ten days' absence, Alex?' she murmured incredulously.

'A whole ten days indeed, Stella. Ten days, four hours and –'

'Sixteen minutes precisely?' she drawled, correct to the second, and damned if she cared what Alex would make of the knowledge.

His smile spread. 'Oh, Stella,' he observed gleefully, 'I do believe you've been missing me.'

'Like a hole in the head,' she retorted sweetly, and, since she'd managed to talk herself into it, reluctantly accompanied Alex across the road.

The village pub was packed – hardly surprising, she supposed, squeezing her way into a space in the corner of the snug as Alex cut a swathe to the bar, and, sure enough, she couldn't help but notice, the massed ranks did indeed make way for the great man himself.

'Cheese and onion or ham?' he enquired on his return, hitching his stool much too close for comfort.

'You decide,' Stella insisted, a churn of nerves and immensely glad they weren't alone.

Alex did. Using the knife provided, he sliced the crispy rolls clean down the centre, swapped a cheese half for a ham half and offered a plate to Stella.

'Thank you.'

'My pleasure.' He nudged a glass towards her. 'Cider. I'm sorry, I should have asked. You probably hate cider.'

'I love cider, but not usually by the pint.'

Alex grinned. 'No problem. Just look on it as two halves.'

Ah, well, lady she'd never be, Stella decided, gripping the glass carefully in both hands – hands that shook despite her best efforts, and a reaction not missed by the man sitting large as life and every bit as devastating practically elbow to elbow with her.

No sleepless nights for Alex, she decided, stealing a sideways glance. No sodden pillows, no recurring nightmares. Yet why should there be? Alex had everything he wanted in life. Money, power, a woman he adored – a woman he'd soon be marrying, she recalled with a vicious stab of pain.

A woman's voice rose above the hubbub. 'Alex, there you are!' A boom of a voice, a boom of a lady, in tweed skirt and cashmere sweater, threading her way through the crush. 'I was hoping to catch you.'

Alex grinned, stood, offered his hand, though the offer of his stool was airily waved away. 'Lady Rogers. Another resounding success, I see. You must be pleased.'

'Over the moon, dear chap, over the moon.' Catching sight of Stella, she gave her a broad wink, clapped Alex heartily on the shoulder and proceeded to thank him for his contribution. 'An astronomical amount,' she acknowledged, and, leaning forward, lowered her voice confidentially, at the same time managing to ensure that half the population of the village learned the precise value of 'astronomic'. 'More than generous,' Lady Rogers beamed, Alex's lightning flash of annoyance somehow passing her by. 'And as for throwing open Freshfields . . .'

As fast as she'd arrived, she breezed away, and Alex regained his seat, turned his inscrutable gaze on Stella.

Only Stella wasn't swallowing that 'sweet and innocent little me' act. She bristled. 'But you said . . .'

'Yes, Stella. What did I say exactly?'

'You said you'd cancel,' she reminded him huffily. 'No feature, no fête, no funding.'

'So I was bluffing. A means to end. I wanted you here. Short of waving a magic wand, how else was a guy to manage it?'

'You bullied me –'

'Persuaded.'

'Why?'

'Why, what?'

'Why did you want me here?' she ground from out between gritted teeth.

'Why, simple, Stella. A tiny matter of absence, heart and its growing fonder – maybe.'

Irritating man. Stella flushed, decided to ignore him, instead nibbling at a corner of her roll, sharply aware of his thoughtful gaze – a heated gaze, she hastily corrected, risking a glance through the veil of her lashes and too late wishing she'd stifled the impulse. Heaven forbid Alex gained the impression she was really missing him. Her hazel eyes oozed defiance, a demeanour matched by the aggressive jut of her chin.

Generous lips quirked at the corners. 'You're looking good,' he surprised her by admitting. 'It must be the new hairstyle.'

With cheeks glowing fit to toast muffins, Stella

inwardly squirmed. Compliments on her appearance, when she'd done her best to appear cool, calm and unflappable! She might have known she was wasting her time, that Alex would take one look at that uncompromising pleat on the back of her neck and demolish the hands-off, keep your distance signal with a careless turn of phrase.

Still, no need for Alex to know that he'd unnerved her. Stella simply nodded, managed to finish her roll without choking, and, taking her cue from Alex, matched him sip for unhurried sip.

As she swallowed the last mouthful – a local brew, and stronger than she was used to – she decided she wouldn't risk Alex offering a second and scraped back her stool. 'Thanks for the lunch,' she murmured casually.

'My pleasure,' he insisted pleasantly. 'Despite the ulterior motive.'

'Oh?' The hairs on the back of Stella's neck began to prickle out a warning.

'That theory I was testing,' he reminded her casually. 'I'll let you know when I've had time to process the results.'

Impossible man. Stella flushed, flounced out without replying, so caught up in her silent rantings and ravings that she careered full pelt into a man rounding the corner.

'I'm terribly sorry – Danny!' she exclaimed with a surge of elation. 'What on earth –?'

'Just doing my bit for my adopted village,' he explained, smiling broadly, steering her safely across the road. 'Local celebrity and all that stuff. Would you believe I'm judging the Best-Dressed Stall competition? Come on,' he insisted, linking her arm through the crook of his and urging her towards the rank of brightly decorated stalls arranged around the green. 'You can cast an expert eye and give me your opinion.'

'How's Carly?'

'Blooming. But you don't have to take my word for it. Why not drop by for lunch tomorrow? Make up for the one you missed last week?'

'I –'

'Still haven't recovered from that tummy bug you picked up in Paris?' Danny's black eyes narrowed thoughtfully. 'Yes, come to think of it, you do look a bit peaky.'

Stella flushed. 'It – was just a twenty-four-hour thing. The usual, you know.' And just a tiny white lie on her part. Because, heading home from Paris, Stella had known she would never be able to face her sister without breaking down, pouring out her heart, and giving Carly a wealth of worry in the process.

There was a sudden silence, and she glanced up, realized Danny had been speaking and flashed him a smile of apology. 'I'm sorry. I was miles away.'

'So I noticed. But it wasn't important. Just a throwaway remark on life's coincidences. Giff was in Paris too last weekend.'

'Giff?' Stella murmured incredulously, her heart skipping a beat.

Danny nodded. 'My partner in crime. The other reason I'm here today – keep the guy with the controlling share of the business sweet. Heaven

Help-U,' he explained, sensing her confusion. 'You mean Carly didn't mention it? Giff's the main investor.' Danny's infectious smile spread. 'Bit of an Angel, as they say in the business.'

Positively saint-like, Stella acknowledged silently, sourly, Danny's use of Hannah's pet name for the moment passing her by.

Which begged the fifty-thousand-dollar question. Why? And why should Carly choose to keep Stella in the dark? Why? *Why?* she repeated incredulously. Since Beth and Carly had been in open cahoots at the wedding, over the unmentioned invitation to Alex, the reason was glaringly obvious. They were meddling. And yet, wouldn't Stella be more likely to mellow towards Alex if she *knew* about his good side? If he had one, she tagged on sourly, preparing to doubt his motives. Because men like Alex, she'd early discovered, rarely did anything without good cause. And then something else popped into her mind. That comment from Danny at the wedding that he'd killed in mid-sentence. One less bill for Stella to worry about. The wine. Profuse amounts of the stuff, courtesy of his new partner. Giff.

Well, stand up, Alex Gifford, and take a bow. The man was unbelievable. He was like one of those monsters in a horror movie, she decided, creeping into all aspects of her life and taking over. Her sister's wedding, her brother-in-law's career, her cousin's favourite charity, and, last but not least, Stella's job. Stella's mind and body too. But she was letting that pass for now.

Leaving Danny to his adoring public – the crowd of teenage girls who'd gathered eagerly round the moment he showed his face at the green – she headed back to Freshfields.

Popping her head round the stable door, she waved to Hannah, paused to watch as a child was lifted from his wheelchair into the specially adapted saddle astride a placid Marbles, and, recalling whose idea it had been to give the kids a treat, went in search of her cousin at the pool – a fully operational pool at that.

'You must be really proud.'

'I am, as it happens, but not so proud that I don't recognize a dig when I hear it,' Beth countered mildly, brushing a stray lock of hair out of her eyes. 'Want to tell me about it?'

'No, Beth, I do not want to tell you about it. What I really want to do is take you by the shoulders and push you into the water,' Stella confided a mite testily. 'The deep end.'

'Why?'

'You *know* why.'

'Maybe,' Beth conceded warily. 'But I should hate to be accused of reading things wrong.'

' "Reading things wrong" is what you're good at, Beth Austin. You've been scheming –'

'Hardly scheming, Stell.'

'Along with Carly –'

'Just a hint of wishful thinking. And you can't blame a girl for hoping.'

'Fine. So do us all a favour, wave a magic wand and wish Tamara out of the picture.'

'Ah-ha! Got you. I *knew* you were pining.'

'Past tense –'

'Liar!'

'So I'm lying. So I love the guy. So I'd crawl a million miles on my hands and knees if I thought I'd get a look-in. But I wouldn't.'

'Because of Tamara?'

'Because of Tamara,' Stella conceded flatly. But even without the shadow of Tamara she was wasting her time with hope. Alex despised her. Understandable, really. Stella's reputation was in tatters, and she wasn't holding out for a miracle. Saint-like Alex might be, but at the end of the day he was as vulnerable as Stella herself.

The end of the day. A long day. A surprisingly pleasant day, all things considered, and, having waved Beth and Connor off, along with hordes of tired but happy children, Stella said goodbye to Hannah and Mandy, gave a flagging James a poignant hug and cast a final glance at the house she didn't expect to see again. Dipping into her jacket pocket, she fished out her car keys.

'Stella! Leaving without saying goodbye?' Alex. Appearing out of nowhere and crossing the yard in a dozen easy strides. 'Surely not,' he chided lightly. 'Besides, it's barely seven. Come inside and let me fix you a drink – for old times' sake, of course.'

'Thanks, but no thanks,' Stella demurred, glad of the fading light to mask her glowing cheeks. 'I'm driving, remember?'

'Coffee, then, or a bite to eat? Supper? You won't

believe the treat Mrs E has in store, and I bet you've eaten nothing since that sandwich in the pub.'

'I –'

'You could always say yes,' he suggested casually, hands thrust just as casually into the pockets of his jeans.

'So I could,' she conceded lightly.

'Only you won't.'

Statement, not question, but Stella had the sense to let it pass. 'Another time maybe,' she insisted brusquely.

'More lies, Stella?' Alex bit out. 'I thought –'

'You thought . . . ?'

'That you might have turned over a new leaf. You know, made a new resolution.'

'Well, maybe I have at that,' she scorned, the tight fold of arms across her chest an unwitting give away. 'How does "Give all newly engaged guys a very wide berth" sound?'

'Enlightening, Stella,' Alex almost purred, his whole expression lifting. 'Exceedingly enlightening. But if you're sure I can't twist your arm? It seems a shame to eat alone when there's more than enough for two.'

'Soft lights, dreamy music and a tickle of toes beneath the table? Sounds every girl's dream. And, talking of dream girls, where is the dear lady?'

Alex angled his head politely. 'And which dear lady is that, in particular?'

'You know very well which,' Stella needled. 'The blushing bride herself.'

'Oh, you know.' Alex waved an airy hand. 'She's around here someplace,' he conceded vaguely.

Minus car? On the day of the village fête – the sort of event a loving fiancée should surely have supported. Not Tamara's thing at all, Stella decided waspishly. So, knowing Tamara, she was merely waiting for the hordes to disperse before heading for home and that cosy candlelit supper.

Ignoring Alex, Stella swung herself in behind the wheel, turned the key in the ignition and waited for the reassuring chug of the engine. Nothing. Stella counted to ten, then tried again. Still nothing. Suppressing a wave of panic, she cast an enquiring glance at Alex.

'AA, RAC?' he murmured unhelpfully, clearly the exception that proved the rule when applied to men and their love affair with engines.

Stella shook her head. Since she rarely travelled without her mobile phone, she'd never worried about the perils of breaking down in the middle of nowhere. Still, no problem. She'd call out the local garage.

Alex's turn to shake his head. 'It's Saturday,' he pointed out, equally unhelpfully, when Stella put her thoughts into words.

'I know it's Saturday.'

'They close at four on Saturdays. Four o'clock sharp. And it's now –'

'Six fifty-nine precisely,' Stella supplied dryly, swinging out and activating the central locking system. 'Well, never mind, I'll call a cab.'

'All the way to London? It'll cost.'

'It will be worth it. Besides, I was thinking more along the lines of the nearest hotel.'

'Guildford'

'Guildford?' Stella echoed absurdly. London itself would be just as convenient, yet surely Alton was a scant ten-minute drive away? A market town maybe, but there had to be a small hotel at least. But if Alex knew better . . . 'Village pub?'

Another shake of the head. 'No room at the inn,' Alex told her mournfully. 'Of course, there is another alternative.'

'Oh?'

'You could always stay the night here. In the guest room, Stella. You'll be perfectly safe, I assure you.'

Safe? Alone in the house with Alex? Not quite, she amended, at the same time wondering if the combined presence of Hannah, Mandy and Mrs Edwards would be enough to keep Alex at a distance once he'd made up his mind. Ah, yes, but then Stella had made up *her* mind. It was over. So why not prove it, to Stella herself as much as Alex? And with Tamara due home soon . . .

Which was how Stella came to be sharing supper for two in the study . . .

'So much cosier in here,' Alex had explained, whisking her inside and insisting she made herself at home on the sofa. 'And as soon as Mrs E has made up your bed, you can disappear upstairs if that's what you want.'

It wasn't. But, since Stella wasn't sure what she did want precisely, she held her tongue. Bed. Under the same roof as Alex. When the last time she'd slept beneath the same roof as Alex she'd shared a bed with Alex. First here, then in Paris. Stella's cheeks flamed. And, with that last dreadful scene in mind, asked, 'Why are you being so nice to me?'

'I'm simply being neighbourly, Stella.'

'But in Paris –'

'That was then and this is now,' Alex reminded her provokingly.

Too many reminders. She shouldn't have agreed to stay. Simply being in the same room as Alex was a torment; the thought of trying to sleep just a few doors away from Alex and Tamara was nothing short of madness. Because she loved him, warts and all. Impossible, arrogant, generous to a fault, considerate, loving – yes, loving, she insisted. He loved James, he loved Tamara, he'd even loved Stella in a way – just not the right way, she acknowledged sadly. But all man just the same, and with those tightly fitted jeans all but moulded to his thighs, Stella was having problems keeping wayward thoughts at bay. So, don't allow time for the wayward thoughts to surface in the first place. Fill the void. Talk – small talk, idle chatter, if necessary. Only Alex would know she was twittering and he'd know precisely why. So, she needed a good, safe topic of conversation, and since it had been eating away at the back of her mind all day, she took a deep breath. 'Tell me something,' she said.

'Anything – and everything,' Alex conceded enigmatically, leaning forward to top up the wine – safer than brandy, Stella supposed, assuming she knew when to stop.

'The help you've given Carly –'

'No more than she deserved, as I explained once before.'

'Yes, but that was before I knew about –' Breaking off, she wondered if she was supposed to know. Guessing from the sudden tightening of Alex's lips, she wasn't.

'Knew about what, Stella?'

'You know what.'

'Yes. A little bird – Danny, I suppose, since I spotted the two of you together earlier – has been telling tales.'

'Lies?'

'Since I wasn't privy to the cosy exchange, difficult to say, but, knowing Danny, I'd have to say no.' He sat back, folded his arms, treated her to one of those faintly accusing stares. 'Next question?'

There didn't have to be a next question, but, since he'd asked, and only because he'd asked, Stella put another thought into words. 'All the strange things that had been happening in the nursery,' she mused, swirling the wine in her glass. 'You knew, didn't you, Alex? The moment I mentioned it, you knew who it was?'

'It – didn't take much to work it out,' he conceded carefully. 'It's a strange emotion, jealousy. A bit like love itself, I suppose.'

'Jealousy?' Stella echoed incredulously. But of course! Hadn't she worked it out for herself all those weeks ago? But even so. 'A grown woman, jealous of James?' she breathed, still only half believing.

Alex gave a shrug of resignation. 'Unbelievable, I know – since I practically ignored the little guy. But, yes. She was jealous. Irrational, insecure, in need of love and understanding. Lots of love and understanding.'

'So getting rid of the nannies –'

'Was an attempt to force my hand, have James adopted or fostered . . .'

Or banished to an orphanage on Mars. Yes, Stella acknowledged silently, bitterly. It all made sense now. Tamara. Beautiful but insecure, and probably blissfully unaware of how lucky she was to have the love and understanding of a man like Alex. But, since Alex was openly reconciled with James, Tamara was too, presumably.

Deciding to move before the wine made her mellow, or worse, given the pull of the man opposite, Stella pointedly yawned, stretched and came lazily to her feet. Nice and easy. No sudden movements, no overreaction, and definitely no scuttling away like a frightened rabbit.

Ever the gentleman, Alex walked her to the door.

'Stella?'

'Alex?'

'Aren't you forgetting something?'

'I don't think so,' she murmured warily, sensing a trap and instantly poised for flight.

A strange smile hovered about the corners of his mouth. He leaned casually forward and managed to rest his hand on the door beside her, effectively blocking her escape. 'How about. Thanks for the lovely supper, Alex?'

Stella flushed. 'Thanks for the lovely supper, Alex,' she duly echoed, nerve-endings jangling.

'My pleasure,' he smilingly demurred. 'Like I said, I'm simply being neighbourly – offering food and shelter to a damsel in distress.'

Shelter. Bed. Stella's cheeks were glowing like coals.

'Mind you,' he tagged on provokingly, 'if you really wanted to thank me, actions speak louder than words.'

'I don't thi –'

'But I do,' he contradicted thickly. And then he kissed her.

'Alex –'

'Just a kiss,' he murmured smokily as his arms folded round. 'A kiss between friends.'

A kiss. Tasting, touching, nuzzling, nibbling, touching again. The merest hint of thumbs across her aching nipples. Madness, Stella told herself, torn between common sense and safety and the need to give instinct its head. Because she wanted him, needed him, craved the touch of skin on skin. And, yes, Alex hated and despised her, but right now Alex's need of Stella was very bit as urgent as Stella's need of him. And, oh, hell, how she wanted him. She hadn't the strength to refuse him – how to refuse him when she loved him?

Madness, madness, madness, she told herself, pushing her treacherous body into the hard lines of his, the whimpers of pleasure in the back of her throat a haunting refrain. And she was kissing Alex, fanning the flames. Now soft and persuasive, a rain of tiny kisses, now a fervent exploration of his mouth. Had she no shame? she wondered fleetingly. Throwing herself at Alex, wanting Alex, aching for a man who openly despised her. Shame, shame, shame . . . No, she insisted, closing her mind. Not now. Not ever. Not even in the dark hours, when the pain would return with a vengeance. She loved him. It was enough. And, since Alex clearly wanted Stella . . .

'Stella!'

Laughing, pulling free, dancing out of reach and then back again, she angled her chin, locked her smouldering gaze on to Alex and peeled off her sweater in a single fluid movement.

'Stella –'

'Soon,' she murmured huskily, arching out of reach again, and, reaching for the buttons of her blouse, beginning to snap them one by one.

'No, Stella –'

'Yes, Alex,' she contradicted saucily. 'Sex. Man and woman. You and me – remember?'

'No, Stella,' he chillingly contradicted, stepping back, shadows of doubt – or disgust – chasing about his features. 'No, Stella. Not like this.'

'Why not?' she countered smokily, her insides churning. 'Isn't this what you've been leading up to? Soft lights, dreamy music, a tickle of toes beneath the table. Good food, good wine, good company. And then the main course,' she reminded him huskily. 'Sex. You and me.' She angled her head in challenge. 'Or maybe you're afraid Tamara will walk in and catch you?'

'Tamara isn't here.'

'Oh, but you said –'

'Yes?'

'Nothing. It doesn't matter. Nothing does, I suppose. So –' She gave an offhand shrug of shoulders and snapped the remaining buttons on her blouse.

'I said, no, Stella.'

'Ah, yes, but actions speak louder than words, and *you*, Alex Gifford, don't fool me for an instant. You want me. Please, Alex,' she entreated on a lighter note, a different note, hating herself for the weakness yet wanting this man so badly she was desperate enough to beg. Besides, eating away at the back of her mind was the awful suspicion that something was wrong – very wrong. Unless – ah, yes, Alex was playing hard to get. Just like he had in Paris. Well, fine. Stella knew precisely how to punish him.

Smiling, she stepped forward to run the flat of her palm over the barrel of his chest. Registering the unmistakable shudder of emotion, she felt her heart soar.

'Sex,' she breathed, close enough to rub her breasts against his chest but denying Alex, denying herself just as badly. 'Because you're a man, all man. And I know, *I know* what you want, what we both want. Sex. Good sex, mind-blowing sex. Man and woman. Adam and Eve. You and me. And, since we're consenting adults . . .'

'No!' With a vicious slice of his arm, Alex pushed her away, his whole expression ugly.

'Please, Alex –'

'No, Stella. No, no, no,' he insisted icily, the look in eyes enough to freeze the blood in her veins.

'But you want me –'

'Not like this. Not some cold and clinical arrangement.'

'Ha! It suited you in Paris, I seem to recall.'

'But that was then and this is now,' he bellowed. 'And, *yes*, Paris was wonderful. Paris was everything I'd wanted and more –'

'Then why?'

'Why? *Why?*' he repeated. 'Because I'm crazy. Because I want you. Because I have needs. Who knows why?' he tossed out bitterly.

'You want me?'

'You *know* I want you.'

'Then why can't you take me, Alex? Take me, Alex. Don't ask me to beg. Not again. Leave me some self-respect at least.'

'You and me both, hey, Stella?' he needled. 'No, Stella. No, no and no,' he repeated harshly, snatching at her shoulders and shaking her. 'It's over. No more. Not now. Not ever. Understand, Stella?' he demanded viciously, the expression in his eyes tearing her apart. 'Sex, sex and more sex isn't enough any more. I'm not looking for sex, not even mind-blowing sex – though heaven help me,' he conceded thickly, 'mind-blowing sex is a definite bonus. Only not now. Not ever. Because it simply isn't enough. My problem, not yours,' he conceded bitterly, releasing her abruptly. 'Incredible though it seems in this day and age, but fun-loving Alex Gifford is looking for love. So –' He broke off, folded his arms, smiled a grim smile. 'No love, no sex. Simple.'

Pain. Disbelief. Complete and utter humiliation. He couldn't even let her down gently, Stella realized, squeezing back the tears. He couldn't take what she was offering, take her to bed and pleasure her, kiss her goodbye in the morning and make an empty promise to phone. No pretence, no indulgence. Just the knowledge that he didn't want her. Brutal. So, nothing else for it, girl. Dredge up the remnants of pride and mask it with flippancy.

Forcing a brittle smile, she pulled the edges of her blouse together. 'Fine,' she acknowledged tightly. 'I guess you'll just have to be patient, Alex. Sex I can happily supply, but love –' She gave a disdainful snap of the fingers. 'That's Tamara's department.'

'Wishful thinking, hey, Stella?'

'I beg your pardon?'

'The cop-out. The let-down. Don't beat about the bush, say it like it is. You can't love me, but that's not a problem. Pass the buck, why don't you?'

'Love you? But of course I love you,' she all but bellowed, heedless of the scorn she was openly inviting. 'For your information, you impossible man, I've always loved you –' Breaking off, she logged the effect of her words, the gamut of emotions chasing about his features – doubt, incredulity, a dawning comprehension, a light that seemed to spread to each and every part of him.

With a great whoop of joy, Alex peeled his sweater over his head as Stella backed away in confusion, came up against the solid fabric of the door and all but slumped against it.

'Wh-what are you doing?'

'What does it look like I'm doing?' he demanded gleefully. 'I'm getting undressed. Sex, remember? Mind-blowing sex –'

'Love, *you* said –'

'So I refused to have the one without the other. One of us had to keep a moral perspective. But now that we've cleared up that small problem – sex. As in the mind-blowing version of. Because you love me and I love you.'

'But you can't love me *and* Tamara, damn you.'

'Who said anything about Tamara?'

'You did. All that love and understanding. Lashings of the stuff –'

'Not Tamara, you idiotic woman. I don't, never have done, never will, love Tamara.'

'The engagement –'

'Was a mistake. She'd planned it months ago. Forgot to ask the prospective bridegroom, would you believe, and then forgot to cancel the announcement when she finally faced the truth. Or, knowing Tamara, she probably ran the announcement out of pique. She couldn't have me; she'd sure as hell make you suffer.'

'Me?'

'You.'

'But –'

'Hush. Later.' He pulled her against him, kissed her, hugged her, cupped her face in his hands and dipped his head to kiss her again. 'Later,' he repeated, blue eyes swirling with love – so much love, she conceded happily. 'After the love, Stella. Our love. Mind-blowing love. Love first, talk later. Promise. Come, my love. Let's go to bed. And later . . .'

'More love, Alex?'

'A lifetime of love, Stella. I love you, Stella Marshall. Though how you could ever doubt it –'

'Hush,' she echoed, touching a finger to his lips to stifle the pain. 'Later.'

Alex nibbled the finger, nuzzled the palm, trailed his lips the length of her arm. 'Come on,' he insisted thickly, threading his fingers through hers and tugging her through the door. 'Before I'm forced to ravish you here and now. Let's –'

A blood-curdling scream rent the air. Mandy, Stella identified, jerking round in horror to find the girl frozen in time at the foot of the stairs, the carton of milk she'd been carrying splattered at her feet.

What on earth –?

And then the acrid stench of burning hit the back of Stella's throat, and, mingling with the smell, the scent of panic.

CHAPTER 19

Fire. Madness. An eerie glow at the top of the stairs. Billows of smoke swirling down the stairwell as the frightened faces of Hannah and Mrs Edwards crept out of the darkness at the back of the house.

'Phone for help. The study. Use the mobile. And then get out. Understand, Stella? Get everyone out of the house.' Alex, galvanized into action, darted across to the still screaming Mandy, snatching at her shoulders as Stella dived for the phone, then dived straight back into the hallway because she couldn't bear not to be there, her terse plea for help thankfully connecting at once.

'James?' Alex demanded, shaking Mandy hard. 'For God's sake, Mandy, where's –'

The sobbing girl heaved a great racking sigh and pointed. Upwards.

'Oh, hell.'

'Alex, no!'

'Yes, Stella,' he contradicted tersely, disappearing into the cloakroom and emerging a few moments later with a fistful of dripping towels. Reaching the foot of the stairs, he paused for a moment and raised his head, as if gauging his line of ascent, Stella decided, bringing her hands together to pray as she'd never prayed before.

'No!' An anguished howl from Hannah halted Alex in his tracks. 'You can't,' she screamed hysterically, propelling herself forward. 'You can't leave me. You mustn't leave me. Please, Alex –'

'I can't let him die, for God's sake. He's my son –'
'You fool, of course he isn't. Chrissie –'
'Played around? Yes, Hannah, I know. I've always known. It doesn't matter. I thought it did once, but I was wrong. We're wasting time. James needs me –'
'*Alex!* Please, Alex, wait –'

Fragments of words, phrases. The wail of siren. The fire brigade, Stella realized, not daring to hope that they'd arrive in time. Because the smoke was choking, smothering, was swirling around Alex, and Alex had moved upwards, had dropped to his knees, keeping his head as low as possible, was coughing and spluttering as he inched his way higher still.

'Wait!' An imperative from Hannah, too compelling to ignore. Everything froze. Alex, Stella, even the smoke seemed suspended in time.

Time. No time to waste. A garbled exchange of words that couldn't have lasted more than twenty seconds, Stella decided later, lasted half a lifetime in her mind.

'The nursery stairs,' Hannah was screaming, arms gesticulating wildly. 'The back stairs, Alex –'

Another snatch of words, Alex's reply lost in the

noise, the crackle of flames as he turned his attention to the hell that existed above him. '. . . blocked off years ago . . . too late . . . only hope . . . James –'

'No-o! No! No! No! You can't! I won't let you! *No-o!*' As the last dreadful note died away Hannah had gone, was out of her chair and had disappeared into the darkness beyond the newel post before an astonished Stella had time to blink.

'Hannah!' Alex, magnificent Alex, was poised on the landing, suffocating smoke swirling around his legs – damned if he did and damned if he didn't, Stella realized, crying inside but determined to be brave for Alex's sake.

'Alex. Oh, my love. Please, God. Please, God, keep him safe,' she repeated over and over, somehow drawing strength from the simple litany, and Alex turned his head to lock an anguished gaze on to Stella, as if making silent promise.

Time passed. Seconds, minutes – hours in Stella's mind – as Alex pulled his shirt over his face, securing it in place over his nose and mouth before dropping to his knees for the final ascent.

So near, so far, she realized, the tears squeezing their way out from beneath her lashes, adding another rosary of prayers at the answer to her prayers – the strident wail of the engines that was growing louder by the second. Soon, please, God, make it soon, she silently implored as billows of smoke screened Alex from her sight. And, though she knew she ought to move, to shepherd Mandy and Mrs Edwards out though the back of the house to safety, she refused to leave Alex alone. Yet, catching a sudden movement out of the corner of her eye, she wrenched her gaze from the spot Alex had reached when she'd last been able to see, couldn't believe what she was seeing. Hannah, emerging from the blackness, a whimpering James in her arms, her expression a curious mix of shame and elation. Until she glanced up, realized the danger Alex was in, and then a look of pure terror crossed her face.

No time for Stella to make sense of it all now. James was safe, please God Alex would be too, and yet above the noise came another sound, a terrible sound of crashing timber and – oh, God!

'Alex!' Stella screamed, dashing forward. And then her world exploded in a jagged mass of colour, shape and pain – so much pain that when the blackness came to claim her, she simply hadn't the strength to fight it.

'Trust me to miss out on all the fun.'

'Fun, madam, is the last thing we were having. The house is a wreck –'

'Not a total wreck, Alex, just a bit of a bomb site from what you've been saying, and since you were insured – you *were* insured?' she queried politely, swallowing the piece of chocolate he'd popped between her lips and, like a baby bird in the nest, opening her mouth for another.

Alex nodded. 'Fire, flood and pestilence. Which is probably as well, since all three managed to visit during the course of a single evening.'

'So give it a couple of months and the place will be like new.'

'Better than new. New wiring – God knows, according to the experts, we were living on a time bomb – a new staircase – safely enclosed, in case of the unmentionable – and that other source of danger, the nursery staircase, demolished once and for all.'

'And you never guessed?'

'That Hannah had rediscovered it when the extension was added? It was boxed off before I was born, as it happens, so it never crossed my mind. Though with the benefit of hindsight . . .'

'Hannah's private link to the nursery? When I think –'

'Hush.' Kiss. Soothing noises in the back of his throat. 'Despite how it seemed, you were never in any danger. Hannah wouldn't hurt a fly.'

No. Stella swallowed a smile. She wouldn't need to. Scaring them to death along with the nannies was much more satisfying.

'Time for your nap. Doctor's orders.'

'Doctor's orders, my foot. I'm fine. I've been perfectly fine for days now.'

'You had a nasty blow to the head –'

'So I had a headache. I survived, didn't I? When I think –'

'Hush. Don't. Don't even think it. You're safe, we're all safe, and James –'

'Owes his life to Hannah? Yes, sweetheart,' she interrupted gently. 'I know. And I know what you're trying to say. Hannah needs help.' Hannah – irrational, insecure and in need of love and understanding. Lots of love and understanding, Stella silently recalled as Alex urged her back against the pillows and perched on the covers beside her, his fingers threaded though hers. And, yes, she was tired. She would sleep for an hour, but then she'd open her eyes to find that Alex hadn't moved, and Alex would *smile*, and Stella would smile, and then he'd dip his head to kiss her, and the kisses would grow more urgent, as they had done day by day, more than keeping pace with Stella's own recovery.

Easy to recover knowing Alex was safe, thanks to Stella's scream of warning. So near, so far, Stella realized, shivering despite it all. Just a few seconds later and – no. She closed her mind, nestled down into the pillows. Alex was safe and that was all that mattered now.

Soon, she promised herself, smiling, dozing. Just a few short days and she'd be home with Alex. Well, if not quite home, she amended sadly, thanks to Lady Rogers' offer of help they wouldn't be far from Freshfields. And if Stella's sleeping with Alex caused a few raised brows, it was a small price to pay for being shameless. Anyway, Stella smiled. Sleep was the last thing on her mind. Hospitals, even the horrendously expensive private kind, were obsessed with sleep.

Another day, another visit, another lingering kiss.

Alex laughed as he pulled away, unhooking Stella's arms from around his neck and cradling her hands in his. 'Unfair, Stella Marshall. You know how much I want you.'

'So take me home and prove it.'

'Tomorrow. Or the next day. Or as soon as the doctors allow it.'

Maybe, Stella silently amended. And maybe he'd arrive for another visit and find Stella fully dressed and ready to leave. Tomorrow. Yes, she decided, visibly brightening. She'd had enough. Two weeks of mollycoddling was more than enough for any reluctant invalid. On the subject of which . . .

'I still don't understand how Hannah pulled it off,' she half mused, half enquired, a frown of concentration furrowing her brow. 'Unless – ah, yes! The riding accident. Of course – cleverly timed to put a halt to her sister's wedding. And when *that* didn't work –'

'Wrong, as it happens,' Alex interrupted, dropping the lightest of kisses at her temple, and then another just for good measure on the sensitive spot inside her wrist. 'Yet you're almost right, Miss Marple-Marshall-Poppins,' he smilingly conceded. 'The accident was real enough, and so was the paralysis – the *temporary* paralysis.'

'You knew?'

'Not immediately. Not for quite a while, as it happens. But over the months I had a few suspicions.'

'And you never thought to mention it?'

'Oh, yes, and what was I supposed to say? Dear Hannah, I do believe you're swinging the lead. Besides, if she needed the prop of invalidity, she was clearly ill – mentally ill.'

'And now that she's proved there's nothing physically wrong, she can concentrate on getting better. At home. With us.'

Alex's features lightened. 'You're sure? It's asking a lot, I know.'

'I'm sure. Hannah is family. And she will get better now. James, the stables, coming to terms with you and me. Her jealousy of James was just another symptom —'

'Or resentment of Chrissie and the fact that she was cheating on me?'

'Not to mention wanting you for herself.'

'Yes.' Alex's smile was tinged with sadness. 'Poor Hannah. Who'd have believed she'd go to such lengths just to keep my attention?'

'Precisely. The sympathy vote. Clever Hannah.'

'Too clever. That was the real give-away. Despite facing life in a wheelchair, she was blissfully unconcerned. It's called "*la belle indifference*",' he explained. 'And is a classic symptom, apparently. So when I did get round to making some enquiries —'

'Bingo! Hysterical neurosis. Kind of obvious when you think about it.'

'What's this?' he demanded gleefully, pinning her against the pillows. 'Another string to Miss Practically Perfect's bow? Journalist, nanny, super-sleuth and now psychiatrist extraordinaire?'

'Ex-journalist, ex-nanny, strictly amateur sleuth, and as for the last one —'

'Just a little something you picked up at school?' he teased.

'It could have been,' Stella conceded, smiling. 'But a girl doesn't like to boast about these things. Kiss the man in her life, yes,' she insisted as her arms crept up and around his neck again. 'Waste time on idle boasts, no. And on the subject of boasts, I'm coming home. Tomorrow. Understand, Alex?'

Alex smiled, nodded, gave an enigmatic, 'We'll see,' that didn't impress Stella one jot. He'd see. But she'd leave him to discover that for himself in the fullness of time. Not a very long fullness of time, because she'd made up her mind.

Another kiss, and Alex's hands, as Stella had fully intended, homing in on breasts that ached for the touch of skin on skin. Only Alex continued to deny her, refused to slide his hands beneath the lace of her nightie. Disappointed, frustrated, on the verge of screaming pitch, Stella contrived to loosen the ribbon that held the panels of the bodice together, and, sure enough, Alex's exploring thumbs homed in.

'*Stella* –'

'Complaining, my love?'

'Like hell. Because I want you –'

'Tomorrow?' she enquired archly, the fold of arms across her naked breasts carefully designed to frustrate him.

'Lady,' he acknowledged thickly, his eyes darting from her face to her breasts and back again, 'you drive a real hard bargain. Tomorrow. Though heaven help me,' he added in anguish, 'I don't think I can wait that long. Now do I get to see?'

'And touch, and taste and kiss,' she conceded happily, shamelessly baring all.

And Alex did.

It was a mellow hour. Lovers' talk and idle plans for the future – a future they'd share together.

A heightened sense of the loss they'd almost suffered steered Stella's mind back over the pleasures and pains of the last few weeks. Her night of love at Freshfields, the dreadful scene that had followed, and on to Paris. She was smiling, was snuggling up to Alex, who'd stretched out on the bed beside her, fully clothed – and heaven help him if that sourpuss of a Sister walked in to catch him. Only she wouldn't, of course. Because, surprise, surprise, thanks to the power of money, privacy and private nursing care went hand in hand.

Hand in hand. Fingers entwined, thumbs idly stroking. And she loved him. And she'd almost lost him. All because of that silly misunderstanding about Tamara. And an engagement. Now wait a minute –

Stella sat bolt-upright.

'Sweetheart –?'

'Precisely. Which sweetheart?' she demanded mock severely. 'The sweetheart sitting large as life before you, or the sweetheart whose name was linked with yours in a certain spoof announcement? That morning in Paris, Alex Gifford,' she sternly reminded him, '*you* ordered *The Times*.'

Alex laughed, reached for her shoulders, drew her down beside him. Propping himself up on his elbow, he threaded a finger through a loop of her hair, skirted the tender patch that hadn't quite healed and idly stroked her cheek. 'The *Financial Times*, my indignant one,' he smilingly informed her. 'I needed to check on my investments, decide if I'd made enough money to ask the woman of my dreams to be my wife. All those temporary arrangements had to come to an end sooner or later, Stella. Was it my fault they delivered the wrong paper and you ran out on me?'

'Oh!'

'Yes, oh. You looked, you jumped, and like a fool I let you. Worse than that, I made some pretty revolting accusations.'

'Since the cap –'

'Didn't fit? Oh, Stella!' He caught her to him, almost squeezing the breath from her body. 'Don't you think I didn't know it?' he demanded fiercely, the pain in his voice almost slicing her in two. 'I was hurting, Stella,' he murmured in anguish, lips nuzzling at her temple, a rain of tiny kisses designed to counter the hurt – Alex's as much as Stella's. 'I was hitting out. But I never, ever believed. I just didn't understand. And then I reached home and the phone never stopped ringing.'

'Let me guess. Congratulations on a certain happy announcement?'

Alex chuckled. 'I'd say commiserations fitted the bill better. But, yes. And since it made sense –'

'You left the woman of your dreams to stew for a whole ten days?' she breathed incredulously. 'Alex Gifford, I'm ashamed of you.'

'Guilty as charged,' he solemnly conceded. 'But I still wasn't sure. I thought there was another man, you see. And since I'd made some pretty vile –'

'Don't.' She put a finger to his lips, stifling the pain.

'Don't blame yourself. Don't blame anyone. We're together now. For ever and ever, hey, my love?'

'A permanent contract, hmm?' he murmured, drawing her finger into his mouth and nibbling hungrily, sensuously, sending shock waves of pleasure the length of her arm and into to the very core of her.

'You bet. To love and to cherish –'

'For richer, for poorer –'

'Well, if it's got to be one or the other,' she interrupted saucily, 'can a girl put in a bid for richer?'

'You, my little minx, can put in a bid for whatever you want, as long it's for ever. Understand?'

'Mr and Mrs Alex Gifford? Sounds divine –' She broke off as Alex swung himself upright, perched on the side of the bed and tugged his unbuttoned shirt over his head. 'Alex, now what are you doing?' she demanded, watching in amazement as Alex simply smiled, stood, stripped off completely and utterly, and, pulling back the covers, climbed into bed beside her. 'But you can't – not here.'

'Want a bet?' he countered thickly, pushing her nightie over her shoulders and exposing her breasts with their shamelessly jutting nipples to the full blast of his gaze – a heated gaze, a hungry gaze, the gaze of a man who's waited more than long enough already.

'Mr Alex Gifford and the future Mrs Stella Gifford,' he reminded her mournfully, 'are sadly in need of a little practice. The sort of practice,' he added smokily, burying his face between her breasts while his hands ranged her body, exploring, caressing, inciting, 'that takes a lot of perfecting. Touch, taste, kiss, touch again,' he breathed.

And he was touching, stroking her thighs, sliding his fingers to the apex of her legs, yet, on the verge of making a connection, veering away and round, and down and back ... And upwards, slowly, oh, so slowly, while Stella writhed in exquisite agony – an agony clearly matched by Alex, she couldn't fail but notice, smiling inside. Man. All man. All hers. Soon. Very soon. So near, so far, and –

'Oh, God, Alex!' she gasped as he made the first thrust, paused, pulled back to the very brim and paused again. And then moved – oh, so slowly, and –

'*Alex!*'

'Ready, my love?'

'For you – any time, any place, any which way at all,' she explained with woeful lack of restraint. 'I'm all yours.'

'I know,' he growled, raising his head, locking his heated gaze on to Stella and seeing to the centre of her soul. 'So now I'm going to prove it. And you, my shamelessly insatiable beauty, are going to enjoy each and every moment.'

Reader, you'd better believe it. She did. And, just in case you were wondering, she married him.

THE EXCITING NEW NAME IN WOMEN'S FICTION!

PLEASE HELP ME TO HELP YOU!

Dear *Scarlet* Reader,

I have some wonderful news for you this month – we are beginning a super Prize Draw, which means that you ***could win an exclusive sassy Scarlet T-shirt!*** Just fill in your questionnaire and return it to us (see addresses at the end of the questionnaire) before 31 November 1998, and we'll do the rest! If you are lucky enough to be one of the first four names out of the hat each month, we will send you this exclusive prize.

So don't delay – return your form straight away!*

Looking forward to hearing from you,

Sally Cooper

Editor-in-Chief, *Scarlet*

---

* Prize draw offer available only in the UK. Draw is not open to employees of Robinson Publishing, or their agents, families or households. Winners will be informed by post, and details of winners can be obtained after 31 November 1998 by sending a stamped addressed envelope to the address given at the end of the questionnaire.

Note: further offers which might be of interest may be sent to you by other, carefully selected, companies. If you do not want to receive them, please write to Robinson Publishing Ltd, 7 Kensington Church Court, London W8 4SP, UK.

QUESTIONNAIRE

Please tick the appropriate boxes to indicate your answers

1 Where did you get this Scarlet title?
Bought in supermarket ☐
Bought at my local bookstore ☐ Bought at chain bookstore ☐
Bought at book exchange or used bookstore ☐
Borrowed from a friend ☐
Other (please indicate) _____

2 Did you enjoy reading it?
A lot ☐   A little ☐   Not at all ☐

3 What did you particularly like about this book?
Believable characters ☐   Easy to read ☐
Good value for money ☐   Enjoyable locations ☐
Interesting story ☐   Modern setting ☐
Other _____

4 What did you particularly dislike about this book?
_____

5 Would you buy another Scarlet book?
Yes ☐   No ☐

6 What other kinds of book do you enjoy reading?
Horror ☐   Puzzle books ☐   Historical fiction ☐
General fiction ☐   Crime/Detective ☐   Cookery ☐
Other (please indicate) _____

7 Which magazines do you enjoy reading?
1. _____
2. _____
3. _____

And now a little about you –

8 How old are you?
Under 25 ☐   25–34 ☐   35–44 ☐
45–54 ☐   55–64 ☐   over 65 ☐

cont.

9 What is your marital status?
Single ☐   Married/living with partner ☐
Widowed ☐   Separated/divorced ☐

10 What is your current occupation?
Employed full-time ☐   Employed part-time ☐
Student ☐   Housewife full-time ☐
Unemployed ☐   Retired ☐

11 Do you have children? If so, how many and how old are they?
_____
_____

12 What is your annual household income?
under $15,000 ☐   or   £10,000 ☐
$15–25,000 ☐   or   £10–20,000 ☐
$25–35,000 ☐   or   £20–30,000 ☐
$35–50,000 ☐   or   £30–40,000 ☐
over $50,000 ☐   or   £40,000 ☐

Miss/Mrs/Ms _____
Address _____
_____
_____

Thank you for completing this questionnaire. Now tear it out – put it in an envelope and send it, before 31 January 1999, to:

Sally Cooper, Editor-in-Chief

USA/Can. address
SCARLET c/o London Bridge
85 River Rock Drive
Suite 202
Buffalo
NY 14207
USA

UK address/No stamp required
SCARLET
FREEPOST LON 3335
LONDON W8 4BR
Please use block capitals for address

TEARR/7/98

Scarlet titles coming next month:

MIX AND MATCH Tegan James

Rich, charming, easy-going yachtsman Jet Diamond is unique. Or so Aberdeen thinks when she falls in love with him. But that's before she meets his twin brother, film-maker Jasper Diamond. Identical in looks but with very different personalities, the Diamond twins bring double trouble to the women in their lives. So what does that mean for Aberdeen?

HEAVEN SENT Stacy Brown

Rebellious blue stocking Celeste Wentworth is determined to escape from the dreary life that her stern grandfather is planning for her – a suitable marriage and a family. She resolves to be 'ruined' and falls for notorious rake Simon Barclay, the Earl of Dragonwood. As their relationship develops, they become caught up in the strange web of a secret society responsible for the corruption of society girls, including Simon's own stepsister.

JOIN THE CLUB!

Why not join the *Scarlet* Readers' Club – you can have four exciting new reads delivered to your door every other month for only £9.99, plus TWO FREE BOOKS WITH YOUR FIRST MONTH'S ORDER!

Fill in the form below and tick your two first books from those listed:

1. *Never Say Never* by Tina Leonard ☐
2. *The Sins of Sarah* by Anne Styles ☐
3. *Wicked in Silk* by Andrea Young ☐
4. *The Master of the House* by Margaret Callaghan ☐
5. *Starstruck* by Lianne Conway ☐
6. *This Time Forever* by Vickie Moore ☐
7. *It Takes Two* by Tina Leonard ☐
8. *The Mistress* by Angela Drake ☐
9. *Come Home Forever* by Jan McDaniel ☐
10. *Deception* by Sophie Weston ☐
11. *Fire and Ice* by Maxine Barry ☐
12. *Caribbean Flame* by Maxine Barry ☐

ORDER FORM

SEND NO MONEY NOW. Just complete and send to SCARLET READERS' CLUB, FREEPOST, LON 3335, Salisbury SP5 5YW

Yes, I want to join the ***SCARLET* READERS' CLUB*** and have the convenience of 4 exciting new novels delivered directly to my door every other month! Please send me my first shipment now for the unbelievable price of £9.99, plus my TWO special offer books absolutely free. I understand that I will be invoiced for this shipment and FOUR further *Scarlet* titles at £9.99 (including postage and packing) every other month unless I cancel my order in writing. I am over 18.

Signed ....

Name (IN BLOCK CAPITALS)...

Address (IN BLOCK CAPITALS)...

....

Town.. **Post Code**................................

Phone...
As a result of this offer your name and address may be passed on to other carefully selected companies. If you do not wish this, please tick this box ☐.

*Please note this offer applies to UK only.

Did You Know?

There are over 120 *NEW* romance novels published each month in the US & Canada?

♥ *Romantic Times Magazine* is **THE ONLY SOURCE** that tells you what they are and where to find them–even if you live abroad!

♥ *Each issue* reviews **ALL** 120 titles, saving you time and money at the bookstores!

♥ *Lists mail-order* book stores who service international customers!

ROMANTIC TIMES MAGAZINE
~ Established 1981 ~

Order a *SAMPLE COPY* Now!

FOR UNITED STATES & CANADA ORDERS:
$2.00 United States & Canada (U.S FUNDS ONLY)
CALL 1-800-989-8816*

* 800 NUMBER FOR US CREDIT CARD ORDERS ONLY

♥ **BY MAIL:** Send <u>US funds Only</u>. Make check payable to: Romantic Times Magazine, 55 Bergen Street, Brooklyn, NY 11201 USA
♥ **TEL.:** 718-237-1097   ♥ **FAX:** 718-624-4231

VISA • M/C • AMEX • DISCOVER ACCEPTED FOR US, CANADA & UK ORDERS!

FOR UNITED KINGDOM ORDERS: (Credit Card Orders Accepted!)
£2.00 Sterling–Check made payable to Robinson Publishing Ltd.
♥ **BY MAIL:** Check to above **DRAWN ON A UK BANK** to: Robinson Publishing Ltd., 7 Kensington Church Court, London W8 4SP England

♥ E-MAIL CREDIT CARD ORDERS: RTmag1@aol.com
♥ VISIT OUR WEB SITE: http://www.rt-online.com